Greetings, Oh Reader,

Several years ago I contracted Lyme disease. I wasn't alerted by a tick bite or the classic bull's eye rash, so my sudden poor memory sent me to the doctor in search of a precursor test for Alzheimer's (there wasn't one). A month later, when a hot June day produced chills despite lack of a fever, I asked for the Lyme disease test, and Boom! I had it. No wonder I was spending my days on the couch, exhausted and in pain. I ended up on antibiotics for a *very* long time, and had to leave teaching for a while, but eventually I recovered (Yay!).

During that time, two wonderful things happened. I started exercising to boost my immune system, and I began writing this book.

Creating a story was the perfect accompaniment to languishing on the sofa. I made things up for hours, inspired by songs playing on the radio. Check out **The Playlist** at the end of this book. Those are the actual songs that fueled my fuzzy imagination.

Months later, when I got better, I returned to my day job teaching Environmental Science, the coolest assignment a teacher can get. From that point forward, I joined writing groups, took lots of classes on writing, and wrote during the summers. The book was coming along nicely.

Then I went to my first Renaissance Faire... **Wow**!

Fairly Safe got shoved to the back burner, and I got all fired up about **Fairly Certain**, which popped into my head while I was standing in the middle of the faire. It, of course, ended up being published first. But I couldn't completely abandon **Fairly Safe**. It's too good of a story. So, here it is, in all it's glory, new and improved, waiting to take you to the fair.

Have fun today!

Deborah Ann Davis, Author

www.DeborahAnnDavis.com

On Facebook and Twitter @DeborahAnnDavis

or @WiggleWriter

PS About five years later, I got Lyme disease again. That time
I got rid of it **without using antibiotics**, thanks to Cowper's
Protocol. Check it out.

Fairly Safe

Who is *that, anyway? Her father?* Jacob tried to step around the hopefuls to get a better view of the dark-haired guy. *No, too young. Her boyfriend? Nah, too old. Well, whoever he is, he's pissed. Wait. What's she saying?*

"You can't tell me what to do," she hissed at the man. "You're not my father." *Jab, jab.*

Okay, not her father.

The man colored and released her arm.

"No, I'm not your father." He took a threatening step toward her. "If I *were* your father, you'd be over my knee for taking stupid risks."

Alarms went off in Jacob. He didn't know this guy, but he recognized controlled fury when he saw it. She was pushing the wrong buttons with this fella. Jacob stepped closer. If she needed his help, he was prepared to whip her out of there.

"I'm not taking any risks!" she shouted as she stomped. "It's a kiss on the *cheek*. And *it's not my birthday!*"

She made no sense to Jacob, but several spectators repeated her words and laughed. He eased in closer. This was going to blow up.

"*Listen—*" the suit yelled as he tried to grab her arm again, but she was ready for him this time. Sidestepping him, she twirled away and slammed right into Jacob.

Amidst the hoots from the guys in the line, Jacob's arms wrapped around her as he steadied them both. Her hands splayed on his chest as she regained her footing, her eyes wide. And there it was—the same tingle coursing through his veins he had experienced with her before. For a moment, their gazes locked.

Then the angry suit charged at them...and fast.

The Second Tale in the...

Love of Fairs Series

Fairly Safe

"If it be the anniversary of your birth when you first kiss, that blessed moment over the ancient rune becomes your union of destiny".

Deborah Ann Davis

D&D Universe, llc
PO Box 177
Colchester, CT 06415

ISBN 978-1-942009-05-4

Cover Design by Becca Davis
Cover Graphics by Roxy Ryan
Edited and Formatted by Wizards in Publishing
Fairly Obvious © 2016 by Deborah Ann Davis

Publisher's Cataloging-In-Publication Data
(Prepared by The Donohue Group, Inc.)

Names: Davis, Deborah Ann, 1957-
Title: Fairly Safe / Deborah Ann Davis.
Description: Colchester, CT : D&D Universe, llc, [2016] | Series: Love of Fairs series ; 2
Identifiers: ISBN 978-1-942009-05-4 | ISBN 978-1-942009-06-1 (ebook)
Subjects: LCSH: Mistaken identity--Fiction. | Witnesses--Protection--Fiction. | Man-woman relationships--Fiction. | Young adults--Fiction. | Fairs--New England--Fiction. | Love stories.
Classification: LCC PS3604.A95 F352 2016 (print) | LCC PS3604.A95 (ebook) | DDC 813/.6--dc23

Dedication

To my parents. If it wasn't for you, I wouldn't be here.

Acknowledgements

Thank you to Kate Richards, who continued to help me edit after the fact because "we just want to get the book right."

Thank you to Rebecca for getting published in *Chicken Soup for the Soul*. You made me believe I could do it, too.

Prologue

Destiny's First Kiss

1938

Eleven-year-old William's entire body snapped with anticipation as he peered around the tent pole. Every summer, when the carnival came to town, the carnies reassembled their makeshift settlement. Folks as colorful as their carts raised tents, fed livestock, and erected booths. One and all were in motion—men and women, old and young—busy creating a temporary home in a harvested hayfield outside of town. William inhaled, savoring the unfamiliar smells of exotic livestock, odors that would never grace a New England barn. Could this day get any better?

The lure of the unfamiliar drew the young trespasser deeper into the commotion. Abandoning the concealment of the tent, William crept deeper into the magnificent foreign world. To his delight, everyone outright ignored him, despite the incongruity of his blue eyes and freckled fair complexion amongst the tanned, olive skin of the bustling Gypsies. How he envied the life he imagined they led. His own should be so happy and carefree.

The sounds of a child shrieking with laughter caught his attention. Following the joyful noise, he came upon a swarthy, coal-eyed man spinning circles with a little girl held high overhead, her dark curls glinting in the sun.

"Papa!" she squealed with delight, her small hands clutching his forearms.

From the shadow of a large wagon, William watched, wistful, wondering how such play felt.

A small, olive-skinned woman with happy brown eyes joined the two cavorters, issuing an amused reprimand, her message made all the more mysterious by her foreign Gypsy tongue. The man slowed his daughter's spin, his shrug sheepish. He set her down as if she were delicate porcelain. These must be her parents.

The little girl regained her balance by grabbing a fistful of her mother's colorful skirt. Her father enveloped the woman in a loving hug. Ignoring the cheerful banter from her parents, the youngster turned toward where William stood in the shadows. Fixing a stare on him, the little girl planted her thumb in her mouth, her other hand still clenching her mother's skirt.

Is she going to tell on me?

Perhaps not. Filled with childish curiosity, William returned her stare, mesmerized. *A real carnival Gypsy girl.*

Apparently, she had permission to run around barefooted, a luxury he craved, but was forever denied. The fine, dry dirt of the season covered her bare feet, which, like William's own pale toes, wiggled in the summer warmth. Enjoying the forbidden dirt, he noticed the bright skirt of her dress was slightly tattered, as if it had seen many days of childhood fun. Following the morning's escape from the oppressive atmosphere of home, William's shirt and breeches were still somewhat neat and clean this early in the day.

Her mother's skirts flipped out of the little Gypsy's hand with a sudden twirl executed by her father. Gay skirts whirling below and long ebony hair flying above, the couple engaged in a moment of spontaneous dance, giggling like children.

The father dipped her and paused. "Ana, my own, you remember what we do this day six years ago?"

"Ah yes, Raul, my love." Ana's robust laugh was as foreign as their accent to a boy like William. The man swooped her up before spinning her around again. Then he stopped, and they posed, cheek to cheek.

"We greet the dawn of Olivia's first day, no?" Ana nuzzled her husband's cheek and kissed it.

Yuck. William turned his attention to the little girl. She edged out of range of the swirling skirts, for the moment forgotten by the two absorbed adults. As she drifted, he became alarmed. *What if she wanders off and gets lost?*

Feeling very responsible and grown, he intercepted her and bent over. "Wait, little girl. You should stay near your mother," he said, imitating his officious father.

The thumb popped out of the rosy mouth. "You speak as if I am baby." Her indignation echoed her parents' accent. "I am not. I am six."

Wow, she was little. He had a four-year-old cousin bigger than her. *And cleaner.*

He straightened. "Well, you're a baby to me. I'm twice your age, so I know someone should be watching you."

She studied him. "As you wish." She slipped her hand into his and beamed.

William's eleven-year-old heart puffed with importance. He glanced over at the dancing couple to see if they had noticed how well he was caring for his little charge. However, engrossed with each other, they danced to music only they could hear.

In due course, standing there simply holding her hand was a little boring. He searched for something of more interest—mischief, his father called it. To his delight, his new companion's next words supplied the perfect distraction.

"Would you see where I live?"

"Truly? Oh, yes! Is it far?"

"No. Is near, over there." She gestured toward one of the colorful carts on the side of the field.

"Let's go!" Unbridled excitement welled up inside him. To see how the carnival people lived. Wait till he told his friends. They were going to be so jealous.

Pulling her by the hand, he hurried past the displays being erected, but slowed when a curious sign caught his eye. It hung over some type of wooden platform. "*Birthday Kisses... Married by Christmas*. What's that?"

"You read?" She drew back and regarded him with respect.

"Of course I can read. I'm eleven." For a moment, he basked in her obvious admiration then pointed to the sign. "What does that mean?"

She shrugged.

He circled the platform. "How do you get up there?"

"No stairs because we no go up."

Filled with a sense of adventure, William coaxed, "Why not? How can it hurt? It's just a floor. C'mon. I can pick you up." Receiving no opposition, he wrapped his arms around her little torso. Clutching her to his chest as her toes banged against his shins, he lifted her higher until she cleared the platform, and then plopped her down with a decided *ooomph*!

"You might be little, but you sure are heavy," William muttered as he clambered up beside her on the empty stage. "What now?"

"Birthday kisses," she said.

William snorted. "Birthday kisses? Yuck."

"Is the day of my birth." She tilted forward, presented her cheek, and waited.

"I'm not kissing you. You're a girl."

She stomped her foot, perching her hands on her waist. "Is our custom."

"You sure have strange customs." He peeked over his

shoulder to make sure no one could witness him embarrassing himself. Warm with discomfort, he bent forward to place a quick peck on the offered cheek. Abruptly, she moved her face so his kiss landed on her mouth. Shocked, he jumped back.

"Hey!" he cried, outraged by her mischief. He rubbed his mouth. "You can't do that! I'm a boy."

"Livy, where are you?"

The little girl turned with a guilty start. "My Mama. I go now." She scooted toward the edge of the platform.

"Wait a minute." William hopped off so he could help her down.

"Olivia…? Where are you?" called a male voice.

William's heart thumped in response. If her father was anything like William's, they were in real trouble—especially if they were caught some place where they weren't supposed to be. "C'mon!" Putting his hands around her waist, he staggered under the wiggling burden and lowered her to the ground. Hand in hand, they raced off toward the adults.

"Here she is," he called. "I was"—he wavered under the glare of her father—"watching her for you." He was in trouble. Again.

"And we thank you, young sir." The mother placed a calming hand on her husband's arm. "But, most regretfully, is time to say good-bye to you young friend, Livy."

"He no is young, Mama. He is eleven." William's former charge slipped her hand out of his and skipped toward her mother.

Both adults smiled.

"But, of course, you right, Livy." Raul directed a respectful nod toward William.

William's stomach unknotted in relief. "Give thanks to young man and bid good-bye to him, Olivia."

Olivia whirled around and ran back toward William.

"Thank you very much." She bobbed a cute curtsey. Without warning, she reached up on tiptoe. Putting a hand on each of his cheeks, she pulled his head down, and kissed him. Again.

William's hands shot out to the side, his back stiffening with shock and embarrassment.

"Olivia!" chorused her parents. Her mother snatched Olivia into her arms.

"What? I kiss him before." Olivia looked from one to the other, and back again. "Birthday kisses, married by Christmas."

Ana clapped a hand over Olivia's mouth.

Flustered, William cried, "I told you! You're not supposed to kiss me. I'm a *boy*."

Livy pulled her mother's hand from her mouth, her lashes brimming with tears, "But is my birthday," she wailed.

Oh, no. Tears? Could this day get any worse? "It...It's fine." William wished himself any place but here. Under the scrutiny of her parents, the dirt near his toe became more than fascinating. In the ensuing silence, he looked up in time to glimpse Ana's anxious glance at Raul. She patted Olivia's bowed head.

"You tell me where you were, yes?" she said to the little girl's averted face.

With a slight hesitation, Olivia sniffled. "At booth."

Ana glanced back at her husband.

"Olivia." Her father sounded gentle but firm. "You *near* booth or *on* booth?"

She hung her head. "On booth—"

"It was my fault." William's heart pounded. "I helped her up there."

Her father turned toward him, his jaw tight. "You, too, on booth?"

William gulped. "Y-yes, sir."

"You kiss him on booth?" asked the mother.

Olivia bowed her head and nodded. To William's surprise, she sent him a mischievous glance through her lashes that neither parent witnessed.

Raul scowled at Ana as she lowered their daughter to the ground. He focused on William again. "You name, young man?"

"William, sir. William Randall Hatch, the third." Filled with dread, he squared his shoulders and waited while the two adults argued in a foreign language.

What were they saying? Olivia's face provided no clue, until she hung her head. William squirmed. "Are you going to tell my parents?"

The mother hesitated. "They shall not hear of it this day. You parents will know if and when is necessary, yes?" She gazed at her husband until he agreed.

Still frowning, Raul said, "Is time to return home, William Randall Hatch, the third."

"Yes, sir." William did not need to be told twice. He made his escape, relief singing in his veins. Gypsies sure were strange people.

"Good-bye, William," Livy called after him.

William paused to shoot her a disgusted look over his shoulder, and then dashed off.

***

"Could this mean they are destined?" Ana's heart clenched. This could not be good. Surely Livy would be happier among her own people. This fair-skinned boy knew nothing of the ways of Gypsies, and what they knew of his did not bode well.

"Destined?" Raul watched William's forlorn figure slow to a walk. "But, Ana, it is a fable only, no? And how could it apply to ones so young?"

"I do not know. If unions can be arranged at birth, then perhaps—"

"Ana—" He placed his hands on her shoulders.

"Raul, do not try to pacify me." She waved a finger in his face. "According to the old ones, if it be the anniversary of your birth when you first kiss, that blessed moment over the ancient rune becomes your union of destiny."

"I am well acquainted with the folktale, Ana." He flashed a wry grin. "The question is, does it apply to ones so young, no? I think not."

"Folktale?" That discussion could be saved for another day. She clutched her hands and turned away from his disbelief. "Once, I considered the old ones to be shrewd for converting a tree-carved rune into floorboards. If it had power, what better way to hide it from those who would use it for wrong? And when my grandparents traded for them so many years ago, I thought it clever to disguise them in a kissing booth."

"And profitable," he muttered.

"But we have become complacent over the years." She shoved back her mane of hair. "We do not know this boy, nor his people. If the legend is true—"

"Ana, we shall wait and see." Her husband wrapped his arms around her. She leaned on him, drawing comfort.

Olivia wiggled into the middle of their embrace. Raul lifted her up for a kiss. "What will become of this? Perhaps nothing, eh?" He looked at Ana. "But we shall make a note of the town and the date."

Ana stroked Olivia's hair then reached up on tiptoe to kiss Raul. "The legend brought us together, my love," she reminded him, knowing he did not believe in the power of the rune.

He kissed her back tenderly. It had been a long time since he contested the legend with her, but he was not yet convinced. He smirked. "It would serve them right."

"Who, Papa?" Livy played with a length of her mother's hair.

"I believe he refers to the snobby elite," laughed her mother.

"What does *that* mean?" The child drew her brow.

Ana kissed the small nose. "It is a lesson for another day, little one."

***

William kicked at any rocks in the road foolish enough to get in his way. *Why is everyone so mad? All we did was climb up on a stupid floor.*

He aimed a vicious kick at another rock. *Stupid Olivia.* What did she have to go and kiss him for? *Stupid girl.*

If anyone found out, he'd never hear the end of it. No eleven-year-old boy wanted to be teased all summer. He chose another unfortunate rock and drew back his leg. With any luck, he would never see Olivia again.

***

Fairly Safe

Chapter 1
Lenny's Livery

1998- Sixty Years Later...

Pleased with the level of sleaze verified by her compact mirror, Casey's entire eighteen-year-old body snapped with excitement. Time to try out her southern drawl.

"Okay, *Clarisse*, honey, let's go do a little research." Batting her makeup-laden, dark-brown eyes, she blew a kiss at her transformed self. "Or should I call you Mata Hari instead?"

She snapped the compact closed with a click. *You sure don't look eighteen anymore. Your own mother wouldn't recognize you.*

This was going to be as easy as pie. She had the perfect disguise, except for the itchy blonde wig. With one last check to make sure her dark locks were not exposed, she exited the public restroom and sashayed toward the convenience store exit. Two weeks of practicing maneuvers in spike heels had paid off. Judging by the double take from the young male cashier, she strutted like a pro. Enjoying the attention, she flashed him her most brazen smile and sauntered toward her car.

Sliding into the driver's seat, she kicked off the uncomfortable designer heels. As the engine sprang to life, so did Blondie on the radio. Gleeful, she cranked up the volume.

One way or another
I'm gonna getcha.
"Next stop, Lenny's Livery!"

***

Jacob Kent glanced out the window of the employees' workroom, catching sight of a frail, elderly man shuffling up the sidewalk. The movement of the old gent was so similar to his grandfather, even after so many years, his throat tightened.

Wow, where did that come from? Filled with nostalgia, he watched the gent make his way toward their entrance. *I wonder if he wants a rental?* Walk-ins at Lenny's Livery were unusual. Most limousine bookings came by computer or on the phone. All the same, he was there as the driver on call.

Sighing at the pending interruption, Jacob closed his textbook. And then chuckled. Five minutes ago, he'd been wishing for an excuse to take a break. A healthy twenty-one-year-old male could only be so devoted to his studies on a warm September Saturday.

"Hey, Jacob, our last car rental for the day might be strolling in." Rita Timmons, the office intern, poked her cheery face into the room. "Neville's sure going to be happy."

Clayton Neville—the sniveling, fawning, opportunistic branch manager—bore an unfortunate similarity to Jacob's childhood caseworker. As the only chauffeur left, booking this last gig would mean leaving Rita alone in the office with their boss. Neville fancied himself a ladies' man, and, on more than one occasion, had directed his unwanted attention toward her. Despite being rebuffed, he continued to bump up against her when he caught her alone. To Jacob's annoyance, she clearly did not know how to put a stop to it.

He mentally shook himself. *It's not my job to watch over Rita. It's not like she's my friend or anything.* He did not do friends at work. As a matter of fact, he didn't do friends pretty much anywhere.

Leaning back in his chair, he stretched his arms toward the ceiling. "Hey, are you going to be all right here alone?" *Did that just come out of my mouth?*

"Yes, hero. Don's meeting me for lunch."

"Hero? I'm no hero." She was pushing his buttons, but the reaction popped out anyway. "Neville was getting on my last nerve. Period. End of story."

"Yeah, keep telling yourself that. *I* know better. Besides, Neville hasn't bothered me since you had Don put in an appearance as my jealous boyfriend. I'm grateful." She directed a regal bow in his direction.

"Yeah, well, no good deed goes unpunished." He reopened his book, hoping she'd take the hint and leave him alone.

"Whatever do you mean by that?"

Jacob scowled at her innocent expression. She knew exactly what he meant. Ever since the advent of Don, Neville's attentions had been summarily deflected. In the fallout, Rita had developed an annoying abundance of gratitude. Jacob had tried to explain his preference for his privacy—several times, in fact— but Rita remained undeterred, disrupting his comfortable solitude in the name of friendship.

She stared back at him, refusing to be baited.

"Fine," he said, slamming the book closed. "Once again.... First, there's you, getting all gooey over nothing." He interrupted her protest by slapping his palms on the table as he leaned forward in exasperation. "Then there's Don, my *formerly* perfect roommate. For two years, he did his thing and left me alone. Now, it seems like every time I turn around, I'm tripping over the great big hulk. I sure wish things would go back to the way they were." There were no words to express how much he missed his previously unobtrusive roommate.

She shrugged. "Live and learn. That's what happens when you have friends."

"We're not friends. We're roommates, for chrissakes. And, FYI, I don't need a friend at work. I need my privacy so I can study."

"Too bad. We're friends, and you can still study."

"Why? Ever since you took up with Don, Neville leaves you alone."

Rita blushed as only a blue-eyed redhead could. "You mean because he *thinks* I've taken up with Don. It was *your* idea to have him pose as my boyfriend."

"Yeah, because Don's twice the little worm's size." To the casual observer, Don's broad, six-foot-three frame seemed better suited for a linebacker than his true persona, a graduating medical student with a gentle bedside manner. But Neville didn't know that.

"Shush!" She shot a glance over her shoulder toward their boss's office. "What if he hears you?"

"He won't. He's having too much fun adding up today's receipts. It's not even ten thirty, and almost every car is rented. Weird."

She bobbed her head. "Right? That's got to be some kind of record. How often do the leftovers get rented on a Saturday morning? And today they *all* went, one right after another. Totally weird."

"I'll bet Neville's trying to figure out some way to take the credit."

"I hope the new owners dump his sorry butt."

He grimaced at her reference to the recent surprise takeover of Lenny's Livery. "Yeah, well, *I* hope everyone else will be able to hang onto their jobs." Jacob shared the underlying fear permeating the staff. He ran his fingers through his hair. "I sure would hate to lose this cushy job. Where else are they going to pay me to sit around and study until someone needs me?"

"Oh, Jacob, it doesn't seem fair. You've been here six months longer than me, and you have no job security. But I get to complete my internship—"

"Aw, Rita, don't worry about me. I'm a part-timer. I can get another job, easy. And with a better boss."

She shuddered. "I don't care what you say. I owe you big time for getting that creep to leave me alone."

"Forget it. Really. Please forget it." He waved away her thanks. "Although, I didn't think you were going to fall for him."

"Fall for Neville?" squawked Rita. "I would never—"

"Noooo. I mean Don. You know, my new burly best friend."

She blushed again, a deeper pink. "Who says I've fallen for him?"

"Well, if you haven't, you're going to have a very unhappy medical student on your hands."

"Really?" she squeaked. "What did he—"

The jangling of the bells hanging from the front door announced the arrival of the elderly patron. Rita glared at Jacob's bland expression and stalked out of the workroom without closing the door.

It sure would be great if she got together with Don. She's tall enough. Then the two of them would both *leave me alone.*

The elderly customer maneuvered toward Rita's desk. He wore a rumpled dark suit and a gentle expression.

"Good morning, my dear." His voice quavered with age as he removed a slightly dented hat from his shock of uncombed white hair.

"Good morning, sir. How may we be of service today?" Rita's earlier cheer was restored. She treated every customer as if they were the president.

"You may begin by calling me William, my dear." He lowered himself into the seat across from her.

"Of course, William. How may we be of service?"

"I have a very important trip to make to Massachusetts

today. My friend told me to try your company."

Jacob could hear the smile in Rita's voice. "You're in luck, sir. We have one limousine left."

As they began the paperwork, Jacob picked up his blazer and hat and prepared to fetch the limo. *All the way to Massachusetts? Probably for some doctor's appointment. Oh, well.* Perhaps he could squeeze in some studying while he waited.

More jangling from the front door bells alerted them to the presence of a second customer. Jacob shrugged on his blazer. *Whoever you are, it sucks to be you. You're five minutes too late.*

"Well, good morning," sang out Neville's nasal twang.

Jacob stiffened as his boss scurried into view, brushing breakfast crumbs off his tie. He was a slightly stooped, slightly balding, slightly paunched, middle-aged guy on a power trip. Jacob didn't have to see the second customer to know it had to be a female...predictably, an attractive female. Why else would his boss put in an appearance?

Rita squared her shoulders. "Good morning, miss," she echoed. "I will be right with you."

"Nonsense," interjected Neville. "No need to wait. I'd be happy to help you. Step right into my *private* office."

Rita turned back to William as the second customer stepped into Jacob's view. A pair of spiky heels and a short skirt, topped with platinum blond hair, sailed toward a preening Neville.

Wow! No wonder Neville bothered to leave his office before lunch. The chances of the old guy booking the last limo had just dropped to zero.

A few moments later, Neville stepped out of his office. "Well, today's your lucky day, Clarisse. We have one limo left."

"One moment, William." Rita scrambled to her feet to intercept her boss. "Excuse me, Mr. Neville," she hissed. "I'm already booking the limo for the customer who came in before her."

Jacob's gut tightened as the little dictator's face hardened. Neville would get what Neville wanted. Rita would get caught in the crossfire, and, for all her trouble, the old guy would still be left with nothing.

"*Ahem.* Well, may I see the paperwork?" Neville asked through gritted teeth.

She hesitated for a moment before spinning on her heel and stalking toward her desk. "Don't worry, Mr.—"

"Please call me William, my dear." He patted the hand reaching for the papers.

She relaxed her shoulders. "Don't worry, William. I promise you we will find a way to get you to your appointment." She scooped up the papers, whirled around, and plowed into Neville who was right on her heels.

He snatched the papers out of her hand and leafed through them. A crafty smirk crossed their supervisor's face. Jacob had witnessed this enough times to know what came next. His smarmy boss had found a loophole.

Neville stepped toward the elderly customer. "Everything is in order, sir. All you have to do is provide a credit card."

The older man's gaze flickered from Rita to Neville. "A credit card? I was going to pay in cash." He slid a small pile of wrinkled bills across the desk.

"Yes, sir, but as my associate was about to tell you, we always secure our bookings with a credit card. You know, for security purposes."

"Well, I never had much use for credit cards, young man. Nope, I don't much cotton to going into debt on a whim."

"I'm very sorry, sir, but without a credit card, we won't be able to help you today." Neville shook his head with feigned regret. "Perhaps you could try a car rental agency."

"Oh, no! Please, I don't drive myself, and I must get to Massachusetts."

Neville had already turned away, still wagging his head. "I'm very sorry, sir, but there's nothing I can do. I have to answer to *my* boss, you know."

Jacob had had enough. He headed for Neville, brushing off Rita's restraining hand as he passed by.

"Jacob," she whispered, her face pale.

He ignored her. "Excuse me, Mr. Neville!"

Neville paused outside his office door and snapped, "What is it? I'm busy."

Jacob lowered his voice. "You know the old guy got here first, and he deserves the car. You don't want to help him out because you've got some little hottie in there." Jacob jerked his head toward Neville's office.

"Is there a problem, Clayton?" the hottie simpered at Jacob's elbow.

Neville's face darkened as Jacob's heated. He whirled around to apologize, but Neville's hearty, "No problem at all, Clarisse," all but drowned out his "I didn't mean any disrespect."

Jacob caught a quick peek at the lovely petite blonde before Neville grabbed her elbow and steered her back into his office. It was, however, enough to get an eyeful of her come-and-get-me outfit and the matching glint her dark eyes directed toward Neville. Frustrated, Jacob grabbed his boss by the arm.

"Mr. Neville, you can't just cheat the old guy. He got here first."

Neville slammed the door shut behind Clarisse and reeled around. "Who do you think you are?" he roared, his face an unattractive shade of purple. "I'm the manager, and what I say goes. One more word, and you're fired."

"Jacob," murmured Rita from behind him, but her warning fell on deaf ears. The Nevilles of the world got away with too much.

He crossed his arms over his chest. "Go ahead and fire me. Who'll drive your limo?"

"That's it!" shrieked Neville. "You're fired! Rita, get him out of here. Now!"

Rita blanched. "But—"

"Now, Rita! Or you can go with him!" he bellowed behind a finger brandished in her face.

Chapter 2
The Customer Is Always Right

"Leave her out of this, Neville. I'm going," Jacob ground out. He forestalled any noble statement Rita was about to make by grabbing her arm and steering her into the workroom.

"I'll drive the damn limo myself!" Neville yelled after them before slamming his office door.

"Jeez, Jacob," Rita gasped as he swung the workroom door closed behind them. "Whatever happened to Mr. Don't Get Involved?"

"I know, I know." Jacob paced, combing his hair with his fingers. What had he been thinking? Nothing. He hadn't been thinking anything at all. He had been reacting because some old guy reminded him of his grandfather. *Stupid, stupid, stupid.*

Still pacing, Jacob tried to calm down. He had to figure out what to do next. *I am not begging for my job back.*

Rita leaned against a table, wringing her hands. She kept glancing at the door like she was trying to get up the nerve to do something stupid. He needed to nip that in the bud. There was enough stupid in the room already.

"Hey, I'll be okay." He hoped he sounded a lot more stouthearted than he felt. He palmed his hair, trying to smooth it back down in an attempt to appear less freaked out and closer to normal. "I can pick up another job anywhere…most likely. But, Rita, *you* got to stay out of trouble. You need to complete your internship."

She nodded and sagged a bit.

Jacob cooled his forehead on the window. "This is so messed up. I'm out of a job, and the old guy still doesn't have a ride."

"That's what I was trying to tell you before you went all hero-like," said Rita. "William wants to go to the Springfield area. You could've taken him in my car."

He snorted. "The mom-mobile?" Shaking his head, he folded his arms and sat on the counter.

"Shut up."

"Yeah, well, how were you planning to get home?"

She cleared her throat as she perched on the edge of the table. "Don could pick me up after work." She traced a scar in the wood with her finger.

He stared at her pink face then straightened. "Well, why not? I find myself with some extra time on my hands."

"You'll take him?" She clasped her hands and jumped to her feet. "He can pay you instead of the company."

"Go ask him. If he's game, I'm in." He picked up his cap and patted it into a jaunty angle. "Let's make sure he gets the full treatment every Lenny's Livery customer deserves."

Rita headed back to where William sat clutching the edge of her desk with a white-knuckled grip.

"Umm, sir—"

He raised his hand, prompting her to amend, "I mean, *William*. As you may have heard, we have run into a bit of a problem. But I have a solution, if you can be a little flexible."

"Let me guess." He jerked his head toward her boss's office. "My legs aren't as pretty as hers, so she gets the last limo."

The old guy got that right. Jacob grabbed the keys off Rita's bag and waited.

Rita sank into her seat. "I'm so sorry, William. I should have said something—"

"Now, now, my dear. It seems to me the young driver said quite enough. Where did the boy go?"

"Well, that's what I wanted to talk to you about. He can bring a car around for you now, if you agree."

"But I thought there was only one limo left." William raised an eyebrow.

"There is, I mean, there was. Jacob is bringing *my* car around. If your heart's not set on a limo, it's another option for getting you to your appointment."

"What about you?" William asked.

"Oh, I can have a...a friend pick me up after work."

Jacob grinned as her color changed. She was either blushing again or having a hot flash at nineteen.

"Hmmm." William squinted at her. "I accept your gracious offer. You are an extremely valuable employee, young lady, and I'm going to make sure the owner knows it." He sat back in his seat with a determined nod.

Better make sure it's the new owner. Jacob headed for the back door to get the mom-mobile.

As he pulled the wood-paneled car door open, he tried to picture how Rita was going to explain this one. *"Uh, there's one more thing. I hope you don't mind, but my car is not exactly in the same class as a limo. It's an old station wagon...."*

Jacob brought her car around front as Rita escorted his final customer outside. At least the old guy was laughing. Jacob jumped out and ran around to open the car door. Touching his cap, he saluted his passenger.

The old man held out his hand. "Jacob, is it? I wish to thank you, young man. Not many people would risk their employment for a stranger."

A fresh wave of irritation swept through him as he shook the old guy's hand. Why had he picked today to erupt out of his look-out-for-myself cocoon? *If I'd just kept his mouth shut, I'd still have a job.*

He shrugged it off. "Stranger or friend, what's the difference? It's too bad you had to hear all that...." He gestured toward the office and paused, his hand frozen in midair.

Through the front window, he watched a red-faced blonde smacking the stupid out of a stunned Neville.

"What are you looking at?" asked Rita, craning her neck.

"She just slapped Neville silly." Somehow that lessened the sting of being fired a bit.

"Hah!" Rita crowed. "No means no, Neville."

"So, he got what he deserved." William cackled.

"I guess the limo is available after all, sir, but I'll have to call in another driver," said Rita.

"If it's all the same to you, my dear, these arrangements are more than suitable." William patted Jacob on the arm. "I prefer my money go to this young man after his sacrifice."

"Thank you, sir." Jacob bowed from the waist as he opened the car door.

"Would you mind if I rode in front with you? I'm not much for pomp and circumstance."

Rita and Jacob chorused, "The customer is always right," and grinned at each other.

She giggled. "Have a pleasant day, you two. I'd better get back inside. It was very nice to meet you, William." With a final wave, she scurried toward the office.

This won't be so bad. Jacob closed the car door for his elderly passenger. *I can start job hunting tomorrow,* and *I'll have some extra cash to last me until I get another job.*

"Is she going to be all right in there?" William's brow knitted as he watched Rita's retreating figure.

"Sure she is. Her 'boyfriend' is meeting her for lunch, and Neville likes to stay out of his way." Jacob slid into the driver's seat and checked William's seat belt. "So, sir, what is today's destination?"

"Young man…." William paused, pleasure written all over his face. "Take me to The Big E."

Chapter 3
So, This Is a Fair

The Big E? Jacob blinked at his fare. "What's that?"

"What's that? You've never heard of The Eastern States Exposition in West Springfield? It's only the biggest event in the northeast. Millions of people attend."

"Let me get this straight. You want me to take you to a *fair?*"

"That's right." The reason for his unemployment rubbed his hands together with happy anticipation.

Realizing his mouth hung open, Jacob slammed it shut. *I thought he had a doctor's appointment or something. I lost my job so this old wonk could hang out at a fair?*

William perched on the edge of his seat like a little kid getting ready to blow out his birthday candles.

Was he for real? "Yes, sir. The Big E, it is," Jacob bit out. Trying to regain his composure, he put the station wagon into gear and set out on the three-hour drive.

"Don't you like the Big E?" William watched him.

He had a sudden urge to squirm. "Uh, no, it's not that. I haven't been there." He didn't mind polite chitchat with customers, but not while trying to rein in his emotions over his sacrificed job. "I don't have time for things like fairs."

"I love fairs. I go to them every chance I get." William leaned toward him. "I met my wife at one. Fifty-five years ago. My one true love." He stared out the window. "She kissed me, you know. The first day we met. At a kissing booth."

Jacob chuckled, the sting of the day's events diminishing ever so slightly. "A kissing booth?"

"Livy never did anything in a conventional way." William settled back into his seat, once again gazing out at the scenery.

"Unfortunately, she passed on many years ago." He angled toward him. "Do you have a young lady? Like that nice Rita, perhaps?"

"I don't have time for a girl right now. I'm trying to graduate in three years."

"I'd bet you'd make time for that little blonde firecracker."

As if a babe like that would give someone like me the time of day. "Nah, she's not my type. She's Clayton's type."

"Clayton?"

"Clayton Neville, my boss. My *former* boss."

"Young man, don't worry about your job. I have a feeling much better things are in store for you." William folded his hands and smiled as if enjoying a private joke.

"Well, there's nothing I can do about it now." Jacob shrugged. "I might as well enjoy the ride."

"Excellent attitude, m'boy, excellent attitude. Resilience is what's going to make you successful." He relaxed against his seat. "Now, tell me about yourself, young man. We have a three-hour ride ahead of us. You should be able to fit most of your story in."

Jacob glanced over at William and snorted. "Are you kidding me? I can squeeze my life into fifteen minutes. I'm only twenty-one. Nothing's really happened yet."

His words did not sway his passenger. Instead, under William's gentle prodding, Jacob opened up, recounting the various foster care homes after his grandfather's death. Even decent foster care had always made him feel like a permanent guest. So had his full scholarship at Yale University, but college life had afforded him the unique opportunity to live in the same place for two consecutive years.

As the car approached the Big E gate, William asked, "Shall I call you when I'm ready to go?"

"No, sir. I don't have a cell phone. Pick a time, and I'll meet you at Gate 1 near the Connecticut Pavilion."

"Surely you make enough money to afford a cell phone."

"I do, but I have plans for my future, so I don't spend my money on *anything*. When it's time to go job hunting, I'll have me a decent suit and enough money to relocate wherever the job takes me." He negotiated the car near the entrance. "Yup, when graduation time comes, I'm going to be ready."

"I believe you will, young man. I believe you will."

A mild glow curled inside him. It was nice to have someone believe in him, even a stranger. William somewhat resembled the man who'd raised him; not the healthy, robust Granddad who had enveloped him in love when his parents died, but the quieter, calmer Granddad learning to live with his declining condition.

"Well, I'm off." William shook his hand. "I'll meet you back here in four hours. Go enjoy the fair."

Jacob stiffened as William tried to curl his fingers around several bills. "No, no, no." He tried to return the money. "I'm going to stay in the car and study. You can pay me when I drop you off."

"Nonsense. This is fair fare. You at least need to have something to eat." William's voice and demeanor were firm. "Besides, you'll hurt my feelings if you say no."

Wow. This old coot totally expects to get his own way. Fine. Whatever. "Okay. I'll get something to eat. Thank you. But I don't need this much."

"Excellent." William beamed as he put his hand on the doorknob. "And you do need that much. I guess you haven't been to a fair in a while. They're expensive."

"Oh, no you don't. You get the full treatment today, sir." Jacob leapt out of the car and hurried around to the other side. With a flourish, he opened the door and extended his hand to help his elderly passenger disembark. "I shall meet you back here at five thirty."

"Until then, sir." William twinkled up at him, and stood stiffly and stretched. He sauntered toward the entrance.

Once again Jacob was struck by the similarity of William's gait to Granddad's. He shook his head and headed for the parking lot.

Luck was with him. Almost immediately a spot vacated right in front of him. Congratulating himself on his parking karma, he climbed out of the car and rested against it.

Beneath the beaming sun, he considered his sudden unemployment. *I'll pick up a paper and see what's out there. I wonder if the company taking over Lenny's is hiring. Wouldn't that piss off Neville.*

He rolled up his sleeves and loosened his tie. It was time to find some shade. The beautiful September afternoon sure was getting hot.

Real hot.

Is this too hot for an old guy like William?

"You've already stuck your neck out enough for one day," Jacob reminded his reflection in the car window.

Sighing, he ignored himself and headed for the fairgrounds to search for his customer. *No telling how long I'll be stuck here if the old guy passes out some place.*

He picked up a discarded map and scanned the layout. The fair was huge, unbelievably huge. With no idea of the direction the old guy might have taken, his chances of finding his passenger were close to zero. On impulse, he headed toward The Kissing Booth. With luck still on his side, after about ten minutes, Jacob came upon William sitting at a table in the food concourse, sipping a cold drink, and chatting with a family of little girls.

Perhaps it would be best to keep tabs on William from a distance. Granddad had always acted insulted when he tried to look out for him. Jacob certainly didn't want to insult his only paying customer. He decided to check out menus on the other side of the concourse.

The variety of the food choices staggered him, some familiar, and some strange. Latin food. Chinese food. Indian food. Meat on a stick, meat in a roll, meat wrapped up, or meat on a salad. Veggie plates. Fruit plates. Fried dough. Deep-fried peanut butter and jelly sandwich. Deep-fried cookies. Deep-fried bananas. Ice cream and gelato on cones, as shakes, in sundaes, or deep-fried. His nose yearned for Italian sausage, peppers, and onions; his throat craved fresh-made lemonade, but the strawberry shortcake satisfied his heart's desire.

Swigging his ice-cold drink, he chose a table situated where he could watch William while eating. He relaxed, savoring the play of sweet-and-sour liquid in his mouth and unwrapping his sandwich. His first bite into the sausage snapped the outer skin, releasing juicy salt-and-garlic flavored meat. *Excellent choice.*

Enveloped in the sights, sounds, and aromas of the unfamiliar surroundings, Jacob watched the scene play out before him the way he would enjoy a good movie. It even came with its own sound track comprised of music from a variety of sources floating in the air. Somehow they merged into a blended sound that promised excitement. Little kids alternated between jumping up and down and tugging on their parents. Teens raced around checking each other out. There were several elderly, some resting, some shuffling after waddling toddlers, others staring into space, lost in thought, or memory. Even the squalling baby or two did not disrupt the atmosphere.

So, this was a fair. No wonder they held them all over the states.

After a time, William strolled off with his little friends toward one of the kiddy rides. Jacob hurriedly disposed of his garbage and followed. Trailing behind them, he found his first fair totally charming.

"What do you think you're doing?"

Chapter 4
Mistaken Identity

Out of nowhere, an attractive girl blocked Jacob's path. Her shiny, brown ponytail jutted out the back of a baseball cap, which shaded irate brown eyes. Very pretty, irate brown eyes. She emanated a lot of anger, and all of it in his direction. Surprised, Jacob recoiled from the cute face barely flush with his chin.

"What do you think you're doing?" she barked again.

"What?" Confused, Jacob retreated a step from her hands-on-hips belligerence. To his dismay, she followed him, jabbing her finger into his chest.

"You people think you can do anything you want!"

Hoping to defuse the attention of passersby, he raised his palms in surrender. All the same, a small, curious crowd gathered around them. She remained in his path, blocking his way. He had to do something before he lost sight of William.

In an effort to stem the flow of heated words coming out of her adorable mouth, he made a successful grab for her jabbing hand. A jolt slammed through him, quickening his pulse and making him aware of his suddenly dry mouth. He stared at her, his heart thumping in his chest. She stared back, her mouth forming a perfect O.

Four protective hefty types materialized around them. "Having some trouble, miss?" one of them rumbled.

Uh-oh. Jacob released her hand like a hot potato.

"I…." She wet her lips, relief written all over her face. "I think he's stalking an elderly man."

Ahh. Now Jacob understood. Later, he could consider her sweet concern, but at the moment, his priority was staving off the protective menace closing in. Fight, flight, or freeze?

Fighting was out of the question. Any one of these guys could deck him with one swing.

He tried to back away, but bumped into a living, breathing wall standing behind him. *Whoa!* The flight option had just disappeared.

"Stalking?" Jacob raised his palms again. "I'm not stalking anybody." How had things become so bizarre so fast?

"There you are, Jacob." The familiar, quavering voice came from behind the girl. "Having a little problem?"

Relief flooded him as the girl whirled around.

"You *know* him?" She shot Jacob an embarrassed glance over her shoulder while she mumbled something apologetic about being glad he was safe.

Could she be any cuter?

William drew his brow. "Of course I'm safe, my dear. Why wouldn't I be?" He caught Jacob's eye over her head, and they both shrugged. He was just as puzzled.

"Oh, no," she groaned. She lifted her head and waved a limp hand. "I'm so sorry. This was a case of mistaken identity," she announced to anyone listening. "Totally my mistake. I thought.... You know what? It doesn't matter. It was my mistake."

"So, everything's in order here?" rumbled the wall behind Jacob.

"Yes, everything's in order here," Jacob snapped at a person four times his size, courtesy of the adrenalin rush conveniently provided by the encounter.

"Yes, everything's in order here," repeated William in a level tone. "And thank you. It's so nice to know strangers watch out for each other."

The crowd dispersed, leaving Jacob with a calm William, a red-faced girl, and an unusual thumping somewhere in the vicinity of his chest.

The girl faced him and opened her mouth to speak, but nothing came out. She was oddly familiar. Where had he seen her before? They regarded each other for another moment as he searched for something exceptional and witty to say.

"I'm so sorry," she blurted out, and then dashed off.

"Hey, wait a minute!" He tried to follow her, but, to his great disappointment, William detained him.

Jacob jammed one hand in his pocket and shoved the other through his hair.

Here it comes.

Chapter 5

A New Path

"So, what *are* you doing here?" William's expression was enigmatic.

Warm around the collar in the hot September sun, Jacob cleared his throat. "Well, I decided to come to the fair...like *you* suggested. And I...went through the same entrance you did, so I guess I, um, ended up near where you were...."

William cocked a quizzical brow.

"Yeah, so," Jacob amended. "Basically, I followed you."

"Why?"

How to explain his concern without offending the old guy? *Awkward.* "Well, I sorta...." Jacob stalled, searching for a tactful explanation. He gave up with a noisy gust of air. "Look, I'm sorry. I don't mean to, you know, be rude." William's eyes narrowed, prompting him to continue in a rush. "But Rita's AC wasn't working, and it's almost ninety degrees out here, and it didn't seem like a good idea for you to go off by yourself when, I mean, just in case...." The rush lost its momentum.

"In case the temperature proved to be too much for me?"

Jacob sagged a bit. "Yes, sir."

"It's been a long time since someone tailed me because they were worried about me." William rubbed his chin.

What? That was *not* on the list of expected responses. "Well, I can see you're doing just fine, so I'm going to head back to the car. I can still get in about an hour of studying."

"That will be fine, m'boy. I'll be at the gate at five thirty." William patted him on the arm.

Jacob strolled back to the car, scanning the crowd, hoping to catch a glimpse of the mystery girl and her flashing brown eyes. He couldn't remember ever reacting in such an unsettled way to any girl he knew, let alone a complete stranger.

He reached the car without a glimpse of her. Making one last, hopeful search of the area, he gave up. *Guess my luck ran out.* Filled with an uncharacteristic disappointment, he opened the driver's door, and plopped down on the seat.

And scrambled out of the car. *Yowww!* While he had been at the fair, Rita's mom-mobile had transformed into an oven with four tires.

After opening the windows to cool the car, he eased onto the seat and proceeded to maneuver the car closer to the gate. Watching the slow stream of people exiting the Big E, he settled in to wait for William. Maybe she would pass by on her way out. Opening his book, Jacob reminded himself he didn't have time for...for...for what?

Memorable brown eyes and a shiny brunette ponytail popped back into his mind.

With a guilty start, Jacob watched William gingerly settle into the front passenger seat. *What is he doing back so soon?* Jacob glanced at the clock. *Five thirty-seven? Whoa! Did I really just spend an hour watching for some random girl?* He slammed his unread books shut. "I'm so sorry I didn't get the door for you."

"Don't be silly, young man. When you get to be my age, you take pleasure in being able to do for yourself."

Jacob checked his passenger's seat belt. "Where to, sir?"

"Let's head back, Jacob." William shielded his eyes from the sun's glare. "It's been a long day."

"Yes, sir." He flipped down his passenger's visor while negotiating the traffic leaving the fair.

When they reached the highway, William asked, "Well? What did you think?"

"About the fair?"

"Yes, about the fair. How did it rate compared to the others you've been to?"

Jacob cleared his throat. "Well, actually, I've never been to one before."

"Never?"

Jacob squashed the urge to fidget. "This was my first one."

"Been to a carnival?"

"Most foster homes don't have a lot of spare change."

"Well, that's unfortunate, but not a calamity."

Funny how William's kindness dissolved his discomfort.

The older man sat up and leaned over the console. "So? What did you think?" There was that birthday-cake expression again.

An unbidden grin spread ear to ear. "It was *great*. I had no idea." That launched an exchange of their favorite moments, which lasted until they were almost back.

Later, as they crossed back into Connecticut, William asked, "Out of curiosity, how long did you follow me?"

Jacob glanced his way and squirmed a little. "I guess about an hour."

"An hour?" William sat up straight. "An *hour*? I thought maybe a few minutes. No wonder she overreacted." He slumped back into the seat. "I must be slipping. I've become too complacent. You should not have been able to follow me undetected for anywhere near an hour."

His words triggered a ripple of alarm. "William, are you... are you in some kind of trouble?"

The older man looked at him openmouthed then threw back his head with a hoot. "No, no, young man. *I'm* not the one in trouble. But I sure can cause trouble. Wait until Monday." William rubbed his hands together and paused. "You know, Jacob, come to think of it, I could use your help. I need a car and driver for Monday afternoon. Do you think you could be available to chauffeur me to a meeting in Stamford?" His blue eyes twinkled.

After the briefest of hesitations, Jacob shrugged. "I don't see why not. I don't get out of class until ten, though, so I won't be able to collect you until eleven thirty, at the earliest." He could put off job hunting until later in the afternoon.

"Perfect."

"I'm pretty sure Rita will let me borrow her car again...as long as you don't mind riding in The Mom-Mobile."

"This car has a name?"

"Nah, more like a title."

William peered into the back, taking in the *Baby On Board* sign and the car seat. "Does Rita have children?"

"Nope." He snorted. "She drives The Mom-Mobile to keep the party boys away. A girl like Rita draws guys like bees to honey, but she doesn't want to be bothered. She calls them Good-Time Charleys."

"Good-Time Charley? Sounds more like someone from my generation."

"Well, as far as I can tell, she's an old-fashioned girl with a strong mind for business."

"Good to know, young man. Good to know. I'll keep it in mind."

Keep it in mind? Bewildered, he glanced sideways at his passenger. *Whatever for?*

As they approached town, William directed him to an assisted-living facility. Jacob hopped out and held the door open for him. A stiff-backed man in a white coat came down the walkway to meet them.

"Thank you for fulfilling an old man's wish, Jacob," said William. "We are defined by moments such as these. You wait and see. Because you took the high road today, a path will open up for you that could change your life." He extended his hand.

Jacob shook it, startled by his strength. "Quite a grip you got there, William."

"I work out."

"I guess so," muttered Jacob to himself as the man from the facility drew closer.

"Ah, Hanson. Nice coat," said William. "I'd like to introduce you to Jacob, my new chauffeur."

"Sir." Hanson directed a disdainful nod toward Jacob.

"Here you go, young man," said William as he pressed a wrinkled envelope into Jacob's hand. "And here's the address where you can pick me up on Monday. Hanson will take it from here."

"Yes, sir," replied Jacob, lifting two fingers to his brow in a parting salute. "Until Monday."

He did a smart about-face and headed for the driver's side. Behind him, Hanson drawled, "A station wagon?"

William scolded the haughty attendant as The Mom-Mobile roared to life. "Honestly, Hanson. You could have been a little friendlier."

He chuckled at Hanson's disdainful reply. "But, sir, a *station wagon?*"

With a low whistle, Jacob pulled up to the front entrance of the address William had scrawled for him. An electronic gate swung open to a long, winding driveway bordered by lush landscaping on both sides. He paused to verify the address. *Yup, this is the place.*

He put the car into gear and eased it down the drive, eventually reaching a magnificent three-story brick mansion nestled among lavish gardens surrounded by tall evergreens. Three men in dark, conservative suits came down the stairs as Jacob hurried around the car to hold the door open. One of them slid into the backseat, clutching his briefcase, rigid and dismissive in his demeanor.

The second man turned out to be Hanson. He regarded the dark sedan Jacob had rented for the occasion with a sniff. "I suppose this is something of an improvement over the last vehicle. I shall be riding in the front, if you don't mind."

"Of course, sir." Jacob masked his irritation and opened the front car door. As Hanson sat down, Jacob realized the third man, offering his hand in greeting, was none other than William.

"Good to see you again, Jacob." The blue eyes twinkled.

He gaped. This was not the same fragile William clad in ill-fitting clothes he had met on Saturday. This William was healthy and strong, standing tall in a tailored suit. This William matched the grip of his handshake. Even his voice exuded power. The only thing familiar about him was his beaming grin.

"Mr. Hatch, we should be going," reminded the man seated in the back.

Jacob's mouth dropped open. "Mr. Hatch? William *Hatch*? Your company took over Lenny's Livery."

"Right you are, young man. And, now, it's time to get this show on the road." William seated himself. "By the way, Jacob," he added, with a wink. "Consider yourself un-fired. Welcome to your new path."

"Yes, sir!" Jacob closed the door and hurried around to the driver's side, pleasure bubbling in his chest.

Jacob delivered his customers to a high-rise in downtown Stamford and parked the sedan in a spot labeled *Reserved for W. Hatch*. Although the men had not addressed him further, he surmised from their conversation that Mr. Hatch—Jacob no longer thought of him as William—had been doing what he liked to call "research incognito" by posing as a customer of the businesses they were acquiring. The shockers just kept right on coming when the security guard directed Jacob to follow his passengers. Curiosity and excitement rippled through his stomach as he hurried inside.

"What was your favorite part, Jacob?" Squeezed around a sidewalk table for two with Jacob and Don in Stamford's Ridgefield Plaza, Rita scooped up the last of her celebratory ice cream.

Mr. Hatch had gathered the local staff from Lenny's Livery, as well as those from several other branches, to announce his new changes. Jacob was still reeling from the morning's events. But his favorite part? It was hard to choose between the greenish hue on Neville's face as he watched Mr. Hatch being escorted to the podium, and the rosy pink in Rita's cheeks when Mr. Hatch offered her Neville's position as branch manager when she graduated.

"Wait, I know," Jacob chortled. "The best part was when Mr. Hatch described what had happened at each of his 'research sites.' If you wanted to know who he was talking about, all you had to do was look around to see who squirmed."

"Yeah. And I thought we had it bad with Neville." Rita gave an unladylike snort. She slid an alarmed glance at Don, who was gazing at her in adoration.

Don blinked, straightened up, and refocused. "I can't believe Hatch arranged to have all your limos rented except one. The way he set up Neville." Don clapped his hands. "He's good. He's really good."

Jacob tipped his cup to get the last of his root beer float. "I wonder who the blonde was."

"Blonde?" Rita sniffed. "Hah! Had to be a wig. Brown eyes do not go with that hair color."

"You have nothing to be jealous about, Rita. She's got nothing on you. Right, Don?" Jacob nudged his hefty roommate.

"Oh, yes. Absolutely! I mean, I didn't see her myself, but you...you...." Don bumbled.

Jacob shook his head as he rose to throw out their garbage. Don was hopeless. Jacob tossed their trash and returned to their table where a shaken Don sat alone.

"Rita had to go. She said to say 'bye." Wild-eyed, Don gaped at Jacob. "Jake.... She asked me out," he said, sounding strangled. "To the Big E. On a date. With *her*."

Finally! The perfect ending to the perfect day. Jacob grinned. Don might be clueless, but Rita obviously wasn't. And now they would both be out of his hair.

Chapter 6
Hanson Weighs In

1998- One Year Later...

"Are you sure you can't join us, Hanson?" William rubbed his hands together in anticipation. It was going to be a beautiful day, although Hanson was looking more sour than usual.

"No, thank you, sir. This cold is getting the better of me. I don't want to get anyone sick." He reached for a nearby tissue box. "Besides, you already have Mr. Kent as a traveling companion, who, by the way, is waiting for you in the library." He dabbed at his pink nose.

William picked up his hat and pointed it at his valet. "You enjoy young Kent's company as much as I do. You should come along."

"I never said I did not like Mr. Kent." Hanson produced an odd honking noise as he blew his nose. "I merely said it seems he is here all of the time."

"Perhaps that has something to do with you converting one of the guest rooms into a bedroom for him."

"That was simple common sense," Hanson sputtered. "You were keeping him out until all hours with these excursions to the fairs, and then he had to drive all the way back to New Haven. Not to mention his constant trips out here to get advice on those school projects of his."

"The room was a fine idea." He continued to push Hanson's buttons. Why? Because he could. "You just don't want to admit you've warmed up to him."

"Well, he did not make much of a first impression, did he? He chauffeured you in a *station wagon*."

His trusty valet was turning the tables on him. "Don't

start, Hanson. The boy made a good first impression on me."

"Well, *I'm* not the one who did a background check on him, am I?"

"Hanson!" That came out sharper than he intended. He calmed his voice. "Hanson, you know we have to check out *everyone*. There's no other way to keep them safe." Despite his best efforts, he drooped under the burden of their secret. The sadness he fought so hard to keep at bay trickled into his stomach. "I do so wish I could tell him the truth."

"As do I." Hanson nudged a couple of figurines on a near-by table and wiped away imaginary dust. "He's become more like...." He trailed away as he continued to nudge and dust the same spot.

"It's okay." William sighed, "You can say it. He's become more like family." His unfocused stare drifted toward the window. "It's been nice having young energy around on holidays."

"In many respects, you have become young Kent's surrogate family." Hanson's voice was as subdued as his own.

What was the matter with them? This wasn't a day for sorrow. He cleared his throat, pushing the negative wave aside. "As have you, old friend. Come now. You were as pleased as I to receive his graduation invitation."

"Yes, well, he did quite well at Yale, didn't he, sir?" Hanson pulled down the cuffs of his sleeves with thinly concealed pride.

"Yes, he did." Matching pride filled William. "And he has done quite well since he graduated."

"Yes, sir. I was sure he would."

"Let's go, Mama Bear. Baby Bear is waiting. Get a move on." He planted his hat on his head.

"Mama Bear?" Hanson picked up his bags, frowning in response. "*I* am not the Mama Bear."

Someday—He followed Hanson downstairs to greet Jacob—*someday this huge house will be filled with the sounds of children. Hopefully, someday soon.*

***

I wonder where we're headed today. Jacob gazed out at the familiar manicured grounds of William's estate. *It's too early for The Big E.*

He thought back to his first visit to the fair a year ago, the fateful day he lost his job and met William Hatch…the same day the angry brunette imprinted her pretty brown eyes on him. The real game changer came two days later when William hired him as a part-time chauffeur and became his mentor. When he later offered Jacob an entry-level position in his company, he had jumped at the opportunity. With so many business ideas itching to be explored, what better way to give back to the man who had provided such invaluable guidance?

Little by little, Jacob found himself being pulled out of his shell. Maybe it was living in the same place for so long; or perhaps it was being around people who genuinely seemed to care for him. For the first time in a very long time, he, Jacob Allen Kent, had people in his life he considered true friends. Who would have thought the boy shuffled from house to house would now be juggling his schedule to accommodate holiday invitations? So many things had changed in such a short time. It made his head spin.

Living in the same place for three consecutive years sure will change you. And so does being around William Hatch.

In public, Mr. Hatch, a tough, no-nonsense businessman from old money, expected to get his way. As one of the many chauffeurs in his employ, Jacob rarely drove Mr. Hatch himself. However, after their first trip to The Big E, it was not unusual for his services to be requested for jaunts to a wide variety of fairs. On those days, William would slide into the front passenger seat, and Jacob would spend the day with his mentor.

It had taken quite a while longer to warm up to Reginald Hanson. Fiercely protective of his employer, the enigmatic manservant was more than territorial, but his devotion had taught Jacob an everlasting lesson in loyalty. Somewhere along the line, Hanson had earned his allegiance as well.

Jacob's cell phone rang, and he glanced at the display. "Hey, Dr. Don."

"Hey, yourself," replied his roommate. "So, today's the big day. Where are you heading?"

"I'm still not sure. They haven't come down yet. But you know how Mr. Hatch is. He tells me where we're going when we get into the car. I only know we won't be back until tomorrow."

"Well, then, this is a great time for a reality check."

He groaned. "Just stop. You are not going to med school to be a psychiatrist—"

"Unh-uh. Don't want to hear it. Jake, it's your twenty-first birthday. Time to find yourself a girl. A real girl. A close encounter of the female kind."

"Believe me, buddy, I *always* check out the girls at the fairs," hedged Jacob. He needed to put a stop to this.

"Yeah, well, do something besides check them out. Find one who has a name."

"Whatever." Jacob began pacing the room. His friend's repeated good intentions grated on his nerves.

"I know you better than you think I do, Jake, and I'm telling you, you can't have a future with someone you *think* you *might* run into. Find someone who lives in your neighborhood. Or at least in your state."

"Yes, *Mom.*"

"Hey, how about finding someone who will tell you her real name? Wouldn't that be fun?"

He stopped pacing and growled, "Can we drop this?"

"C'mon, Jake. You hung out with her *one time* at some random fair *last* year."

"Don't forget, I also saw her at that craft fair in Stowe—"

"You *think* you saw her. It could have been anybody. It doesn't count."

Oh, no. It counted. In early October, after The Big E, he had driven William to a fair in Vermont, and twice, while wandering around the fairgrounds, he'd thought he had spotted the girl. As he tried to approach her, she had disappeared into the crowd, but he was sure it had been her. Pretty sure.

Catching sight of her again in early December in New Hampshire had almost a cosmic feel to it—three different fairs in three different states. Jacob had managed to introduce himself, although she coyly had not returned the courtesy. They'd spent several hours together enjoying the fair before she slipped away into the crowd, leaving him with no way to contact her.

Mystified by the meaning of it all, Jacob had been too excited to keep the coincidence to himself.

Big mistake. "I never should have opened my big mouth."

"Yeah, well, that's what friends are for, Jake. Besides, you know Rita is dying to set you up with a date for our wedding."

"Jeez!" He raked his hair in frustration. His second big mistake—one time he let her set him up on a date. One time. Talk about throwing gasoline on a fire…. Rita would not let up. Plopping into an overstuffed chair, he slumped into it and splayed his feet. "Maybe I won't go."

"You're my best man," Don pointed out. "You'll be there. Hey, you could always bring The Nameless Wonder. Oh, wait. You don't know where she lives."

"Stop calling her that!"

"Okay, fine. But what am I supposed to call her? You and I both know she's an excuse for you to avoid dating. And Rita agrees."

Jacob groaned. Of course Rita agreed. "Look, just because you're about to marry your dream girl doesn't mean I...." Jacob paused, distracted by footfalls coming from the hallway. He rose, saying, "Hey, *Mom*, they're coming. Got to go. I promise I'll try to meet a nice girl."

"Shut up!" chuckled Don.

Jacob glared at his quieted phone. Sometimes having friends didn't live up to the hype.

***

William strode into the room with Hanson on his heels. "Ready to go, Jacob?" He rubbed his hands together. This was going to be a great trip.

Jacob spun around. "You bet."

The boy's happy grin reflected William's own enthusiasm. It was a great day for a trip to the fair.

"But, if you don't mind, sir, I have one small matter to take care of before we go."

"Of course. What is it?" William studied the six-foot-one boy-man walking toward him, a folded slip of paper in one outstretched hand, his other hand stuffed in his pocket. Under his guidance, the shy, intense youth with the dark, wavy hair and dark-brown eyes had grown into a handsome, determined young man. More importantly, he was becoming a good man, one who had graduated with honors, and was now shining in his entry-level position. William suspected this was only the beginning.

With Hanson peering over his shoulder, William accepted the paper and unfolded…a check?

"Look." Jacob jammed his hand into his other pocket and took an awkward step back. "When you first hired me, I accepted the cell phone so you could have me on call. That was fine. But when you very generously overnighted a laptop to my dorm, it didn't feel right to accept it…like I was taking advantage of your kindness. But I figured I could put it to good use, and I'd be able to pay you back someday." Jacob cleared his throat. "Well, today's that day."

Despite a tightness in his throat, William managed to smile at the earnest youth before him. He understood the magnitude of his mentee's actions. With respect, he folded the check and slipped it into his pocket. "You've come a long way, m'boy, and you've done us proud." He clapped Jacob on the shoulder.

"Yes, indeed, young man." Hanson's voice wobbled from the hallway. "Quite proud." Hanson blew his nose with a honk. Most likely it was not due to the bighearted, starchy valet's ailment.

"Thank you, Hanson. That means a lot to me," called Jacob.

"How's that cold coming, Hanson?" William snickered.

Jacob mouthed, *Leave him alone,* but William just smirked.

Hanson blew his noise with greater force.

Jacob forestalled William's next jab. "So, where to?" he asked. "You said this was an overnighter."

"We're headed for the Skowhegan State Fair in Maine."

"Maine? I'll bet you'll meet some real characters there." Jacob headed for the door.

"I certainly hope so," muttered Hanson fervently as Jacob passed him.

William tensed as Jacob gave Hanson a questioning glance.

"To the fair!" declared William. He distracted the boy by grasping his arm and steering him toward the door.

"To the fair!" repeated Jacob, brimming with youthful energy.

Masking his relief, William slid into the passenger seat. He shot a warning glare at Hanson, but his valet kept his gaze fixed on the hood of the car. Perhaps Jacob would attribute Hanson's comment to an idiosyncrasy. He certainly had enough of them.

The last thing they needed was for Jacob to become suspicious.

***

Chapter 7
Birthday Kisses

Calliope music and aromas of fried dough and sausages, the essence of the Skowhegan Fair, enveloped Jacob as they emerged from the car. He and William shared a laugh over the heads of a couple of small boys dragging their parents toward the fair's open invitation.

"Well, m'boy, I'm off!" William slid a couple of bills into Jacob's palm.

Jacob had long since stopped objecting to his mentor slipping him "fair fare." Somehow the gesture mattered to William, so Jacob had learned to acquiesce with grace.

Today they stayed true to their ritual. The blinking lights beckoned, and, as per their routine, William sent Jacob on his way before sauntering off by himself. Jacob didn't mind. He enjoyed wandering around, sopping up the sights and sounds of families relaxing and having fun together. Although no longer a foreign experience for him, Jacob continued to appreciate it.

Occasionally, he would catch sight of William in deep conversation with a variety of characters. "Research" William would tell him later with a grin.

As he was about to do justice to his last bite of fried dough, a crowd milling around a nearby sign drew Jacob's attention. Brushing powdered sugar off his hands, he read:

The Kissing Booth
Pucker Up for Charity

The Kissing Booth itself was more like a wooden stage about three feet above the ground, topped with a folding table and a couple of chairs. A bright-blue plastic tarp had been erected overhead to shade the participants, and a heavy red curtain hung behind them, creating a back wall. There were stairs on either side, and the front of the booth was lined with what appeared to be buckets of water.

Two pretty girls, a blonde and a redhead, sat on the chairs, raising money for some worthy cause, one gentle peck on the cheek at a time. About a dozen males of various ages lined up to the left of the stage. Older folks occupied clumps of lawn chairs on either side of the booth, providing an ongoing commentary as they traded quips about the participants.

Brushing wayward powdered sugar off his clothes, Jacob joined the good-natured bystanders next to the line of hopefuls.

And froze.

To his complete and utter astonishment, there was The Nameless Wonder. He held his breath, not daring to believe his good fortune. It was definitely her, in all her glory. Today, the baseball cap was absent, and her shiny brown hair flowed down her back, brushing across her cheeks in the gentle summer breeze. She shook it out of her way, a scowl marring her flushed face as she strode by.

Elated, Jacob moved to intercept her. Then panic set in. What was he going to say to her? After all the time spent hoping he'd run into her, one would think he would've prepared a dazzling opening line designed for this exact moment.

He hadn't.

Apparently she was heading for The Kissing Booth and the merrily waving redhead. A glance established the redhead was gathering her belongings. Horror eclipsed his internal social struggle when he realized the object of his turmoil intended to replace the redhead at The Kissing Booth.

No way! In an instant, harmless fun morphed into inappropriate behavior. Somehow he had to stop her. She wasn't going to kiss a bunch of strangers if he had anything to say about it.

Apparently, someone else was of the same mind. As she approached the side stairs, a strong hand snaked out from a dark suit, grabbed her by the arm, and whirled her around.

"You are *not* going up there," a low, angry voice ground out.

Jacob paused as the line of waiting-to-be-kissed males eagerly turned to watch.

A sixteenish boy next to Jacob elbowed him in the ribs, bouncing with excitement. "This is the best part. Happens every year."

"What?" Jacob asked, focused on the incensed man.

"This." The boy gestured toward the mysterious brunette. "Someone is always trying to...you know...interfere."

"You mean, stop *her*?"

"Nah. It's someone different every year." The kid scoffed in the direction of the finger jabbing the suit's chest. "Who comes to a fair in a suit...James Bond?"

A rotund man behind Jacob boomed, "Yeah, I don't believe the story myself, but what if it's true? I wouldn't let my girl be up there with all those honeys!"

What story was the guy talking about? Not that it mattered. Jacob was concerned about only one honey and, right now, she was making him feel...what? Protective? And jealous? Was he seriously wishing her finger jabbed at him, and those brown eyes flashed at his?

Who is *that, anyway? Her father?* Jacob tried to step around the hopefuls to get a better view of the dark-haired guy. *No, too young. Her boyfriend? Nah, too old. Well, whoever he is, he's pissed. Wait. What's she saying?*

"You can't tell me what to do," she hissed at the man.

"You're not my father." *Jab, jab.*

Okay, not her father.

The man colored and released her arm.

"No, I'm not your father." He took a threatening step toward her. "If I *were* your father, you'd be over my knee for taking stupid risks."

Alarms went off in Jacob. He didn't know this guy, but he recognized controlled fury when he saw it. She seemed to be pushing the wrong buttons with this fella. Jacob stepped closer. If she needed his help, he was prepared to whip her out of there.

"I'm not taking any risks!" she shouted as she stomped. "It's a kiss on the *cheek*. And *it's not my birthday!*"

Her words made no sense to Jacob, but several spectators repeated her words and laughed. He eased in closer. This was going to blow up.

"*Listen—*" the suit yelled as he tried to grab her arm again, but she was ready for him this time. Sidestepping him, she twirled away and slammed right into Jacob. Amidst the hoots from the line, Jacob's arms wrapped around her as he steadied them both. Her hands splayed on his chest as she regained her footing, her eyes wide. And there it was—the same tingle coursing through his veins he had experienced with her before. For a moment, their gazes locked.

The angry suit charging at them...and fast.

Jacob whisked the girl behind him an instant before the man tackled him. The line of males dodged out of the way as the two hit the ground. The whooping around them escalated.

Grappling, the two rolled until they collided with the booth. Jacob tried to get off a punch but instead found himself on his back, choking and sputtering sun-warmed water in front of a cheering throng. His foe was rolling onto his side, doing the same. Standing in a ring around them, the blonde, the redhead, and Jacob's brunette each raised a dripping empty bucket over their heads in triumph as the crowd cheered.

Wiping water off his face, Jacob sized up his coughing foe and his ruined suit. The last thing he expected to see was the man's grin, but there it was.

A babble of voices surrounded them as the hands of strangers reached out to help the two combatants up. "Wow!"

"That was better than the one with that little blonde last year!"

"Yeah, remember that?"

Looks like it's over. Jacob staggered over to the booth and hoisted himself up to sit on its floor. Legs dangling off the side, he shook water off his shirt and out of his hair.

Or maybe not.

The brunette was at it once again, back in the suit's face. "If I want to kiss someone"—*jab, jab*—"I'll kiss him!" she stormed.

This time, the guy raised his hands in a mock surrender, laughing at her. She spun around on her heel and stomped over to Jacob. Before he knew what she was doing, she grasped his face and pulled it down to hers. Their eyes locked, this time hers questioning and his accepting.

He closed the space between them.

Her parted lips were soft and warm. Of their own accord, his arms slipped around her petite waist as he pulled her closer, lifting her off the ground. With his heart thudding in his ears, the rest of the world seemed to drop away. He no longer saw the crowd, or heard calliope music, or smelled the fried food. For this moment, she was his entire world— the sound of her breath, the line of her lashes against the blush on her cheeks, the scent of her mixed with the clean smell of shampoo, the pressure of her impossibly soft lips on his. She slid her hand from his cheek to cup the back of his head, leaving a trail of heat across his skin as she drew him closer. With his heart pounding, he deepened the kiss.

The noise of the exuberant crowd intruded, reminding him they were in public. He drew back just enough to be able to gaze at her. As cool air drifted between them, her eyes fluttered open. They remained entwined in their embrace, their breaths mingling as they tried to control their breathing. He lowered her back to the ground as if she would break.

She stepped back, her brown eyes blinking owlishly at him. He couldn't tell which of them had been more affected, but his irregular breathing matched hers. She took another shaky step away from him, squaring her shoulders, regaining her composure. His composure was long gone.

The cheers and catcalls of the crowd sidled into Jacob's awareness. What were they chanting? "Birthday Kisses! Married by Christmas! Birthday Kisses! Married by Christmas!"

What's that all about? That's when he noticed a second sign:

Birthday Kisses.
Married by Christmas

What the? Not sure what to do next, he glanced at her. She and her red face looked royally pissed. *Oh, no. What have I done?*

She whirled around and hollered at their audience, "It's not my birthday!" With that, she stalked off.

Baffled, he watched the top of her head flounce through the crowd. The butterflies in his stomach faded, leaving it feeling hollow. *I shouldn't have kissed her.* "Yeah, well, it's *my* birthday." That was some birthday present.

Overhearing him, an older man clapped him on the back. "Well, then, birthday boy, what are you waiting for? You better go after her."

"But I don't even know her name." He swung his head in the direction he had last seen her. What *was* he waiting for?

The teen who had poked him in the ribs earlier once again stood by his side. "Yeah, well, you better find out before Christmas. You'll need it on the marriage license."

What have I got to lose? She's already mad. Jacob flashed him a grin, hopped off The Kissing Booth floor, and bolted after her, once again searching for The Nameless Wonder.

***

The elderly Gypsy wrapped her shawl tighter as she gauged the mood of the crowd. Satisfied the skirmish was over, and all was well, she turned her attention to the main players. She was itching to identify who had been involved and, more importantly, who had kissed one of her girls. Aided by her cane, she rounded the booth in time to catch the girl's shiny brown hair flouncing off. Was she the one who had received the kiss, or was she angry because someone else had? Although both were common scenarios at her kissing booth, most likely, this girl had received the kiss. It felt like her time.

And the fighters? Engrossed in watching her girl's angry departure, the two adversaries created quite a humorous picture as they dripped under the summer sun. There was nothing like a face full of water to interrupt a battle. The old ways were the best.

The boy was still on her booth with his back to her. Although she could not see his face, she had the perfect vantage point to view his opponent. The girl's protector stood to shake water off his suit, wagging his head with a rueful chuckle.

Out of the blue, the boy announced it was his birthday. As the implications registered, the Gypsy hurriedly tapped her cane on a couple of ankles to get by. She needed to see the boy's face so she would recognize him in the future. Despite the energy of the crowd, people obliged her by stepping aside. Before she could reach him, however, the boy jumped down from the booth and raced off into the crowd, pursuing her girl.

The Gypsy was disappointed, but all was as it should be. She sent a blessing after the disappearing boy and turned back to the girl's protector. All color had drained from his face. He understood what the kiss represented, but he was a fool to think he could reroute a union of destiny. As he and his soaked suit melted into the crowd, she sent a blessing after him as well.

There would be trouble, but there was nothing to be done about it now.

Destiny would decide.

***

Jacob's short-lived search failed. Instead, about twenty minutes later, an upset, red-faced William found him first and demanded they return to Greenwich, pronto. When they reached the limo, not only did William retire to the back seat, but he also closed the window between them. Jacob drove back in silent confusion, wondering, about William, about the girl, about an incredible kiss.

When they arrived at the mansion, seven silent hours later, Jacob opened William's car door.

"Sir…." He hesitated. "Is something wrong? Is there something I can do?"

"I wish there was, but what's done is done." William leaned heavily on Jacob's outstretched hand.

What could be wrong? Had William received bad news

from work?

His mentor drifted toward the house. "Not to worry, dear boy. It all comes out in the wash," he called over his shoulder.

Hanson met him at the door. William directed a brief nod toward Jacob, and, with drooping shoulders, he and Hanson disappeared inside.

Jacob parked the limo and got into his car. He sat for a moment, drumming his fingers on the steering wheel, feeling like he was acting in some weird movie without a script. Reaching a decision, he reset a course back to Skowhegan and pulled out of the driveway. He'd spend the night in the car and then devote tomorrow to tracking down The Nameless Wonder.

The next day he began by seeking out the person who ran The Kissing Booth. Miss Ana, a small, elderly woman with impish brown eyes, was the quintessential Gypsy, complete with shawl and colorful skirts.

"You seek you true love, yes?" she asked, taking his hand in both of hers. Rather than examining his palm, she lightly caressed it while mesmerizing him with her intense gaze.

His face heated up. Uncomfortable, he tried to ease his hand free, but her grasp tightened. "Look, no offense, but you don't have to do the whole act for me. I just need some information."

"Oh, no, young man, is not all act," she insisted. "You seek you true love? Or you no seek you true love?"

"No...I mean, yes. Actually she's not my—" He tried to stem the rush of words. "Look, are you the one who signs up the girls for The Kissing Booth, or not? I need to find one of them." He managed to free his hand and shoved them both safely into his pockets.

"Ah, no. With regret, I not know the names my girls use,"

she said with her musical accent. "I not know how to contact them." A smile played at the edge of her lips.

Why would she know? After all, The Kissing Booth was used as a fundraiser for some local charity. She wouldn't have the names of the individual girls.

"No worry, young man." She winked at him and began to hobble away. "If young lady chosen for her birthday, true love will find you."

"Oh, that's just great." *What a waste of time.*

"Ah, yes, the young ones are, how you say, without patience." Miss Ana waved a dismissive hand.

"Yeah, well, even if I believed in this stuff—which I don't— it wasn't her birthday, okay? It was mine."

Miss Ana tottered back to him. "Ah, so you the one, yes? Yesterday was *you* birthday? Oh ho!" She slapped her knees. "And you back for her today."

Once again, Miss Ana snagged his hands in hers. She intoned, "If it be the anniversary of your birth when you first kiss, that blessed moment over the ancient rune becomes you union of destiny."

"Wh—what?" He didn't know whether to be excited or creeped out.

"Is you time to find her, but is not yet her time." She shrugged. "No matter." The Gypsy reached up and patted his cheek. "She is you true love. She will find you again." She released his hand, and with one final pat on the cheek, instructed Jacob to enjoy the fair.

"Is that a hint?" he asked, hope rising.

"No, is only good idea." She laughed and turned away, leaving him standing there like a fish with a bicycle.

She was probably making fun of him, but Jacob spent the rest of the day wandering around the fairgrounds, searching for the girl. As the carnival started to close down for the night, he corralled his disappointment and headed for his car. Who goes to a fair two days in a row anyway? Besides him?

It didn't matter. He had seen her at four different fairs in four different states. What were the odds? Yup, he would see her again. Hopefully, William would schedule another trip to a fair *very* soon.

Meanwhile, knowing Don and Rita, life would be a lot simpler if he just kept all this to himself.

Chapter 8

The Good Samaritan

2002 - Three Years Later

Why did they rush William to the hospital? With anxiety morphing into anger and impatience, Jacob's fingers dug into the gearshift as he negotiated a sharper-than-anticipated curve on a back road in Connecticut's Fairfield County.

What's wrong with these people? Haven't they ever heard of a highway?

Glancing at the speedometer, he forced a calming breath and slowed down for the next bend. It would only make matters worse if he ended up wrapped around a tree while speeding to William's side.

The low afternoon sun sporadically dappled between the treetops. Depressing the brake for another curve, Jacob crested a hill, only to be blinded by the sun's glare. He slammed on the brakes, flipping down his sun visor as he swerved around a pile of garbage on the side of the road. At that moment, his peripheral vision caught sight of something scampering into the brush.

Hold on. Something? Or someone?

Topping the hill, he glanced at his rearview mirror. More movement.

A little kid? Alone out here? Nah. The light through the trees is playing tricks on me. He hadn't exactly been focused on the road.

He coasted up and over the next hill. *C'mon. I'm in the middle of nowhere. It wasn't a kid.* All the same, he lifted his foot from the gas.

It's none of my business what people do with their kids, he reminded himself, creeping around the next curve. Besides, he had to get to William.

But what if another car comes zipping along, and…. Jacob pulled to the side of the road and stopped. *I really don't need this right now.* And, he hadn't actually seen another car in quite a while. Nevertheless, something compelled him to go back. He couldn't just leave a child alone in the middle of nowhere.

"Five minutes," Jacob muttered. "I'll give it five minutes, and then I'm out of here."

He topped the hill in time to see a skinny kid pull an even scrawnier kid into the brush. Jacob parked near the heap of trash and stared into the roadside overgrowth. Impotent fear created by William's sudden hospitalization funneled into anger. *Why the hell are they playing in the road? They could cause an accident!*

Thrusting the door open, he unfolded his frame from the sedan.

"Hey!" he called out. "You shouldn't be playing in the road."

Silence.

He peered into the brush as he strode back and forth, trying to spy their location. Hands on hips, he glanced at the collection of litter with disgust. It was, in fact, a mass of old clothes, apparent escapees from the back of someone's pickup truck.

William's in the hospital, and I'm checking out recyclables? He blew an impatient breath as he peered at the array of bushes and vines. *I'm outta here.*

"Hello?" he yelled one last time.

The pile of rubbish near his feet shifted.

"Whoa!" Jacob jumped back. He nudged the heap with his foot, uncovering a third boy. This one was older, a teenager perhaps. A matt of tangled blond hair and several days' worth of grime obscured his face. He was breathing, but he was laid out cold.

Jeez! What the…? Maybe it was a hit-and-run.

Crack!

Jacob whirled around to find a bullet-sized hole in his passenger window. He didn't need military training to recognize an attack. He scrambled behind his car and hunkered down into a poised-for-action squat near the front tire.

"Stop it!" A small boy burst out of the bushes, clambered up the embankment, and ran around the car toward Jacob. "He can help us."

Angry howls from the underbrush followed him as he hurled himself at Jacob then clung to his neck. Off balance in his squat, Jacob threw one hand behind him for support while securing the weeping missile with the other. They landed in the middle of the street. A series of pinging and cracking noises claimed the other side of his car. He shifted position to wrap both arms around his slight bundle, and rolled them toward the protection of the front tire.

I need to get us inside the car and out of range of…pebbles? Since when does a pebble put a hole in a window? "Hold on!" he shouted. "I'm not going to hurt anyone."

The pinging stopped.

"I told you so," intoned a muffled voice in the vicinity of his chest.

"Let him go, get back in your car, and leave!" ordered one of his hidden attackers with an unfamiliar accent.

"You're squishing me," complained the squirming body in his arms.

Jacob loosened his grip to find a tear-stained face staring back at him. "I won't hurt you," he murmured.

"I know," sniffled the child. "You're gonna help us." He patted Jacob on the cheek.

That hadn't happened before. An odd protective reaction

to the boy's hand on his face curled in the pit of his stomach. "Don't worry. I'll get us out of here." Satisfied there were no signs of panic in the young face, Jacob focused on the situation.

The assailants might not have a gun, but whatever put a hole in his window sure could put a hole in him. He wasn't even sure whether they were attacking or protecting the unconscious boy. "I've got to get *that* kid out of range." He craned his neck to see what kind of cover the other side of the street provided, further loosening his hold on the child.

"I'll make 'em stop," declared his bundle and, with a determined wiggle, he squirmed free.

"Hey, get back here," Jacob hissed, making an unsuccessful grab at the slight figure scampering toward the exposed front end of the car.

Eluding him, the youngster shouted, "I said he's gonna help us. Quit messin' with him."

A moment of silence greeted his announcement, followed by a clamor of comments. "Are you sure?"

"How do you know?"

"We don't need his help."

"Get back here."

How many of them were there? Was he about to be rushed by some kind of gang? *And what the hell are they doing in the woods in the middle of nowhere?*

With an **exaggerated** roll of his eyes, the kid bent to inspect a bug bite on his leg. "I'm *sure*," he shouted. "Stop it or you'll hurt him. He's not gonna help us if you hurt him!" He looked over his shoulder at Jacob and raised his palms with indignation. "You see what I have to put up with?"

The murmuring resumed in the underbrush. Jacob inched over, intent on retrieving the flea-bitten kid before he got injured.

"Hey, back off!" Another *ping* on his car accompanied the shout from a deeply accented voice in the brush.

The small boy straightened in surprise. "He's not gonna help us if you keep doing that!" he admonished shrilly into the brush.

Jacob raised his palms and peeked over the hood of his car. "Everybody stay calm, all right? What happened? A car accident?"

"None of your business. You need to leave. We got this. My—our dad is on his way," ordered a nearby bush.

Right.

"No! Don't go." Bug bites forgotten, the boy ran back to Jacob. He grabbed his hand and tugged him over to the motionless bundle on the side of the road.

Remaining vigilant, Jacob allowed himself to be led toward the unconscious form. He reached down to check for a pulse. *Wow, this kid is burning up*! But the pulse was there, slow and faint.

"It's a fever, right?" A thin boy of about twelve had appeared at his elbow.

How many are there? "Yeah. He needs to go to the hospital."

The two boys started shouting at him.

Jacob raised his palms in the classic surrender position. "Okay, I get it!" he roared over the din. "No hospital." What now?

Eying each other, the boys looked as indecisive as Jacob felt. He had to get to William, but he couldn't just leave them here. William would say, *Choose your battles, m'boy.*

This is going to take longer than I thought, William, but I'll be there as soon as I can. First, he had to get them into the car, and then they could negotiate the hospital. Someone else could deal with them there.

"How many of you are there?" He peered into the brush, producing snickers from the grungy duo.

"Just us." The smaller boy spoke with a heavy accent.

"Just us," the larger boy repeated with a deep man-like imitation.

"Really?" He scowled. "Just two of you?" They had played him. *Okay, I can handle this.* "Fine. You two get into the car."

The two faces in front of him shuttered as the boys shuffled closer together.

Ignoring their reaction, he gestured toward the bundle on the ground. "And I'll get...."

"K.C.," enunciated the little one helpfully, ignoring the glare of the elder boy.

Jacob waited.

"I'm Robin," chirped Jacob's earlier squirming ally. "And this is Sam." He gestured toward the older boy whose mouth had formed a stupefied O.

"Are you crazy? He doesn't need to know our names!" Sam snapped as Robin pulled Jacob down toward the pile of rags named K.C.

"Don't get all hyper, kid. I'm just trying to help. You guys get into the car, and I'll get K.C." Jacob knelt, watching them move toward his car. "So, what happened here?"

"Don't waste time with stupid questions." Sam planted his hands on his hips. "Are you going to help us or not?"

Jacob and the boy stared at each other in a silent struggle for dominance.

A noisy sigh from Robin interrupted them as he opened the back door of the car. "*C'mon,* you guys!" He scrambled in behind the driver's seat.

Heaving his own more resigned breath, Sam and his parting glare followed.

While Sam buckled Robin in, Jacob took a moment to run

his hands along K.C.'s limbs, checking for problems. Jeez, he was hot.

"Hey, what are you doing?" cried Robin.

Sam leaped out of the car and charged. Jumping to his feet, Jacob raised his palms again as he retreated from the boy's attack. "Whoa! I'm just checking for broken bones."

Sam positioned himself between Jacob and K.C., ready to do battle. "There was no accident!" he shouted. "I said it's a fever."

"Okay, *okay!*" Jacob tried to rein in his exasperation. He was not accustomed to having his actions questioned, and never by a mangy brat. All this arguing delayed his reaching William. "Look, kid, you're not the only one who has an emergency to deal with," he barked. "I don't need all this hassle. So, why don't we all just get into the damn car and get K.C. out of this heat?" Jacob began to silently count to ten. At five, Sam turned his head toward the car.

"Are you sure?" he asked the small occupant.

"I'm *positive.*"

Jacob continued to glower as Sam studied him for a moment. The boy shifted his stare to K.C.'s motionless form and shrugged. "Fine. Works for me."

Behind Sam, Robin settled against the seat cushion.

Why was the youngest of them all making the decisions? *Who cares? As long as it gets them into the car.* Jacob scooped K.C. up in his arms and positioned him in the back seat. An anxious Robin cradled his head, and a sullen Sam held onto his legs. Ignoring the suspicious eyes watching his every move, he secured the center seat belt around the unconscious form, ran around the car, and slid in.

"He better not try nothing," Sam muttered.

Jacob started the car and hightailed it for Norwalk Hospital.

Chapter 9

The Hospital

Sam broke the terse silence. "What town is this?"

"Somewhere near Ridgefield or Weston," Jacob bit out, trying to concentrate on driving while digging out his cell phone to check for a signal.

"Where's Greenwich?"

"It's a few towns over. Why?" Jacob watched his rearview mirror for a response.

"That's where we're going," Robin volunteered. "That's… umm…." He faltered at Sam's warning look.

"Our cousins live there," Sam said.

"Yeah," agreed Robin in a rush. "Our cousins."

Jacob glanced again at Sam. *Weird. I think I've seen that kid somewhere before.* "Is there someone you want me to call? I should have a signal in a few minutes." Another glimpse in the mirror revealed an agitated Sam shifting in his seat. Jacob waited.

"I…we don't know the number. K.C. does," said Sam. "But we have the address." He rummaged around in his pockets, producing a piece of paper.

Jacob reached for it as he pulled up to a stop sign. He examined the scrap of newsprint, registering a familiar face in the photograph and an address scrawled across it. *No way. What the hell is going on?*

"It's 537 Cherrier Lane. Can you take us there?" said Sam.

He knew the address very well. *What are these kids up to?* "Sorry. I'm taking you to the hospital," he ground out.

"I knew it!" Sam exploded. "I knew we shouldn't trust you."

"We have to go to the hospital," Robin murmured, barely

above a whisper. "I can't feel K.C. anymore."

Jacob tried to angle the mirror to include Robin, but he was too small to be seen. Sam expelled a noisy breath and slammed back into his seat. Jacob checked his cell phone again. *At last!* A couple of flickering bars. They were close to service range. He punched in the number of his assistant, Margaret Fuller, and briefly explained the situation.

"They want to be taken to 537 Cherrier Lane."

She gasped.

Oh, yeah, she understood the significance as well as he did. "I'm taking them to Norwalk Hospital. One of them has been unconscious for quite a while."

No response.

"Maggie?" Dammit, he had lost the signal again. Exasperated, he put the phone away.

"If you take us to the hospital, they'll try to split us up," Sam hissed. "We're a family. We have to stay together. *Please* take us to…um…." He inspected the piece of newspaper with William's picture again. "To Cherrier Lane."

The kid was right about the system Jacob knew so well. The thought made his stomach drop, but what could he do about it? These kids were not his responsibility. And he had to get to William. "I'm afraid that's out of the question."

"I know what," exclaimed Robin. "We'll go to *your* house."

"*What?* No way. Not *my* house." What was he supposed to do with a bunch of kids? "The hospital will make K.C. better. No more discussion."

They rode in silence punctuated by an occasional sniffle. A fleeting peek in the mirror confirmed Sam angrily dashing away tears. Jacob didn't care.

No one waited for them at 537 Cherrier Lane. That was William's address. The closest things he had to family were Hanson and Jacob. The man definitely didn't have any kids.

The wrinkled article Sam carried honored William for his philanthropic efforts. Maybe the scam was to tap his boss for money. If so, Jacob was now in the best position to run interference.

After five years with William Hatch, from part-time chauffeur during college to William's business protégé after graduating, Jacob had helped his mentor's business grow. But today William had collapsed— something to do with his heart— and a hollow pit the size of the Grand Canyon lodged in Jacob's gut.

He downshifted again. He had to get rid of these kids ASAP.

William was so vibrant, so full of life and energy, like Granddad had been when Jacob was little. As an adult, Jacob understood Granddad had been hiding the seriousness of his condition, but, as a child, he hadn't noticed the changes. Had he missed similar signs of decline in William? Usually the older man was healthy and strong.

Except for a couple of years ago, when William had been so short-tempered and miserable most of the time. Hanson had confided their boss wasn't eating or sleeping well. The two older men were constantly going at it. During those months, Jacob's visits were less frequent due to the toxic atmosphere in the mansion. Quite a bit of William's workload shifted over to him as the businessman rarely showed up at the office. Then, a sudden reversal took Jacob by surprise. In his relief, he had brushed the whole thing off.

But now, William had collapsed. What did it mean? Granddad's collapse had been the beginning of the end. Jacob couldn't imagine William waning like Granddad, the energy and life fading from his twinkling blue eyes. What if…what if….

Emotionally, there was no way to prepare for the huge hole

William's loss would create. As far as business was concerned, Jacob did not have a choice. Too many people depended on him to rein in his emotions. Without William, the outside world would perceive the organization as existing in an unstable state. If not handled strategically, leakage of William's collapse could make their stock plummet. Handling this situation with his head, and not his heart, was imperative. He would have to cope with his emotions later.

This should not be too hard to contain initially, Jacob mused as he entered Norwalk. *As of right now, only a few people know what's happened, and Maggie will help to keep it hushed for as long as possible.*

Ms. Margaret Fuller, executive secretary, had come with his first executive promotion. About twenty years his senior, she was prim, starched, and ruthlessly efficient. No doubt she would have matters well in hand by the time they reached the hospital...if she had heard his message.

He negotiated the traffic in the more congested area of Norwalk, desperately trying to rein in his mounting apprehension. He pulled into the area marked *Emergency*. Maggie waited with good old Dr. Donald McNamara inside the lobby. *Yes! The cavalry to the rescue.*

The doors slid open for a couple of nurses with a gurney just as Jacob shut off the engine. Under Dr. Don's supervision, they deftly removed K.C. from the backseat and wheeled him away. Sam moved to follow, but Margaret stepped in his path. One look at Margaret's tall, imposing business-suit-clad frame, topped by her snapping I-mean-business hazel gaze, and Sam slumped against the car.

Ignoring the others, Jacob opened the car's back door and unbuckled Robin. For a moment, they stared at each other. Then, the child's brown eyes welled up.

"Everything will work out," Jacob said without conviction.

The little arms reached out to him. Without thinking, he lifted the boy, holding him until the soft sobbing subsided. He had never held a child like this before. He was so…so little. His arms were little, his legs were little, and his body was little, but his distress was so huge.

Striding toward the hospital entrance, Jacob didn't bother checking to see if Sam followed. No way would he let the grimy kid in Jacob's arms out of his sight. He set Robin down in the waiting room, and the two boys huddled together. Jacob signaled Maggie to keep tabs on them. If she could handle the most temperamental of their rich and famous clients, she certainly could handle these two.

Jacob didn't know what kind of plot these kids were trying to hatch, but, for some reason, he wanted to make sure no harm would come to them.

Chapter 10
Ms. Fuller Takes Charge

"Who are you?" Sam placed himself between Margaret and Robin.

"Are you going to take us away?" The young voice behind him quivered.

"My name is Ms. Fuller. I'm Mr. Kent's assistant." Her statement produced blank looks and exchanged glances. "The man who drove you here?" she hinted.

"Me." Jacob waved his hand. "That's me."

"And, yes," she continued, "I am going to take you away. A hospital is no place for healthy people. And you are?" she asked the littler child who now stood at her side.

"I'm Robin. That's Sam."

"Why not just tell everyone?" muttered Sam with a baleful scowl.

"Will K.C. be okay?" Robin stared at the door closing behind the older boy's gurney.

"Mr. Kent will go find out. Then he can be on his way," hedged Maggie.

"Right," affirmed Jacob. *What the hell should I do now?* Dr. Don had followed the gurney. That seemed like a good place to start. Raking his fingers through his hair, he headed down the hallway.

***

Emerging from the darkness, she tried to open her eyes despite the skull-splitting throbbing pain behind them. A sense of movement confused her fuzzy head. She fought off nausea. As the darkness tried to reclaim her, she struggled to remain conscious.

Where am I? Her intermittent thoughts blended in a quagmire of twilight sleep. She forced her eyes open, but was greeted by institutional fluorescent lights speeding by. More nausea.

A hospital? Or someplace else…?

Waking again, she battled to remain alert. When her forward movement ceased, she once again opened her eyes. This time, two sets of broad shoulders greeted her. One wore a white coat, his curly dark head bent in discussion with a suit.

What is he *doing here?*

Impossibly, the pounding in her head increased. *Where are….*

Darkness encroached on her consciousness again.

The stories are *true….*

***

"Don." Jacob elbow-steered his friend away from the nursing station.

"What happened to your car? Did someone attack you?" Don asked quietly, his brow drawn.

"My car?" Jacob gaped up at Don. "Sort of." He had more important things on his mind.

"Well, who—"

He jerked his head in the general direction of the two boys commandeered by Ms. Fuller.

"Those kids did it? What's up with that?" Don snorted. "Better not let them near Mr. Hatch's cars."

William. He had to get to William. "Don, I have to go. Right now, okay? Something's happened to Mr. Hatch, and I have to get out of here. Please don't say anything."

"Sure, sure. You can count on me." He glanced at the dirty bundle being assessed in triage.

"Look," said Jacob. "That's K.C. Uh...he's...an old family friend, see? I'll take care of the bill. I just need this all kept quiet for now. Okay?"

Don nodded. "Was it a car accident?"

"I don't think so." Jacob raked his hair with his hands. "His brothers...." *When did I decide they were brothers?* "They said it was a fever, and he was burning up."

Don pursed his lips. "Yes, we've already started an IV to increase his fluids."

His friend always came through. Jacob turned to go, but Don clapped him on the shoulder. "Give the nurse his info before you go."

His info? "Sure." Jacob didn't have the kid's info, but he knew who would. Heading for the nursing station, he pulled out his phone. It went off in his hand. "Margaret Fuller, you have perfect timing, as usual. I need—"

As he listened to Maggie's intel on the patient, an attractive nurse waited. If her encouraging smile was anything to go on, she wasn't put off by his rumpled suit and unkempt hair. No matter. He hung up and stared at the curtain concealing the eldest brother until the nurse politely cleared her throat.

"Oh, right," Jacob acknowledged. "The patient's name is K.C. Thatcher. He's twenty-three years old." Unbelievable, but that's what Maggie said. He could have sworn he'd been lifting a kid. Jacob himself had not sprouted up until late high school, so he had borne his share of height-related barbs. At least he had finally grown, but this guy was already twenty-three and had hardly any muscle on him. Maybe it had to do with his illness.

"I don't know the blood type or allergy history," he continued, ignoring the nurse's unspoken invitation. He shared the contact and billing information, and then hurried toward the cafeteria to tie up loose ends with the rest of K.C.'s family. Why they had been out there in the woods in the middle of nowhere wasn't his business. He just needed to keep them away from William.

William. His chest tightened. He had to get out of there.

The unexpected scene in the cafeteria derailed Jacob's resolve to simply walk away. The unflappable Margaret Fuller sat ramrod straight next to Robin who blathered away while playing with the woman's salt and pepper waves. Who'd have thought a pocketsize chatterbox would crack her veneer? Calling her Maggie all these years hadn't loosened her up at all.

Sam slumped in a chair across from them, nibbling on a huge brownie. Could Sam be in high school? After being so mistaken about K.C.'s age, Jacob needed to reevaluate these two. Sam's size was more like a middle schooler, but he had shouldered the responsibility of taking care of their family when K.C. went down. He could be either. Robin was tiny, but his babble hinted he might actually be school age. From across the room, both boys had the same blond hair and dark eyes— probably brown. Although on the skinny side, and in sore need of a bath and a good haircut, they appeared healthy enough.

Sam pushed the brownie aside and put his head down on the table. Maggie reached out a slow hand then hesitated and withdrew it. Her movement caught Robin's attention. Looking past Maggie's shoulder, Robin froze, staring at Jacob. Following the boy's gaze, Maggie rotated in her seat toward her boss. Was she blushing?

His phone rang. Sam jerked toward the sound and sat up. A malevolent glare radiated from his pale face as Jacob received Don's report on the patient.

Robin launched off his chair and barreled into Jacob's legs, beaming up at him. *What the hell?* Jacob looked to Maggie for help. As she rewrapped her bun, a smirk flitted across her face.

Jacob untangled Robin from his legs. "Good news," Jacob said as the boy led him to their table, "Dr. Don thinks he knows what's wrong with K.C., Lyme disease and dehydration." *Don sounded extremely...cheerful. What's that all about?*

"Maybe that's what's wrong with Sam," piped up Robin.

Sam hunched over the table with his arms wrapped around his abdomen, scowling at the world.

Reaching across the table, Jacob touched the nearest shoulder to check the kid's temperature. His arm registered as normal before Sam shook him off.

"There's nothing wrong with me. I'm *fine*," he spat out.

Robin rolled his eyes. "There's always something wrong with you."

Sam shot to his feet and stomped off to another table.

Wow, where did that come from?

"Close your mouth, Mr. Kent." Margaret nudged Jacob's jaw closed. "I'll handle this."

He sank into a seat at the table. Margaret joined Sam at his. After a few minutes with their heads together, Sam shot them a furtive glance, shook his head, and stood up. As Margaret and Sam walked out the door, she put a tentative arm around the boy's shoulders. After first stiffening, he leaned against her.

Okay, that's something you don't see every day. Who knew Maggie had a soft side? A tug on his sleeve drew his attention to the other kid. Jacob wanted information, and, like it or not, Robin was going to give it to him.

Fifteen minutes later, all he had gotten out of the flighty kid was that K.C. had gotten sick while the Thatcher family had been on a "lonnnng camping trip." That, and their ages. They were all vertically challenged. Despite their diminutive size, Sam was fifteen, and Robin was eight. That is, *if* Robin was telling the truth.

By that time Margaret and Sam returned, Jacob's man-to-man approach had produced exactly squat. *Are all kids so distracted? Or is he doing it on purpose?* Jacob had his suspicions.

Sam looked better, and Maggie was back to her prim Margaret Fuller persona. As they sat down, Sam took a deep breath and quietly apologized for his behavior.

Robin yelled, "Group hug!" and ran around to the other side of the table. Sam produced an "Ooomph!" as they collided.

"Lyme disease?" Margaret enquired over their heads. "How did they know?"

"There's one of those bull's-eye rashes on K.C.'s back. They're testing him now to see if he can handle antibiotics." Jacob paused to find the other two observing their conversation. These kids did not miss a thing. "Do you know what I'm talking about?" he asked them.

"Yeah," said Sam. "We know all that stuff from school."

"Right." Jacob stood. "Maggie, what do you have for me? I've got to go."

Maggie whipped out the permanent notepad which somehow was always just out of sight. "I've called Gregory, who is preparing rooms at your place for them. Mrs. Tucker is obtaining more suitable and *clean* clothing. Isadora is getting age-appropriate groceries even as we speak. I notified the hospital about your delay."

The high decibel protests of the two boys completely drowned out Jacob's. "Now, wait just a minute!"

But Ms. Margaret Fuller informed them no one would remain at the hospital to wait for K.C. to recover. The government would not have to split up the children because Mr. Kent's house had plenty of room. Mr. Kent would come in and check on them when he returned, and everyone needed a good night's sleep.

"Isn't that right, Mr. Kent?" she concluded.

Maggie sounds more like a den mother than a high-paid assistant. Fine. He needed a den mother so he could leave. If she was forming some type of attachment to these kids, he'd be stupid to interfere.

"All right, as long as *you* spend the night," he bargained.

Margaret hesitated and then nodded. Jacob still needed to get to their boss.

"Then I…I'd better go." What did the next hospital hold? Dread flooded Jacob, leaving a sour taste in his mouth.

The small hand slipping into his startled him.

"Don't be sad," whispered Robin.

That's a lot of insight for a little kid. Feeling awkward, Jacob uncurled the little fingers from his. "Um…sometimes you can't help it."

Sam came over and put an arm around Robin. "We know what you mean," he muttered as he led the little boy back to the table.

Once more, Jacob's previously nonexistent protective side surfaced.

As quickly as it appeared, he squashed it. *No way. These kids are not my problem.*

He spun on his heel and strode out the door.

Chapter 11
An Unwilling Patient

"Finally!" Jacob swung his car into the Greenwich Hospital parking lot, anxiety flooding him. He headed for the cardiac unit, pausing at the nurse's station to ask directions to William's room.

"Follow the noise," snapped the exasperated nurse, pointing to a door where bellowing followed Hanson into the hallway.

Of course William's loyal personal valet was here. A tidal wave of relief washed over Jacob as he hurried over. "How is he, Hanson?" How bad could it be if the patient could holler?

"Judge for yourself." Hanson stepped aside so Jacob could enter.

"I'm glad you're here, Hanson." Jacob squeezed the man's shoulder as he went by.

"Yes, well…I…."

Was Hanson flustered? He took a closer look at the man who served as the eternal buffer between William and the outside world. Hanson had been with William decades longer than Jacob had known him. Today his drawn countenance made the man appear much older than usual. A closer look revealed deep shadows under his gray eyes. Jacob paused. "Have you had anything to eat? When did you sleep last?"

Hanson stiffened, and if possible, his chin seemed to incline a bit more than usual. "I am fine, thank you, sir. If you please, perhaps now would be the time to see to the *patient*, Mr. Hatch, instead of concerning yourself about me."

"Of course." *I'm going to have to keep an eye on the both of them. William would be lost without Hanson.*

Stepping into the hospital room, Jacob stopped short, his

stomach dropping. William had morphed into the frail senior he had impersonated when they first met. Slumped against the pillows, garbed in a pasty-colored gown, tubes jutting out of his arms— this was his grandfather's last month all over again. It took Jacob's breath away.

"Don't be put off, boy." William growled. "Hospital gowns make everyone look like an invalid, but these things…." He shook his arm, making the attached tubes and wires dance in the air. "Don't you worry. I'll be fogging up the mirror for a few more years."

His tone helped focus Jacob on the still-present twinkle in William's eyes. He was pale, yes, and tired, but he seemed hearty enough.

Somewhat calmer, Jacob asked, "How long have you been here?"

"Too long!"

"Long enough to drive Hanson crazy?"

"It's his own fault." William jerked his blanket smooth. "I'm *fine*, but noooo. He wouldn't leave it alone."

"Leave what alone?" Jacob pressed.

William sat forward. "It's nothing, I tell you. *Nothing.*"

"'*Nothing*' doesn't require me to pick you up off the floor." Hanson's haughty interjection came from behind them.

William pointed at him angrily. "You forget who works for whom, Hanson. I am *fine.*"

Hanson sniffed, crossed his arms, and propped himself in the doorway.

This was getting Jacob nowhere. "What hap—"

"*Nothing* happened!" William roared. "I *tripped* over something and hit my ribs on a table. Hanson the Hissy saw me on the floor holding my chest and *assumed* I'd had a heart attack." He glared at Hanson. "You are so pigheaded some-times."

"Sometimes?" Hanson brushed nonexistent lint off his jacket sleeve. "I must be slipping."

"You tripped over something?" Jacob repeated. "You?" No one would expect clumsiness from William Hatch. "Over what?"

"Well, I'm not sure. I was thinking about...something." William shot Jacob a sidelong look. "And the next thing you know, Hanson's trying to see how far he can go before he gets fired."

Hanson gave another aloof sniff, but Jacob caught the valet's worried expression. That settled it. Regardless of what William said, he was going to follow the doctor's orders. Jacob prepared to do battle.

An hour later, faced with an impenetrable wall composed of Jacob, Hanson, and his doctor, William caved—but with conditions. He agreed to spend the night in the hospital as long as Jacob and Hanson made sure business functioned as usual. All attempts would be made to keep the story out of the media as long as possible, and Jacob would shoulder some of William's workload.

Hours later, the skeletal night shift reminded them visiting hours were long past, and the patient needed to get his rest. An adamant nurse, with hands on her hips, refused to let William continue issuing orders, finally allowing his visitors to escape. Still, it was well past midnight before the hospital doors closed behind them.

Jacob wagged his head. "I didn't realize William handled so much himself. Why doesn't his staff do some of this?"

"That's probably why his blood pressure is up. He's been so...distracted." Hanson looked over his shoulder and smirked. "To tell you the truth, I did see him trip. Saying it was a heart attack was the only way to get him to the hospital. I was actually concerned about broken ribs." He sobered. "I was not expecting the high blood pressure or the dehydration. He hasn't been sleeping well for the last couple of months, not since...."

"Since?" prompted Jacob.

"Pardon me, Mr. Kent." Hanson reddened. "I am speaking out of turn. Good evening, sir." He curtly nodded and headed down the stairs.

Jacob knew better than to try to get information out of Hanson if he didn't want to share it. "Hanson," he called after him.

The older man paused. "Yes, Mr. Kent?"

"I'm going to stay at William's place for a few days to get a handle on this stuff." He waved his list in the air.

"Very good, sir."

"I'm also going to have Magg—Ms. Fuller lend a hand."

"Yes, Ms. Fuller is exceptional,"

Hanson was complimenting someone? "Yes, she is. She will—" He smacked his forehead with his palm and yelled, "Maggie!"

Hanson jumped. "Where?"

"I forgot about Maggie!" Jacob spun on his heel and sprinted for the car, leaving Hanson to draw his own conclusions.

Chapter 12

A Crash Course in Family

"Yeah, you look innocent enough, but *I* know what's lurking inside," Jacob muttered to his unlit condo as he pulled up. He checked his clock: 1:05 a.m. Of course everyone was asleep. *What was I thinking?*

Tomorrow, he would talk to Maggie about finding a place for the kids to stay until K.C. could discuss their care. Tomorrow, he would tend to the business demands of William's list. Tomorrow, he would worm information out of Hanson.

But, tonight, he was going to bed.

He slipped in and looked around. The spacious three-bedroom townhouse had way more room than he needed. It, like Margaret Fuller, had come with the job, and sometimes provided lodging for a client or two as well. Maggie had been right when she'd said he had plenty of room for the boys, but he didn't want them there. They were someone else's responsibility. This was only a temporary stop.

In case she had given his room to one of the impromptu guests, he opened his door with caution.

Empty.

He sagged in relief. Stepping inside, he pulled it closed behind him.

Almost. Robin was tugging the door back open.

Cute kid, he thought despite himself as he surveyed the messy hair and sleepy countenance topping off his Dave Matthews Band T-shirt. He released the door. "What are you doing here?"

Robin stepped back, rubbing his eyes. "I waited up for you," Robin stage-whispered.

"I see that. Why? It's late." He hoped he sounded authoritative as he whispered back.

"Because you were sad, and you need someone to tuck you in."

Jacob cleared his throat. "How about you go back to bed, and we can both get some sleep?"

The small boy extended his hand. "Works for me."

Jacob smothered a smile at hearing an echo of Sam in the small boy. Feeling awkward, he took Robin's offered hand. "Which room?"

Robin pointed. "Miss Fuller is in here, and we're in there."

Jacob peered into the guest room and found Sam sleeping, sprawled in and around a tangle of covers in the queen-size bed. Robin scrambled up while Jacob gently tugged the bedcovers out from under his brother. Robin slipped in and closed his eyes. Jacob spread the covers over the two kids. Robin opened one sleepy eye and snuggled next to his brother. Then, just like that, he was asleep.

Jacob let himself out of the bedroom and retraced his steps. Moments later, he slid between his own sheets. Although the last twenty-four hours had been a roller coaster of emotions, something told him this was merely a prelude. His life had been turned upside-down, but there was no sense in losing sleep over it.

The sun streamed through the window as loud music poured through the wall, waking Jacob. Someone was messing with his stereo system? He shot up in bed as memories of yesterday came rushing back. Time to take his life back. Leaping out of bed, he threw on a bathrobe over his sweatpants and T-shirt and went searching for Maggie. She had done this. She could undo it.

Following the music, Jacob came upon a heap of rags stacked at the top of the stairs similar to the pile he'd mistaken for garbage on the side of the road. With a sense of déjà vu, he nudged it with his foot. Nothing. Just a mound of the grubby clothing previously worn by his unwelcome houseguests. A second nudge for verification toppled what had been a neat pile. Satisfied, he used his foot to shove them back into a less-than-neat pile and continued downstairs.

He found Sam in the dining room, clad in Jacob's favorite Gorillaz T-shirt, reading the newspaper comics and bobbing his head in time to the music. He looked up when Jacob cleared his throat.

"That's my newspaper," Jacob said. *I sound like Hanson.*

"Well, duh. It's your house." Sam pushed the paper toward him. "Wouldja like some of it?"

He automatically reached for the offering. "Where are the others?"

"Robin's still sleeping for some reason." Sam paused for a moment, shrugged, and continued. "Mrs. Fuller is in that room with the books and the computer." Sam gestured to the right. Jacob's head swiveled toward the indicated direction.

"And Isadora is in the kitchen." Again, Jacob's head swiveled after Sam's thumb. A guy in his twenties didn't need a cook, but Isadora came with the place. He turned back to find Sam watching him warily, ignoring the comics. Jacob stared back, at a complete loss for words.

Sam broke the silence. "You're not the family type, are you?"

He hesitated. "No, not really."

"Well, you did good last night," said Sam gruffly. "Y'know, with the covers and stuff."

"Oh. Thanks. I mean, I thought you were asleep."

Sam rolled his eyes. "Like you can sleep with someone yanking the covers out from under you."

Isadora emerged from the kitchen, beaming over a tray

laden with food.

"I *love* English muffins!" Sam jumped up to hold the door wider, pure adoration on his face.

Blushing, the cook set down a spread capable of putting the finest restaurant to shame. Jacob grinned at her palpable pleasure. He rarely ate breakfast, lunched at the office, and usually had dinner out. Isadora typically only cooked for Gregory, the butler, Mrs. Tucker, the housekeeper, and herself. Today, she had an entire household to feed. Oh, yeah. She was definitely loving it.

Sam dove in, a vision of complete bliss. Jacob gave himself a mental shake and frowned. He did not want these kids to get used to being here. As soon as possible, Maggie had to find a place for them. And he wanted those T-shirts back before they left. He headed for the study to tell her so.

Storming in, he realized Maggie was on the phone and quietly closed the door behind him. She caught his eye and nodded as he sank into the leather easy chair by the window.

"Thank you very much. Good-bye now," she murmured, hanging up. After jotting down some notes, she flipped the pages in her notebook.

Here we go.

"Good morning, Mr. Kent," she said brightly.

"How come you're so…so…unruffled?" He smoothed his own sleep-tousled hair. "Good morning, Maggie," he added, as an afterthought. "We need to talk about where the boys will stay—"

"Ah, yes, the children." She flipped to another page in her notebook. "The clothes I've ordered should be delivered soon. They'll be able to wear something clean that doesn't belong to you. I'm sure you'll agree we cannot have them put those dirty clothes back on now that they've washed up. Mrs. Tucker said she doesn't mind the extra laundry, and the children have proven to be very neat." She marked a check on her pad with her typical flourish. "Sam asked if they could use your computer, but I said to wait until I asked you." *Check.*

No way! They weren't going to be here long enough to need it. He opened his mouth to speak, but she pressed on before he could voice his thoughts.

"Gregory did show Sam how to use the sound system. It's much more efficient than having Gregory change the stations for them." *Check.*

"What?"

She ignored his weak attempt to stem her flow. "Both of them have been very evasive when I ask them about their family. As far as I can tell, there isn't anyone they want to contact regarding K.C." *Check.*

No family? That means.... His gut tightened. Elbows on his knees, he propped his head in his hands. Her next words confirmed what he knew was coming.

"I've tried to contact the State Welfare Department. Since it's the weekend, their office is closed. They have an emergency number, but since this doesn't qualify as an emergency, I suggest the children stay here until it reopens." *Check.*

His head shot up in panic, followed by his body. "I don't know what to do with a house-load of kids!"

"Nonsense. You can manage for one weekend. You certainly have the space. And I don't mind staying until the authorities settled the situation."

The authorities. He slumped in his chair. He had bunked many times with foster boys who had been separated from their siblings, and that never worked out for anybody.

A knock interrupted them. "Breakfast is served," said the butler through the door.

"Thank you, Gregory." Margaret shot to her feet.

"Hold it." Jacob's voice was low.

She froze.

"No Welfare Department. They need to stay together."

"Very well, Mr. Kent, I shall try my best. And until then?" She waited.

He blew through pursed lips, the sound following his intentions right out the window. "They can stay here."

"Yes, Mr. Kent." She grabbed for the doorknob and a quick escape.

"And don't think I don't know what you're pulling with that welfare crap," he growled as she stepped out.

"Yes, Mr. Kent." She closed the door behind her.

Now what? Jacob ran his fingers through his hair. *I have to find out K.C.'s condition. I can't figure out what to do with those two 'til then.* For now, he could outright avoid them. He reached for William's list in his briefcase, tabling the unwanted-guests problem for later.

Concern furrowed Jacob's brow as he reviewed his tasks. This list was way too long. Seeing his mentor in the hospital last night had been a distressing wakeup call. In hindsight, he recognized there had been an ongoing deterioration, too gradual to notice. No wonder, with William driving himself like this. "Oh, yeah." He shook the list. "We definitely need to talk."

He stood and stretched towards the ceiling. A shower and a shave, and he'd be on his way.

Cheerful noise from the dining room greeted him as he emerged from the study. Despite his intentions, Jacob drifted toward it and peered through the door. At Maggie's insistence, Gregory and Mrs. Tucker were joining her and the older refugee for breakfast. Isadora was setting out dishes for them. The scene had a peculiar family feeling to it, which suddenly made Jacob feel like a guest in his own place.

He turned away, nearly colliding with Robin. His little face beamed above Jacob's T-shirt and his feet peeked out below it.

"How extremely fortunate my T-shirts fit you," grunted Jacob.

"We must be the same size," Robin responded with a cheeky grin, and held up his hand in a universal invitation even Jacob understood.

Feeling awkward, he took it. As Robin led him into the dining room, Jacob decided to join them for breakfast. After all, why disturb William by arriving too early?

"Pardon me, Mr. Kent," said Gregory, rising with a guilty start.

Mrs. Tucker held her napkin to her lips with a deer-in-the-headlights stare. Isadora glanced at Maggie and then looked uncertainly at Jacob. Sam sat between the lot of them, English muffin poised in midair.

Jacob waved his hand. "Sit, Gregory. It's all good. Makes no sense for you and Mrs. Tucker to have breakfast in the other room."

Glowing, Isadora disappeared into the kitchen. Jacob settled Robin into the seat next to Maggie, while Mrs. Tucker loaded food onto the boy's plate.

Isadora returned bearing a fresh plate of hot cakes. When Jacob realized she would hover until he tasted it, he added some syrup and took a bite. *Nice.* "This must be why they say breakfast is the most important meal of the day. Dee-licious."

His cook responded with a pleased blush. As if a dam broke, the cheerful racket killed by his appearance returned with gusto. Jacob sat in the middle of it, savoring both his hot cakes and the moment. *So, this was what family feels like.* He sensed the too-knowing gaze of Ms. Fuller upon him, but he didn't care. He was enjoying himself.

Chapter 13
Girls, Girls, Girls

Following breakfast, the glow of the morning meal faded fast as Mrs. Tucker and Maggie argued as to whether "the poor dears" should clear their own plates. When both women sought Jacob for support, his survival instinct kicked into high gear, and he hastily excused himself. Backing out of the dining room behind his raised palms, he turned and sprinted up the stairs to his room. No way he was going to get sucked into that one.

Several phone calls later, he stood up and reached for the ceiling. *What is up with Don? He sounded like he was trying not to laugh when he was going over K.C.'s condition. It's as if—*

Blaring music from the guestroom assaulted his senses as he opened the door. *Again?* He frowned at the smattering of empty bags and boxes scattered around the hall leading to the guest room door. Vexed, he snatched up a couple of bags and headed toward the noise to tell them to clean up after themselves. He stopped short as he caught a glimpse of them jumping on the bed through the partially open door. *Are they for real?* It was time to take control of the situation. He swung the door open with an exasperated shove, and froze.

What the hell? Jacob stared, open-mouthed, at the youngsters happily shouting along with some song, hopping up and down on his mattress in time to the music.

He heard, but didn't register "They call me Stacey. They call me Jane. That's not my name. That's not my name."

Stunned, he registered two kids prancing around like a couple of girls. Cleaned up and dressed up, it was painfully obvious to any moron.

These *were* girls.

Forget about the new nail polish. Forget about the ribbons in their hair. Boys didn't wear leggings…or tank tops…or cute little sundresses. His bed was covered with jumping girls.

And, they had lied to him. He had taken them into his home, and they had *lied* to him. They gave him fake names, and—

Jacob continued to stare, bewildered. For the first time, he noticed a composed Maggie sitting to the side folding clothes.

Well, I suppose Robin could be either male or female…. And Sam could be short for Samantha…. And, I suppose, K.C. could stand for anything….

Maybe those *were* their real names.

The song ended and he heard a choking sound from Maggie. He glared at her as she dabbed at the corner of her eye. Ms. Margaret Fuller…*giggling?*

"You knew."

His words drew the boys'—no— the *girls'* attention to him. They stood on the bed uneasily watching him swing his gaze back and forth between them and his traitorous executive assistant. Another song started up, but Margaret shut it off. The two girls hopped to the floor, chattering as they descended upon him.

"Mrs. Fuller said we could jump on the bed."

"Are you mad at us?"

"Don't you just love that song?"

"Sorry about the music. It was way too loud."

"Don't I look pretty?"

"Wait a minute!" Jacob hollered, and the girls fell silent. The last comment had been from Robin as she smoothed the front of her new sundress. Sam was wide-eyed, her hands clenched in a white-knuckled grip. He took a deep breath.

"*If* Ms. Fuller said you could jump on the bed, fine. But don't do it again. No, I'm not mad at you…I don't think. Yes, the music was too loud. No, I never heard that song before, okay? And, yes, you look very pretty."

"And *you*." He leveled his glare at Maggie. "When were you planning on telling me?"

"Oh." She sat up straighter, regaining her composure. "I fully expected you to figure it out on your own."

Jacob stared at the three of them and reached a decision.

"Okay, everybody take a seat. We need to talk." He sank into a chair twin to the one occupied by Maggie. *That turncoat.* The girls clambered back onto the edge of the bed, settling in while Robin continued to preen.

How could he have missed it? They were pretty little things with delicate features. They had similarly shaped brown eyes, but of different shades of chocolate, which seemed at odds with their stark blonde hair. Sam had somehow intertwined a ribbon through her boyish hairstyle, making it look chic.

Jacob cleared his throat. Unsure of how he would be received, he blurted, "I thought you were boys."

"You were supposed to," laughed Sam.

"K.C. said it would be safer to travel—" began Robin, executing small bounces as she spoke.

"She means..." injected Sam, "it would be more fun to camp in the woods if we pretended we were boys."

"So we bleached our hair," exclaimed Robin, hopping down to the floor, "so no one would reco—"

"Because blondes have more fun," Sam interrupted again.

"Uh, right." Robin stopped bouncing. "Because we wanted to have more fun."

Looks like the fun just disappeared. "And did you?" Jacob asked, his tone gentle, leaving the faux pas for later.

"Did we what?" asked Robin, focused on Sam. She sat back down on the bed.

"Did you have more fun?"

"Oh, yes." Robin resumed a halfhearted bounce. "I *love* camping."

With the new direction of the conversation, Sam relaxed back onto the bed.

Jacob paused as another realization dawned. "I suppose K.C. is a girl, too?" The two girls smirked as he answered his own question. "Of course she is. A twenty-three-year-old *guy* would be a lot bigger."

In the face of the smugness dominating the room, he aimed for diplomacy. "Look, K.C. was right. It's not safe for a herd of girls to go *camping* alone without supervision."

"We had supervision. K.C.'s an adult." A frown accompanied Sam's sullen tone.

"Yeah, but then K.C. got sick," Robin lamented.

"I understand. But when that happened, you should have gone to the nearest police station or hospital and gotten help. I mean, she didn't get sick overnight, right?"

The girls exchanged glances.

"She didn't want to ruin our camping trip, so she didn't tell us right away," said Sam.

So, they were not going to tell him the real story. "I'm just saying you should've found someone to help you. That's all."

"But we *did* find someone. We found you." Robin beamed at him again.

"But, Robin, you don't know me. You didn't know if you could trust me."

"Oh, *I* knew we could trust you," said Robin then shrank away from Sam's glare.

"Why are you so sure of me?" he pressed. "You shouldn't trust adults you don't know. Sam, *you* are old enough to know better."

"You wouldn't hurt us," said Sam sulkily.

"No, I wouldn't," he confirmed. "But *I'm* the only one who

knows that for sure. *You* don't know me."

To his confusion, the two girls snickered. Robin hopped off the bed and came to lean against his knee. She reached up and patted him on the cheek, exactly like she had done on the side of the road the night before.

"We can trust you," she said.

He glanced at Maggie, who gave a slight shake of her head. He decided to hold off until later. Why scare them with possibilities that had not occurred? Besides, he still needed to visit William.

"Okay, whatever." He stood up. "I'm going out for a while. I have to go to the hospital to—"

A chorus of requests interrupted him.

"No, you can't come. I have to go to a different hospital to see *my* friend, and, afterwards, I'll go check on K.C." He paused. "What does K.C. stand for, anyway?"

Why were the girls looking confused?

Margaret stood also, her features still carefully schooled into a benign, neutral expression. "It's Cassie, Mr. Kent. C-a-s-s-i-e, not K-C."

The giggling resumed as Margaret herded the girls past him toward the hall. "Why don't we see what we can find to do until Mr. Kent returns?"

"Oh, that'll be just dandy," Jacob muttered. He headed down the stairs and out the door, his shower forgotten.

He slid into his car and just sat, playing back the morning's events. "So that's what Don thought was so funny. Great." It was going to be a *long* time before good ol' Dr. Don let this one go. He started the engine.

Girls?

Chapter 14
By the Light of Day

"Don't say it, Don. I mean it," Jacob growled into his cell phone.

"Sorry! Sorry," Don snorted as he gasped for breath. "But *you* said Cassie was a family friend. I didn't know you meant the family of man...or should I say, the family of woman?" His howling laughter resumed.

Jacob drummed his fingers on the steering wheel, waiting. "Don!" he finally hollered. "Can you give me some information here? I've got two more at home who want to know—"

"Wait, wait, wait. You mean, they're *all* girls? That's even worse." Another uncontrolled burst of laughter followed.

He willed himself to be patient. After all, how long could this last?

Don's hysterics outlasted Jacob's patience. "DON!" he bellowed. "What the hell?"

"*Okay.* Okay." Don panted. "Wait a sec. My eyes are watering."

Oh, great. That's twice today I made someone laugh till they cried. This day is just keeps getting better and better.

"Okay." Don cleared his throat and continued. "Okay. *She's* responding well to the fluids, and *she* hasn't had a reaction to the antibiotics. *She* has to stay on them for three weeks." The mirth disappeared as he transformed into Dr. Don. "Listen, the only way to fight this bug is to be aggressive with the treatment."

"Thank you, Doctor," he barked. "So *she's* going to be all right?"

"Yes. Cassie is a strong and healthy young *woman*."

"When can *she* leave the hospital?"

"Well, it depends on where *she* is going. Cassie is going to need a lot of bed rest. It would be a bad idea to just send her on her way."

"I guess she can come stay at my place. What's one more girl in the herd?" Jacob heard the words come out of his mouth, but couldn't believe he had said them aloud. What in the world was he doing? He cherished his privacy.

"You?" Don asked. "*You're* going to keep three females at your place?"

Don knows me too well. "Yeah, well, believe me, this is temporary. I'll get Maggie to supervise the Herd of Girls." Someone had to keep tabs on them. No doubt they were up to something. He ignored Don's mirth gurgling through the phone. "I'm going to stay at William's for a while anyway, until we get a handle on what's happening with him."

"I'm pulling an evening shift at Greenwich Hospital. I'll check on him before I go on duty."

"You know, William didn't have a heart attack. He fell and hit his chest on the coffee table. But his blood pressure is way up, so they decided to run some tests on him last night."

"Hmmm. See if he'll tell you when he last had a checkup. If it's been a while, I'd have them do a complete work-up…if you can get him to cooperate."

"Yup. That's a big *if*. I'm on my way there now."

"It'll all work out, Jake. The girls should be fine at your place. Mrs. Tucker will love having a patient to boss around, and Isadora will have someone to cook for."

"You're right." A smiled tugged at him as he remembered breakfast.

"Of course I'm right. The doctor's always right," Don teased. "But a word of warning, buddy—"

"I know. Make sure they have something to do besides watch TV."

"I was going to tell you to be careful with them, unless you are ready for a pre-made family. Kids can be heartbreakers, and—"

"Don't worry about me. My heart is safe."

"Yeah, well, that's a discussion for another time," muttered Don. "I'm just trying to say, be careful you don't break *their* hearts. They're dealing with something—something big—and I don't think you know what it is."

"You're right." An image of Robin's vulnerable face popped into his mind. "I'm in uncharted territory here. I want to help them, but I don't want someone else's family. I want my own family with—" He caught himself too late.

"Oh, right. You're still pining for The Nameless Wonder," said Don with ill-disguised disgust.

"I never should have told you about her," he said for the hundredth time.

"Yup, that was stupid. Almost as stupid as spending your time going to fairs to find—"

"Lay off. I have enough to deal with right now without you adding to it."

"You're right," said Don. "I apologize. I just want you to meet a normal woman in a normal way."

"I understand," he said with more patience than he felt. "Some of us are married to the women of our dreams. The rest of us are still searching."

"I'm just saying there are plenty of women who don't go to fairs. Take me and Rita, for example. We met. We fell in love. We got married. We're happy. No fairs involved, and we still managed to get it right."

"But the first time you kissed her was at a fair."

Don paused. "No, it wasn't."

"Yes, it was. And at a kissing booth."

Another, longer pause ended with, "So what? I kissed her

at a kissing booth. Whatever. It wasn't our first kiss."

"Yes, it was."

Another pause, shorter this time, and then, "Did Rita tell you?"

"Who else?"

"I told her not to."

"She told me that, too. She said you didn't want to feed my Nameless Wonder fantasy."

Don muttered something about how he and Rita were going to have a talk tonight. Louder, he retorted, "Whatever. Let's not forget the real issue here. You had three—count 'em, *three* females in your car, and you didn't even know it. *Three Females.*"

"Grow up. I'm going to Greenwich Hospital to have a sit-down with William about his workload. I'll swing by Norwalk and check on Cassie after. Good luck with that talk with Rita."

***

I'm in a hospital.

She jostled her blurry thoughts through a killer headache and a wave of nausea. Something needed her immediate attention, but what? Her head was fuzzy and unfocused. She remembered trying to cross some road. The road to perdition? The yellow brick road to perdition! Had she been hit by a car on the highway to hell? Cars were nice. Especially red ones.

She groaned as she tried to move her arms. *What's that on my hand? And why can't I move my legs?* She felt enormous panic. *I can't move my legs!* Blankets. It was blankets weighing down her legs. Relief flooded her. No casts meant no broken bones. Or maybe not.

She rolled her head, but it made her ache all over. More nausea. *I need to burp. Or toss my cookies. Or cook some cook-*

ies. Mmmm. Hot chocolate chip cookies. No! Snickerdoodles are way better. Is a snickerdoodle a cookie or a dog? Maybe it's a cookie shaped like a dog. And what's with the tube sticking out of my hand? Not pretty. Not pretty at all.

Maybe it doesn't matter. I just need to put another TV in my bucket. She drifted back into the darkness.

***

Girls?

Jacob pulled into the hospital parking lot, feeling his predictable existence slipping away. *And Margaret Fuller knew.* He remained in his car for a moment, drumming his fingers on the steering wheel, reviewing the last couple of days. He sighed. It was time to go a round with William over his work list. With shoulders set, he strode toward the building, preparing for a skirmish of epic proportions.

He found his boss bantering with the nurse taking his vitals while Hanson glowered at him from a chair by the window. Wondering what was going on, Jacob beckoned to William's domestic and stepped back into the hall.

"You appear to be in capable hands, *Sire,*" the valet said. "I shall return momentarily." Hanson appeared in the doorway, followed by William's bellow, "Chicken!"

Hanson stiffened, sniffed, and marched towards Jacob. Dr. Sal Tujay joined them.

Jacob extended his hand to William's golfing buddy. "Glad you're here, Doc. What do you think?"

Waggling his head from side to side, Dr. Tujay shook his hand. "We need to get a full workup done on my old friend while we've got him here. That's what I think."

"Good luck. Mr. Hatch has not been to a doctor in years," drawled Hanson.

"Well, he's here now, so let's take advantage of it," said Jacob. "He's been driving himself too hard. Some downtime will do him good."

"Very good, sir." Hanson raised one eyebrow. "May I suggest *you* tell him?"

"Me?"

"I'll come with you," encouraged Dr. Tujay. "It's for his own good."

Jacob drew a deep breath and clapped Tujay on the shoulder. "All right. Let's do this." It was going to be a long battle.

Fifty-five minutes later a weary Jacob found Hanson in the waiting room, wrinkling his nose over a cup of hospital coffee. He plopped into the chair next to him. It sure felt good to sit. "I have good news about our patient. William has agreed to let them do as many tests on him as they deem necessary."

"Oh, very good, sir." Hanson relaxed back in his chair. "How many times did he fire you?"

Dr. Tujay entered and sank into another chair. "Only three times. Well done, Jacob." He slapped him on the back. "I've been trying to get that stubborn old goat in for routine tests for years. You're a miracle worker."

He shook his head. "It wasn't me, Doc. It was all Hanson. He got William here. And, miracle or not, you only have until six o'clock tomorrow night. Then he's leaving, and I quote, 'come hell or high water.'"

Dr. Tujay slapped his thighs and stood. "Well, then, we'd better get started."

Hanson rose and dumped out his cup. "I had better get in there." As he passed Jacob, they high-fived like members of a tag team.

No rest for the weary. It was now time to go check on the mysterious Cassie.

***

She looked around at the sterile surroundings. *A hospital?* That couldn't be good. Panic crept into her fuzzy head. She needed answers. *Hospitals have nurses. Nurses have call buttons.*

No, wait. Hospitals have buttons that call nurses. That was it. There had to be one around here somewhere, but she couldn't see it. Maybe she could prop herself up on her elbow.

Hey! Someone taped a tube to the back of her hand. *Ick.* It was sticking in her. She gingerly raised her hand and lowered it. Nothing hurt. *How long is this thing?* A mild shake made the tube execute a fascinating little dance. *I could hang our laundry on that. But not all of it. Just the whites.* She looked at the sheets enveloping her body. Way too many whites.

Oooh, her head pounded. She closed her eyes to ease the throbbing. *Wait. What was I trying to do?* She noticed a tube sticking out of the back of her hand. *What's that? Truth serum? They won't get anything outta me!* She was about to pull the tube out when she realized They would know she was on to them if she did.

She paused for a moment to test herself. *I'm a guy…*She waited. *Wow, I can still lie. That means…I'm immune to truth serum!* She was delighted. *No problem. I'll just escape before They interrogate me. There must be a way to call for help around here someplace. I'll just roll over and…*she spied a call button tied to the bedrail. Of course! There it was, hidden in plain sight. They thought They were so clever.

She tried to reach for it, but despite her best efforts, she rolled back. It was insidious how They placed it just out of reach.

I'll rest for just a moment. Then I'll….

She closed her eyes and drifted back to sleep.

Jacob hesitated in the doorway watching the eldest sister jiggle her IV and then struggle to reach the call button. "What does one say to a fugitive?" he muttered, imitating Hanson's haughty tones. A flash of sympathy shot through him as she gave up and rolled onto her back, apparently asleep.

That's when every particle in Jacob's world collided. Shock glued his feet to the floor. Through the instantaneous utter and complete chaos, he was aware of two things—his heart pounding so hard he could barely breathe, and his beloved Casey asleep in front of him in a hospital bed.

What was she doing here? Where was Cassie Thatcher's room? He took a step out to check the room number. This *was* Cassie Thatcher's room. He stepped back in, drowning in excitement.

"So, you're calling yourself Cassie now." And she was pretending to be a guy. A blond guy at that. And she had two sisters pretending to be boys.

Who were at his place.

He gazed at the motionless form. To think when the boys— no, the girls—had called her K.C., he'd had no clue at all.

Maybe they had said Casey. *K.C. sounds like Casey.*

It didn't matter. Cassie, K.C., Casey. Whatever her name was, she was *here*. After not being able to find her at fairs for the last couple of months, she shows up in Norwalk.

Jacob stole to her bedside and leaned over her. "Where have you been?" he whispered. "I've been so worried. I don't know what the hell is going on, but I promise I won't let anything happen to you. Or to your bro—sisters."

He traced the outline of her face, his blood pumping. When she stirred and murmured something unintelligible, he snatched his finger away. He wasn't ready for her to see him yet. Life as he knew it was about to radically change, and he had some major arrangements to make.

He flipped over a paper placemat from the bed stand and jotted a note in case she woke before he got back. She was too weak to leave, but he didn't want to take the chance of her slipping away. Bending closer, he wedged it next to the call button where she would be sure to find it.

Hearing a quick intake of air, he turned and caught her gazing at him, radiating love. *What?* She never let her emotions show. It had to be the hospital meds.

She placed a hand on his cheek and drew him to her. He brushed his lips over hers, stroking her short hair, and enjoying the rush of her proximity. With a sigh, she relaxed into the pillow. Her hand slid back onto the sheets, and just like that, she was fast asleep.

What was that? Straightening up, he stared at her, ignoring his still-thumping heart. *So she* does *love me!* Gleeful, he slipped out of the room to find Don to tell him the news. The Nameless Wonder was in the house!

***

Fretful, Casey emerged from the darkness again. Something was missing. What was it?

Her sisters. Where were her sisters? She felt for the call button she remembered finding earlier. Her hand hit a piece of paper. She picked it up and read,

Your sisters are safe and happy. All you need to do is get better. I will bring them to visit you when you are stronger.

Who wrote that? She fumbled for the button again. A few moments later, a matronly, middle-aged nurse swept in.

"How are you feeling, Cassie?" She scanned the equipment behind the bed.

"Where are my sisters?" she managed to croak out.

The nurse patted her hand. "Your sisters? I'm sure they're fine, honey. Your family must've taken them home."

"My family? What family?" *Oh, no.*

"I don't know. Some guy in a dark suit," she said, jotting down something on the chart at the foot of her bed.

Casey's aching head commenced pounding. She pressed her palms over her eyes and tried to control her reaction, willing herself to calm down. *What are the chances the girls have been taken? Small.* They had been very careful to travel undetected from Albany to Connecticut. No one even knew they had a destination, so no one would be trying to intercept them. *Stop panicking.*

What about the note? A fresh wave of anxiety erupted from deep within. Was the author a friend? It seemed so. An enemy would not alert her.

Oh, if only she wasn't so weak. She was in no condition to face an enemy.

"Does your head hurt, dear?" the nurse asked.

"Yes," whispered Casey. She needed to remember something else. Something important.

"I can fix that right up." The nurse reached behind her to manipulate some medical gizmo. Before Casey could protest, the pounding ceased, and darkness swallowed her once again, a blessed relief from the burden of trying to protect others, when she couldn't even protect herself.

***

Chapter 15
The Nameless Wonder

A level head. That's what Jacob needed. Feeling akin to a lit, but yet to be exploded box of fireworks, he was far from levelheaded. He sprinted up the stairs to where Don was doing rounds. Bursting out of the stairwell, he spotted him at the end of the corridor. "Don! Don! It's her. She's here!"

"*Sir*, this is a hospital. Lower your voice," admonished a frowning nurse.

"Oops. Sorry." He hissed the apology over his shoulder as he skidded to a stop and grabbed Don's arm.

Shrugging him off, Don commandeered Jacob's arm and maneuvered him into an empty room. "Let me guess. You saw The Nameless Wonder."

"I did." Astonishing! Don had gotten it on the first try.

"Seriously?" Don staggered back a step. "Where?"

"Downstairs. In Cassie's room. I mean—"

"She knows Cassie Thatcher?"

Jacob grabbed him by both shoulders. "She *is* Cassie Thatcher." He grinned at his best friend, waiting for a reaction. Don did not disappoint.

"*What*? You mean that girl you brought in here yesterday?"

"Yes, yes, yes! It's her." He bounced twice.

"Cassie Thatcher is The Nameless Wonder?"

He bounced again. "Yes, yes, y— Stop calling her that!"

"Okay, fine. Cassie Thatcher is the paragon over whom you have been mooning?"

"That's what I've been trying to tell you." Jubilant, he slapped Don on the shoulder and started to pace.

"Jacob." Don snapped his fingers in the air. "Jake!"

He stopped pacing, a bit dazed.

"Are you sure it's her?"

"Oh, I'm sure." He shoved his palms skyward. "I know. I know. It's crazy. I actually picked her up and drove her around in my car and didn't even suspect it was her." He rubbed his head and resumed his laps across the room. "Of course, her hair is shorter. And blonde. You know, it's supposed to be brown."

"I know. You've told me once or twice."

"And she never mentioned having sisters. That kind of threw me."

"Yeah, that, and the fact she was disguised as a *guy*."

"That's right!" Jacob paused to pound his fist into his palm, and realized Don had been watching him pace back and forth like he was a racket sport. "Well, no wonder I didn't recognize her."

"I hate to burst your bubble, but you don't know how this girl feels about you."

The comment opened the floodgates of indignation. Jacob folded his arms across his chest. "Sure I do. She feels the same way I do."

"Really? She told you that."

"Well, okay," he amended. "*Probably* she feels the same way I do."

"Probably?"

"All right already! I don't exactly know how she feels about me. Satisfied?"

"Jacob, has the girl given you any indication about any-thing?"

"Sure she's given me indications. Lots of times. Well, maybe not lots. I only see her a few times a year." The anxiety dial was creeping up. "But she always seems happy to see me. Well, unless we have a fight." Indignation gave way to doubt.

He sank into a nearby chair as he mulled over his interactions with Casey. Brightening, he straightened up. "Hah! She just kissed me. *That* is a definite indication."

"She's awake?"

Why was Don amazed by that? "Well, for a moment, you know, for the kiss. Then she fell back asleep."

"Okay. Jake, buddy, that's only a definite indication she's on meds." Don sat next to him, frowning.

Jacob scowled back and then sagged in his chair. "You're right. For all I know, it might've only been a series of summer flings to her." He shifted to the edge of the chair to face him, willing his friend to understand. "But don't you see? This is my chance to find out. And this time, it won't be at some fair where she can appear and disappear. I don't know where she's heading, but she can't go anywhere for the next few days."

"A series of summer flings? Jake, three random encounters does not a series make."

"About that…. I stopped telling you when I ran into her so you'd get off my back."

"Fair enough. So, I take it there were more than three encounters."

"Yeah, a lot more." Jacob grinned and raked his hair. "Like thirty or forty more."

"No way! Are you kidding me?"

Jubilance returned. Jacob pounded the good doctor on his chest. Don was beginning to get it.

"So what are you doing here?"

Jacob shot to his feet. "Right. I wasn't thinking. I should—" He bolted for the door.

Jacob pulled a chair next to Casey's bed and sat down. He spied his note clutched in her hand and slipped it out of her grasp.

She won't be needing that. Next time she wakes up, I'm going to be right here.

Settling back, he studied her face, a thinner version of the laughing girl from last summer. Were she and her sisters in some type of custody battle? Were they in danger? Runaways?

He laid his questions to rest. *It's a waste of time to keep guessing. She'll be able to tell me when she wakes up.*

Jacob rested his head in his palms. *But will she tell me? She's never told me anything else.* Over the years, Don had made no secret of his disdain for The Nameless Wonder. He claimed Jacob used her to keep interested females at arm's length. Was it true? Perhaps. He'd never had a problem getting a date, but none of them had made him feel like *she* did.

He had taken to referring to her as "she" because every time he found her, she gave him a different name. He settled on calling her Casey, the first name she had used when she had finally introduced herself, and no matter which name she subsequently chose, he usually thought of her as Casey.

Jacob used to think the name games were an unfamiliar form of flirtation. However, traveling around the country disguised as a guy waved a major red flag.

I want to help you, but how can I get you to tell me what's going on? He continued to stare at her face. Something registered. It had been there, right in front of him the whole time. In her sleeping features, he recognized Sam's pert nose and chin. Now, he understood his uncharacteristic reaction to Robin, whose big round eyes were fringed with long lashes just like Casey's.

I assumed you were an only child like me. You never mentioned anyone else. Don's right. Jacob stared at the monitors behind the bed. "I don't know how you feel about me. I'm just fooling myself," he muttered. "I don't know anything about you. Except you go to a lot of fairs. I don't know where you're from, or what you do for work. Hell, I don't even know your real name."

Casey mumbled something unintelligible, clutching at her blankets. Wherever sleep had taken her, turmoil had been waiting. Jacob captured her hand as it waved in the air.

"Everything's okay, Casey." He didn't want to wake her, but perhaps his words could pierce her distress. "Everyone is safe now."

Casey's hands dropped to the sheet. He reached over to smooth the frown gathered at her brow. She relaxed back into her pillow. Satisfied, he sat back, wishing he could do more.

Okay, so I don't know anything about your life. But I do know you.

She was smart, well-educated, and funny. Personal experience vouched she could be provocative and clever in an argument. She definitely had a temper, but she also was thoughtful and caring for people less able. Jacob loved the way her face lit up with undisguised pleasure when she spotted him at a fair, and how she had taken to tenderly kissing him good-bye. He believed she cherished their time together, as fleeting as it was, as much as he did.

His thoughts drifted to their early years. Captivated by Casey long after their first encounter, nothing had prepared him for the delightful shock of running into her later that very same year—at a different fair in a different state. Coincidence? The Kissing Booth prophecy? Fate? He didn't care. He was just so pleased to see her.

Over the next couple of years, their occasional encounters seemed more like a series of snapshots than an ongoing relationship. Casey had blossomed into an extremely desirable young woman who possessed all the qualities he treasured, with the exception of her secrecy.

She had teased, dodged, and parried all of his attempts to

learn about her. She never gave him a way to contact her, instead insisting he appreciate the fact she had not given him a bogus number. Each time they met, Jacob pressed his telephone number into her hand, hoping she would contact him, but she never had. They would part, not knowing if, or when, they would meet again.

For the first few years, he'd persisted in trying to extend their visits, but Casey adhered to some kind of inflexible timetable. At first he felt slighted, imagining her meeting someone else later. However, at some point after she had begun greeting him with a bear hug, she started to cling to him when it was time to part, and he stopped wondering about other guys.

He had failed at trying to figure out a way to kick their relationship up a notch, but now he had her here, outside of the sporadic world of fairs they shared and inside his world. Today, the possibilities seemed unlimited.

Hope pulsed through him. *Oh, yeah. Your sisters are at my place, honey. You can't take them and disappear on me because you don't know where I live.*

✳✳✳

Casey awoke to the sight of Jacob staring into space with a smile on his face.

This is too weird. Where did he come from?

A million thoughts rushed through her at once, but as she opened her mouth to speak, his gaze locked on hers. Feeling the air rush out of her lungs, she closed her mouth. How did he do that to her every time? So unfair.

Jacob reached over and stroked her hair. "Your sisters are safe," he murmured.

She closed her eyes. Out of all of the things he could have said to her, he chose the one she needed to hear the most.

"Where?" she croaked out.

"They're at my house."

Jacob with her sisters? That wasn't right. The foggy edges of sleep began to close in. But there was something else… something else…something…. She struggled back awake.

"What's wrong—" she managed.

"You have Lyme disease, but you made it worse by getting dehydrated," he said, again nailing the answer she needed.

"'Kay."

"They have you on fluids and antibiotics," he added in a faraway place as sleep closed in again. She was not sure she was still awake when he said, "You're going to be just fine."

His lips brushed across her forehead after his tender whisper, and she gave in to the enveloping sleep.

***

Jacob had some serious planning to do. He began a mental checklist.

Get my room ready for when Casey leaves the hospital.

Have Maggie rearrange my schedule. She can tell everyone I'm out of town.

Figure out a way to intercept William's mail so he won't keep loading up on projects.

Have Hanson set up a dinner date for Dr. Tujay and William for a little casual observation.

Ask Don when Sam and Robin can visit Casey.

Tell Maggie to settle the girls into my place for a lot longer than expected.

He would wait to tell William about the Herd of Girls until he understood all the circumstances with his old friend's health, and until he had a handle on the real story behind his new houseguests.

His mind drifted back to the morning's events.

You're not the family type, are you? Sam had observed.

He had been dreaming about a life with Casey. She came with some kind of significant baggage, but he had not expected a ready-made family. As she lay recovering in the hospital bed next to him, he realized it didn't matter.

I might not be the family type now, but I will learn. Oh, Casey—if that's your real name—I'm going to have to move slowly so I don't scare you off.

"You have to stop doing that," Casey rasped, her eyes still closed.

"Stop doing what?" He scooted a bit closer.

"Stop watching me while I sleep."

"Sorry." *What am I supposed to look at?* "It's just that I can't believe you're really here." He slid the chair alongside her bed.

She opened her eyes at the sound and rolled her head toward him. And there it was. He spotted it when their gazes met in that unguarded waking moment. She loved him.

He suppressed an erupting grin. *I know we can make it work. And wait until William meets you. He is going to* love *you.*

***

Chapter 16
The Missed Connection

A wave of panic hit Casey as she broke free of sleep. She scanned the corners of the room as if Jacob might be hiding there, but of course he wasn't. It had only been a dream. *Then I still don't know where the girls are.* Unbidden tears threatened as she fumbled for the call button, a sob escaping.

"What is it? What's the matter?" It was Jacob, rushing over to her bedside.

Confusion, relief, and something else flooded her. "Oh, Jacob," she squeaked past the lump in her throat.

Reaching over the bedrail, he enveloped her in a reassuring hug.

She wrapped her arms around him and gave in to her tears. "I…I thought I…I dreamed you," she said between sobs.

"No, no. I'm right here." He sat back a bit and peered into her face. "Do you remember I told you I have the girls, and they're fine?"

She nodded, and he moved closer again.

"I'm so sorry I scared you. I just stepped out for a hot minute. I didn't think you'd wake up right then."

She interrupted his apology with insistent shushing. They clung to each other, their embrace quieting her fears for a moment. The rest of the world disappeared, leaving them with an elusive moment of peace, just the two of them…

***

…And the figure spying on them from the door.

He stepped back and headed for a phone. Thrumming his fingers for a moment, he tried to decide what to do. Reaching a conclusion, he leaned forward to dial.

"We have a guest here who would interest you very much." Don frowned into the receiver, hoping he would not live to regret this move.

***

By late afternoon, snare drums had replaced the kettledrums pounding in Casey's head. Jacob stayed long enough to make sure she consumed her fair share of Jell-O and broth. When her eyes began feeling heavy again, he left, promising to bring the girls by the next day. He had not asked any questions, and she had not provided any answers. She fell asleep, a rare feeling of security wrapping around her like a child's blanket.

She awoke later that evening to a white-haired, thick-waisted nurse bustling around with a clipboard.

"How ya doing, honey?" the nurse asked.

"I've been better." She tried to sit up. "But I've also been worse."

The nurse handed her a control to manipulate the bed. As she rose to a sitting position, Casey asked, "How long have I been here?"

"Oh, a couple of days." The nurse fluffed pillows and straightened sheets.

"A couple of *days*?" Horror filled Casey. "What day is it?"

"Why, it's Sunday."

"*Sunday*? Oh, no! What time is it?"

"It's, um, after ten thirty."

"Oh, no. Oh, no. Oh, no," moaned Casey as she rocked back and forth.

"Honey, are you all right?"

"I...I was supposed to call someone at seven thirty." Casey drew a shaky breath. "Is there a phone I can use? Does it call

411?"

When the nurse hesitated, Casey grabbed her by the arm. "Oh, please. Can you find me a phone book? Please, please, please. He might still be there."

"Sure, honey. I think there's one at the desk. You stay put. I'll be right back."

The nurse hastened out, leaving Casey to cope with the kettledrums in her head now banging in time with her thumping heart.

***

"We should go, sir."

Hanson placed a gentle hand on his shoulder, but William couldn't summon the energy to respond.

Punctual Casey, for the first time, had missed a call.

"Sir, it is ten thirty. It has been three hours." Hanson's face was pale.

"Go check again. Maybe she called while the phone was busy." William's fingers trembled as he clutched at Hanson's arm. "Maybe the bar took the call. Maybe...."

"Yes, sir." Hanson left the table and headed for the maître d' to inquire once again, but the results were the same.

They had traveled to the restaurant rendezvous from Greenwich Hospital, arriving thirty minutes early for this long-anticipated appointment. The message had said to expect a call at seven thirty. The appointed time had come and gone, and still they waited, their hopes dimming with each passing second.

If only I had stuck with the plan, William agonized. *Then we'd know where Simon's children are.*

It was the ultimate irony. William had married his secret Gypsy love, and now he had to secretly meet with his grandchildren. Being introduced to eighteen-year-old Simon then discovering the young man was William's son, had been almost as big a shock to Hanson as it had been for William. Fate had whisked Simon out of reach, concealed behind a new identity provided to protect him after he agreed to testify for a crime he had witnessed. Just a few short years after William met his son, the Witness Protection Program had robbed them of their budding relationship.

But Simon had inherited determination from both of his parents. Taking matters into his own hands, he had faked his death and initiated secret meetings with his newly found father. William's favorite pastime became the vehicle by which Simon could be part of his forbidden family. With his guidance, they rendezvoused at fairs, always in a variety of states and always at different times of the year. During these visits to the fairs, Simon had introduced William and Hanson to his bride, Dorothy, and later, to their precious children. Hanson was devoted to William's family like they were his own, protecting them fiercely as they tried to defy the odds.

In due time, Casey had enrolled at Northeastern University in Boston under an assumed name. Through NEU's Co-op Program, she secured internships at different companies owned by William. The interoffice courier became a conduit for communication between grandfather and granddaughter, but, more importantly, they were able to talk on the phone during business hours, knowing phone records would show no unusual activity.

Then, overnight, everything changed. A car crash took the lives of Simon and Dorothy. Although the police later declared it a random accident, William's grandchildren had disappeared without a trace. And so the nightmare had begun.

Were the children alive, or had they become victims of a vindictive crime boss? With no way to contact them, William and Hanson had been miserable, hoping against hope. Every time the grandchildren did not show up to a prearranged rendezvous, their fear and frustration mushroomed. Over a year later, they received a smuggled note. So what if the message asked William not to search for them. It was evidence of their survival.

The eldest had inherited the double whammy of protecting her siblings, and holding her grieving family together while she mourned. Almost six months later, she reinitiated communication. At first, they maintained contact by phone, a call from one random location to another predetermined location. In time, they began to risk an occasional rendezvous at a fair. The younger ones took on the role of researching fairs and creating ways to let their grandpa and Hanson know when and where to meet them. In turn, the two men strove to do everything they could to help the children remain undetected and to help them heal. William provided more than enough money for them to buy new IDs, to set up a home, and to travel whenever and wherever needed. Neither man knew the names on the IDs, nor where the girls had moved, but the smuggled messages kept them satisfied the youngsters were safe.

Tonight at the restaurant rendezvous, with three hours of silence weighing heavily on them, William and Hanson were reluctant to leave. Leaving would be admitting the unspoken. Although neither said it aloud, both men knew something was wrong.

The grandchildren were in trouble.

***

That's it. Casey underscored the restaurant's phone number with a quaking finger. She misdialed, hung up. *Take three deep breaths. I can do this.* She dialed again. When a speaker on the other end regretted to inform her no one answered the page for Mr. Children, she returned the phone to the cradle, her head pounding worse than ever.

Poor Grandpa and Hanson. She knew what this would mean to them, especially after her last message had informed them she and the girls were once again on the run. They must be frantic. Her shoulders drooped, and tears brimmed, but before the first fallen tear hit the sheets, she squared her shoulders. Yes, there would be a world of worry for Grandpa and Hanson until she contacted them. She would simply have to get a message to them as fast as she could.

The nurse watched her with a furrowed brow.

"Excuse me, but is there something I can use to write a letter?" Casey asked, trying to steady herself.

The nurse pursed her lips. "Sure. Let me grab something."

Settling back against the pillows, Casey tried to gather her thoughts for the task at hand. She would give the letter to Jacob to give to Sam. Sam was resourceful. She would figure out a way to get it to Grandpa.

The nurse reappeared. "Now don't you overdo it," she cautioned as she handed over a pad of paper.

"I won't. Thank you so much." Casey pressed her palm to her temples as the nurse bustled out. How was she going to structure the message? It had to appear like an innocent communication in case someone intercepted it. Writing something and translating it into code was hard enough without her head pounding like this.

After several tries, Casey gave up. She relaxed back into her pillow to rest for a moment, trying to ease her headache. Her fingers went slack, and the pen slipped from them. Sleep overtook her once again.

I'm so sorry, Grandpa. I'm so sorry, Hanson....

***

Chapter 17
Jacob's House Runneth Over

Jacob drove from Casey's hospital, his mind bouncing between problems. He checked his watch—6:30 p.m. No doubt William and Hanson had left the other hospital by now. No power on earth could change William's mind once he set it. *I hope he doesn't set it against Casey and The Herd.*

He pulled up in front of his townhouse, trying to picture William meeting his recently acquired Herd. He had never shared anything with his mentor about Casey, a decision prompted by Don's ridicule. There was no way to predict William's reaction to hearing about her secret life, especially right out of the blue.

Jacob was in no hurry to find out.

He hoped they would get along, but Casey and William both possessed strong personalities. *Too bad if they don't mix.* Seeing them in shifts would have to work because giving up either of them was out of the question. He wagged his head. How had he gone from a foster kid who barely spoke to five people a month to a guy trying to...to....

Omigod...Hanson! He doesn't like anybody. Hanson was nice enough to kids at the fairs, but what if he didn't like The Herd?

I'm not sure I like them. He chuckled as he heaved himself out of the car. *But I sure like Casey, and this is a package deal.*

Jacob tried to picture Hanson's snooty sniff combined with Sam's hypersensitivity. Oh, yeah, that spelled disaster. He rubbed his head. Maybe he could just make sure The Herd never met Hanson.

Right. That wasn't happening. Hanson and William came as a set. No doubt about it. This was going to be a mess if either of them didn't like The Herd.

Speaking of a mess, it would probably be better not to tell the girls he and Casey were already well acquainted. *I'll leave it up to her to decide how she wants to handle her sisters, but one way or another, it is going to be handled.* Whether they were ready for it or not, Jacob was joining The Herd.

He opened his front door with caution. Gregory met him at the foyer. All appeared calm, and something smelled great.

"How're things going, Gregory?" The corners of his mouth quirked. His butler had been the only male in the condo all day.

"Interesting day, sir." Gregory was noncommittal as he reached for the briefcase. "I'm sure Ms. Fuller will fill you in."

Fill me in? That didn't sound good. He followed TV noise to the den where he found Margaret reading a book on the settee with Robin beside her. Sam lounged on the floor with her back against the settee, wedged between their legs. The two girls sat engrossed by the television while Margaret read.

It was a peek into the future. *So this is what it's like to be part of a family. It doesn't look so hard. I can do this.*

Sure, he didn't have any actual experience with a family of his own, but he watched families on TV. He knew the drill. Besides, he'd have Casey and Maggie to lend a hand.

Who was he kidding? He didn't know anything about girls either.

Hell, he didn't know anything about kids in general. *He* would be the one lending the hand.

He glanced at the TV. Did they spend the whole day in here? They were mocking the "Wax on, Wax off" scene from *The Karate Kid.*

"Oh, brother." Sam gave a snort.

"Yeah, right?" Robin giggled.

"What is it?" asked Margaret absently, her gaze sharp. Jacob focused his attention on their conversation, remembering Margaret never did anything absently.

Sam gestured toward the screen. "Nobody who is untrained would have reflexes like that."

"Yeah," chimed in Robin. "And if he wasn't used to all that waxing, his arms would be too tired."

"I understand," said Margaret, "but wouldn't the fear of being struck make him react?"

"Yeah, he'd react," explained Sam, "but a normal reaction would be to protect your face. Plus, his T1 muscle fibers would have fatigued without endurance training—"

"Yeah, and a couple of days of chores is not exactly endurance training," grunted Robin.

"Shhh. I can't hear," said Sam.

Their exchange bewildered Jacob. *Not exactly a* Brady Bunch *conversation, but I guess they pay attention at school.*

Gregory appeared behind him. "Dinner is served, sir."

"Dinner?" He wasn't usually home at this hour. As if on cue, his stomach rumbled.

"Mr. Kent!" shrieked Robin. The TV forgotten, the girls scrambled toward him amid a clamor of questions.

"Hold it," commanded Margaret. "Bathroom first. Go wash your hands. Mr. Kent will talk to you at dinner."

Despite a mildly sullen glance from Sam, they bolted from the room to do her bidding. Robin paused to wrap her small arms around his legs and beam up at him. Wow, those were Casey's brown eyes, no doubt. Surprised by how her simple, affectionate act touched him, Jacob awkwardly patted the top of her head. As she skipped out, the spell weakened, but did not completely dissolve.

Margaret rose, smoothed her skirt, and approached him. "We have to talk," she mouthed at him as she walked by.

"What's up?" Frowning, he followed her into the room

across the hall and closed the door.

"Mr. Kent, do you know what the girls did all day?"

Uh-oh. "What?"

She paced the room. "They *trained.*"

"Trained? What do you mean trained? For what?"

"I don't know for what."

"Maybe it's some kind of exercise."

She smiled at that. "Well, in fact, Sam called it exercise. Robin said they were playing Army." She shook her head.

"That doesn't seem so bad," he offered. Where was this going?

"No, Mr. Kent," Margaret replied impatiently. "It's not a *bad* thing. It's an *odd* thing."

"Ms. Fuller," he teased. "Perhaps, when you were a child, they didn't consider it, er, proper for young ladies to play Army, but I assure you, we've crossed several gender barriers since then."

Margaret drew herself up as he grinned down at her. "I'm not from the dark ages, Mr. Kent," she retorted. "I am telling you, what they were doing was odd."

She was obviously bothered by what she had seen, and if time had taught him anything, he could rely on Margaret Fuller's observations. Jacob stopped teasing. "Sorry. Go ahead."

"Well, they constructed some type of obstacle course around the apartment using your furniture." She resumed pacing. "First, Sam took Robin through the course to make sure she knew how she had set it up. Then they took turns timing how long it took them to complete it. After that they started racing the clock. When Sam seemed satisfied with their times, they each started to change the course secretly. When I asked why, Robin said so they could learn to adapt at a moment's notice." She paused and fixed her gaze on him. "Mr. Kent, this was not a game. They were *training.*"

Pounding on the stairs alerted them to the returning girls. He nodded his understanding, and opened the door in time to watch the two youngsters race into the dining room. *They seem like normal kids…except for their hair being cut to disguise them as boys. What kind of life are they leading?*

Jacob followed Maggie to the table. Isadora beamed as he took his seat at its head. Between her hovering and the two girls watching him, he felt like he had a spotlight on him.

"Busy day?" he asked, nodding at the impromptu houseguests.

"Nothing I can't handle, sir." Pink tinged the cook's cheeks.

"Isadora's the best," stated Robin. "You wouldn't believe how we've been eating." She glanced at him. "Oh, I guess *you* know. You eat here all the time."

He cleared his throat. "Unfortunately, business usually keeps me away from Isadora's fine cooking." He ignored Isadora's muttering something about him needing to settle down and get a life as she marched back into the kitchen. Instead, he picked up his fork, his mouth watering in response to the heavenly aromas, and dove in. Jacob slowed his eating moments later, again watching the scene unfold before him. He'd been doing a lot of that lately.

"How is your employer?" Margaret asked.

"He agreed to stay in the hospital and let them do tests on him. He said he was leaving after six, no matter what. Short of them knocking him out, I'm sure he's already on his way," he chuckled.

Weird. Neither of the girls had asked him about Casey. "Don't you want to know how your sister is?"

"Oh, she's good," said Robin behind a mouth of mashed potatoes.

As she closed her eyes to savor a bite, her sister nodded behind the drink she was guzzling.

Jacob met Margaret's eyes across the table. Her drawn brow indicated she was as mystified as he by their nonchalance.

"Really?" he finally asked.

"Yup. I know how she feels—" Robin looked up as she reached for a second roll, locking gazes with Sam who had just tuned into the conversation.

"Because Robin had me call the hospital." Sam's smooth filler was accompanied by a subtle, but not invisible, warning look at Robin.

The little girl hunched her shoulders as she buttered her roll, alarm flitting across her face.

Jacob diverted the conversation to save Robin any more distress. "How resourceful of you."

The tension at the table dropped with his words.

Another item for the Things To Ask Casey *list.*

After dinner, the girls cleared the table and insisted on helping in the kitchen. Clearly, Maggie had won that argument. Jacob decided to take a quick tour of the condo to see what mayhem they had caused. He returned a while later and joined her in the den.

"What did you notice?" she asked.

"Well, they're very neat," he said. "But…oh, I don't know…. A little too neat, maybe?" He thought about his words. "Is there such a thing as 'too neat' when it comes to kids?"

"Think about it, Mr. Kent," Margaret urged. She clasped her hands in her lap and leaned forward.

Frowning, he thought about the rooms the girls were occupying. Everything had been neat as a pin. He contemplated their 'training' and looked up, feeling a little dazed.

"There's no trace of them. Anywhere," he whispered. "If they were to walk out the door this minute, there would be no evidence they were ever here. I'll bet they've even wiped everything down for fingerprints."

"They're hiding from something," agreed Margaret, her voice hushed. "They're not training for fun or exercise—"

"They're training for survival."

They sat still, listening to laughter float up from the kitchen. Responding to a twinge in his gut, he leaned forward, scooping up Margaret's hands.

"I'm not going to let anything happen to them." He hoped his words conveyed how far he was willing to go.

She reassured him with a squeeze of his hands. "*We're* not going to let anything happen to them, sir."

He stood and pulled her to her feet. On an impulse, he gave the older woman a quick hug.

She tsk-tsked him as she brushed imaginary lint from his sleeve. "Maybe you are the family type after all."

"You heard that?" A bit of heat flushed his face.

"Mr. Kent, when are you going to learn I hear everything?"

"I'm learning. I'm learning." He laughed as he escorted her to the door.

"They didn't ask, but I will. How is your Miss Cassie?" she asked.

"Miss Cassie? Oh! Miss *Cassie*. Right, Miss Cassie. Wait. *My* Miss Cassie? She's not *my* Miss Cassie. I mean, we just met. I don't *know* her." Jacob didn't seem to be able to recover from his fumble. "I mean, I know her because I just met her, but I don't *know* her."

"It's only a figure of speech."

"Oh. Right. Only a figure of...I mean, I thought you...." *Lame. I sound lame.* "Never mind. Let's go see what The Herd is into."

He rushed for the door and paused to hold it open for her.

"The Herd?" Margaret followed her boss, her eyebrows arched. "I'm going to have to get a better look at that Miss Cassie."

Jacob inwardly cringed. *Oh, great. This just keeps getting better and better.*

***

Chapter 18
Crafty Men

"Hanson! You have got to get that boy out of here." William seethed exasperation. "We have serious work to do, and I can't have him constantly underfoot."

"First of all, 'that boy' is twenty-five years old," Hanson reminded him. "Secondly, he is here because he is worried about your health, which he wouldn't be if you took better care of yourself."

"Don't nag!"

"Thirdly," he continued as if William hadn't spoken, "I don't understand why you don't tell Jacob your family is missing and let him help you."

"Lower your voice, Hanson. He'll hear you." William threw a furtive peek over his shoulder. "I can't simply tell him I have a family after…what? Five years?"

"Well, why not? His background checked out. He is who he says he is."

"It's not that. I trust Jacob completely." He paused, his chest tightening. "It's just that…." *Enough of this.* He cleared his throat. "Let's discuss this later." Trying to close the conversation, he crossed the room.

Undeterred, Hanson followed him. "It's just what?"

He expelled a slow breath. "I don't want to hurt the boy."

Hanson waited.

"I've taken him into my confidence, into my life. I couldn't be any prouder of him if he truly was part of my own family." He sighed and turned toward a window. How he wished he could get about the business of reconciling his two lives.

"I am certain young Mr. Kent knows that, sir. Just as I am positive he does not expect to be versed on all aspects of your life."

"Sure, sure. But this situation isn't simple, like…like taking a Gypsy girl to my first formal dance. Let's face it." William swatted at the curtain. "Having a family I visit in secret…. He's going to feel betrayed when he finds out about them." He lapsed into silence, his thoughts chasing each other. After a few moments, he added, "You remember back when we bought Lenny's Livery?"

Hanson nodded. "The day we met young Mr. Kent."

"I had my granddaughter with me." William chuckled. "Doing 'research.' She was all gussied up with a blonde wig. That jackass manager didn't know what hit him. Literally." He smirked at the memory and then cackled. "I had to leave her high and dry because Jacob and Rita came to my rescue." He smiled, recalling the gangly boy-man whose sense of integrity had cost him his job, and for a complete stranger.

Hanson listened without comment to the familiar story.

William fell silent then resumed reminiscing. "She was so protective. She got right up in his face. Hanson, you remember that cartoon where the little chicken hawk kept attacking a huge rooster? She looked just like that, standing there, poking Jacob in the chest. She thought I had a stalker. Ha! Can you imagine Jacob as a stalker?" He sank into a chair.

Hanson took a seat across from him, still silent.

"Jacob didn't recognize her at the fair. The way he stared at her, I thought he had figured it out, but…." He wrung his hands. "Oh, Lord, I hope they're safe."

"She has a lot of gumption, sir, and she's very resourceful, like her father. I'm sure they will meet us at the appropriate time, and then you can clear up this unfortunate misunderstanding."

"The baby is too young to remember being on the run. She must be so frightened. I hate to think of them hiding someplace…alone…afraid…."

"They aren't helpless, you know," Hanson said with a touch of impatience. "The older ones are well versed in self-defense. They can take care of themselves. Most likely, the little one thinks they are on an adventure."

Hanson's looking on the bright side?

"If I may say so, sir, *they* don't know the threat has been eliminated," Hanson continued, "They probably spotted your bumbling private investigator. Undoubtedly, that's what sent them back into hiding."

William crossed to a desk and fished out a couple of well-worn newspapers he kept hidden. He selected one dated back to three months ago. Once again, he studied the familiar headlines.

Salvador Maletti Dead: Local Crime Boss Killed in Prison Riot.

"Our problems should've died when you did," he hissed at the dead mobster who'd almost destroyed his family.

He resumed staring out the window. "I should have waited until our next rendezvous to tell them instead of trying to track them down. I see that now. I thought when that...that *monster* died in prison, all our problems had ended with him. I was too damn eager to bring my family home."

William chose a much-older newspaper from the stack, a feeling of pride warming him as it always did.

Simon Hatch to Testify

"Livy and I didn't do so badly, did we, Hanson?"

"Simon was a fine young man, sir," he said, a mournful quaver revealing his own sadness. The man had been with William through thick and thin. He loved them all as well, no matter how aloof he acted.

William put his hand on another newspaper, but his

clenching heart would not allow him to open it. It contained a short article about a couple killed in a tragic car crash two years earlier, identifying them with their fake names, reporting no next of kin, protectively omitting three devastated children, one heartbroken father, and one grieving valet.

"What if it wasn't an accident?" William murmured for the hundredth time.

"Then they are better off in hiding," Hanson replied for the hundredth time.

***

Jacob spotted Hanson in William's den. He shrugged on his jacket as he headed over.

"*Ahem!* Good morning, Mr. Kent," Hanson blared.

Jacob caught a glimpse of William stuffing some papers out of sight before Hanson stepped in to neatly block his view. *What could he possibly need to hide from me?* A chill washed through him. *It must be the test results from the hospital. They found something bad.* Jacob controlled his expression. It was still William's private concern.

"Good morning, Hanson," he replied to the extraordinarily innocent-looking valet. "Good morning," he repeated to an exceedingly nonchalant William.

Had the doctor sent bad news while he was out yesterday? He had gotten in late last night after making sure The Herd was tucked in. *Might as well be direct.*

"How are you feeling, William?" Jacob asked.

"I'm fine, m'boy. Just fine." William seemed a bit too bright. "Breakfast?" he offered, nodding toward the dining room.

"No, thanks, just coffee." Jacob did his best to mask his concern. If he acted suspicious, William would get cagier, and if pressed, his sidekick, Hanson, would back his boss.

I'm sleeping over here until I know what's going on. You're not going to overdo it on my watch. Jacob grimly turned toward the coffeepot. *Besides, I am* not *living with The Herd of Girls. That nightmare is Maggie's assignment.*

Maggie, Mrs. Tucker, Isadora, and two girls—he didn't envy Gregory one bit. *Correction. Make that* three *girls.* Don said Casey would be ready to come home tomorrow.

Home. He stilled, coffeepot poised in midair. It did something to his stomach to think of Casey sharing his home.

He shook his head ruefully and began pouring. Of course, *he* wasn't going to be there. It didn't quite seem appropriate somehow, especially with the younger girls around.

And Maggie.

And Mrs. Tucker.

And....

He gave himself a mental shake. *I am definitely* not *staying with The Herd of Girls.*

Besides, Casey needed to acknowledge her love for him on her own. Jacob sensed a fragility about her, which had nothing to do with her illness, and he didn't want to pressure her. Just thinking about her warm brown eyes and her delicately shaped lips made him—

A throat cleared behind him. "Is there anything you require, Mr. Kent?" asked Hanson.

He was still holding the coffeepot in midair. "No, no. Everything is fine. No problem here." He replaced the pot and took a sip of coffee. *Slow down, Kent. Let the girl recover.*

Too bad Sam would be cramping his style this morning. The girls had decided only she should visit Casey. That must've been tough for Robin.

Oh, well. I guess I'll get some work done while Sam visits. I'll just have to get my quality alone time with Casey after I take Sam back.

Once Casey got to his place, he'd have to share her with her sisters. Their private time would become an endangered commodity. Not to mention he would have his hands full with the new work William had assigned him, and without Maggie. The Herd and their strange activities occupied all of his assistant's time.

He didn't mind the extra work, but his mission to lighten William's load would only be effective if William didn't create more work for himself. Now seemed as good a time as any to discuss it.

Jacob took a deep breath and crossed the room to sit by William. "Sir, may I suggest you relax at home until you hear from the doctor about your test results?"

Annoyance flashed across William's face. Jacob caught movement by the door in the corner of his eye as Hanson made a hasty retreat. Jacob braced himself.

William's expression became contemplative. "Y'know, m'boy, you may be right." He tapped his fingertips together. "That might be precisely what I need."

Jacob's heart fell. The lack of protest on the elderly man's part could only mean one thing. The doctors must have found something terribly wrong. He took a deep breath. Whatever it was, he would support his friend the whole way. "Yes, sir," he promised. "My staff and I will have no problem handling the work you gave me. We should be through most of it in two to three weeks."

"Two to three weeks? Excellent. I'll rest here...with Hanson, of course." William leaned in and lowered his voice. "He's been looking a bit peaked, don't you think?"

"Yes, I thought so, too." Jacob stood up as Hanson walked back into the room. *I can see I'm going to have to keep tabs on both of them.* "I can bring you anything you need from the office. Every day, if you'd like."

"Fine. Fine," said William, his expression smug. "And you can have Connor at your disposal," he added with a magnanimous wave, referring to his executive assistant.

"Great." Jacob tugged on his cuffs, imitating William's demeanor. "You have nothing to worry about, sir. Between us, everything will run smoothly until your return." He bade William good-bye and headed for the door.

Yes! Now I can screen everything sent to him. With Connor and Hanson's help, we'll make sure he maintains a light load.

He paused in the doorway. "Uh, sir, in all probability, I'll be working late nights for a while," he said, his tone casual.

"Don't overdo it yourself, m'boy," said William with an offhand wave.

"No, sir. I won't." *Perfect!* gloated Jacob as he left. *Now I can keep William from overdoing it, and visit Casey without raising questions. You are one crafty character.*

Perfect! gloated William, watching Jacob take his leave. *It's not going to be so hard to keep the boy out of my hair after all. We'll be able to work full tilt with him out of the way.* Ignoring Hanson's rolling eyes, he smiled to himself, proud of how crafty he was.

***

Chapter 19

Sam Reports

An enigma sat next to Jacob in the passenger seat. Sam looked and sounded like a typical high school teenage girl, but she wasn't. Her combat persona had crammed her training in early so she could visit Casey. It didn't quite gel with the teenage persona who had commandeered his car radio the second she got in.

And I was wondering what I'd talk about with a teenage girl. There was no talking while Sam surfed the radio waves and belted out tunes. Unless you counted the occasional shriek of "Oooh! That's my song!" Lyrics did constitute a conversation as far as he was concerned.

He lowered the volume as they pulled up to the hospital. "This is it. You know—"

"'Scuze me, Mr. Kent," interrupted Sam, "but do you know which room she's in? 'Cuz I need to go to…you know…."

"Oh." He took in her somewhat flushed face. "Right." *Awkward.*

"How 'bout I meet you there?"

"Sure. Um…sure." He gave Sam the room number, and she slid out of the car.

As she sauntered off, he tried to picture Casey at her age. Sam shared the same air of confidence he remembered in a younger Casey, but was much more flamboyant than her older sister. Today, little spikes of hair stood at attention all over Sam's head. In his opinion, she wore an awful lot of makeup for a morning jaunt to the hospital, but what did he know?

That girl is going to be a heartbreaker. Jacob wagged his head. *I do not envy the teenage male population one bit.*

He made his way to Casey's room, wondering again why

he had never met any of her family. Of course, he didn't have any family for Casey to meet, but he should have realized she had some. Casey had never asked about his family, and for the first several years, he hadn't been interested in anyone but her anyway.

Casey's flirtatious games had usually charmed him. She'd introduced herself with a new name every time they met at a fair. Sometimes she would have him move around the fair as if they were spies. They once were able to tail someone for two hours without detection. He had played along, caught up in the thrill of having found her again. In more recent years, he had grown more curious about her life outside of the fairs. She had been evasive when asked and irritated when pressed. He'd never learned anything concrete about her, like her real name. Or the fact that she had sisters.

His stride faltered. *What if there're more of them?* He halted midstride. *What if Casey has a boyfriend somewhere?*

Jacob's *Things To Ask Casey* list was growing by leaps and bounds. Spurred by budding anxiety, he hurried to her room. He skidded to a stop outside Casey's doorway, smoothed his ruffled hair, and entered. His heart rammed north into his throat as his stomach took a dive south.

Casey was gone.

Except for a nurse making up an empty bed, Jacob stood in a vacant room. Panic crowded his attempts at rational thought, his head pivoting in a futile attempt to spot her. *Maybe Sam got here first, and they cut out together.* As his alarm mushroomed, his brain went numb. He had no idea what to do.

"*Where is she?*"

From behind him, Sam's cry mirrored Jacob's reaction, oddly flooding him with relief. They hadn't ditched him.

Sam shoved past him and repeated his scan of the barren

cubicle, her face pale and her breathing rapid and shallow. She stepped back through the doorway. "Are you sure this is the right room?"

Her distress ratcheted Jacob back up to panic.

"Who are you looking for, honey?" asked the nurse, shaking out a pillowcase.

"Me." Casey stepped out of the bathroom.

Sam burst into tears. Jacob allowed himself to be pushed aside as she rushed by him and threw herself at her big sister.

I know what you mean, kid, he thought as he tried to corral his own runaway emotions.

Casey rocked and hushed until Sam's sobs subsided. The baffled nurse propelled them both toward the freshly made bed.

He remained at the door, feeling like an awkward intruder in the presence of the display of raw female emotion. What a luxury to be able to release her sudden panic like that. His heart was still charging along at top speed.

Jacob politely cleared his throat as Casey eased into bed. "I guess I'll leave you two to catch up. I've got some calls to make." No one acknowledged him. A bit deflated, he slipped out of the room. Shoving his hands into his pockets, he started down the hall, trying to decide where to go.

The sound of running made him pause.

"Mr. Kent," called Sam. "She wants to see you. I'll be right back. I gotta fix my face, and then I'm getting a soda."

"Sure." Trying to mask his pleasure, he forced a casual tone. He hurried back to Casey's room, a more cheerful emotion quickening his heart.

"Why did you leave?" Casey's brow furrowed as her fingers clutched her sheets.

"I didn't want to intrude." His confession seemed petty even to his ears, in light of her anxiety.

"Intrude?" She cocked her head. "I'll never understand you."

He pulled a chair close to her bed, sat down, and took her hand in his. "Maybe not." He was so happy to be with her. "But I'm going to make sure you have fun trying."

***

Jacob's deep-brown eyes glowed from his summer-tanned face. Casey smiled back, knowing she was responsible for his joy, and, for once, taking pleasure in it instead of trying to squash it.

With Sam returning soon, she needed to redirect the conversation. "Jacob—"

"I know, I know. We have to talk."

Theirs had to be the most bizarre relationship in the world. It didn't seem to matter that she lived a clandestine life. They both could complete each other's sentences and understand each other's moods—an extraordinary feat for two people who spent barely any time together.

Over the years, they had kept running into each other at random fairs—different months, different states. At this point, she pretty much expected to find him there. What she didn't expect was the magnitude of her disappointment when she didn't.

But how could he be here in her hospital room? It redefined bizarre.

With the danger she faced, Casey could not afford to indulge in an exploration of her feelings for Jacob. She had to be strong enough to say what needed to be said. Regardless, against her better judgment, she discovered she didn't want him to disappear before things were sorted out.

"Jacob—"

"Wait. I have something to tell you before Sam gets back." With a quick glance over his shoulder, he angled over the bed to brush his lips across hers then kissed her. He lingered long enough for their breaths to mingle, conveying a question she was not ready to hear. Despite her attempts to not react, she wanted more. Yielding, she closed her eyes. A delicate rush curled in her stomach. To her disappointment, he pulled away. His lopsided grin affirmed his reluctance to stop, but who wanted to risk Sam walking in on them?

"What…what did you want to tell me?" she asked, somewhat breathless.

"That was it," he said. "I'll fill in the rest later, when we can be alone."

Focus, Casey. "Jacob, my life is very complicated." She ignored his sarcastic grunt of agreement. "I have things I have to take care of…and sort out…and—"

He captured one of her hands punctuating the air along with her agitated statements. "Sweetie, all you have to do is get better. I will help you with everything else," he assured her.

Oh, how I wish you could. She slouched against the pillows. "How are they doing?"

"It's hard for me to say." His thumb caressed the back of her hand. "I've just met them, so I have nothing to compare." His eyes narrowed. "There *are* only two of them, right?"

Casey nodded as she plucked at the sheet with her fingers. What must he be thinking?

"That's a relief," he answered cheerily. "I can tell you they're eating well, but the rest I'll leave up to Sam to fill in."

"Speaking of the devil…." She drew her hand away.

Jacob looked over his shoulder to see the middle sister coming down the corridor. Turning back to Casey, he bared his teeth and raised his brow in a stage smile and sat back.

"Hey." Sam appeared fully recovered.

He rose to offer her the chair. Forgetting Sam, Casey clutched his arm. "Where are you going?"

He patted her hand. "Right now, I'm going to find a place where I can make a few phone calls for work. I'm leaving you in Sam's capable hands for about a half hour. Then I'll bring her back to my place so she can fill in the rest of The Her—I mean, *the others*. This afternoon, after work, I'll come back and keep you company, okay?"

Casey relaxed into her pillows. "Sounds great. Just don't disappear on me."

"I could say the same thing to you." He strolled out the door, leaving Casey to deal with Sam's perceptive gleam. Too bad she couldn't escape with him.

After Sam settled into his vacated chair, Casey began, "I missed Grandpa's phone call last night. He must be going crazy. I wish I had told you the arrangements before I got sick."

"What are we going to do?" Sam understood all too well the ramifications of the missed connection.

"We need to send him a note. I didn't feel up to writing it last night, but I started it this morning. You finish it. You're quicker at it than I am." She reached under the food tray to fish out a paper.

Sam read it quickly. "Sure. What else do you want me to tell him?"

"First, go online and choose a fair. It can't be sooner than two or three weeks. I don't know how fast I'm going to recover, and I don't want to risk being out there in a weakened condition. Pick an afternoon and set up a rendezvous."

"What about delivery?"

"Hmmm. Have you assessed the situation geographically?"

"The hospital is about a half-hour's drive from Grandpa's house. It's also about forty minutes from Mr. Kent's townhouse. That's where we're staying."

Had they really made it so far? Was their hike from Albany almost over? Imagine Jacob living so close to Grandpa. Totally freaky. "Ja—Mr. Kent already told me both of you were over there. How is it?"

"The part where we're staying, it's a three-bedroom apartment…a really big three-bedroom apartment. There's direct access from both the front and back, and through the garage. All three bedrooms have fire escapes. There's an alarm system, but there are too many points of egress to be totally safe. The upside is, there're lots of ways to escape if we need to."

"The other part?" asked Casey.

"I haven't seen that part yet, but I think it's where Gregory stays. He's the butler. Robin is going to try to get a tour of it today."

"Who else is there?" Casey's unease grew. They always tried not to involve other people. This had too many moving parts.

Sam counted them off on her fingers. "Isadora's the cook. Mrs. Tucker's the housekeeper. I'm not sure what Miss Fuller does. She's staying in one of the guest rooms like us. She works for Mr. Kent, but I'm pretty sure she's only there to babysit us."

Great. More moving parts.

"Oh, yeah, and the hospital, Grandpa's house, and Mr. Kent's house make, like, a triangle. It's maybe a half-hour from Mr. Kent's to Grandpa's."

"Good job, Sam." She sat up. "Hey, can you get the note to Grandpa?"

"Sure. I'll do it today."

"What does Mr. Kent know?"

"Not much. We've made a few slipups, but he doesn't ask a lot of questions."

"No, he doesn't," Casey murmured. "But he will."

"Besides, this morning, I did the teenager-thing with the car radio so he wouldn't try to talk to me."

What a perverse concept—Sam acting like a teenager as a ruse. At fifteen, she should be acting like a teenager because that's what she *was*.

Samantha wouldn't be getting her chance to be a real teenage girl any time soon. Until they confirmed they had shaken off the stalker from Albany, none of them could relax. Almost two years had passed since the death of their parents. Despite remaining hidden all that time, somehow, they had been traced. And, now, Casey's weakened condition made it impossible for her to protect them.

"But Ms. Fuller sure does," said Sam, fetching Casey from her thoughts.

"Does what?"

"Asks a lot of questions."

Casey frowned. "You mentioned her. Is it Mrs. or Miss?"

"I'm not sure. It doesn't seem like she's married, 'cuz she stays overnight with us. She doesn't carry a pocketbook, so there's nothing we can go through. She keeps a notebook in her skirt. I told Robin to find a way to get hold of it today, so we can see what's in it."

"Good. Odds are she's reporting back to Mr. Kent, but we can't be too careful. See what you can find out about her from our regular sources. Wait. You know what? Check them all out." A wave of fatigue washed over Casey.

"Sure thing." Sam studied Casey for a moment and resumed. "So far, we've managed to stay inside. We told Miss Fuller we wanted to be near the phone in case the hospital called. Which was true," she added under her breath.

This whole thing must've been a nightmare for Sam. Casey reached out to squeeze the teen's hand, and was rewarded with a lopsided grin.

"Today should be no problem because it's rainy. For the rest of the week, we can take turns not feeling well."

Something tugged at Casey's heart. It had been a long while since she had seen Samantha smile. "It feels safe?"

Those slender shoulders shouldn't have to bear this burden. When she'd been Sam's age, their parents had been alive. Her name had been Casey Clark, and, for the most part, they had led a typical middle class existence. At fifteen, she'd enjoyed being a big sister, never contemplating how toddler Sam actually got there. But, when she learned Robin was on the way, she had been horrified and embarrassed. Old people having sex? Gross!

Oh, how her minor fifteen-year-old issues paled in comparison to the ones Samantha now bore.

"Safe?" Sam hesitated. "It *feels* safe, but, honestly, after you got sick, I was scared. I mean I was so worried about making a mistake and putting us all in danger...." Sam directed a guilty side glance at her big sister. "Like, I *really* wanted someone to take care of us. It's possible I'm not objective enough to evaluate."

"Oh, Samantha! You've done a wonderful job. Because of *your* decisions, everyone is safe and healthy. I'm so proud of you." Casey sat up so she could hug her, trying as hard as she could to convey reassurance while at the same time trying to draw some of Samantha's strength for herself. They sighed in unison and smiled at each other.

Casey fingered Sam's spiky hair. "That's quite a statement."

Reclining, Sam smirked and shrugged. "It works for me. I figured I'd be harder to identify if I went kinda Goth."

"How about Robin?"

"She's fine. Ms. Fuller is really nice to her. We're worried about you. Are you going to be okay?"

She opened her arms, and Samantha climbed right into

the bed with her like she used to when she was little. They both needed to snuggle. "I'm fine, especially because I know *you* are taking care of everything."

"Is it all right that we went to Mr. Kent's house? I didn't know what to do, and Ms. Fuller just seemed to take charge of everybody, including Mr. Kent."

"Yes, it is," Casey affirmed. "The way you met him was far too random for him to be suspicious."

"Good. I didn't bring Robin because I thought we'd be too easy to identify if we were all together." Her tone became smug. "So I told Mr. Kent we didn't want to overwhelm you."

"What else have you noticed?"

"Well, it seems our Mr. Kent doesn't spend much time at home. He's some kind of business god, according to Mrs. Tucker." She propped herself up on her elbow and altered her voice. "*It's none of MY business where he spends most of his nights. I'm supposed to clean up after someone who doesn't come home.*"

Having never met Mrs. Tucker, Casey could rely on Sam's imitation of the busybody personality. It was what her sister did. "Doesn't come home at night?" repeated Casey. "I wonder what that's all about."

"Maybe he has a girlfriend," speculated Sam. "He hasn't spent the night since we got there."

"A girlfriend?" Casey squeaked. *Well, of course Jacob could have a girlfriend. He's a good-looking guy, obviously successful.* A thread of insecurity wound around her gut.

Samantha's eyebrows arched. "Why?"

Oooh, she sounds suspicious. "Oh, it's just that would mean another person in the mix. It keeps getting more and more complicated."

"I'll find out." Sam squinted at her. "If there is a girlfriend, I'll have her checked out, too."

"I'm so lucky to have you."

"Lucky enough to tell me what's going on with you between Mr. Kent?"

"What do you mean?"

"Getting tired of waiting for me?" Jacob stood in the doorway.

Talk about perfect timing.... How long has he been there?

"Never mind. We'll talk later." Sam climbed out of the bed, avoiding Casey's IV tube. She headed for the door. "Casey needs to rest now."

"Oh. Okay. Well, get some sleep and feel better." Jacob cast a glance at Casey but followed Sam as she swept out of the room.

How strange to see Jacob and Samantha together. He seemed to be taking it all in stride, but he would want details when he returned. She had to decide what to tell him about their peculiar story.

On one hand, if she hid the truth, he would know. He always knew when she tried to deceive him, so she never did, choosing instead to be vague. On the other hand, he might not react too well to her being a fugitive. Either way, she could lose him. Her throat tightened.

You can't lose someone you don't have.

But, yesterday, something had changed. During those moments of panic when she had confused his presence with part of a dream, she understood the truth for the first time. Despite her best efforts to minimize their involvement all these years, Jacob Kent had crept under her skin. It was too idiotic. There was no way things could work out for them. Her eyes began to burn with unshed tears.

So, what was she going to tell him? The first tears fell.

Chapter 20

The Nameless Wonder is Named

"Do you have a girlfriend?" Sam buckled her seat belt with an innocent expression.

Jacob knew an ambush when he saw one. However, recognizing an ambush did not equip him to handle it. "Uh, yes... well, no, not really...um...sorta." Calling Casey his girlfriend was a little presumptuous.

"Is '*Sorta*' the reason you don't sleep at your house?"

"Yes," he blurted. "I mean, no! I mean, I don't sleep at my house because it's been overrun by a herd of females disguised as boys." He reached over and cranked up the radio.

Sam flopped back in her seat for a moment then kicked the teenager thing into high gear, belting out the song flooding the car.

He slid a glance toward the adolescent bouncing in the front seat, keeping time to the music. *Casey at fifteen*. She would be as pretty as she was now, if her sisters were any evidence. She'd probably had a ton of boyfriends in high school. He tried to visualize a teenage him meeting a teenage her.

Back then, short and pretty withdrawn, he had not exactly been a babe magnet. Constant shuffling from school to school as his foster homes changed had contributed to his lack of experience with the mysterious gender. By the time he'd reached college, his sense of self-preservation had pretty much made the dating scene something to actively avoid. For the most part, his existence satisfied him. Focusing on his studies and keeping under the radar offered a comfortable life.

Until Rita and Don had wormed their way into his life, attempting to help Jacob become as happy as them with one fix-up offer after another.

Okay, blaming Don isn't fair. It was all Rita.

One time, only one time, Jacob had caved and let her fix him up with some girl. Big mistake. His acceptance had lit a fire under Rita, who turned finding a girl for him into a career.

His second mistake was telling Don about his mysterious Casey encounters at different fairs. Since Don didn't approve of The Nameless Wonder, he encouraged Rita's attempts. It was like pouring gasoline on a fire.

But all Rita's blind dates paled next to Casey—or Cassie or Candy or Carol or Cathy—whatever she called herself on any given day. Unlike Rita's parade of hopefuls, at least, with Casey, he knew where he stood.

She never led him on. She never gave him a fake phone number or address. Of course, she never gave him *any* phone number or address. She never promised to make time for him. She never said yes, and she never said no. In that respect, she was totally predictable. And adorable. True, she was un-relenting about keeping her personal life secret, but she had shared something much more important. She had let Jacob learn about her.

Strolling around the fair, holding hands, they had talked for hours. She'd shared her passions, her philosophy, and her dreams. He'd reciprocated. The way she'd listened had made him feel like the most fascinating person in the world. They had admired and challenged each other. Agreed and debated. Solved the world's problems with strategies that made sense only to college coeds.

At first, every random reunion had a cosmic feel to it. They never knew if they would meet again, but as the years passed, he came to expect the unplanned encounters, as if destiny lent a hand. When Casey wasn't at a fair, fear would fill him; fear they had already experienced their last encounter.

The absolute worst was two years before, when he couldn't find her all summer. Not once. Each fair passed, leaving him more and more frantic. The reality of never being with her again slapped him in the face, and he had no idea how to handle it. How had he become so attached to her under such weird circumstances? He didn't do attachments.

He shifted in his seat. *I didn't used to do attachments.* Things had to change. No more games. He wanted to take their relationship to the next level.

"Are you okay?"

Sam's question startled him out of his thoughts. *What the hell?* "Yeah. Sure. Why?"

"You're holding onto that steering wheel like you are trying to choke it or something."

"No, I'm not." He loosened his white-knuckled grip.

"Yeah. Whatever." She interrupted a commercial to surf the radio stations. "Ooh, I love this song!" She resumed singing and bouncing.

Jacob went back to pondering her big sister.

Almost a year later, they'd finally encountered each other at the Barnstable County Fair in Massachusetts. One minute she was staring at him from across the concourse. The next minute she was in his arms, clinging to him. Through a haze of relief, he had wiped away her tears, secretly cherishing them as evidence of her feelings for him. Nevertheless, she remained as steadfast as ever, deflecting every attempt to discuss their situation. She wanted to continue as if nothing had happened.

But that year apart had changed her. Where she used to cheerfully block his attempts to pursue her, she now responded with an agitation that escalated into immediate anger. Despite his own anxiety over the prospect of losing her, Jacob backed off. After all, any type of relationship was better than nothing.

Yeah, all that was moot now. He had her sisters, and Jacob was going to take full advantage of the situation, whatever mess they were in. She wasn't going anywhere before they had an opportunity to talk. His instinct told him there was never going to be a better chance than this for the two of them.

In the middle of surfing the radio stations, Sam settled on a song he recognized from the fateful bed-jumping revelation. She wiggled and sang like she didn't have a care in the world.

I don't understand the teenage female. He turned down his street. *I need to add eight-year-old females to that list.* Shoot, who was he kidding? He didn't get any female, except Casey.

Arriving at home turned out to be easier than leaving it again. After Jacob delivered Sam to Maggie, Robin coaxed him into struggling through the obstacle course she had designed. He stopped by the kitchen to tell Isadora he might be late for dinner, and he had to promise the entire Herd to check back in later.

Dodging around the obstacle course on his way out, he jumped back into the peace and quiet of his car, rubbing a bruised shin. If he was going to keep The Herd, he was going to need a yard.

***

"How's the patient?" The large man in doctor scrubs spoke softly, but he startled Casey who was staring at the far wall. He pulled up a chair next to the bed and started to flip through a chart labeled *Cassie Thatcher*. He looked up in time to catch her wiping tears from her face and silently handed her a tissue.

"I'm still a little tired." She dried her cheeks. When he didn't respond, she looked up to find him studying her.

Oh, no. Not again! complained the little voice that always accompanied the *Uh-oh* feeling. Years of experience had taught her to pay attention to that feeling of being targeted. She strove for an unsuspecting air for the benefit of the sizeable man at her bedside impersonating a doctor. Every fiber of her being readied for an attack.

How had they tracked her? *Not important.* Did they know where the girls were? *Very important.* But, first, she needed a plan of escape.

To keep him role-playing, she choked out, "How soon will this Lyme disease be gone?"

She half heard him begin an explanation when she spotted his nametag. Startled, she raised her eyes to his. For a moment, they stared at each other. Trying to decide how to proceed, Casey broke the silence. "You're his friend, aren't you? Dr. Don?"

The side of his mouth quirked. "And you are?"

"The Nameless Wonder, in person," she said, not bothering to hide her weariness.

Don had the good manners to blush. "Oh...Jake told you about that, huh? I didn't mean—"

She halted him with a raised hand. "You were being his friend."

He fiddled with something on the chart, waiting.

She expelled a breath, unfisted her sheet, and smoothed it out. "Call me Casey."

He looked up. "Why?"

"Because it's my name!"

"Casey Thatcher?" he pressed.

"Close enough."

He looked back at the chart in his hand. "Are you going to break his heart?"

She gasped. This Dr. Don did not mince words. "I...hope

not," she whispered, turning her head away, trying to control the lump in her throat.

He handed her another tissue and sat in silence.

She pressed the thin square of paper to her face as the tears eked out under her palms. In a rare moment of unveiled vulnerability, she wailed, "I don't know what to do."

Don thrust the entire tissue box at her. "I've sat next to hundreds of beds like this, but I have no idea what to say here," he confessed. "What kind of trouble are you in?"

"I can't say," Casey moaned. "What if—" She gulped. "What if you got hurt because I told you?"

"Can you tell me?" Jacob stood in the doorway.

"*Jacob*," she squeezed out. "Oh, Jacob, what if they hurt *you*? I don't think I could stand—"

Jacob was by her side before she could finish. Scooping her into his arms, he sat on the edge of her bed, holding on for dear life.

This is crazy, Don fumed as he watched his best friend comforting his patient. *Jake has no idea what he's up against. If this girl's in danger, so is he.* Don caught his friend's eye over Casey's head, but Jacob shrugged helplessly, his face distraught. This was too much.

As she reached for another tissue, Don stood up. "I still have my rounds to do. I'll check back later."

Jacob grabbed his arm. "When can she leave?"

"You want me to tell you today, but I don't feel quite comfortable with her progress yet." Don turned to Casey. "I'm waiting for some test results, and I'd like to see your fluid levels stabilize first. If all is well, you could be discharged tomorrow afternoon. But, if I were you, I'd plan on Wednesday."

She laced her fingers with Jacob's. "I guess I'm okay staying another day or so. I just got rattled because I thought Dr.

Don was one of *them*. But that's ridiculous. No one knows I'm here." She sniffled.

"One of *them*?" Anger rippled through Don. *Jeez! I need to get her away from Jake before he gets hurt. The sooner she's gone, the better.*

"Yeah. Sorry." She took a deep breath. "It should be fine as long as you don't tell anyone I'm here."

"Uh, sure," said Don, "I won't tell anyone." *Anyone else.*

"My house staff knows, but they won't say anything," assured Jacob.

Casey looked at him, eyebrows raised. "You don't talk to Mrs. Tucker much, do you?" she gurgled. "Telling someone like Mrs. Tucker not to mention anything is like alerting the media."

"What do you mean?" he asked. "You've never met her."

"Samantha told me."

"Whatever. Look, if we stress the importance of this, Mrs. Tucker will be discreet. We can make this work, Casey. I know we can. You can be safe here."

Don gritted his teeth. *No one's safe while she's here. This is getting out of hand.* He excused himself. "Let me get to my rounds. I'll check back later."

No matter what fantasy Jacob spun for himself, Don recognized leaving mode, and Casey reeked of it. Better she go before the poor idiot got too attached.

He walked into his office, squashing his discomfort. *You'll thank me later, Jake.* He stared at the phone, trying to work up the nerve to follow through. He had already crossed the line once he'd figured out Casey's identity. That was before he understood the danger associated with her, but it was too late to stop the momentum now.

If I'm going to get rid of her, I have one more phone call to make.

"It's for his own good," he muttered as he dialed, trying to justify his actions to himself.

Casey was right about Mrs. Tucker. If things blew up, he could always blame it on the nosy housekeeper.

"Hello? It's me again," he said, clutching the receiver.

***

Jacob was scared. For all he knew, Casey was mere moments away from deciding to bolt.

"What's with him?" Casey asked as Don disappeared.

Jacob shrugged, not interested in discussing Don.

"He's your friend. Did he seem…I don't know…kind of funny to you?"

"I don't know. He's probably as surprised as me you're here." He gave her another squeeze. "Hey, Casey, I, uh, have a few questions, you know."

Casey lay back on her pillow. "Please, Jacob, I can't handle it right now," she groaned, pressing her palms to her temples. "I need to think, but the meds have my head so fuzzy." She pulled out the pillow and covered her face with it. "I can't decide what I should tell you and what would be safer if you didn't know."

The pillow muffled Casey's words, but he received her message clear as a bell. "Look," he said, "can you at least promise me you won't leave without letting me know?"

She didn't answer right away. Finally, she lifted the pillow. "I can't promise."

"Casey—"

Sitting up, she put a finger over his lips, quelling his objection. "I can't promise because I have my sisters to think of. Their safety has to be my first priority."

What could he say to that? Nothing.

"But I can promise I will try to never lie to you."

"Can't you even tell me what you are running from? Or what your real name is? Or about your family?" he asked. "C'mon! We've known each other for over five years. Throw me a bone here."

Casey blew through pursed lips, once again holding her sheet in a death grip. "What can I tell you that won't put you in any danger?" Catching sight of her hands, she pulled the sheet flat. "Okay. My current identity is Cassie Thatcher, but my real name is Casey. I'm not sure why the girls told you their real names. They're never supposed to. But, for some reason, they did." She paused. "For some reason, *I* did. But I'm not going to tell you our last name."

At his nod, she continued. "We're in the Witness Protection Program, but I'm not going to tell you why."

"The Witness Protection Program?" He hadn't guessed that one. "Wow. That explains a lot."

"No, it explains a little," she corrected. "About two years ago, our parents died in a car crash. I don't know if it was a vendetta or an accident," she said with a hitch in her voice, "but we've been hiding ever since."

"Two years ago?" He did the math in his head. Understanding dawned. "The summer I couldn't find you. I hated that year," he muttered, remembering the fear. He stared at her hand entwined with his. When he lifted his gaze to her face, her cheeks were pink.

"What?"

"Nothing." She ducked her head.

"Hey, you promised you wouldn't lie to me."

"I lied." She grinned.

He chuckled and hugged her. After all she'd been through, she still had such spirit. "Seriously, Casey, if you left without telling me, I'd go nuts worrying about you. Please give me a way to reach you. You know, a Plan B."

Casey relented. "Plan B, huh? Okay. In case something happens."

"Nothing is going to happen," Jacob declared. "It's only backup."

"Sweetie, contingency plans are the backbone of my family. That's what's kept us safe all these years. We'll pick a place and time to meet…as backup."

"Right. Fine. It just takes some getting used to," he said. "Did you call me sweetie?" Jacob snapped his fingers. "Hey, how about the top of the Empire State Building?"

"*An Affair to Remember*?" Casey teased. "You're a closet romantic."

"Nope. *Sleepless in Seattle*. And there's no closet here. I'm a confirmed romantic where you're concerned."

"Well, forget it," said Casey. "Deborah Kerr gets hit by a car trying to meet her love there. I don't want to take any chances."

"I know. How about Niagara Falls? On Labor Day?" He smiled at her. "Do you think that's a safer place to meet your love?"

Casey's color deepened, but she laughed. "Oh, no. We just came from that direction, and it took us almost three months to get this far."

"Wow! All right."

"How about The Big E in Springfield? On the last Saturday in September," she offered.

"The Big E, huh? That's my favorite fair." There was hope here.

"Focus, Kent," she ordered. "I'm talking about a contingency plan here. Don't you understand the significance of this?"

"Of course I do." He tilted closer. "That's the fair where we met."

She closed the distance between them, stopping a hair's breadth from his lips. His blood sang in his ears.

"But the Skowhegan Fair is *my* favorite fair. That's where we first kissed," she murmured against his mouth before pressing her lips to his.

"Well, I guess you're feeling better." The unfamiliar male voice chuckled.

Jacob and Casey sprang apart.

"Oh, don't let me interrupt," the male nurse said. "I'll be out of here in a minute."

"Actually, I have to go." Jacob jumped to his feet, energized. *Oh, yeah. She loves me.* He shoved the chair back and grinned at Casey. "I never made it into the office today. I have to stop there before I get home."

She nodded, stifling a yawn. "I'm ready to sleep some more anyway."

"I have that effect on women." He headed out the door. "I'll try to come back by after, but I did promise a certain brown-eyed beauty I'd try to be home for dinner tonight, so I don't want to be late."

Casey cocked an eyebrow.

"Eight-year-olds can be so demanding." Jacob blew her a kiss as he left.

Chapter 21
That Empty Feeling

Casey hated to admit it, but she felt empty when Jacob left. He sure could fill a room. Although, technically, she hadn't been inside with him anywhere but this hospital cubicle, so she didn't have much for comparison. All the fairs had been outside.

How the years had changed Jacob. Tall and slender, more like a gangly colt when she'd first met him, he'd still done crazy things to her pulse. But the idea of being more than friends? Ridiculous. Where could it lead? How could she ask anyone to share her life?

Why in the world had she kissed him?

True, her mother had met, fallen in love with, and married her father despite his being in the Witness Protection Program, and they had been happy together. But her dad had been a single guy with no kids. Casey came as a package deal, presenting a hurdle significant enough for normal people leading normal lives. Jacob didn't seem to be too put off by their bizarre relationship, but how could they fit their lives together? Without question, he had no concept of her world. Even setting up an ordinary daytrip to a fair was as complicated as planning a three-week safari.

Her sisters selected fairs attended by GrandAna, their father's maternal grandmother, and her kissing booth. Despite her age, their great-grandmother and her kissing booth traveled from state to state. From what Hanson told her, Grandpa and GrandAna hadn't gotten along for many years, but called a truce when Daddy had gone into hiding. Her father later confirmed it, but Casey never detected any issues.

Casey would pick up the girls and head for the predetermined rendezvous. Upon arriving at the fair, they would split up, Sam taking one direction, and Casey checking out a second with Robin in tow. After their reconnaissance, they'd meet back at a different location to report anything suspicious.

Although they never ran into anything conclusive, sometimes one of them would get an *uh-oh* feeling, so they'd scrap their plans. Robin was especially sensitive. Of course, an *uh-oh* feeling from a small child, too young to be entirely aware of their situation, raised doubts about the necessity of leaving. Whether due to Gypsy intuition or childish imagination, it was too risky to ignore her concern. A hastily posted *Save the Children* advertisement near GrandAna's booth would alert Grandpa. Better safe than sorry. And there was always another rendezvous scheduled.

Otherwise, they would locate Grandpa from the coded message he'd leave for them at The Kissing Booth. Casey would spend an hour or so with them and then leave. Grandpa, GrandAna, and, more often than not, Hanson, would play with the younger ones while she rechecked the area. The family never tired of the fair activities. Even as she got older, Casey relished their fair ritual.

Until Jacob.

"How are you feeling tonight, Cassie?" The nurse bustled in, stethoscope around her neck, and unfolded the blood pressure cuff hanging above Casey. "Are you still experiencing any pain?"

"I still have a headache, but it's much milder."

"Would you like something for that?" the nurse asked.

"I don't think so." Casey wanted her wits about her and needed to avoid any kind of mind-muddling medication. "I'm feeling pretty sleepy already. I think I'd prefer trying to fall asleep on my own."

"As you wish, honey." The nurse checked her temperature, gave a satisfied nod, and sailed out of the room.

Casey's thoughts drifted to the first night in the hospital when she had mistaken Jacob for a dream. Was it a coincidence Jacob, and not some arbitrary stranger, had rescued them on a random back road in Connecticut? Maybe it was Kismet. GrandAna would say it was the Legend of The Kissing Booth.

Casey didn't remember when she'd first heard the story. According to her great-grandmother, planks cut from some "magical" tree made up the floor of the booth, and if you kissed someone while on it, *and* it was your birthday, you would find your true love.

GrandAna did not invite Casey to attend the booth until after her nineteenth birthday. Popping up and down on her toes with delight, she'd jokingly mentioned since her birthday had passed, no good would come of it.

"Ah, then, no one object, yes?" GrandAna had said, a mischievous glint in her eye.

Oh, but Casey's parents had objected, and in a major way. She'd stormed off like a lunatic, fuming at parental injustice. Her folks went to find Grandpa to have him speak to his special girl, hoping he could defuse her obstinacy. Uncle Scott had followed Casey.

Scott Burleson, her father's best friend and college roommate, had gotten a job right after graduation working for some branch of the government. When Daddy decided to testify against some crook named Salvador Maletti, the decision had put his life in danger. Uncle Scott was instrumental in procuring a brand new life and brand new identity for him through the Witness Protection Program, becoming Daddy's handler with the agency.

Occasionally, Uncle Scott would arrange to show up at one

of the fairs for some special family occasion, like a new baby or Casey's graduation. On this occasion, he was there to introduce the family to his new bride. The two of them were making another stop at a bar mitzvah, so they were a little overdressed for a fair.

Uncle Scott must have kept a safe distance from Casey—a suit at a fair stands out like a sore thumb. She never noticed him as she stomped through the fairgrounds, muttering about her parents acting pigheaded over something so inconsequential. And wondering why she had responded like an emotional flake.

He didn't interfere until she made it to the booth where he humiliated her by grabbing her arm and jerking her away from the platform. And in front of hundreds of people. *Okay, maybe not hundreds.*

Casey had spun away from him and collided with a warm male body. To her surprise, she recognized him from somewhere. Funny how she remembered his unruly brown hair, his warm brown eyes, his cute face, but she couldn't place him.

Jacob had stood his ground, protective arms steadying her, staring at her with wide eyes.

And then, Uncle Scott had charged. Jacob had thrust her behind him right before Uncle Scott took him down. The crowd went wild.

GrandAna always lined The Kissing Booth with buckets of water to quell any altercations. Adhering to their training, Casey and two kissing-booth girls each grabbed a full pail. On *three*, they drenched the two combatants. The soaked males separated, spitting out sun-warmed water. Jacob kept a wary eye on Uncle Scott while the spectators roared their approval.

Casey was so incensed she could barely breathe. As Uncle Scott stood up, she got right up in his face and declared, "If I want to kiss someone, I will!"

And what did Uncle Scott do? He laughed. Oooh, she was pissed! Before she lost her nerve, she marched right back over to Jacob where he sat on the edge of the booth floor. She placed one hand on each of his cheeks, wet with water, rough from late afternoon shadow, and warmed by his flush. Her pulse started a staccato rhythm. She drew his face down toward hers, wondering if he would pull away. But he didn't.

Their gazes had locked, and he closed the distance between them. He lifted her off the ground, his lips met hers, and the world melted away. As the ground disappeared from beneath her feet, she clung to him. An immediate rush of heat and energy surged through her while her heart pounded in her ears. She wrapped her arms around his neck, responding to a need to be closer to him. The kiss ended, and he lowered her back to the ground. She experienced the chilly feeling of loss as she stepped back.

More like staggered back.

And then the noise of the crowd had intruded. "Birthday Kisses! Married by Christmas!"

She felt awful as she watched Jacob's face flood with color. She had embarrassed him. Whirling around, she tried to silence the crowd by yelling, "It's not my birthday!" As the bystanders continued to chant, she stalked off, escaping to the concourse.

When she finally met up with her family about an hour later, everyone was in a tizzy. Grandpa had left early, upset— so her father had told her—by her carelessness. Tight-lipped, the rest of them prepared for their customary routine of leaving separately to avoid drawing attention. Her parents took four-year-old Robin. Eleven-year-old Samantha was entrusted to Casey.

As they headed out, Sam confided, "Aunt Patti really yelled

at Uncle Scott for ruining his suit before the bar mister."

"Bar mitzvah," Casey corrected automatically. "And it serves him right."

Sam skipped along with Casey's angry strides. "Uncle Scott said he saw you kiss a boy. Is that why everybody's mad?"

"Yes," confessed Casey, slowing down and taking the younger girl's hand.

"At The Birthday Booth?" asked Sam, familiar with the popular story.

"The Kissing Booth," Casey corrected. "Well, near it. But you know the story. You have to be *on* the floor for the magic, and I wasn't exactly on it. And, besides, it's not my birthday, so there's nothing to worry about."

"Yeah, but Uncle Scott said it was his birthday," said Sam in a you're-in-trouble voice.

"Why should I care if it's Uncle Scott's birthday?" Casey bit back her irritation.

"Not Uncle Scott." Sam giggled. "That boy you kissed. It's *his* birthday."

Casey stopped and gawked at her little sister. "Are you sure?"

"Sure I'm sure."

"How does he know?"

"I dunno. I guess he told Uncle Scott." Sam shrugged. "Does that mean you're gonna get married on Christmas?"

"*No!* It does *not* mean I'm going to get married on Christmas. I'm not getting married at all. It's just a fairy tale, like *Cinderella*. It's not real."

"Then why is everybody mad?"

"Because they're all superstitious." Casey resumed marching. "But I'm not."

"But what if—"

"Sam! There's no what if," snapped Casey, turning Samantha toward her. "I don't even know the boy's name. You can't marry someone if you don't know his name, right?"

"I guess so." Sam kicked a crumpled cup in her path.

Casey exhaled a calming breath and continued their exit stroll through the fair.

"Sooooo." Samantha perked up. "It's okay to kiss boys you don't know. That's good, 'cuz there's a boy in the fourth grade who hit me last week. I think he likes me." Her face held a faraway look. "But I don't know his name, so I'm gonna kiss him."

Ten years of training, and two years of college, but Casey still couldn't follow the logic of an eleven-year-old.

Her thoughts returned to present-day Samantha. At fifteen, she'd accepted her lot in life. She was dependable and capable. Their little hike from Albany, New York, to Greenwich, Connecticut, would have been impossible without her there to help. Somehow, someway, Casey would find a way to make it up to her.

And what about Jacob? How could she set things right with him? He didn't belong in her life, but he kept popping up. Like at the Annual Oyster Festival in Long Island a couple of months after that earthshaking kiss. She had been in the middle of doing a reconnaissance sweep after visiting with Grandpa when she caught him staring at her from across the concourse.

Like her, he was dressed for the October weather in a jacket, jeans, and sneakers. Her training triggered alarms in her head. Running into him in New York was too much of a coincidence to be accidental. Nevertheless, instead of dodging him, she had been rooted to the ground. He approached her slowly, stopping about three feet away, his hands shoved into his pockets, rocking back and forth on his heels.

Why didn't I run? When he said, "I've been looking for

you," *I should have felt scared, not pleased.*

Because his warm brown eyes had held no malice—shy and pleased and hopeful, but no danger.

Under his gaze, calm had engulfed her adrenaline rush. When he asked her what she was doing, she told a half-truth about just hanging out. Then she broke with protocol by accepting his offer to accompany her.

As they chatted away, their stroll took them past The Kissing Booth, where GrandAna waved merrily at them. Embarrassed by their shared memory of the kiss, Casey focused straight ahead and fell silent.

He cleared his throat and asked, "Are you working at the booth today?"

She snorted. "After the drama it raised the last time? Not likely."

"Who was that guy anyway?"

"A friend of the family." Changing the subject, she asked him if he believed in the legend.

"What legend?"

"About The Kissing Booth magic." She took on a low, spooky tone, ominously wiggling her fingers in the air.

He laughed, a warm comfortable sound. "I guess I don't know that particular story. Why don't you tell me?"

"Well, according to Miss Ana, the Gypsy lady who owns the booth, its floor is made out of planks from some magical tree, and if you kiss someone, while standing on it, *and* it's your birthday, you will find your true love."

"Birthday Kisses, Married at Christmas?"

"Yeah, something like that." Casey shrugged, cheeks heating.

"Well, it's a good thing we were only sitting on it. I want to finish college first." He winked.

"Me, too." She smiled back, her embarrassment evaporating.

"So, what's her record like?"

"Her record?"

"Yeah. Does it work? Have a lot of people met their true love through The Kissing Booth?"

"Actually, yes, but I'll let you in on a little secret. In each town, Miss Ana interviews local girls to staff the booth. She picks them according to birthdays and romantic interests, if you get my drift."

"Oh ho. The old broad stacks the deck, eh?"

"Definitely. And get this—sometimes she says no to some of them just so they will report back to their friends that it wasn't 'their time.'"

"Ah, yes, thus furthering the mystical allure of the booth," said Jacob in a spooky imitation of Casey's previous attempt.

"Yup, sweet old Ana has got quite a racket going for herself." She was enjoying the camaraderie developing between them. Enjoying it, that is, until she remembered she couldn't afford to let him get to know her. It wasn't safe for her, her family, or him.

So, she kept the conversation light and flirtatious, coyly refusing to give him her name that day, but promising to give it to him the next time they met. They talked about college, but she wouldn't tell him which one she attended. He was two years older than her, although he didn't look it. Neither of them talked about their families. He accepted the parameters she imposed, and she enjoyed herself. It was an odd but fun couple of hours, and then she had to go meet the others.

They faced each other, hands in pockets, eyes averted, not quite sure how to end their time together. She had gone out of her way to guarantee he would not be able to find her again, but now was sorely resenting the lifestyle that made it necessary. The promise of The Kissing Booth legend would be unfulfilled for them.

He reached out one finger and traced an outline of her face in a slow circle, as if he was trying to memorize it. He smiled crookedly. "See you next time."

And just like today, she had felt empty when he left.

It wasn't supposed to be like this.

****

Chapter 22
The Men in the Mix

"No, I'm not having second thoughts." Don did not bother to hide his irritation, regardless of the consequences. He *was* having second thoughts. And third thoughts. Being questioned only made it worse. "The best I can do is to recommend she stay until Wednesday, and I've already done that. I can't guarantee she'll be here tomorrow morning. For all I know, she still might try to leave," he huffed into the phone in a rush. "I have to get back to work. I've done my part. The rest is up to you. We both know once she leaves here, she might disappear again, so it will have to be tomorrow morning. Oh, and don't forget to transfer the money to my account."

He rang off and sat behind his desk. *Am I doing the right thing?*

***

"When is Jacob going to leave?" asked William, his frustration growing.

"He's having his breakfast in his room so he can take care of a few matters while he's eating." Hanson handed him a cup of tea. "It appears he is going to be a while."

"Can't we just kick him out?" muttered William.

"Whatever you wish, sir."

William shot him a baleful glare and continued to fume.

"Why don't we get to work anyway, sir? What does it matter if Mr. Kent sees it? We will merely tell him this is how you plot out your itinerary for the fairs. After all, he doesn't in fact know your procedure. He will be none the wiser."

Of course. William rubbed his hands together. "Excellent

idea, Hanson. That's why I keep you around." Pleased, he headed for the door.

Hanson followed him. "That, and no one else would put up with what I have to put up with."

"I heard that." He waited a beat and called from the hallway, "And do stop rolling your eyes, man. We have work to do." He had caught Hanson's ritual enough times over the years to know what went on behind his back.

Hanson emerged from the room. "Yes, *Sire*, I am coming."

***

Jacob checked items off on his mental list as he came downstairs a couple of hours later.

Look in on William and Hanson to make sure they're taking it easy.

Sort William's mail before I leave.

Stop by the hospital to see how Casey's doing.

Swing by my place and give Maggie a breather.

He located William and Hanson in the drawing room. At least, it used to be a drawing room.

Can you say Commando Headquarters?

They had propped up a map of New England on a chair and another map of New York State by the bookcase. A smattering of documents covered the table, and more papers had been posted on the wall next to the computer. Color-coded pins depicted locations on the maps, perhaps coinciding with color-coded, highlighted excerpts in the documents. Hanson sat in a corner on the telephone, taking notes. William stood next to the New England map, tracing out a route with his finger and checking it against a pad of paper in his hand.

"Hel-*lo*." Jacob cast about the room for a clue. *What the hell is all this?*

Hanson acknowledged him with a raised brow and continued his task.

William hurried over. "Now, Jacob, I know what you are thinking, but I *am* taking it easy. This is a...a little project."

"*This*...." He swept a hand toward the room. "Is *one* project?"

"Yes, yes. It's about fairs." William nodded vigorously.

He surveyed their work. "Fairs?"

"Well, fairs and business. I love to go to fairs, so I thought, why not combine the two? I'm analyzing the market for providing a shuttle service at different fairs." William gestured toward the map. "Look at all the fairs in New England alone. The different colors are different months. What do you think?"

"It's an interesting prospect." Jacob crossed his arms. "But, please, William, no 'research' until your test results come in, all right?" He knew firsthand about William's penchant for approaching a new business venture in disguise in order to make undetected observations.

"Oh, no. I wouldn't dream of it."

"Okay. Sure." *What a snow job.* "Don't overdo it, all right?" He'd have to try to worm the real story out of Hanson later.

"Absolutely. Wouldn't think of it, m'boy." William put his hand on Jacob's shoulder and steered him toward the door.

"I get it. I get it." He laughed. "Don't let the door hit me on my way out."

William sent him a sheepish grin. "Son, you're too young to understand, but slowing down makes someone my age feel old."

Jacob patted his friend's thin arm. "I'll keep that in mind, sir." He looked across the room at Hanson hanging up the phone. "Take good care of him."

"Of course, Mr. Kent. I always do."

Jacob allowed himself to be ushered out. As the door

closed firmly behind him, he detoured to the foyer, grabbed the morning mail, and thumbed through it, listening for the two men. He pulled out everything he could and neatly stacked the rest, pausing as usual, undecided about the junk mail— Keep it or toss it? If it was his choice, he'd chuck the whole worthless waste of a good tree right into the garbage. *But it's William's junk mail, and he has a right to it. I'll just have Connor add it to the pile.*

A plain, hand-addressed envelope from the *Save the Children* organization caught his eye. Even the return address was handwritten—simplicity itself distinguished it from other junk mail. Great idea. He'd have their marketing department take a look at it.

His cell phone vibrated. *I've spent enough time on this.* He tucked the mail into his briefcase and headed out the door, phone to his ear.

***

Hurry up and leave, Jacob. "Well?" asked William. "Who was it?"

Hanson's face creased into a smile as they listened to the boy's footsteps fade. Hopefully, that meant good news.

"We finally have a bit of luck, sir. That was Rivers."

"The private investigator? I hope this one's better than the last one you hired."

"*You* hired the last one, sir." Hanson's sour expression reflected his words.

"Don't waste time," snapped William. "What's the news?"

"Rivers checked with that restaurant where we waited for their call Sunday night. A call asking for Mr. Children did come in, but close to eleven o'clock. So she *did* call."

William's eyes stung with tears of relief. He faced the map

to hide his show of emotion. Clearing his throat, he asked, "Anything else?"

Hanson hesitated and walked over. "Yes, sir. Rivers accessed the phone records from the restaurant. He traced all of the incoming calls, including that one." He paused.

William rotated to face him. "Tell me, Reginald," he said quietly as dread curled in his gut.

"The phone call came from a hospital."

He sank heavily into a chair. Hanson knelt by his side. "It does not necessarily mean anything dire, sir. After all, she made the call."

William nodded, grateful for the support from his longtime friend. He didn't bother to contradict him. A call from the hospital could mean any number of things could have happened to any one of the girls. And if nothing had been amiss, she would have called on time. *My poor babies.* William cleared his throat. "What's next?"

"I'm not sure. I couldn't speak with Mr. Kent in the room." Hanson got to his feet. "We have to wait for Rivers to call back."

"Then we'll wait," he murmured. "I sure hope this PI doesn't go to the hospital to find them. That's how the last one scared them off."

***

Chapter 23
Moving Target

A hospital is not the place to go for a good night's rest. Casey peered at the morning nurse then yawned. Without sleeping medication, last night had been interesting. Years of living in hiding had taught her to rouse ready to escape danger. Every time a nurse crept into her room, her fight, flight, or freeze response kicked into high gear. After each visit, it took a while to calm down before she could drift back to sleep, feeling vulnerable and exposed behind the flimsy curtain. It was almost as if the diligent staff timed their next visit with when she finally dozed off.

Casey yawned again. *I'm going to have to ask Jacob to take me home so I can get some sleep.*

Home. Where could they call home now? They couldn't very well go back to Albany. She had hated pulling the girls out of school when they were doing so well, but they could be homeschooled. They wouldn't be able to live with Grandpa without drawing attention to themselves and possibly endangering him. Jacob's place was definitely out. A bachelor and a ready-made family? *Unh-uh.* Besides, she could not bear the idea of placing him in danger.

With her train of thought rocking her, Casey needed to move around. After all, exercise would speed her healing and help her regain her strength. Wrapping the hospital gown around her, she decided to go visit the maternity ward. A room of fresh, new beginnings would cheer her up. She shuffled toward the stairs, testing her limits.

She headed down to the main floor to look up the nursery location. She cracked open the stairwell door and peered through. A few people stood in line at the information desk, and none of them wore hospital garb. Being the only person in pajamas was not exactly the best way to keep a low profile. "What were you thinking, Casey? Finding babies isn't happening today." Giggling, she started back up the stairs.

By the time Casey reached the first landing, her mirth dissipated as the full impact of her body's weakness hit home. Her heart pounded with the mild exertion, and she panted after only one flight of stairs. Thank goodness for the support of the railing.

All future plans had to be contingent on her current limitations. Until she regained her strength, whisking the girls away on another lengthy camp-out was not an option. She sat down on the landing to consider the alternatives while she rested up for the next flight of stairs.

Someone shoved a door open on an upper floor. The sound reverberated throughout the stairwell as a crisp female voice rained down. Her terse words made Casey's blood freeze.

"I *was* in Cassie Thatcher's room. I'm telling you she's not there.... Of course I checked with the nursing station. She's gone.... No, I'm certain she didn't see me. I was very careful.... No, I'm in the stairwell. No one can hear me. What next?"

Casey held her breath. She had run out of time.

The woman's grim voice continued. "Knock it off, Dr. Don! I'm going back to check the whole floor. Then I'm going to camp out in the lobby until I hear from you. You check the floors below me. I am only going to give you a half hour, do you understand me? Thirty minutes. That's it."

Click! It sounded like a cell phone snapping shut. The stairwell door opened and closed, leaving Casey alone with the inescapable truth. She was a target once more.

Dr. Don? Jacob's best friend? Had he betrayed her deliberately or by accident? Not that it mattered right now. She had to get out of there. Too bad she hadn't seen the woman's face. The enemy could identify her, but she could not spot the enemy.

She took a calming breath to keep panic at bay. *First things first. I need clothes.* She slipped through the stairwell door to the second floor, snatched a set of blue surgical scrubs and changed in a closet. A little water in her hair to smooth it out, squared shoulders, a confident stride down the corridor, and she blended right in. Around the first corner, she grabbed a parked gurney. She steered it into the nearby elevator, using it to prop herself up.

Five minutes later, the hospital was history.

***

Chapter 24
Derrick Rivers, Private Eye

Derrick Rivers liked his job. He was good at it, so he got to pick and choose the types of cases he handled. He turned a pretty penny for a while staking out the unfaithful for the rich and famous, but he had tired of it. Ten years of confirming suspicions had taken a toll on his view of relationships. He had to get out before the effect became permanent.

Now the self-proclaimed finder of lost loves, his favorite cases reunited siblings who had been separated in their youth. He had tried reuniting adoptees with birth parents, but it was too much like opening Pandora's box. Nope, give him a simple case where both parties wanted to be reunited.

"So why are you working for William Hatch?" he asked his reflection in the car mirror. True, as one of the Greenwich gentry, Hatch could afford to pay well, but there was nothing simple about this case.

According to Hatch, the party he sought consisted of three females sheltered by the Witness Protection Program. First of all, Derrick could not verify they were actually Hatch's granddaughters.

Second, Hatch told him their threat had been eliminated, so they no longer needed to hide. Also unverifiable.

Third, Hatch's son and daughter-in-law, the alleged parents of the three females, had died in a car crash a few years back, also unsupported because the death certificates reflected their fake identities. Though Hatch had shown Derrick an obituary he claimed confirmed the deaths of his son and daughter-in-law, not only did it use their cover names, but it neglected to mention any children. For all he knew, Hatch had cut a random obituary out of the paper.

There was not a lot to go on, and the entire case smelled

bad. Hatch knew neither their current names, nor where they had been living at the time of their parents' deaths. He had zero pictures of the children, and he was pretty sure they would be in disguise.

Derrick had taken the job anyway. If the story proved true, both parties would benefit from a reunion. However, if Hatch and his man, Hanson, were not on the level, and were in fact hunting down the children themselves, they would simply hire someone else to do their dirty deed if he refused the job.

According to Hatch's story, his son Simon had testified against *the* Salvador Maletti. When Simon realized he would have to disappear into Witness Protection, he concocted an intricate system by which they could secretly contact each other, though the rules forbade it. Simon then faked his death to protect his father, putting him out of reach of even the government. Father and son had been in contact ever since.

The car crash changed everything. Were Simon and his wife Dorothy victims of the original vendetta, or casualties of fate? Hatch and Hanson professed they didn't know. It didn't matter. Before anyone could take a breath, the sisters had disappeared. It had been too risky for them even to attend the funeral.

Eventually, Hatch and his grandchildren had reestablished contact. Double precautions protected every meeting. Their elaborate system had functioned just fine until a couple of months ago when an unrelated prison incident took Maletti's life. Hatch was able to establish Maletti's successor felt "unsympathetic" toward his predecessor and his vendettas. His family was finally safe. The excited grandfather didn't want to wait to tell his granddaughters in person. Instead, he went out straightaway and hired some flatfoot to find them.

As far as they could tell, the amateur had somehow given himself away. Most likely the girls thought Maletti sent the idiot. They vanished, surfacing long enough to get a coded message to Hatch and Hanson. The note alerted them to protect themselves and gave details for last week's phone connection. When the youngsters missed the long-awaited phone call, the men feared some harm had befallen them.

Derrick took the case.

A little digging revealed a call for Hatch had been placed to the restaurant, but it had been three hours late. Although Hatch wanted to believe the girls had gone to California with its confusing time zones, Derrick doubted it. The oldest granddaughter seemed to be on the ball. That type of glaring oversight conflicted with what he understood about her.

The alternative? She had made the call out of desperation, despite it being past the time for their appointment. Discovering the phone call originated at Norwalk Hospital was his first good lead.

Derrick adjusted his florist delivery cap and grabbed a bouquet out of the backseat. He had already located the room from where the call originated—belonging to one Cassie Thatcher—and identified the occupant of the room next door—one Nellie Jones. This was Nellie's lucky day. She was about to get an unexpected bouquet of flowers.

Derrick sauntered into Cassie Thatcher's room with the flowers for Nellie. The room was empty except for a nurse making the bed. *Uh-oh.*

"Hey, there." Derrick oozed friendliness with a relaxed stroll and sideways grin. "Where's the patient?"

The nurse glanced at the bouquet in his hands. "I'm sorry, but she's checked out."

"*Checked out?*" *Jeez.* He was too late.

"Oh! No, not dead. I mean, she's gone…. She left."

"She left? Where to?"

"I'm sorry, sir, but I'm not at liberty to say."

"Is there a forwarding address where I can deliver these?" He jiggled the flowers.

She let loose an exasperated puff of air. "I just came on duty, and I can't get anyone to explain to me what's going on, so I can't help you."

"Oh, well." Derrick flashed his most charming smile. "Poor Nellie. Her loss." He shrugged and turned, pretending to leave, and waited for her response. She didn't disappoint him.

"Nellie? Nellie Jones? Oh, her room's next door. This is Cassie Thatcher's room." She accompanied him out.

"Oh, so ol' Cassie's gone AWOL, not Nellie."

"Yes. It was the strangest thing. She left sometime after morning rounds."

"Well, I hope she is healthy enough to be running around."

"It's hard to tell with cases like this."

"Like what? Did she have an accident?"

"Oh, no. She came down with a particularly nasty bout of Lyme Dis—" the nurse caught herself. With an embarrassed flutter, she said, "Look how I carry on, and you still having to make your delivery. That's Nellie's room right over there. I won't keep you. Have a nice day." She spun on her heel and rushed off.

So no accident. Cassie got sick. If she's the missing grand-daughter, she must've stashed the others somewhere, but where? He moseyed into Nellie's room with the flowers. *I might as well drop these off.*

Seated in a chair by the window, Nellie turned out to be a delicate, elderly woman with sharp, bird-like eyes at odds with her softly wrinkled face.

"Delivery for Ms. Jones," he said, offering her the flowers.

She reached forward, presumably for the flowers. Instead, her slender hand grabbed his wrist with amazing strength for one so frail. "You're no delivery man."

Taken by surprise, he almost dropped the bouquet on her.

"I beg your pardon, ma'am?"

"You're looking for the girl next door." As he opened his mouth to protest, she released his wrist and waved her hand in a dismissive manner. "Don't bother. Your cover is blown."

Derrick closed his mouth, and waited to see what direction they were heading. He removed the delivery cap and folded it into his back pocket.

"How did you know?" He went over to a cupboard to find a pitcher for the flowers. Locating one, he filled it with water.

Nellie refolded a tissue in her lap. "Because I have no one," she said as he placed the flowers next to her bed. "There's no one left to send me flowers."

She reached out a hand to stroke one of the blossoms then turned away, touching the tissue to the corner of her eyes. "You're my first visitor."

"How long have you been in here?"

"A little over a week."

"I'm so sorry."

"It is what it is." She folded her hands in her lap and fixed her gaze on him. "So, who are you, really?"

He reached into his pocket and showed her his identification.

"Ahh." She nodded toward Cassie's room. "They brought her in two days after I arrived."

He checked over his shoulder. What luck. Her seat provided a perfect view of any hall activity. "Do you know why?" he asked, holding his breath.

Nellie regarded him for a moment, and then handed back his ID. "Lyme disease. But she also had gotten herself dehydrated."

He took the seat across from her.

"They brought her in unconscious." She grinned. "But I guess she's up and about now. She slipped out of here this morning."

"Do you have any idea why she left?"

"Nope, but I'm guessing she needed to get out and stretch her legs a bit."

"Ms. Jones—"

"Oh, please." She waved her hand imperiously. "Call me Nellie."

"Nellie," he corrected, "did she have any visitors?"

"A couple. A strapping young man comes by every day, sometimes twice a day." She nodded her approval. "She should snatch that one up. He's a keeper."

"Oh, yeah? What makes him 'a keeper'?"

"He loves her so much." She leaned forward and lowered her voice. "He's in cahoots with that young Dr. Don, you know. I hear them talking in the hall. I think she's in some kind of trouble, and they're trying to keep her safe. They moved a security guard up here to keep an eye on her room. That poor boy is going to be shook for sure when he finds out she's gone."

"A security guard? How did she get out of her room without anyone knowing?"

Nellie shrugged. "I don't know. Doughnut break? Bathroom break? He wasn't there when she left."

"Any other visitors?"

"Mm-hmm. A girl. A teenage girl."

Derrick sat up straight.

"I think they're related. They have the same bone structure." She bobbed her head. "Yes, a definite strong family resemblance. I think the young man brought her here to visit."

Now we're getting somewhere. Only one more girl needs to be accounted for.

"How did she look?" Derrick asked.

"Blonde, spikey hair. Way too much makeup for this time of day, if you ask me. Short, about this high."

"But, did she look healthy? Safe?"

Nellie nodded. "She's too skinny, and you know what? She's definitely scared about something. I think when she showed up, the girl couldn't find Cassie. She must've been in the bathroom, so the poor thing didn't see her at first. I guess Cassie came out because she went running in there. I could hear the little soul crying her heart out all the way in here."

She gazed at the flowers for a moment then spent the next few minutes describing Cassie and her two visitors for Derrick while he jotted notes on his pad.

"Nellie, did you see what time Cassie left this morning?"

"I'd say about eight-ish. Now *she* is fragile. *I* look stronger than she does. Lyme can be nasty." Nellie wagged her head. "I wouldn't have guessed she was leaving the building. She didn't move like she was sneaking around, and she wore her hospital clothes."

An orderly bustled in, carrying Nellie's lunch tray. "Good afternoon, Mrs. Jones. I see you have a visitor today," he said brightly.

"Yes." Nellie buried her face in the flowers and inhaled. "I guess I do."

Derrick shifted his weight and fiddled with his watch. Almost noon. "Umm, I should get going, Nellie. Thank you for everything." He took her hands in his. "It's none of my business, but are *you* going to be all right?"

Her eyes widened, and then she smiled. "How nice of you to ask. I'm going to have a little procedure done tomorrow, and then I'll be out and about soon."

A *little* procedure? Did people stay in hospitals over a week for a little procedure? But it wasn't any of his business.

She patted his hand. "*You* are definitely a keeper."

Heat rose in his face.

"Now, off with you, young man." She waved toward the

door. "You have things to do, and I have a sumptuous feast to tend to." She inclined her head toward the hot but bland-looking meal.

He bowed to her and left. Mulling over what he had learned, he paused outside Cassie's empty room.

"Friend of Mrs. Jones?" a deep voice behind him asked.

"More like a fan." Derrick turned to find a gladiator-sized man in a white coat. The nametag indicated he had found Dr. Don McNamara, Cassie's physician. *Excellent. Another chance to collect more info on the elusive Ms. Thatcher.* The universe was smiling down on him today.

Or not.

"I'm sorry, Mr. Rivers," repeated Dr. McNamara ten minutes later, "but, again, unless you are a member of Ms. Thatcher's family, I am not at liberty to say."

"I understand, Doctor." Frustrated, Derrick fished in his pocket. "If you don't mind, I'd like to leave you my card. You know…in case you think of something you *can* tell me."

"Certainly." The doctor gazed past Derrick's shoulder, a sorrowful expression suddenly dropping the corners of his mouth. "But like I said, you got here too late," he finished softly. "She's gone."

Was the doctor actually talking to him? Derrick checked over his shoulder to see what had caught his attention, only to find an empty hallway. This was a dead end.

Derrick excused himself and headed for Patient Services to take care of one last thing before he left the hospital. Stopping at the desk for Friends of Norwalk Hospital, he arranged for someone to stop in to visit Nellie twice a day for the rest of her stay. Then he headed out. He had work to do, and some serious leads to follow.

Chapter 25
Welcome to My World

From the lobby, Jacob caught sight of Don escorting a man toward his office, engrossed in conversation. Don always noticed everything on his shift, so when he didn't spare even a fleeting glance at Jacob stepping off the elevator, the hairs on the back of his neck rose. Don's civil manner certainly did not convey it, but something about the angle of his head alerted Jacob. He could see what the stranger wouldn't. Don was very upset.

Jacob strolled past the two men in time to hear Don emphasize, "Mr. Rivers, unless you are a member of Ms. Thatcher's family...."

Oh no! He's after Casey. Heart pounding, he decided to take a roundabout route in case the guy was not alone. He dawdled at the bathroom before heading to her room, trying to quell the fear rising in the pit of his stomach. He made a beeline across the empty hall. Don's strange behavior had already clued him in, but the sight of the stripped-down bed still made him stagger.

She's gone.

He leaned against the doorway for support. Through a heartbroken haze, he still felt thankful she had gotten away. How close they had come. He shuddered around the hollow pit in his stomach.

Hold on. She's not completely gone. There's no way Casey's going to leave her sisters behind. Maybe she was headed toward his house right now. Hope soared.

And then crashed.

If they had traced Casey to the hospital, they might have linked her to him. The younger girls could be in danger, too.

Trying not to let the fear rising in his chest overwhelm him, he darted into the room and dialed Maggie's cell phone.

"C'mon, c'mon, c'mon," he muttered as the phone rang. Impatient, he propped his forearm on the window, rested his forehead on it, and stared at the parking lot below. He snapped to attention. There was Casey, slouched down in the front seat of his car, her eyes closed.

"Margaret Fuller here," said the voice in his ear. "How may I help you?"

Yes. Yes. Yes! Casey hadn't disappeared out of his life.

"Hello?" Maggie said when he didn't respond.

"Hello?" he parroted, preoccupied by his heart leaping into his throat.

"Hello? Mr. Kent, is that you?"

"Yes! Yes, Maggie, it's me!" he shouted, giddy with relief.

"Mr. Kent?"

The sound of her confusion refocused him. "Maggie, I'm bringing Casey home. I think. I want you to keep the girls quiet and inside. I'll fill you in when I get there."

"That won't be so easy, boss."

Uh-oh, she called me boss. "What is it, Margaret?"

"Sam is gone. She asked me if she could go for a walk. I told her to wait and ask you. I thought she was upstairs watching TV all this time. Robin kept me distracted so I didn't notice her leave. She's been gone about three hours, but I just found out."

"Okay. There's nothing we can do about it now. One thing I've learned about this family is they don't do anything spontaneously. See what you can get out of Robin. She should at least be able to tell you when to expect her back. I'll be there as soon as I can. Oh, and, Maggie?"

"Yes, Mr. Kent?"

"Tell the staff not to let anyone in the house."

Hanging up, he ran out of the room and right into Don.

***

Don waited until the elevator door closed behind Derrick Rivers then headed for Casey's room to see how he could help his buddy. *I knew she was going to break his heart. I knew it.* But try as he might, he had not been able to prevent it. He'd expected to find Jacob crushed and unhappy, not barreling out of the room with a dopey grin, heading for the elevator. He grabbed Jake's arm.

"Don, what happened? Who was that guy you took to your office?"

"He's a private investigator looking for Cassie Thatcher. He says he represents her family." Was his friend holding up okay? His good cheer seemed pretty inappropriate for the circumstances. "Jake, she's been gone since about eight. Rita was the first one who noticed."

"Rita? You mean, *your* Rita?"

Don couldn't hold eye contact. "I told her Casey was here. But that was before I knew she was hiding out. Rita came down this morning before work. You know how she is. She wanted to see The Nameless Wonder for herself, but Casey was already gone."

"But why? Did Rita see anyone else? Someone suspicious?"

"I don't think so. That PI guy showed up less than an hour ago, or at least that's when I noticed him."

"All right," Jacob turned. "I'm outta here. I have to make sure her sisters are safe."

"Hang on, Jake. You'll need this." Don detained his friend with a hand on his chest. He could feel Jake's heart thumping double time through his shirt.

Don waved for an approaching nurse to hurry. She came

running toward them with a small bag in her hand. "Don't worry. I'm sure she's with her sisters." He took the bag from the nurse and nodded his thanks.

"Here, her antibiotics. She has to take them *exactly* like it says on the bottle. Make sure she finishes it." He handed the bag to Jacob, guilt and concern for his friend engulfing him. "Jake—"

"Don't worry about me, Don. I haven't given up yet. Casey is The One. I just have to figure out how to make it happen."

He couldn't suppress a negative wag of his head.

Jacob's brow furrowed. "Sure, she might have to sneak the girls out of here and disappear, but if that's what she has to do to be safe, I'll help her any way I can, even if it means being without her."

This was not the happily-ever-after scenario he wished for the guy who'd introduced him to his wife.

Jacob clapped him on the arm and headed for the stairs at a trot. As he swung open the door, he called over his shoulder, "Besides, we just set up a secret meeting place in case something like this happened. Go figure."

"Where?" called Don after him, "The top of the Empire State Building?"

Jacob laughed. "That's what *I* said." And he was gone, the pounding of his feet quickly fading.

***

Yup, she's asleep. Good thing he had parked in the shade.

Although he made no noise, Casey shifted, opened her eyes, and yawned.

He unlatched the car door and slid in beside her. "You've had a busy day, doctor," he said, plucking at the shoulder of her scrubs. He handed her the bag of medicine. "Compliments of Dr. Don."

"Thanks, Jacob." She heaved a weary sigh. "Let's get out of here."

"You bet!" he said in fervent agreement. Casey remained slouched low while he eased the car out of the parking space. Jacob took out his cell phone and pretended to talk into it in case anyone was watching. "I think you need to take one of those pills," he said to the phone.

"Look at you, all James-Bond-like." Casey giggled. She opened the bag and scanned the directions as he handed her a water bottle.

"Wow. This is a full-service getaway," she quipped, opening the water.

"What happened back there, Casey?"

"Oh…. Well, my thoughts chased me out of bed *really* early this morning, so I went for a short walk. But when I was in the stairwell, I overheard someone targeting me."

She gestured toward her outfit. "I had already figured out trotting around in a hospital gown was not the way to keep a low profile, so I re-outfitted myself and then snuck out. The rest is history," she said lightly.

He slid a glance at her. How could she be so calm when he was feeling so freaked out? "Who are these people?"

"I'm not sure. I don't usually hang around to find out." She popped the pills into her mouth and took a sip.

"You know, Casey, I heard some guy in there say he represents your family who's trying to find you."

She pulled the bottle away from her mouth and growled, "They're not my family, and we don't want to be found. Please, can that be enough information for you? Because I can't tell you any more. It's too dangerous for the others." She put a hand on his knee. "And it's too dangerous for you, too. Please, just take me to the girls."

"Don't you worry about me. I can take this James Bond thing *pret-ty* far." He gave her a cocky wink.

"Be serious, Jacob. I don't even want you to tell the people close to you about us. That includes Dr. Don."

"Yeah, well, about that. He probably expects you to go to my house because that's where the girls are."

Casey exhaled slowly. "Okay. Well, there's nothing we can do about that now. They should be fairly safe there."

Or were they? He cleared his throat. "I was thinking. If they traced you in the hospital, they might be able to link you to me." He looked sideways at her past the phone. "What if they're able to find the girls?"

"I've been thinking about that, too. I want to call them and tell them to clear out."

She couldn't leave yet. Not before she understood they were meant to be together. "Yeah, well, Sam went for a walk. It's been over three hours, and Maggie hasn't heard from her."

"Who's Maggie?" Casey asked.

"Uh, it's actually Margaret. She's my right hand. I call her Maggie to rile her up." He grinned. "She needs to be a little riled up occasionally." He turned his concentration to negotiating his entrance onto the busy Merritt Parkway from a ridiculously short on-ramp.

"Don't worry, Casey," he assured her. "Maggie's trustworthy. I left the girls with her because she is completely dependable. You should have seen her handle them the day we brought you to the hospital."

"Can you get this Margaret on the phone?"

"Sure." He hit speed dial.

"I need to talk to Robin," Casey whispered at him.

Moments later, he handed her the phone.

"Hello?" said Casey. "Report." She listened silently, no expression on her face. With a final, "That's fine," she hung up the phone.

Jacob was beside himself with curiosity. "What did she say?"

"What?" asked Casey. "Oh, it's fine. Say, how far is Greenwich from your house?" She dug a map out of the glove compartment.

"About twenty miles. Why? Is that where she went?"

"Yup."

"Why?"

Casey rearranged the map before answering. "Oh, she's a typical teenager. You know teenagers. She heard there were some nice shops there."

Her evasive answer offended him. "Casey, there is a huge shopping area in Norwalk, and that's half the distance," he snapped. "And Sam is *not* a typical teenager. She's like G.I. Joe in a miniskirt. You don't have to lie. Please tell me what is going on."

Casey bit her lip and gave him a sidelong glance. "We might have a contact in Greenwich who can help us on our way. If Sam isn't back by the time we get to your house, then I'll worry."

She gripped her hands in her lap. "We have to leave, you know."

"I know." He reached over and stroked her blond hair. To his surprise, it felt brittle and dry. "But it's different this time. Now we can begin working together."

"Working together? On what? And keep your eyes on the road, Mr. Bond."

"Work on us." There. He said it.

"Jacob, there can be no *us*," she sputtered, rattling the map in her hands.

Jacob ignored her comment. He looked over at her, scrunched up in the seat. She was so cute, and he loved her so much. It was so totally unbelievable, he had to say it out loud. "How in the world did I miss it?"

"Miss what?"

"You. I picked you up and carried you to my car. I buckled the seat belt around you. I checked you for broken bones. How could I have not known it was you? It's so obvious."

"It's obvious now because everything is in context. It's the same principal as performing magic. Misdirection. The magician distracts you with movement and talk, and makes you think one thing, while something completely different is going on under your very nose."

"Magic, huh? Right."

"I'm serious. You weren't checking for a girl from the fair who had no family. You saw one of three brothers. The girl you know had long brown hair, not short blonde hair. You get it? Misdirection. If you had been hunting for *me* that day, no disguise would have made you miss me."

"Like how we always seem to run into each other at the fairs?"

"Right. Out of all of those people, I always look for your face, and I find it."

"Hah! I knew it!" said a very smug Jacob. There was definitely hope here.

Casey frowned. "You know what I mean—"

"Don't bother with the retraction," he interrupted happily. "You search for me at the fairs, just like I search for you."

"Don't read something into it that's not there, Jacob." She scowled at the map.

"Don't worry. I'm not." He didn't care if his cheerful grin belied his statement.

She frowned at the dashboard. "You're deliberately being difficult."

"You always say that when I don't agree with you."

She folded her arms across her chest and slid further into her seat, but his grin didn't fade. They rode in silence until he exited the highway.

As they waited at a traffic light, he noticed a slender figure walking down the side of the darkening street. The light changed to green, allowing him to merge into traffic. "Hey! That's Sam." He steered toward the curb.

Casey grabbed his knee. "Don't stop, Jacob."

"Why not?" He scanned both sides of the street as he slowed. "Hey, where is she?" he asked, checking the mirrors.

"She's hiding because she saw a car slow down."

"Maybe she doesn't remember what my car looks like." He started rolling down his window to call to her, but Casey placed a restraining hand on his arm.

"She won't answer. She has no way of knowing whether or not you can be trusted."

Incredulous, he turned to her. "Me? She doesn't trust me? After I opened my home to her?"

"Look, Jacob, try to understand. If they grabbed Robin and told you to help them or they'd hurt her, what would you do?"

A cold feeling spread inside his stomach. Films turned this type of dilemma into some kind of thrilling adventure, but there was no thrill here. Real fear and helplessness were not fun.

She patted his hand in his silence. "She has no way of knowing whether you have been compromised. The kindest thing you can do is to keep driving and let Samantha figure out her own way back to your place."

Jacob linked his fingers with hers and sped up again.

"Welcome to my world," Casey intoned. She untangled her hand from his and covered her face. "Oh, I'm such a fool."

"Why do you say that?" Jacob asked, shivering in the warm

late afternoon air.

"Oh." She peeked at him. "For a little while back there, I actually fantasized about having a normal life. Not being on the run. Not having to plan everything. Thinking about a permanent future with—" She blushed.

His heart leapt. "Yes?"

"Um…with the girls."

"Or maybe with me?"

"No," she declared. "It's not going to happen. My life is too complicated."

"No," Jacob corrected with equal firmness. "It's not going to happen *yet*."

Casey looked away.

Time to change the topic. "How did you know this was my car?"

"Easy. Sam told me the make and license plate. I broke in and made myself at home."

"I can see you're going to be handy if I ever lock my keys in the car."

"You have no idea." Casey replaced the map in the glove compartment. "By the way, what happened to your car?"

"My car? What's wrong with it?"

"The passenger side. It's all dented. And one of your windows has a hole in it."

"Oh, that," grunted Jacob. "That's your sister's response to my trying to help you."

"Oh, no." She covered her cheeks with her palms.

He glanced at her. "What did she use?"

"From the size of the dents, probably a slingshot." Casey smothered a laugh as Jacob's jaw dropped. "They're pretty good with them."

"Slingshots? Who uses slingshots?" He pulled into his driveway.

"Wow," breathed Casey. "Business must be good."

"Yeah, well," laughed Jacob. "This place and its staff come with the job." It was way more than he needed, but William wanted someone in the place, so Jacob had moved in. It took some getting used to, but now he was pretty comfortable here.

"Staff?" repeated Casey. "Business must be *really* good."

He maneuvered his car into a spacious garage and closed the door. From there, they could enter his condo without being seen by the outside world.

Casey sat up and stretched, no longer vulnerable to spying eyes. "Finally!" she said.

Jacob came around and held open her door. "Welcome to my world."

Chapter 26
Reunited

Casey stepped into another universe when she entered Jacob's home. It was huge. It had nine or ten rooms. It had a live-in butler. It had a cook and a housekeeper. But most important-ly, it had Robin. Casey passed through to the main foyer, lis-tening for her.

From the top banister, her baby sister shrieked, "Casey!" and bounded down the stairs. She skidded to a stop in front of her. "Hold up. Are you okay?"

Casey opened her arms wide in a loving invitation. The two girls transformed into one big hugging, tearful mess.

"Don't cry. Don't cry," crooned Casey, tears streaming down her own cheeks.

"I was so scared," hiccupped Robin. "We couldn't wake you up, not even in the hospital. You didn't do anything. I couldn't even feel you."

She squeezed the little girl tighter, her throat aching. She tried to squelch the anger rising inside her; anger that Robin had been subjected to such distress; anger that Samantha had to make her way back to them alone in the dark; anger at the distance she had to keep from Grandpa. Her inability to protect her family suddenly suffocated her. They all depend-ed on her, and she could barely stand up for fifteen minutes. Overwhelmed, all she could think about was the need to sit for a moment.

"C'mon, little women. Let's find a place to sit." Jacob peeled Robin off her. "Casey is still getting her strength back." He lift-ed Robin into his arms, and the two of them peered at each other as if trying to decide if the move was appropriate. Robin hiccupped again, and buried her face in his shoulder. Casey blinked at him through her tears, watching him awkwardly pat her baby sister on the back. An unfamiliar longing filled her. Normally she would squash that kind of feeling, but today exhaustion prevailed.

She allowed him to steer her into a comfortable room with a large sofa. Her sister plopped down next to her once she settled against the arm of the couch.

As they snuggled, Robin announced, "Sam's home. Now we can all be together."

Jacob lowered himself into a chair across from them. "We know Sam is—"

"Very sorry I took off without permission," said Sam from the doorway.

Robin jumped up and ran to her, grabbed her hand, and led her toward the couch. "Wow! You need this more than I do." Robin pushed Sam into her former spot.

"Thanks, Tidbit." Sam buried her head in her big sister's shoulder. As Casey's arms enveloped her, Sam covered her face with her hand, only the gentle shaking of her shoulders betraying her tears. Casey's heart ached as she bowed her head over the younger girl who bore so much.

Hearing a sniffle, she looked up. Robin stood over them, wringing her hands.

Jacob cleared his throat. "Come here, Robin. I feel lonely." He reached a hand toward the forlorn little soul. Robin clambered up into his lap and put her head on his shoulder. He gingerly wrapped an arm around her, his movement less awkward than before.

"Why is everybody so sad? Isn't this a happy time?" Robin asked. "We're all together again."

"I'm not sure, Robin," said Jacob. "Why don't we wait until we all feel better, and then you can ask, okay?"

"'Kay." Robin positioned herself to better see her sisters

and then suddenly jumped out of his lap. "Wait. We're not all here." She turned and ran from the room as they regarded each other in confusion. She returned, dragging behind her a slender, middle-age woman in a gray sweater set and skirt.

"C'mon," Robin insisted as the woman hesitated at the door.

"I don't want to intrude," she demurred.

"I don't know what that means," said Robin, "but you should sit over here."

Robin tugged her toward the other chair.

"Please, Maggie." Jacob indicated the chair.

So, this is Margaret. A wave of gratitude swept over Casey. This woman had cared for her family when she could not. She would never be able to repay her. And, as soon as the lump in her throat relaxed, she would tell her so.

"*Now* everyone is here," said Robin with a satisfied air. She leaned toward Margaret and stage-whispered, "I'm gonna go sit with him because you already had your turn."

"Very well," Margaret stage-whispered back. "Fair's only fair."

Robin skipped back to Jacob and clambered back into his lap.

Margaret fetched a box of tissues and set it down on the couch, carrying a couple to Robin before taking her seat. A comfortable silence settled over the room, punctuated by the occasional sniffle from the girls. A weight lifted off Casey's shoulders. After keeping everyone hidden and safe all by herself for so long, she had no idea how to receive help. But help abounded here, making her a lot less overwhelmed.

Robin turned to Jacob. "Doesn't this feel like one of those families you see on TV?"

He looked at her, his eyes wide. "I was just thinking that."

"I know," she said, cuddling up in the crook of his arm.

Shaking his head, he caught Sam and Robin exchanging quick looks and grins before Sam buried her face again. He gave Casey a quizzical glance. She just shrugged. She had no idea what they were about, and, right now, she didn't have the energy to find out. Margaret's curious gaze was on her.

"I am Margaret Fuller. You must be Cassie. I—"

"Yes, you're Jacob's right hand," Casey finished for her. "And, you can call me Casey. It's my…my nickname."

"K.C.? As in the talking horse?"

"No." She laughed. "That would be Casey, as in…in—"

"Casey typeface?" Margaret offered.

"Casey typeface?" repeated Jacob.

Margaret blushed. "It's a font used by railways for…never mind. Is it C-A-S-E-Y?"

"Yes, that's right." Casey tried to smother her mirth. It figured an executive assistant of Margaret's caliber would have oodles of factoids at her fingertips. "I can't thank you enough for all you've done."

"They're lovely children," said Margaret. "You should be very proud."

"I thought you said we were odd." A familiar glint of mischief had returned to Samantha's watery face.

"I *never* told you that," huffed Margaret.

"No, you said it to Miss Isadora."

Jacob chuckled. "Little pitchers have big ears."

"She meant you were unusual and unique," said Casey.

"Yes, I did. Thank you," said Margaret, relaxing back into her seat.

Just a few minutes in Margaret's presence, and Casey understood Jacob's tendency to tease her. She was unyieldingly formal, prim in all her mannerisms. But her unexpectedly warm heart had kept Robin company, left alone in this strange place without either of her sisters. "Oh, no, *thank you.* It must have frightened them terribly when I got sick. We were so lucky they had someone like you to be with them. I don't know how to repay you," said Casey, the lump returning.

"No thanks necessary." Margaret colored.

"Why, Maggie. You're blushing," teased Jacob. "I do believe I don't thank you enough."

"Mama used to say you can never be too kind," Robin said through a yawn.

Jacob caught Casey stifling an answering yawn. "I think we could all do with some rest." He stood up and hoisted Robin over his shoulder like a sack of potatoes. As she gasped and giggled, he reached down and pulled Casey to a standing position. "You're going to be staying in my room."

"No way! Absolutely not!" *He's crazy if he thinks we're sharing a room.*

As Casey indignantly began to sputter, Sam said through a sniffle, "Don't worry. He's been sleeping over his friend's house. His friend's been sick, so Mr. Kent has been making sure he doesn't overdo it."

"How did you know that?" asked Jacob.

Sam smirked. "Bigger pitchers have even bigger ears," she said, a bit more of her bravado returning.

Casey eyed Jacob. "Do you always take care of everybody?" This side of him was new.

"No, no....this is totally out of character for me. Margaret is the one who takes care of everything."

"Well, that's my job. Mr. Kent, why don't you get on the road? You have a bit of a drive ahead of you. Miss Casey probably would like to get cleaned up and get some rest after her long day."

Casey was exhausted, so she didn't protest when the ever-efficient Margaret Fuller took charge.

"I'll help the young ladies get ready for bed, and then

they'll be in to say good night." Margaret gently tugged at the younger two, who followed her without fuss.

Casey grabbed Jacob's hand, alarm spreading through her. "You're leaving?" she hissed.

"You'll be fine, Casey. No one knows you're here. And if everyone is very careful, you can be fairly safe here for quite a while, at least long enough for you to fully recover." He gently traced the outline of her face. "I'll be back tomorrow morning as early as you want me."

Casey clutched his other hand. "Okay, then nine o'clock. Sharp. No, wait. Eight o'clock."

Jacob laughed and raised her hand to his lips. "I'll be here at seven and wait for you to wake up." He brushed his lips across the back of her hand.

Self-consciously, Casey removed her tingling hand from his grasp and put it behind her back. She peeked around his shoulder to see if the others had noticed, but the girls were making their way upstairs with Margaret.

"Go with them," Jacob urged. "I'll be back before you know it."

"C'mon, Casey. Wait 'til you see our room," called Robin from the top step.

As Casey moved toward the first step, she heard the door close softly behind Jacob. Once again, she was struck with an empty feeling only his presence could fill. Remembering how difficult the stairs had been at the hospital, she squared her shoulders and palmed the banister.

"May I be of assistance, Miss?" asked Gregory, materializing at her side. Embarrassed, Casey was about to decline, but common sense reared its head. Thanking him, she took the offered arm, and they made their way slowly toward the second floor.

***

"Leave me alone." Samantha shook off her little sister's hand, her throat tight.

"What is wrong with you?" Robin lowered her voice. "Did you deliver the note to Grandpa?"

Sam nodded curtly as she shut the door. "Listen, Robin. You can't tell anyone, okay?" she whispered. Her better instinct told her to keep quiet, but her agitation made her want to share her pain with someone. Besides, she couldn't hide what she was feeling from Robin anyway.

"Not even Casey?"

"Especially not Casey...at least, not until she gets better, okay?"

"What is it?" Robin regarded Sam, wide-eyed.

"Promise?"

"I *promise*. What is it?"

Sam hesitated, tears springing forth. "Grandpa changed his mind. He doesn't want us anymore."

Chapter 27
The Unwanted

"You're crazy." Robin dismissed Samantha's statement with a wave of her hand. "Of course Grandpa wants us. Whatever you heard must've been him trying to trick somebody."

"That's what I thought, too." Sam wrung her hands. "At first. But you weren't there. You didn't hear him."

"What did he say?"

"That he wants to be by himself and 'everyone should get the hell out and leave him alone.' He said he didn't want anyone else in his house because it wasn't big enough to keep people out of his business. He went on and on."

"Was he yelling? Maybe he was having a fit."

Sam swallowed past a lump in her throat. "He was yelling at first. Then he got real calm and said it all over again, real patient, like he was talking to a little kid or something."

"Did you leave the note anyway?"

"Of course. Casey told me to, so I did. I put it right on top of his mail so he couldn't miss it. I'll bet he doesn't answer it."

Robin dropped her head. "I thought he loved us."

Uh-oh. She's too young for this. "Of course he loves us, Tidbit. But just because you love someone doesn't mean you want to live with them."

Robin climbed up on the bed, pulled a pillow into her arms, and buried her face in it.

Why had she burdened her little sister? "You know, you're probably right. He was just trying to throw somebody off our trail."

"Yeah." Some of Robin's buoyancy returned as she raised her head. "'Cuz I think someone has been snooping around. Mr. Kent called after you left and told Miss Fuller not to let us go outside and not to let anyone in."

"Really?" said Sam. "Hmmm. I'll bet that's why he brought Casey here so soon. She doesn't look strong enough to be out of the hospital yet."

"What do *you* know about it?" Robin said fiercely, squishing the pillow. "She's fine. Besides, she'll heal faster if she's around us."

"Absolutely, Tidbit." She didn't want to upset her again.

Robin fluffed up the pillow and rested her chin on it.

"No sense in worrying about Grandpa, either." Sam spoke firmly but remained unconvinced herself. "Let's wait and see what his answer is, okay?"

***

Jacob drove the route back to William's house out of sheer habit, one hundred percent preoccupied by a single topic—how to keep The Herd safe. They couldn't stay inside forever. William was his go-to mentor when he had to hash out a problem, but obviously Jacob couldn't bother him about this now. Until William had a handle on his health issues, he didn't need anything else added to his plate.

Although William had not had an actual heart attack, something was terribly wrong. He was too intense, too easily riled, too pale. If he was sleeping well, he wouldn't have those shadows under his eyes. Or be so thin. Could it be cancer? He made a note to check with the cook to see how he was eating. William didn't want anyone checking up on him, but he'd have to move heaven and earth before he got rid of Jacob.

He parked his car, braced himself, and headed into the house. Nowadays, he didn't know what to expect when he showed up. Tonight he planned to keep out of the way as much as possible. That left Hanson to cope with whatever crap William dished out.

"He's in a foul mood," Hanson warned him at the door.

"Do you know why?"

"Something to do with his project not going as planned."

Dead end. "I thought you were going to keep his projects down to a minimum."

"I'll tell you what, sir. I will go out tomorrow and do your job. *You* can stay here with Mr. Hatch, and *you* get him to lower his workload."

Jacob held his palms up in mock surrender. "No, no. I'm sure you're doing all you can. We both know how stubborn he is. Do you think I should stop in and see him tonight? I have to leave around six-thirty tomorrow morning."

"Only if you want to get your head chewed off, sir."

"No thanks. After the day I've had, I'm heading to bed."

"Very well, sir. With any luck, Mr. Hatch will do the same shortly."

As he spoke, Jacob noticed the shadows under Hanson's eyes. "How many times did he fire you today?"

Hanson waved a casual hand. "Oh, two or three...dozen. I lost track."

"Wow. I guess I'm not the only one who had a tough day. I hope you don't let him drive you off."

"And why would I want to start over, sir, at my age?" Hanson shared a rare smile. "We've become accustomed to each other."

"That's a relief. Good night then, Hanson."

"Good night, sir," he replied as Jacob headed up the stairs.

Reaching for his doorknob, Jacob heard William come into the foyer. "Reginald, old friend, I know I owe you an apology for my behavior today—"

"Several, in fact," interrupted Hanson, his voice neutral.

Jeez. Jacob closed his door with a soft *click*. *I'm glad I wasn't around here today.*

***

Chapter 28
Threatened by the Bell

"Does anyone recognize the black sedan parked outside?" Gregory's words put Casey on alert, although his manner had not changed. Was this a black-sedan kind of neighborhood? Unwilling to alarm Jacob's unsuspecting staff, she covertly scanned for her sisters. Robin was across the hall in the den, creating art. Sam was upstairs composing a message to Grandpa.

Across the living room, Margaret was on the phone discussing something to do with work. She answered with a shake of her head.

Isadora poked her head into the room. "I noticed that black car when I came in. The man driving it was over at the Millers' house."

Gregory nodded and walked out.

Casey cocked an eyebrow. *Is this the way they normally are, or do they suspect something?* The girls had been careful not to reveal their fugitive status, providing excuse after excuse why they should remain inside. *I'll have to get Jacob's take on it when he gets back. Meanwhile—*

The doorbell rang.

Before an alarmed Casey could throw off her blanket, Margaret was on her feet, the phone forgotten. "Casey, wouldn't you be more comfortable in your room? It's so sunny this time of day."

Casey found herself being ushered up the stairs by Margaret just as Isadora swept into the den and collected Robin. From the second-floor landing she could see Mrs. Tucker scurrying around to collect their belongings as Robin and the cook trotted up the stairs. Nodding to Gregory, the housekeeper disappeared into the den. As the doorbell rang again, Isadora closed the bedroom door behind Margaret and the two sisters, and left.

Humming a song, Robin spread out her materials on the bed and resumed coloring. Margaret returned Casey's book then sat in a wing chair. Pumping adrenaline, Casey remained by the door straining to distinguish the male murmuring downstairs.

A few minutes later, Sam poked her head into the room. "No worries. It was some pushy door-to-door salesman, but Gregory wasn't having it. The guy's dearly departed. He's headed next door." Then Sam and her grin were gone, leaving the two women to breathe a sigh of relief.

"I'm going back to my spot." Robin scooped up her paraphernalia and left.

Casey settled in the chair opposite Margaret and tried to process how she had ended up in the upstairs bedroom. "Umm...Margaret, what just happened?"

Margaret looked up from her book. "Happened? Nothing happened. I simply thought you'd be more comfortable up here."

"Uh-huh. Sure you did. How long have you known we're hiding out?"

Margaret closed her book. "I've suspected since the hospital."

She tried to smile. "We must be slipping."

"Nonsense. Those were very unusual circumstances. The girls conducted themselves admirably. You should be proud."

"The others obviously know. Did Jacob tell them?"

"No. He only told us not to let the girls go outside the day you came home." The older woman leaned forward. "There's no reason why you cannot remain here until you are fully convalesced. I don't want to overstep boundaries, but we—

Mrs. Tucker, Gregory, Isadora, and I—we've been talking. The girls need to get out and move around. And so will you when you are stronger. We've come up with a plan."

"A plan?" *Too many complications. Too many people getting involved.*

"Yes, a plan to get all of you out of the condo, undetected. In shifts. Mostly with one of us. But only if you are comfortable with the idea, of course."

"I feel like I should explain—"

Margaret held up a forestalling hand. "Not necessary. Mr. Kent has hosted somewhat quirky houseguests before, all in the line of business. We have always accommodated them."

Casey licked her dry lips, trying to decide which tack to take. "Okay. Let's hear your quirky plan."

Chapter 29
The Family Man

How does a guy go from being solitary and single to juggling a job and two households? Jacob could handle his own work. No problem. All appointments requiring decisions had been rescheduled. He shifted everybody possible into research and development projects. At least for a while, they would merely require him to check on their progress. With work under control, he could direct his attentions to his two "families," neither of which belonged to him.

Mornings were spent in Greenwich where he would have breakfast while he worked. After William's mail arrived at around ten o'clock, Jacob would announce he was going to the office, sort through William's mail when no one was looking, and escape the melancholy and often volatile atmosphere of the once peaceful residence.

Every day, Jacob dropped off the mail at the Stamford office to William's assistant, Connor. There, he reviewed the previous day's progress with both Connor and Patrick, Margaret's assistant. Everyone else had been told Mr. Hatch was on vacation, and, coincidentally, so was Ms. Fuller. Connor and Patrick knew that wasn't true, but they were only privy to varying degrees of the actual situation.

Even with William's extra work, Jacob managed to spend only a few short hours at the office. Then he would head home to Westport, where Maggie, Isadora, Mrs. Tucker, and Gregory were trying to keep the girls under wraps and entertained while Casey recovered. With so many people at his place, Jacob had suggested Casey consider relocating to where he was staying. After all, William's mansion had several unused rooms available, perfect for a little peace and quiet. But Casey had been adamant about not being separated from her sisters while a threat existed, and he had not pursued the matter, especially since William had become so morose lately.

Meanwhile, Maggie and his house staff continued to devise ingenious ways to take the girls outside for short periods of time. Whenever they had an errand to run, they spirited away a small body with them, hidden under the dashboard disguised as a blanket. Having agreed on a two-hour time limit for the business part of these excursions, the staff let the girls use any extra time available for fun activities like visits to the playground for Robin or to a basketball court for Sam. Who would've thought Gregory played basketball? A couple of times, Margaret bundled up Casey and took her to Sunset Tai Chi on the Sound.

Those left at home kept busy with a multitude of library books provided by Mrs. Tucker. Once, Jacob came across a pile of books set out by the door, waiting to be returned. Thumbing through the titles, he realized Mrs. Tucker had selected stories in which insurmountable odds had been conquered as well as a couple of organic cookbooks for Sam, who had become Isadora's shadow in the kitchen. Together, they had set up the kitchen so recyclables could be disposed of efficiently. Isadora nowadays made organic choices when buying produce, and Jacob's love affair with junk food was now a faint memory.

Casey was the easiest to entertain. She took a couple of long naps every day. Mrs. Tucker or Margaret would rouse her to take her medication and encourage her to move around a bit. Samantha would serve her a meal before she went back to bed. Robin's job was to read her a story until she fell back to sleep. Little by little, naps shortened, and the time between them increased as Casey regained her strength.

Jacob watched and learned how to contribute to the household. One day, he brought home piles of crayons, markers, and coloring books. He cleared a table in the den for Robin and declared it her spot.

"Thank you very much," she said, fingering the markers. "I like these, but I don't need the coloring books right now."

"Robin!" admonished Casey. "That's not polite."

Robin's earnest voice derailed Jacob's pacifying response. "He doesn't mind. He wants to know why."

"Well, yeah. That's right." *How does she know that?*

"I only use coloring books when I'm sad. I don't have to think when I'm coloring inside the lines. It keeps me busy when things go wrong, and I need to feel better. And I don't need them right now."

"No problem. I got this. I'll be back in half an hour." Undaunted, Jacob strode out the door. He returned with a bag filled with drawing pads, colored paper, scissors, and glue. Delighted, Robin settled into her spot and busied herself with a creation.

"Hah!" He had triumphed.

Jacob enjoyed the memory as he drove toward home. *Home.* It had a totally different meaning lately. Energy and laughter filled the condo. His staff walked around with a bounce in their step. Everyone seemed to have adjusted well.

Except Sam, the enigma.

The middle sister participated in activities, read the books suggested, exercised, and basically did everything asked. But in the midst of it all, Jacob perceived an air of isolation about her. Her energy and buoyancy diminished as the days passed. Was this teenage-girl stuff or something else? But one thing he did know…. Sam's melancholy affected Robin.

The youngest fugitive spent most of her days skipping after Mrs. Tucker or playing on the computer. But whenever Sam entered the room, Robin changed, shoulders drooping and tone hushed, as if the middle sister's presence reminded her of the reality lurking outside the condo.

Jacob checked the time. If he hurried, he could get home before they dismantled today's obstacle course. One of these days, he was going to make it all the way through. If they could do it, so could he.

Besides, he had come up with an exceptional scheme for getting them all to the beach after dark this evening to witness the Perseids. The August sky put on this meteor shower spectacle every year. Tonight promised to be clear and warm, perfect for viewing the peak of the meteor shower. A night of wishing on falling stars would be the perfect thing for "his" family. Later, he would slip into William's house for a few hours of sleep then repeat his routine tomorrow.

This dual life could not last forever, but Jacob had decided to make the best of it for as long as it was fairly safe. Meanwhile, he prepared for the inevitable. With Maggie's permission, he opened a bank account in her name with an ATM card for Casey's anonymous use. Hopefully, Casey would always have access to funds.

Jacob also investigated real estate, searching for isolated vacation getaway cabins in the surrounding states. This would give Casey several options for hiding places, should they need it. He made sure each location was in the vicinity of a fair. Sooner or later, the girls would have to disappear, but now he'd be able to locate them again.

As it turned out, Sam had been wrong about him. Jacob actually was the family type.

Chapter 30
Forget the Fair

"Good morning, Jacob." William sounded cheerful as he came down for breakfast.

The sunny tone surprised him. "Good morning, yourself."

"I'm glad you're here, Jacob—"

"Oh, really?" The sardonic quip popped out before he could stop it.

"I don't mean I'm glad you're constantly fluttering around me like a midwife trying to deliver triplets." William irritably waved his hands in the air as he stalked toward the food on the sideboard. "I'm fine. Go home! Live your own life."

Jacob grinned as he took another bite. He felt pretty sunny himself. Things were going so well at his place, he sometimes forgot the girls were in hiding. He tried to picture William's face when he told him he was getting married.

For that matter, he could hardly wait to see Casey's expression when he asked her. She would say no, of course, because of her situation. *But I'm ready for that.* He chuckled as he fingered the ring box in his pocket.

"What's so funny?" asked William as he sat across from him.

Hanson appeared in time to move the salt out of William's reach. Ignoring William's glare, Hanson greeted Jacob with a nod.

Before William could get into it with Hanson, Jacob reminded him. "Why are you glad I'm here, sir?"

"What? Oh. The Skowhegan State Fair is coming up."

Jacob cringed inside. A jaunt to Skowhegan, Maine, usually lasted three days and included a hotel stay. That was a long time to be away from Casey, especially when he didn't know how much time they had together.

"The only day I can go is Monday. Are you free?" William looked at Jacob expectantly.

"Monday? Sir, we set up the preliminary meeting for the S&D merger in New York on Monday. It's too late to change it. I think we'll have to miss Skowhegan this year." What a shame. A trip to Skowhegan was just what William needed to get him out of his funk. Regrettable, yes, but it would give Jacob more time with Casey.

"Oh, that's right, the meeting. I do so hate to miss that fair again this year." William rested his elbow on the table and propped his chin in his palm.

Hanson stood behind Jacob. "If you would pardon me, sir," Hanson said with exaggerated politeness. "I believe I may have a solution."

"Yes, Hanson, what is it?" said a very innocent-sounding William.

Whoa. That was way too much nonchalance for one room. *What are these two up to?*

"Why don't *I* accompany you to the Skowhegan Fair, and Jacob can join you for the Renaissance Fair in October."

"Good idea, Hanson, that is, of course, if Jacob wouldn't feel put out. After all, it's a bit of a tradition, the two of us on an end-of-the-summer excursion to the fair."

"I'd love to go traipsing around with you, but that's a great idea. Why don't you go with Hanson? It would be a shame for you to miss it because of the meeting."

"Yes, that would be a shame, sir. But didn't you set up that meeting yourself?" Hanson asked William.

Jacob masked his resurging apprehension. *A mistake like that is not normal.* Was Hanson trying to tell him something?

"I suppose I did." William glared at Hanson as Jacob rose to refill his coffee. "Whatever was I thinking?"

"You've had a lot on your mind, William," Jacob said. "Anyone can make a mistake."

But William Hatch did not make mistakes like double-booking his schedule. Perhaps it was time to arrange another dinner date with Dr. Tujay. William's declining health was plain to see. He seemed to be thinner and paler with each passing day, and more irritable than ever. It had been almost a month since the incident at the hospital, and Jacob still didn't know what the tests had revealed.

Although lately, the old William seemed to be reemerging. An increased appetite; strolling around the grounds; getting fresh air and exercise. A trip to the fair was exactly what the old guy needed.

"If you're sure you don't mind—" said Jacob.

"Oh, no, not at all," William and Hanson chorused and then shot each other reproachful glances.

What's going on with them? The sound of the mail delivery diverted his attention. He'd have to figure this out later. He pushed back from the table. "All right, then. I should head to the office. Don't kill each other while I'm gone."

As Jacob sorted through the mail, he noticed another "please contact us" flyer from *Save the Children*. He had to hand it to them. Plain and simple stood out in a handful of colorful glossy competitors. *I need to show this to the Advertising Department and get their take on it.* He stuffed the mail into his pocket and left.

***

"What the hell were you trying to do?" hissed William at Hanson.

"Me? What about you? Could you have been any more obvious, *sir*?"

"All you had to do was offer to drive me to the fair after he realized there was a conflict. You didn't have to get theatrical. You upset him."

"I realize that. I certainly did not mean to," said Hanson. "I saw his face. Poor boy doesn't realize you scheduled the meeting so he wouldn't be able to come."

"Well, he's worried now, thanks to your big mouth. We can't tell him what's going on until my grandchildren are safe." Anxiety flared once again. William turned away to stare at the window sash. "I wish I knew why they haven't contacted us. Something must be wrong."

"They still don't realize the threat has been removed. Most likely they are hiding until the next rendezvous."

William brightened. "Of course. They've probably been traveling to Skowhegan all this time." He rubbed his hands together in anticipation, suppressing the worry that still clung to everything. "Just think. By Monday, this will all be over."

***

"Is this the last week of August?" Robin asked Casey.

"Mm-hmm," Casey murmured, enjoying a rare moment alone with her baby sister. Margaret had spirited Sam away to enjoy some time away from the condo. Casey sat with her arm around Robin's shoulder, examining Robin's pictures, astonished at how her skills had improved.

"Aren't we going to the fair this week?"

"Hmmm?" Absorbed in Robin's work, Casey half heard the question. Robin had some serious talent for someone so young, especially with faces. How Casey wished Robin was old enough to remember their parents clearly enough to draw them. They never kept photos when they moved in case they could be used against them. Having to leave everything behind when they went on the run was par for the course.

She picked up a drawing of a Ferris wheel. "This is an amazing picture, Tidbit." Casey marveled at its details.

"Are we?" persisted Robin.

She looked down on Robin's head, noticing the brown roots beneath the bleached blonde hair. "Are we what?"

"Are we going to the fair this week?"

"No, not this time."

"But we always see Grandpa in August and next week is September."

"You're right, sweetie, but we had to change our plans this year. Don't worry. I sent Grandpa a message so he knows."

Robin sat for a few minutes, digesting this information. "This doesn't feel right, Casey. What if Grandpa didn't get the message?"

She hugged the child close. "Sweetie, Grandpa knows. I even sent him a second message to firm up where to meet us."

"Where's that?" Robin's forehead creased.

"We're going to meet him at the Renaissance Fair here in Connecticut. Do you remember that one? You got to dress up in old-fashioned clothing? The one with knights on horse-back?"

"I remember." Robin bounced with excitement. "We went there when I was seven, and I got a turkey leg. Will GrandAna be there?"

"Oh, yes. A kissing booth is totally their style." Casey's gaze drifted. The mention of GrandAna's Kissing Booth brought Jacob to mind. He was so—

"Casey!"

She jolted out of her reverie. "I'm sorry, Tidbit. What did you say?"

"I said, when is that fair?"

"That one goes from the end of September to Columbus

Day Weekend in October."

Robin thought for a minute, her hands tightly clasped. "Casey, what was the fair we went to last year? You know, like now?"

"You mean in August? Umm, the Skowhegan Fair in Maine."

Squirming out of her embrace, Robin faced her on the couch. "We have to go to *that* fair, Casey. We have to see Grandpa right away."

"Robin, I told you I cancelled that fair. He's not going to be there."

Robin jumped up and cried, "Forget the fair. Can't we just go see Grandpa? How far away are we?"

"Robin, what is the matter with you? We *never* go to Grandpa's house!" To her shock, the child's eyes brimmed with tears, so she continued more gently. "He always meets us at a fair. Things are a little different right now, with us staying at Mr. Kent's place. We've had to make different plans. We're only staying here until I get better. Then things will go back to normal." *Normal?* The way they lived was anything but normal.

"Casey, *please*, let's just go see Grandpa. He *needs* us." Her first tears fell.

What would upset Robin so? They had never been too explicit about their situation because of her age, so Casey wasn't too sure what the eight-year-old understood.

"We'll see him at the Renaissance Fair in October," Casey said firmly. "Now, stop this."

Robin whirled around and ran out of the room, colliding with Jacob at the door.

"What's this?" he asked of the tear-stained face.

"Nobody listens to me!" wailed Robin, breaking free and running up the stairs.

Jacob checked Casey for a clue, but her deer-in-the-headlights pose conveyed she was as bewildered as he. They listened to the bedroom door slam shut behind Robin.

"Trouble in paradise?" He joined her on the couch.

"I don't know. Something is spooking Robin. I think we're going to need to make some changes soon." Sadness enveloped her.

"Don't do it, Casey," he murmured. "Don't disappear."

"I told you I can't promise that." Her heart ached, but there was nothing she could do about it. Reality had reared its ugly head.

For a moment, poor Jacob's face fell as his world fell apart. But only for a moment. He wrapped his arms around her as if his protective embrace could keep her safe.

"I understand, Casey. Tell me what you want me to do."

***

Chapter 31
Gotcha

"Gotcha!" cried Derrick Rivers to nobody in particular. He had put in too many hours chasing down worthless leads, most of which had been generated by the phone records from Cassie Thatcher's hospital room. Apparently, some of the hospital staff made unsanctioned private calls from the rooms of unconscious patients, but Derrick's perseverance had finally produced a real lead.

A phone call had been made from Cassie's room phone *after* she disappeared to the cell phone of one Margaret Fuller. A little research had identified her as an employee of William Hatch, specifically the executive assistant of none other than Jacob Kent, Hatch's right hand company man. Why would someone be calling Kent's assistant from the hospital room of Hatch's missing granddaughter? It was time to pay Mr. Kent and Ms. Fuller a call.

Ms. Fuller, it turned out, was on an unexpected vacation—to where, no one seemed to know. Derrick decided to check out the biz-wiz kid until she returned. A butler type rebuffed his door-to-door salesman routine at Kent's place. *So much for getting inside and snooping around.*

There sure was a lot of activity at the townhouse. After watching it from the anonymity of his vehicle, it seemed like every couple of hours, someone was coming or going.

He didn't mind the stakeout as long as it produced clues. He brushed veggie wrap crumbs away as he swigged his organic carrot juice, idly watching a car approach. Sitting up straight, he choked on misdirected juice. *This is a pretty strange place for Ms. Fuller to be vacationing,* he thought as she pulled into the driveway.

Perhaps he could approach one of the women when they were away from the apartment.

Be careful what you wish for. Derrick grinned as one of them exited from the front door and got into her car. Easing his vehicle into traffic at a safe distance, he cruised behind the conservative older sedan all the way to a toy store chain in Norwalk.

Aha! Derrick smirked. *Shopping for something for an eight-year-old, perhaps?*

***

Casey felt fairly safe, a dangerous mode for anyone on the run. Deep down, she knew the time had come to make the decision. Off the antibiotics and returning to normal, she had even resumed exercising. But Jacob's presence clouded her instincts. She was happy, and she didn't want it to end.

Nevertheless, they were prepared to disappear when the time came. And it would come. The next rendezvous did not require her to travel very far. The Renaissance Faire in Hebron was about ninety minutes away from Westport. Grandpa would meet them there and give them enough money to buy new IDs and make a new start. Together, they would plot out the subsequent rendezvous, and then she and the girls would vanish. No doubt disappearing would destroy her growing relationship with Jacob. It had always been inevitable, but was much more difficult to prepare for now.

When Gregory announced he had noticed a strange SUV outside, everyone went on alert. Better to be a safe paranoid than a naïve target. However, a suspicious door-to-door salesman knocking solely at their door transformed their daily excursions into a very bad idea. Mrs. Tucker, Gregory, Isadora, and Margaret continued their pattern of leaving and returning to allay suspicions, although without hidden passengers.

Were they being overly cautious? Perhaps, but now that Robin was beginning to spook, Sam was urging Casey to go. Still, she procrastinated, unwilling to give up her time with Jacob.

Then the day came when a black vehicle followed Mrs. Tucker.

They had waited too long.

***

Derrick strolled inside the well-lit toy store behind Mrs. Tucker. Too bad this was business. She was exactly his type—about forty, a little on the plump side, and wearing sensible shoes. Her face was shiny and pleasant, with big eyes. Too many women today valued the decorated-scarecrow image. He didn't see it. This was a much healthier style. For some reason, he wondered what she sounded like. *Stop getting distracted. Pay attention!*

"Excuse me, miss," he said in his most humble, benign voice, "Would you mind if I ask you a quick question?"

Mrs. Tucker turned toward Derrick, taking in his middle-aged, rumpled countenance as he held up two baby outfits.

"It's Mrs.," she answered stiffly. "Ask away."

Looking into her gray-blue eyes, a vague twinge of disappointment flickered in him. *Focus, Romeo.*

"Yes, uh, how important are the years on these things?" He waved the two outfits. "I'm picking up something for someone in my office who has a six-month-old."

Softening, she relaxed her stance. "It's confusing. The labels say three to six months, or six to nine months. Go for the larger one. The baby can grow into it."

"Thanks. I appreciate your help."

"You don't have any children?"

"Oh, no." He smiled. "Didn't quite seem fair."

"Not fair?"

"Well, first of all, I'm not married. And second of all...." Why did he feel like a tongue-tied teen? "Well, I guess there is no second of all when you're not married." He shrugged.

Face brightening, she steered him toward better-made brands. They chatted through the checkout counter and into the parking lot. When holding her there would become awkward, he reached out his hand to shake hers.

"My name is Derrick, by the way. I sincerely enjoyed making your acquaintance, Mrs...."

"Tucker. Helene Tucker. Well, good luck with the baby shower, and— Oh, my. How foolish of me. I can't believe I forgot to buy what I came in for." She shook his hand quickly, sounding a little breathless. "Please excuse me. It was very nice meeting you. Bye now." Spinning around, she darted back into the store.

Derrick stood there with his mouth open. He couldn't very well follow her back in. *Oh, well. This can still work out just fine.* He would sit in his car, wait for her to come out, and resume following her. In fact, it worked out better this way. If she didn't recognize his car, she wouldn't realize she had a tail.

He carefully placed his purchase in the trunk so it wouldn't get messed up before he gave it to his secretary. After all, she did have a six-month-old. He settled into his car to wait.

Mrs. Tucker, I hope your husband appreciates what a good thing he's got.

***

"Yes, officer, I'm sure." Inside the store, Helene Tucker

cupped her hand around her cell phone to muffle her call. She identified the make and model of Derrick's car for the police.

"I think he's selling drugs in the parking lot. You know, like one of those predators you see on TV."

She told him where Derrick's car was parked and hung up. She shook her head mournfully. "And he seemed like such a nice man."

***

Derrick spied Mrs. Tucker emerging from the store.

"Gotcha!" he said cheerfully.

As he started his car, a police cruiser pulled up in front of him, blocking his exit. A glance in the rearview mirror revealed a second cruiser behind his car.

What the hell?

***

From her car, Mrs. Tucker adjusted her rear view mirror so she could see Derrick Rivers being searched by the police.

"Gotcha!" she said with satisfaction and headed back to Westport.

She opened her cell phone and hit a speed dial code, a lump in her throat. "It's me. The coast is clear. He won't be back today. Tell the girls I said good luck and be safe."

***

Chapter 32
Disappearing is Easy

Casey and Margaret argued long and hard about whether to contact Jacob at his big business meeting in New York City. However, when Casey confessed she might not be able to make the decision to leave with him there, Margaret reluctantly agreed to break it to him when he got home.

So it was decided.

The girls disappeared into the bathrooms and emerged a couple of hours later, completely transformed. Three darker-haired boys had replaced three blonde girls. Robin sported light-auburn hair, Sam's hair was black, and Casey's, light-ash brown, compliments of Nice 'N Easy Hair Color. Dressed in unremarkable T-shirts and jeans and carrying old, faded sweatshirts, they bore no identifying logos or distinctive colors. The girls did a thorough sweep and cleared out any evidence of their presence, carrying everything with them, destined for the nearest public garbage can or Goodwill bin. They left the condo in the usual mode—one by one, hidden under blankets—to be driven to a nearby train station.

Sam was the first to sneak out, chauffeured by Gregory. She remained hidden the entire trip to the Stamford Goodwill Store, listening to the butler heave repeated sighs. She waited while he dropped off their new clothing, packed into three garbage bags, remnants of their temporary life together. From there, he drove her closer to the train station. They waited until a Mack truck parked next to them before she slipped out of the car. The sound of his vehicle pulling away accompanied her as she briskly headed for the stairs without a backward glance.

Sometime later, Isadora headed for the grocery store with Casey hidden away in the backseat. After parking, the cook paused for a moment to check herself in the mirror. She made no sign of noticing the back door softly opening or closing. Touching a tissue to the corner of her eye, she gave a huge, tremulous sigh, flipped back her hair, and exited the car.

The last one to leave was Robin. Buried under blankets, she rode with Margaret to the Westport train station. They slid out of the car separately and walked to the platform. Robin stood next to a family with three children, and Margaret stood behind her, reading a book.

The train arrived, and everyone boarded. Robin took a seat next to the children. Margaret stood in the aisle by the door, still reading. At the next stop, Casey got on. She drifted between Margaret and Robin, looking like a bored and sleepy teenage boy. Ignoring her, Robin began to color in one of her coloring books, focusing on staying inside the lines.

Without a backward glance, Margaret got off the train at the next stop. As other people entered the train, Casey sat across the aisle from Robin and continued to idly read the signs posted on the wall.

Robin did not acknowledge Casey, but watched Margaret's back until she disappeared. As the train lurched forward, Robin set her features and resumed coloring inside the lines. Anyone glancing at her would see a small boy with nothing better to do than to color while on a train trip. They wouldn't notice the sad eyes or pale face Margaret had glimpsed before she left.

Margaret knew Casey and Robin would get off the train together at another stop. Nevertheless, once she could no longer hear the train's rumble in the distance, her tears began to flow.

Disappearing was easy. Finding people to love was not.

***

Chapter 33
They're Not Here

Jacob was doing an unavoidable sardine imitation on a New York City train platform, trying, like the other sardines, to board the next train to Connecticut. His meeting had lasted a lot longer than anticipated, so instead of leaving the city during the early afternoon as planned, he had ended up in rush-hour traffic.

As another train rumbled out of the station without him, he raised his phone over his head, searching for a signal. Realizing even if he could get through, he still wouldn't be able to hear anything anyway, he decided to put it away. As he lowered his arm, the jostling of the crowd amped up in anticipation of yet another train. Someone knocked Jacob's arm, and his cell phone flew out of his hand. It bounced off a man's shoulder and disappeared under the feet of the crowd.

Jeez, I don't believe it. He groaned.

He had no hope of retrieving the phone. Even if he could touch it with his foot, the crowd was too tight to bend over to pick it up. *It's as good as gone. Maggie will have to order me another one.* Fortunately, he kept his phone synched with his laptop. He clutched his briefcase closer to his chest.

The next train opened its doors, and Jacob managed to graduate from being a mere sardine on the platform to being a sardine in a can. He settled in for the ride, pressed against strangers. By the time they reached Stamford, the crowd had thinned considerably, but not enough for him to find a seat.

Man, am I lucky I don't have to do this every day, he thought as he debarked.

Twenty minutes later, he crept toward home along the highway with the top dropped on his convertible. Although he tried to appreciate the sunset, a vaguely uncomfortable feeling kept cropping up in the center of his chest. He pushed it aside, attributing it to rush-hour impatience.

Two hours later, his entire world crashed.

***

William and Hanson arrived two hours ahead of the long-awaited appointment at the Skowhegan Fair. Casey always had them meet someplace where William could sit down. They posted an encrypted message at The Kissing Booth and then wandered around for a while before settling at the tables by the concessions. Unwilling to face what he already knew, William barely glanced at the activity around them.

Hanson, on the other hand, was restless and talkative. "How are you going to tell them they can come out of hiding? I can hardly wait to see their faces. It's been too long since I've seen them. Miss Robin was only seven, and now she's going into the third grade. And Miss Casey...."

William was staring into space when it registered that Hanson's voice had died away. He looked at the man who had become more of a friend and confident than an employee. It was most fitting that he'd be here today.

"What is it, sir?" Hanson asked.

"I don't know, old friend," William almost whispered. His chest ached. "I don't have a good feeling about this. They're running away from some place, but I don't think they're headed here."

"Nonsense! You are simply feeling the long ride. Next time, we'll break it into a two-day trip."

He could no longer deny it. Time to face what his heart was trying to tell him. "They're not here, Reginald."

"But how can you say that? We both check the mail every day. There's been no message. And we still have twenty minutes until the rendezvous."

"I feel it. I've been trying to ignore it, but I can't. They're not here, and I don't know how to contact them anymore."

"Just wait, sir. You'll see." Hanson shot off the bench, his face pale. "I'll get you a cool drink, and you'll feel better. You'll see. There is nothing to worry about. You'll see. You'll see." Hanson hurried off to the nearest concession stand.

The purpose of his friend's words had not been to convince William, but to convince himself. It did not work. He could see Hanson at the concession stand, staring at the drinks in his hand, forgetting the line of customers behind him. *Hanson knows.* Every now and then, William would "get a feeling," and, whether he ignored it or not, it was always right.

An overwhelming wave of sadness swept through him, leaving him weak. *What do I do now?*

***

Jacob sensed something was wrong the minute he stepped into his condo. It was too quiet.

"Sir." Gregory approached hesitantly, glancing over his shoulder.

Behind him Mrs. Tucker and Isadora walked into the room, their faces red and puffy, watching Jacob.

He knew. Without them saying a word, he knew. He recognized it in their deep sorrow.

"Oh no," moaned Jacob. "No, no, no, no!" He bolted up the stairs shouting, "Casey!" He dashed toward her room, praying she was there. *"Casey!"* Flinging open the door revealed a view of his room, not her room. He ran to the dresser, jerking open a drawer with such force, it slid free and fell to the floor.

Nothing. The bedroom had been completely stripped of her presence. A change of clothes for Jacob covered the pillow where she had laid her head.

"*Samantha!*" Turning on his heel, he dashed to the girls' bedroom. "*Robin!*"

The door crashed open under the force of his desperation, revealing a tearful Margaret sitting on the bed with some library books. There was no evidence of the girls other than the little recycling trashcans in each room.

"Jacob. Mr. Kent—"

He strode over to her, and, grabbing her by the arms, pulled her to her feet. "Where are they, Margaret? Where did they go?"

As she shook her head helplessly, he released her and ran out to the landing again.

"*Casey!* Sam! Robin...." Jacob couldn't stop going through the motions, but he no longer expected a response.

Margaret came to stand behind him. She tentatively put a hand on his arm. As he sank down on the top step and cradled his head, she whispered what he had been dreading.

"They're not here, my dear. They're not here."

Chapter 34
Watching the Empty Nest

"All right, what happened?" asked Jacob as he walked into the kitchen. The others had gathered there in silence, waiting for him to collect himself.

Gregory pulled a stool over to the island so he could join them. Isadora brought him a cup of tea. By unspoken consensus, Margaret described the events that had transpired. The most difficult part was hearing Casey's request he not be told of their decision to leave, but he listened without comment, staring at his cup. He reached over to squeeze Mrs. Tucker's hand when Margaret described how she had gotten rid of the man who had been watching them. Margaret concluded with the details of how she had left Robin in Casey's care and fell silent.

Jacob cleared his throat and stood. "Well, we'll just have to find them." He started to leave the kitchen.

"But, Jacob—Mr. Kent," said Margaret, "they don't want to be found."

"They're my family now, Maggie, and I'm not going to lose them." He headed for the door, but paused before leaving the kitchen. "One thing I've learned from these past few weeks, I've been too narrow in my definition of the word 'family.' I always defined it by the TV shows I watched when I was a kid because I didn't have a family of my own. But *family* is the people who care for you, and you care for...like the four of you." He inclined his head toward them. "You honor me," he said, and left.

He had no expectations of hearing from The Herd, but now that he had access to a phone once again, he sat in his bedroom and checked his messages. Any glimmer of hope was soon dispelled. Hanson had left the one message of con-sequence, informing him he and William would be spending the evening in a hotel because the day's events had tired them. Hanson sounded as depleted as Jacob felt.

Jacob sat staring into space at the place where Casey had slept. The change of clothes which had been left out for him almost seemed like an attempt to erase the past and focus him on the present. Well, that wasn't happening. *I'm not pretending you weren't here.*

Restless, he stood up and raked his hands through his hair. *What to do? What to do?* He aimlessly walked around the room, eventually leaving it to wander around his home. Every room held a memory—the girls beating him on an ob-stacle course, Robin showing him her pictures, Sam hovering over him as he tasted her newest culinary experiment, nightly karaoke, setting up his place for recycling, the kids jumping on the bed to that ridiculous song on the day he realized they were girls…. He shoved his hands into his pockets and fin-gered the ring box that had burned a hole there for the past few weeks.

Casey. Her presence was everywhere, in every room. Each corner he turned provided fresh pain. He opened the door to her room and sat down. He had to believe he would find her again. He just didn't know when.

Or how.

Or where.

Jeez! He had to either get out of the condo or go crazy. Stuffing the clothes from the bed into his overnight bag, he headed downstairs.

"I'll be at Mr. Hatch's place," he shot at Gregory on his way out the door. "You can reach me there."

The door slammed behind him, and, like The Herd of Girls, he was gone.

***

Get a grip, Kent. Get a grip. Jacob forced the mantra through his head. He should be glad they were gone if it meant their safety, but the onslaught of his own, very personal loss consumed him. Casey was his love and his future. She had always affected him, ever since the beginning. But how had the other two wormed their way into his heart so fast?

As Jacob negotiated the street leading to the Hatch estate, he squinted at a utility van parked on the side of the road. Yesterday, it seemed like the neighbors were getting an awful lot of work done. Today it occurred to him he was being watched.

Once inside, he carried a phone to the kitchen sink, and, while running the water, dialed the police. Taking a cue from Mrs. Tucker, he reported a suspicious van that appeared to be dealing drugs. He then ran upstairs to peer through the drapes overlooking the street. With no little satisfaction, he watched the van peel away. If they *were* watching him, it probably meant they did not yet realize the girls were on the move.

On the other hand, what if he wasn't being watched? Perhaps the van leaving moments before the police arrived was a coincidence. Maybe he needed to get a serious grip on his paranoia. And ease up on the spy movies.

Jacob awoke with a groggy start. *This is weird.* For starters, it was dawn and he was still in his clothes. And sleeping in a chair in William's County Fairs Commando Center. He gingerly straightened up as the previous day's events came flooding back. *Oww!* His arm was asleep.

He had wandered in here last night, the vast data bank on fairs making him feel closer to Casey. *Owww!* This morning, his neck regretted that decision. As he rolled his head to appease it, an earlier conversation with Robin popped into his mind.

"This is where you sleep?" she asked, patting his pillow. "Right here?"

He nodded. "Yup."

"On *this* pillow?"

He laughed then. "Yes, ma'am, right there, on *that* very pillow and no other."

"Why do you keep going to sleepovers with your friend instead of having a sleepover with us?"

At the time, the idea of a sleepover with The Herd had made Jacob's toes curl. Now he would like nothing better. Shaking the pins and needles out of his arm, he grinned as he imagined what Robin would say about where he had spent the night. Moving like an old man, he rose from the chair that had hosted him all night. He rubbed his face briskly and smacked his cheeks a couple of times.

It was true. Things really did look brighter by the light of day. Casey and her little family weren't gone. They were temporarily displaced. Jacob had made it his mission to find Casey at fairs for years. Why should he stop now? All he had to do was to figure out where they would go, and meet them. If push came to shove, he always had Plan B.

He wandered into the kitchen to make himself a cup of coffee. Twenty minutes later, the startled cook found him there, staring out the window holding a coffee filter in his hand, deep in thought. Loosening the filter from Jacob's grip, the cook finished making the coffee and added the grounds to the new compost bin while he paced, mulling over possibilities.

Nearly every time he encountered Casey at a fair, he had been on a trip with William. He didn't have to do a statistical analysis to figure out they had similar tastes in fairs. Perhaps examining William's data might provide a clue as to where to head next.

Thanking the cook, he headed back toward the drawing room, blowing on his coffee. He stood in the doorway and surveyed the room. This was great. He had everything he needed right here.

Jacob paced around the room, studying William's layout. Funny, but after all of these years of chauffeuring William to fairs, Jacob had never been curious as to how he picked them. Did he go through all this effort every time?

He froze in the middle of the room, lips still pursed for another cooling breath for his coffee. *Jeez!* He made a quick sweep of the room, taking in the level of detail and attention this one project had garnered. A different kind of alarm rippled through him. *Oh, no.*

This was too much, way too much. He was not viewing a simple project. It was an obsession, and it looked like it was draining the life out of William. His old friend and mentor was gradually unraveling, and he had been too self-absorbed to notice.

First things first, as William would say. He made a direct line to the computer. *Right now, I need to locate the girls and make sure they're safe. I'll tend to William when he gets home tonight.*

Accepting the cook's offer to be served where he worked, Jacob rolled up his rumpled sleeves.

"What is it with the men in this house and fairs?" the cook muttered as she left the room.

A few hours later, Hanson called to inform him William wanted to attend the fair one more day, and they would be home tomorrow. Elated, he wished them a good time and rang off. He took a much-needed stretch and then rubbed his hands together. They had just granted him another twenty-four hours to figure out Casey's destination before William reclaimed his commando center.

***

The next day Margaret arrived at the Hatch estate in search of Mr. Kent. She was shown to the drawing room where her disheveled boss working feverishly. She wrinkled her nose. He wore the same clothes he had worn to the meeting in New York two days earlier, and his hair stuck out in a variety of directions. She waited for him to reach a stopping place and then realized he didn't know she was there.

"Mr. Kent."

Despite her soft words, a startled expression flashed across his face. He jumped up and rushed toward her. A flicker of alarm shot through her as he grabbed her and clamped a hand over her mouth. She stiffened and began to struggle.

"Hi, Maggie." His calm voice was a stark contrast to his wild behavior. "Here, read this." He mouthed *please* at her. He was begging her to recognize something, but what?

"Whaddya think?" he asked, emphatic nods cuing her understanding. Tentatively, she nodded back, and he loosened his grip. She relaxed, conveying he could let go. Releasing her, he put a finger to his lips.

"Well, I'd have to see more before I could say anything." Judging from the pleased look lighting up his face, she'd said the right thing.

"Fine. No problem." He drew her over to a chair near him. "Here's the rest. I'll wait until you read it."

Sitting opposite her, he started scrawling on a pad. Her heart thumped as she took the pad from him. For about twenty minutes, they punctuated the silence with comments befitting their role-playing while they communicated undetected on paper. Finally, she patted him on the arm and stood up.

"Where is Mr. Hanson?" she asked. "And Mr. Hatch?"

"They decided to stay at the fair one more day." He grinned weakly at her. "I hope *they're* having a good time."

"I see. I'll be going now, unless there is something you need brought to the office."

He shook his head.

"Very well. And at what time shall we expect you for dinner? Isadora was quite upset when you didn't show up last night." She grasped his hand to make sure he understood her point.

Jacob got it. "I'll be there on time tonight. Not to worry."

"Thank you, Gregory," said Margaret as he relieved her of her things. "Please call Isadora so I can tell her what Mr. Kent wants for dinner." Margaret gestured wildly as she spoke, pantomiming for Mrs. Tucker to silently follow her. "I'll be in the TV room."

Gregory nodded his understanding and headed for the kitchen as the two women entered the den. By the time he and Isadora joined them, the news blared in the background while Mrs. Tucker read her boss's note.

Trying to figure out how to find the girls. Both houses are being watched so it might mean they don't know they've left. Following the same routine as if the girls are here. They might be listening in. Use background noise with discussions. Destroy all notes. Be safe.

Gregory checked to make sure everyone understood then lit a match under the note. After processing Jacob's message, the four conspirators took to role-playing like they had been born to it.

"Very well, Ms. Fuller. Mr. Kent shall have his stroganoff tonight. Thank you for letting me know," said Isadora with a sparkle. As she made to leave, Gregory and Mrs. Tucker slid through the door with her. Margaret settled back on the couch with her pad, ignoring the talking reptile in the insurance commercial.

That evening, Jacob joined them for dinner, bearing assignments for each one. Assembled in the kitchen with the radio playing dinner music for cover, he explained.

They were to maintain the established pattern of comings and goings. If someone believed the girls were here, Jacob wanted to keep their attention as long as possible. Meanwhile, on their days off, they would be taking the train to a variety of destinations. There they would make cash withdrawals from the ATM account he had set up for Casey. If someone were to access the account records, they would not be able to distinguish Casey's withdrawal location from the others. Hopefully, when she checked the account online, it could yield at least one emergency use with minimal risk.

After dinner, he headed back to William's house and the county fairs' headquarters. Time was running out, and he had a huge puzzle to solve before it did.

Chapter 35

The Trail

The last few years had been interesting for Margaret, to say the least. In the middle of the hostile takeover of her former company, she'd first met Mr. Hatch posing as a craggy deliveryman. Her former boss had become more unglued as the inevitable loomed closer, leaving it to her to single-handedly keeping everything afloat.

After the transition, she had been reassigned as the executive assistant to a former part-time chauffeur barely out of college. A promotion or a demotion? She couldn't tell, but she still had a job, which was more than most could say. When youthful Mr. Kent began by asking her what an executive secretary did, she assumed she had been saddled with another version of ineptitude. She was so wrong.

Her intensely focused fledgling boss learned how to use her skills and proceeded to launch a business skyrocket which had no end in sight. As she recognized the genius in him, it warmed her soul that Mr. Hatch had acknowledged her skills by assigning her to this position.

Mr. Kent was a loner with no family, clueless about the unwavering loyalty he created in those around him. Even Reginald Hanson, who seemed to tolerate no one except Mr. Hatch, cared for the young man.

Frustrated, Margaret sat with Mr. Kent's house staff as they tarried over coffee in the kitchen. She hated this helpless feeling. It was unfortunate Mr. Hanson wasn't there. He would be such a comfort at a time like this.

Isadora passed the sugar and cream, the unhappy expression in her brown eyes reflecting what they all were feeling.

Shielded by music, and the sounds of the dishwasher,

Margaret felt free to talk softly as they shared a hot drink. "You know, when I went over to Mr. Hatch's place today, the funniest thing happened." She smiled sadly. "I turned on my car, and the next thing I knew, my stereo was playing one of the girls' favorite songs."

Gregory raised his head, cleared his throat, and reached for the sugar. "You mean, on the radio?"

"No, on one of the CDs they burned for us." She half smiled. "I guess they didn't get to dispose of *everything* before they left."

"Me, too. They left a CD in my car." Gregory stared into space as he stirred sugar into his coffee. "I thought it was odd they had missed it."

Margaret paused mid sip. *I'll say it's odd. They are not careless people.*

"Maybe it wasn't an accident," said Isadora. "Maybe it was a present."

"Nice thought, but not likely." Gregory added more sugar. "Too risky."

"We just weren't as thorough as we thought." Mrs. Tucker paused to sip. "It seems like I keep bumping into things that remind me of the little dears."

"I know what you mean," said Isadora. "Sam left bookmarks in some of my cookbooks." She traced the rim of her cup with her finger. "The things that girl found interesting."

They fell silent, each lost in their own private memories of their temporary guests.

After a few moments, Gregory cleared his throat and addressed Mrs. Tucker. "By the way, one of the library books got left behind. I can drop it off for you on my day off if you'd like."

"Thank you, Gregory. I'd appreciate that." She stared at the steam rising from her cup. "Which one was it?"

"Casey, the Utterly Impossible Talking Horse."

They chuckled together at the irony of the title and once again lapsed into silence, but an odd excitement began building inside Margaret.

"Funny that was the one left behind, eh?" Gregory frowned as he reached for the sugar once more. As Mrs. Tucker nodded in response, Isadora stopped his hand. "Gregory, you don't take sugar in your coffee."

"Hmmm?" He looked down at his cup as if he didn't recognize it.

So, he was feeling it, too. Margaret had to know. "Isadora, what things did Sam find interesting?"

"Oh, she looked up the weight of a cooking skillet in one book. Did you know people throw them? In a competition? In another book—"

"Where do they compete, Isadora?" Mrs. Tucker banged her cup into the saucer.

"At fairs and such." Isadora held a napkin to her mouth, her eyes wide.

A chill went down Margaret's arms. *Oh, my.*

They sat quietly in the kitchen staring at each other.

"Okay, we're all thinking it. I'm just going to say it." Gregory whispered. "Are these clues? Are they trying to tell us something?"

They looked from one to another for an answer they did not have.

"Don't be silly." The hope blooming on Mrs. Tucker's face negated her words. A responding smile spread across Isadora's face. Margaret stood and began to pace.

"Do you really think they want to tell us how to track them?" Isadora whispered as she looked nervously over her shoulder.

"Who knows?" hissed Mrs. Tucker. "Who cares? Doing

something is better than sitting around wondering." She turned toward Margaret with an unspoken question.

She stopped pacing. "I agree." She put a finger to her lips. "If we're right, they're depending on us to be clever. Make a list of everything you've noticed. Every detail. Keep your eyes open and stay sharp."

The others nodded.

"Isadora, see what's on the pages Sam marked. Get page numbers or anything else that might have a sequence."

"Have you listened to your CD all the way through?" Gregory asked.

Margaret shook her head.

"Neither did I. We should do that first. And, if you can, make a note of what song or verse was playing when the car started."

Margaret nodded and held up her hand. "Do you think we should tell Mr. Kent?"

The four shared anxious glances.

Gregory slowly shook his head. "I don't believe so. Not until we are positive."

Isadora and Mrs. Tucker nodded their agreement.

"I'll check to see if they left me a CD, too." Mrs. Tucker veered toward the door. "Then I'm going to go back over this place with a fine-tooth comb."

"All right, then." Isadora began pulling cookbooks off the shelf.

Margaret needed to retrieve the CD from her car. "Let's meet back here in one hour."

Sixty minutes later they stood around the kitchen table huddled up like a football team. Before them, spread across the tabletop, were the fruits of their labor—an assortment of objects and notes. Were they clues or coincidences? With renewed hope, the triumphant huddle decided it was time to call Mr. Kent. Three pairs of eyes gleamed at Margaret as she reached for the phone. The goose bumps had returned.

They were back in the game!

***

William's cook approached Jacob again after lunch had been cleared. "Excuse me, sir—"

Without glancing up, Jacob cut her off. "I'm fine, thanks."

"Yes, sir. I mean, no, sir."

At Jacob's puzzled glance, she whispered, "Sir, there is a call for you. On *my* cell phone." She handed him the phone. "She *told* me to whisper."

He leaped to his feet, heart pounding as he reached for the phone. "Casey?" he whispered as the cook hurried from the room. To his colossal disappointment, Maggie's excited voice replied. He sank back into his chair.

"Jacob, Mr. Kent, we think they left us a message. We kept running into things that reminded us of them, and when we put them together, it's obvious...we think."

"There's a message?" he asked as he leapt to his feet.

"No, not exactly. It's a set of clues, but we think we can piece something together. You need to go through your routine and see if they left anything for you."

His thoughts strayed to his conversation with Robin about where he slept. "I'll check around here, but give my bed a once-over, especially my pillow. Call me right back."

Carrying his clothes back and forth for the past couple of weeks was now part of his routine. He dumped out his packed bag and rummaged through it. Nothing.

Sitting back on his haunches, he retrieved the clothes he had flung to the side.

Crackle.

It came from his jacket pocket. Holding his breath, he pulled out the *Save the Children* advertisement he had meant to leave at the office. Disappointed, he crumpled it and hurled it at the wall. He shook out a pair of pants, and something fluttered to the floor. Jacob grabbed at the small white paper. A partially filled-out Sudoku puzzle sheet? *I don't do Sudoku puzzles.* Exhilaration bubbled up inside him as the phone rang.

"Yes?" he whispered.

"You were right," said Margaret. "I found a small ceramic robin hidden in your pillowcase. You were probably supposed to find it when you went to bed."

"What else?"

"Oh, I don't think we should discuss this over the phone."

"You're right. I'm heading your way."

He hung up, trying not to get his hopes raised prematurely but it was difficult to contain himself. He strode around the command center gathering up his work, stuffed his clothes back into his bag, returned the cook's cell phone, and left. He had his own Commando Center to set up.

Jacob's "team" was busy working in what was formally known as his dining room. His computer and a CD player had been moved in, and maps hung on the walls. Gregory had posted a sheet of large paper, one for each fair under consideration. Isadora followed him, recording dates and locations. From the computer, Mrs. Tucker provided them with information.

"Wow! You've been busy. What have we got?" He handed the Sudoku puzzle to Mrs. Tucker. She grabbed a pencil and settled in a corner to work on it.

Margaret turned up the music and then referred to her ever-present pad. "First, let's talk about the CDs left in our cars. They weren't the ones the girls listened to. We think they were specially designed as clues. Each one has several versions of a single song, over and over. Since none of us are musically inclined, we assumed the clue must be in the lyrics, title, or artist."

"Tell him about mine!" cut in Mrs. Tucker.

"I was just getting to that." Margaret turned to Jacob. "The song is about Mrs. Tucker and Sam—she goes and gets him on Saturday night."

Gregory and Isadora paused to watch Jacob as he absorbed this piece of info. Gregory reached over to the CD player and started a song by The Manhattan Transfer called "Ray's Rockhouse."

"Do we know which Saturday?"

"No," said Gregory.

"Maybe we do." Mrs. Tucker beckoned them over with her hand. "Here are the numbers from the Sudoku puzzle."

They gathered around to view her work.

9 1 2 1 3 1 4 1 5 2 2

"Is it a date?" asked Isadora.

"No, too many numbers," answered Jacob.

"Not if it includes the time," Isadora said, pointing to the paper. Mrs. Tucker took out a fresh paper and handed it to her. Isadora slid into the chair next to her, and they got to work.

"Maggie, what was your song?" Jacob asked.

"'Walk Like an Egyptian' by The Bangles." She raised her palms. "I know there's a clue there, but I can't figure out what it is. I looked up the lyrics online. There's a reference to police and doughnuts, but nothing jumps out at me. I don't think they want us to call the police."

"Okay, we'll hold that one aside until later. Hey, see if there are any fairs with kissing booths at them."

She nodded and slid behind the computer.

He clapped his butler on the shoulder. "Gregory, what else do we have?"

"Sam marked some pages in Isadora's cookbooks. At first Isadora thought they were favorite recipes, but it's more like a collection of random facts. Then she noticed all the recipes she marked were winners at county fairs."

A grin spread across Jacob's face. "That sounds like a nudge to me."

"That's not all, sir. Sam also earmarked iron skillets, several times in different books. One of them had a picture of a skillet torn from a magazine." Gregory shook his head. "She's telling us something, but we can't figure out what."

Frustrated, Jacob sat back. "I guess we'll set *that* one aside for now, too." He fingered the little robin that had been left on his pillow, trying to piece it all together. What did it mean? Something? Nothing?

"Ooh, I think we got it!" cried Isadora. "If we're doing this right, it's September 12, 13, 14, and 15. It's a lot of numbers because it's several dates, not a time."

"Are you sure?" asked Jacob as the others came over.

"Well, if we insert a zero into the empty boxes, this is the number sequence." Mrs. Tucker showed him their paper.

0 9 1 2 1 3 1 4 1 5 2 0 0 2

"I see it!" Jacob tried to calm his excitement. "2002 jumps right out at you." He rubbed his hands as he stared at the wall. "Gregory, what do we have for fairs from September 12th to the 15th?"

Gregory hurried around the room snatching specific papers off the wall. Returning to the table, he spread them out. Margaret reached over and rearranged them by states.

"But which day?" asked Gregory.

"Why, Saturday. From my song," beamed Mrs. Tucker.

They stood around the table and read the choices, not knowing where to go next.

"Margaret, did you find any with kissing booths?" Isadora asked.

"Dead end," she replied.

"Well," said Mrs. Tucker, "I guess we'd better research each of these and see if we can dig up some more clues."

"Fine. Start with that fair," he said pointing at Four Town Fair. He had four people working with him on this. Why not?

Moments later, Margaret had it up on the monitor. The others crowded around to peer over her shoulder.

"What do we look for?" Mrs. Tucker expressed their thoughts.

"I'll start at the top." Margaret clicked on *Events*.

"Maggie, your song!" shouted Jacob, pointing to the fair's address on the screen: *56 Egypt Road (off Rt. 83) Somers, CT.*

"'Walk Like an Egyptian,'" Margaret cried, clapping her hands.

"Look, look, look!" Isadora shook Margaret's shoulder in her excitement. "They have a women's skillet-throwing contest."

"A *what*? You've got to be kidding." Gregory thumped Jacob on the back. "Oh, this is it. This has *got* to be it!"

"Oh, it's *definitely* the one." Jacob held up the little ceramic robin. He put it in his palm and turned it over. The bottom held half of an inscription. The rest had been filed away, but the visible portion read: *Made in Somers.*

Five pairs of eyes returned to the address of the fair on the screen.

"Guess I'm going to Somers on Saturday, the fourteenth." Jacob put an arm around Margaret and squeezed.

Gregory clasped Margaret and Isadora's hands. Isadora and Mrs. Tucker hugged each other in jubilation, while the unflappable Margaret hopped up and down.

"By the way, what song did they leave you, Gregory?" asked Jacob.

"A song by Aerosmith," Gregory chortled. "'Dude (Looks Like a Lady).'"

"Ahh, our Herd of Girls is disguised as a Bevy of Boys," giggled Mrs. Tucker.

"Mr. Kent, what was your song?" asked Margaret.

"'Wipe Out,' by the Safaris." Jacob sobered as he named the song the girls played when running through the obstacle courses. No doubt about that message. From their expressions, the others had drawn the same conclusion. It was a clear warning to be careful.

Chapter 36

Wipeout!

Heart pounding, Jacob stepped out of his car as he scanned the fair on the far side of the parking lot. What if he had misinterpreted the clues and was at the wrong place?

As with many country fairs, the parking lot was no more than an abused pasture. This one was almost the size of two football fields. Fair employees decked in bright yellow directed the early trickle of cars to their temporary berths. Jacob ignored them, choosing instead a parking spot near the exit. The possibility of needing a quick getaway outweighed a pimply teen's attempts to redirect him.

The rides twirled and spun above and around the strolling families. Despite the morning sun, the lights flashed merrily, beckoning to young and old. At ten in the morning there wasn't much of a crowd. This was as good a time as any to review the plan.

First, he would walk through the fair to familiarize himself with the layout they had printed out. Then he would adjust the escape route to where he parked the car. After assessing the grounds, he'd plant himself somewhere along the concourse and watch the crowd. That's how he had always found Casey in the past, and that's how he was going to find her today.

A voice came over the loudspeaker, momentarily dimming the carnival noise. "Would the owner of a red ford pickup truck, license plate DAG537, please return to your vehicle? Your lights are on."

Jacob tensed. Was that some kind of clue? He looked over the parking lot. No, he could see the lights of the red truck from here. He smiled ruefully as a portly balding man, radiating exasperation, marched toward the older truck.

Get a grip, Kent. Intellectually, he acknowledged he and his team could have pieced together a bunch of randomly forgotten objects into a fantastical story, but emotionally, he couldn't help but believe the items they collected served an ultimate purpose. If The Herd was here, he was going to find them. He also knew if he wasn't careful, he could spend the entire day jumping at shadows and following dead ends.

Like that little commotion over by the edge of the fair. To his over-active imagination, that simple game of tag resembled a child the size of Robin trying to escape from the evil clutches of—

"Ha Ha Ha Ha Ha Ha Ha, WIPEOUT!" sang out over the loudspeaker.

His head jerked up. As the pounding drums from the familiar song drowned out the carnival music, all doubt was erased. In this surreal moment, the same song they had used for obstacle course training piped out like background music in a movie. The loudspeaker was sending out a warning.

His eyes darted back toward the commotion he had noticed. *That's no game of tag.* That was a child trying to escape a man in hot pursuit. Jacob couldn't be positive at this distance, but the kid moved like Robin. With his heart in his throat, he broke into a run, zigzagging between cars, trying to intercept the youngster fleeing toward the other side of the lot. This was no movie track. This was reality, where a real menace was gaining on his small victim. Caught in his own nightmare, Jacob was watching Robin run for her life, and he was still too far away to help.

As the predator and prey crossed the area between the fair and the parking lot, the longer legs of the adult closed the gap between them, but once they reached the cars, the advantage became hers. Robin's small size and training put some distance between them as she dodged around vehicles. However, her constant change of direction made it difficult for Jacob and his burning lungs to maintain a course of interception.

Good girl! She was trying to head back toward the fair. Silently applauding Robin's decision to get closer to a populated area, Jacob altered his course accordingly.

So did Robin's pursuer.

With one swift maneuver, her stalker clambered up and over two pickup trucks, landing an arm's length away. Skidding, Robin veered around another vehicle with the man on her tail. As Jacob frantically tried to reach her, what looked like a brunette Sam suddenly popped out from behind a car and neatly took the man out with one magnificent sweep of a skateboard to the head.

Where did she come from? Stunned, Jacob skidded to a stop, wheezing for breath. He rested his hands on his head as he tried to calm the burning in his shoulders.

With a quick high-five, the sisters raced back to the fair. Jacob tried in vain to get their attention, but he hadn't quite recovered enough breath to formulate sounds louder than gasps. Here he was, a complete wreck, but they were able to *run* off.

He bent in half, hands on his knees, as he tried to ease a painful stitch in his side. *And I was going to rescue them?* He would have chuckled if he could breathe. *What was I thinking?*

Recovering somewhat, he trotted over to the man staggering to his feet. With rage marshaling all of his strength, Jacob drew back and smashed his fist into the man's face. The unexpected pain radiating up his forearm was nothing compared to the satisfaction of making Robin's assailant drop like an anchor.

Shaking the ache out of his hand, Jacob aimed a vindictive

kick at the guy's ribs. Ordinarily, he might have qualms about hitting a man when he was down, but when it came to someone threatening his girls, those thoughts were nonexistent.

Satisfied the man no longer posed a danger, Jacob took off in the direction he had seen the two disappear, trying to calm the fear rising in his chest. He doubted the man laid out in the parking lot had come alone. It went without saying Casey would draw the same conclusion. The girls would be getting ready to disappear. *I have to find The Herd before they do.*

Sunlight glinted off the speaker perched atop a telephone pole. Jacob skidded to a stop and stared at it. *Of course.* When Robin had been trying to escape, that same speaker had been blasting out "Wipeout," but now it pumped innocuous carnival music. It was time to stop believing in coincidences. Someone at the fair must be helping them. If he could reach that person, he'd be able to find the fugitives. He took off at a trot.

I need to get into better shape if I'm going to have a family.

Chapter 37
Jacob Finds the Girls

"Hey, buddy. Got a minute?" A firm hand on Jacob's shoulder tried to detain him.

Jacob shook it off and faced its owner. Alarm coursed through him at the sight of the bodyguard build and dark sunglasses. "Nope. Sorry. Gotta go."

He plunged into the crowd, dodging between booths in an eerie repeat of Robin's chase scene. Checking behind him, he slowed to a brisk walk and entered the main concourse of the fair. No one followed. Perhaps the guy really wanted to ask a question. Oh, well. There was too much at stake to worry about it.

Jacob needed to reconsider his strategy. Hanging out and scanning the crowd for three familiar faces no longer made sense. He needed to get some altitude for a better view, and fast. He grimaced as he fixed upon the solution—the carnival rides. The Ferris wheel and the Tower Drop were the highest. The Tower Drop would be faster, but the last thing he needed was to lose his lunch in the middle of saving The Herd. With the cheerful blinking lights in his sites, Jacob hurried over to the Ferris wheel.

If that didn't work, he could—

Wham!

He saw it coming from the corner of his eye, but couldn't react in time to avoid it. The moving force of the tackle deftly carried him between two booths and out of the main concourse. They rolled until they hit a wall. With the wind knocked out of him, Jacob could not get off a single punch, although his attacker seemed more intent on restraining him than harming him.

Unexpectedly, he was drenched with water. As both men choked and sputtered, the assailant's grip loosened. Jacob tucked a knee up toward his chest, planted it on his attacker, and, with one determined kick, freed himself. Scrambling out of range, Jacob recognized the man with the sunglasses who had tried to detain him earlier. His foe was on all fours, shaking water out of his eyes.

And chuckling?

"I'm getting too old for this." The man sat back on his haunches as he warily watched an elderly woman holding an empty, dripping bucket.

Jacob scanned for more adversaries. Aside from a small curious crowd, the man appeared to be alone, and the little old lady with the bucket didn't seem a probable threat.

Groaning, the man got to his feet. Jacob watched his slow, limping approach, an uncomfortable wave of déjà-vu rippling through him.

"I apologize, okay? I need you to answer a few questions away from the crowd." His attacker put out a hand to help him up, a benign but unconvincing expression on his face.

Ignoring the outstretched hand, Jacob clambered to his feet and struck a fighting stance he had learned from Sam. "Who are you, and what the hell is going on?" He was new at this game, but he was pretty sure the enemy wasn't supposed to be friendly.

"Relax." The man raised his palms and retreated a step then winced. "Let's try to keep this civil." He reached down and massaged his knee.

"Civil? Why don't *you* answer some questions?" Jacob did not drop his guard.

"Look." The man glanced up at Jacob. His jovial tone did not quite reach his scrutinizing eyes. "I just want to know how you got to the girls. How long have you been hiding them?

We've been searching for them for months."

Alarm buzzed in Jacob's head. *This guy's trying to trick me into giving away something.* "What girls? I don't know what you're talking about. I'm here to enjoy the fair."

"*Sure* you are." The man leered as he straightened up. "And how are you enjoying it so far? *Yow!*" His yelp replaced his smirk when the empty bucket clanged against his injured knee.

"Scott Burleson, you stop teasing the boy. You explain," commanded the elderly bucket wielder in a foreign accent.

"Yes, ma'am." With an unabashed grin, the guy hopped out of range of the bucket.

"*What's going on?*" Jacob was about to explode. "Who the hell are you?" he directed toward the limping man. "And who the hell are you?" he directed toward the elderly woman. He was rewarded with a well-placed bucket to the hip.

"You talk respectful to you elders." She glared up at him.

"I'd back up, if I were you," suggested Jacob's adversary, who had resumed rubbing his knee at a safe distance.

Rubbing his hip, Jacob complied, skirting the bucket as he went. For some reason, the glaring woman reminded him of the woman who ran The Kissing Booth, but there wasn't one at this fair. *It must be the bucket of water.*

"So, what's your story?" The man's eyes narrowed as he started to limp in a circle around Jacob. "I couldn't figure you out," Burleson said. "Why would you put yourself out for complete strangers like that? It didn't make sense. So, I ran a check on you. You're not connected to the mob. As a matter of fact, you're not connected to anyone except William Hatch, of all people. Yup, you turn out to be some kind of business wiz kid who works for good ol' Mr. Hatch." He loomed toward Jacob. "So what's your angle? Pretty damsel in distress? Trying to get in good with the boss?"

Jacob stood unflinching, despite his rising anger and the confusion Burleson's words created. "I don't know what you're talking about." He hoped he sounded unruffled. "Why don't you just go your way, and I'll go mine, and we'll call it a day?" He took one cautious step.

In a blink of an eye, Burleson grabbed Jacob's collar and morphed into a complete and absolute threat. "They didn't randomly pop into your life, did they? What's your game, you little sh—"

A foreign expletive erupted from the little woman who had been monitoring their exchange. Scurrying over, she pried her way between Burleson and Jacob, forcing the latter to back up a step. With an angry tirade in a language he didn't recognize, she reached up and grabbed Jacob by the chin.

"Look at him, Scott," she demanded, switching to English. She waggled Jacob's face at Burleson with her surprisingly strong grip. "This Casey's boy."

"What? No way!" Scott recoiled, shock splashed all over his face. "That was *you* at The Kissing Booth?"

"What Kissing Booth?" managed Jacob through her hold on his jaw. "I—" Jacob stiffened as he placed Scott Burleson. He was a little older, but this guy was the suit who tried to keep Casey off The Kissing Booth the day she had first kissed him.

"Whoa!" Shock reverberated through Jacob's core. "That was *you* at The Kissing Booth?"

"Hah!" The elderly woman released Jacob's chin. Patting him on the chest, she shared a smug smile. "Birthday Kisses, Married by Christmas." She picked up her bucket and brandished it at Jacob's attacker. "Now, you behave."

"Oh, man." His former adversary pressed his palms on his temple and tilted skyward as she sauntered away. "Someone up there has one unbelievable sense of humor."

Jacob's head spun. *Unreal. The girls were on the run, hiding somewhere at the fair. This guy shows up. The Kissing Booth lady is here without her kissing booth. This must be how Alice felt when she fell down the rabbit hole.*

Snapping to attention, Scott chose a formal tone to couch his sarcasm. "We've never been properly introduced. My name is Scott Burleson, and I work for the Witness Protection Program. Simon was my best friend."

"Hold up." Not quite ready to transfer the guy out of the threat category, Jacob waved his palms in front of Scott's face. "Who's Simon?"

Scott raised his brow. "Who's Simon? The girls' father. He and Dorothy, their mother, were killed in a car accident two years ago. At the time, we didn't know if it was a contracted hit or an actual accident. The girls assumed the worst and fled. Besides, we suspected the contract on Simon included the children."

"So you relocated them."

Scott scratched his head. "Not exactly. Casey relocated them in case there was a leak on our side. They've been off radar for a very long time, and we haven't been able to find them." He paused, distracted by two men slowly approaching them, one supporting the other. The hairs on the nape of Jacob's neck rose as he recognized the limping man from the parking lot.

"What happened to *you*?" asked Scott.

"Carl got beat up by a girl."

"Shut up, Bret!" The injured man groaned as he leaned heavily on him. "For your information, it was *two* girls."

Uh-oh. "Friends of yours?" Jacob asked Scott.

"Not when they embarrass me like this." Scott helped Bret settle Carl in a nearby seat. "This is the pathetic Carl, and that's his sidekick Bret. They also work for the program, but technically, this isn't their case."

The elderly woman reappeared, her bucket replaced by a first-aid kit. "I tell you no chase them." She frowned as she began to tend to Carl's injuries.

"I was just trying to tell her it's safe to come in." Carl winced as she applied some foul-smelling salve to his bruised face.

Wrinkling their noses, Bret and Scott sidled away.

Desperation filled Jacob. However well intentioned, Carl's bumbling would surely send The Herd into hiding. "They've been on the run all their lives. They know how to protect themselves. How am I supposed to find them if you've scared them off?"

"Don't worry," Scott assured him. "I've already told Casey."

"Told Casey what?"

Scott gave Jacob a genuine smile. "That it's all over. Due to extenuating circumstances, the threat to the girls no longer exists."

"Yeah, an extenuating prison riot," snorted Bret.

"What are you talking about?" *What the hell is going on?*

"Simon witnessed a crime perpetrated by Salvador Maletti, a local crime boss," said Scott. "He was the real deal when it came to bad guys. In exchange for a testimony, the FBI agreed to protect Simon. We put Maletti behind bars, but he still wielded a lot of power, even from jail, so the family remained hidden.

"A few months ago, Maletti was killed in a prison riot. Word has it he was murdered by his competition. This particular competition won't honor Maletti's unfulfilled contracts, so that's that. It's over."

"It's over?" The Herd was finally safe? No more hiding, or making secret rendezvous or faking medical records, or.... "Where are your other men?"

"I don't have any other men. It's just us three," said Scott. "Maletti killed Bret's father in the line of duty."

"Yeah, and he was responsible for the death of Carl's brother," added Bret.

Jacob's gut tightened. "I hate to tell you this, friend, but if everyone is here, it's not over yet. Someone's been staking out my place and following me around for a couple of weeks. I called the police on a van parked outside my boss's place."

Bret raised his hand. "Guilty as charged," he grinned. "No worries. That was us. We thought it was an old biddy with nothing better to do than harass us poor little stalkers."

He was rewarded with a sound smack to the side of his head by the elderly woman nursing Carl. "You respect you elders," she murmured as she returned to her ministrations.

"Yes, ma'am." Bret rubbed his head while putting a greater distance between them.

Jacob needed to lay all possibilities to rest before he could shift gears. "But I don't recognize any of you from the hospital. And who did Helene Tucker have arrested at Toys R Us?"

The three agents exchanged puzzled glances.

"Hospital? That wasn't us. Is there another player in this game?" mused Carl as he winced under the woman's hands.

Bret frowned. "Maybe their grandfather?"

What? Had Jacob heard wrong?

Scott shook his head. "Do you really think he would risk everything after that last fiasco? Something's not right."

"What did he say when you told him where the girls were?" Bret asked.

"I haven't told him yet. I haven't been able to reach him. This is too strange. Bret, locate their grandfather. Now." With his companions already murmuring into their devices, Scott glanced at Jacob, who was staring at him, mouth agape.

"*What?*" cried Jacob.

"What?" repeated Scott.

"There's a *grandfather*?" asked Jacob. "What grandfather?"

"Of course there's a grandfather. Are you being funny?" Bret snorted.

Scott raised his hand to interrupt him, his brow drawn. "How could you not know?"

"Not know what?" asked Jacob. What was going on now?

Scott's reply was interrupted by a PA system announcement. "We would like to invite you to a Kent family reunion under the Karaoke Tent, starting immediately."

"*Yes! Yes! Yes!* That's Casey!" shouted Jacob. He bounded over to Scott and clapped him on the shoulders. "I gotta go!" And before anyone could say anything, he was gone.

***

"I'm telling you, that's a girl," the convinced teenage male insisted.

"That's not a girl. That's a fruit loop with an identity problem," snickered his friend.

"Shut up! There's no way that's anything but a girl."

Jacob followed the boy's admiring stare from where they stood at the side of the tent. There, on the stage, Sam pranced, disguised as a brunette boy in full adolescent female glory, vamping it up to their favorite jump-on-his-bed song, singing, "That's not my name!"

The first kid was right. Despite Sam's boy disguise, pure femininity was belting out that karaoke song. That other kid was crazy.

Instead of dashing forward, he corralled his heart, biding his time as he waited for the next verse of the song. His patience was rewarded when, right on cue, Robin appeared, mic in hand, dragging a chair. Setting it down, she plopped into it, demurely crossing her ankles, and joined in the song.

Casey would be close behind, but, first, his part was next. Jacob's heart was full. This was *his* Herd of Girls now, *his* family.

He slapped Sam's admirer on the shoulder before running to the front. "Good eye, kid."

Leaping on the stage, he joined the song. The girls whirled around at the sound of his voice. The song forgotten, they raced over to him and sandwiched him in an exuberant hug.

And then, there she was. Microphone in hand, Casey sashayed toward them, singing her heart out. His very own Casey. The full impact of her love and joy radiated from her. It was finally over.

Like a lumbering six-legged creature, Jacob and the girls dragged themselves toward Casey. She gave up trying to sing as the happy group absorbed her. The crowd recognized a happy ending when they saw it. Enthusiastic clapping and stomping accompanied the rest of the lyrics.

"Take your bow," shouted the emcee.

Joining hands, they swept downward and upward and then slammed back into their happy clump. Scuttling off the stage, they ran out of the tent into the welcoming sunshine.

"You found us! You found us!" Robin jumped up and down with delight.

Sam laughed. "Of course he found us. We left a trail even the FBI could trace."

Jacob followed her shrug toward the tent and saw Scott standing at the exit.

Robin tugged on Casey's shirt. "Something's wrong, Casey."

Jacob looked at her with surprise then noticed a grim Scott striding toward them. He must've spooked the little girl. "Casey, do you know that guy?"

"Hush, Tidbit. Everything's okay now. That's just Uncle Scott. He's an old friend of Daddy's," Casey confirmed.

Unsatisfied, Robin tried her other sister. "Sam," she said. "*Sam!*"

But Sam's attention had shifted elsewhere.

"Hey, uh, you looked really good up there." It was Sam's young admirer from the tent. He shifted his weight from foot to foot as Sam's eyes narrowed in her pink-tinged face. Jacob was all sympathy for the poor guy.

"Um, thanks, I guess." Sam exuded discomfort. "Okay, I appreciate you coming over and everything, but, uh...." She jutted out her chin. "I'm not what you think. Actually, I'm a—"

"You're a beautiful girl." The kid ducked his head. "And you looked really good up there."

A pleased smile spread across Sam's face as her blush deepened. "How did you know?"

"You're kidding, right?" He looked up in surprise then examined the ground next to his big toe with a matching blush.

Casey blocked Jacob's eavesdropping by leaning over to whisper, "Are you sure you want this whole package? I have no idea what life will be like with no one hunting us."

Jacob answered her with a loving kiss. He didn't care who saw.

"Casey!" Robin tugged on her sister's hand. "Something's *wrong!*"

When Casey still didn't respond, Robin shrieked, "Mr. Kent! Something's *wrong!*"

Jacob broke off his kiss with Casey just as his cell phone rang. It seemed to punctuate the crumbling of their happy ending. *Now what?*

"Hang on a sec, Robin." He fished for his phone so he could silence it.

"No, no, no!" Robin burst into tears. "Something's *wrong*."

"What is it, Tidbit?" Robin's anguish had finally broken through Sam's moment of personal fluster. With two steps she gathered Robin into her arms. "It's okay. We're all here, and we're all safe."

Tears streamed down Robin cheeks. "We're *not* all here. Something's wrong with *Grandpa,* and no one will listen to me!"

Jacob's cell phone resumed its insistent demand for attention, amplifying his feeling of foreboding. He scooped it out of his pocket and found Hanson had left two messages. He stepped away from the group to listen, his heart revving. There was only one reason Hanson would call him. Something was wrong with William. As he retrieved his messages, he watched the others gather around Scott. Casey held Robin, who was hiccupping into her shoulder. Their expressions spoke volumes. More bad news? *How could things change so fast?*

"What is it?" Jacob asked Scott. Putting his personal anguish aside, he wrapped his arms around Casey and Robin. Sam's admirer moved to stand behind her.

"It's our grandpa." Sam's face was pale. "You followed our clues, but he didn't. He should be here. Robin's right. Something's wrong."

Scott confirmed Sam's fears with a brusque nod. Jacob's heart dropped further. These poor girls couldn't catch a break.

He felt a hand on his arm.

"You got bad news just now, didn't you?"

Jacob looked down at Sam's sympathetic face and nodded. This one didn't miss a thing.

"What is it, Jacob?" asked Casey.

Reluctant to add to their newest dilemma, he hesitated. "My boss, my *friend,* is in the hospital again. I'm sorry but

I need to go to him. He's the only family I've had for years, until you all came along. I have to go, but I can't just leave you guys."

"We should all go," announced Robin, lifting her head from Casey's shoulder. "Grandpa's in the hospital, and he's scared. He needs us."

"Hush, Robin," said Casey. "You don't know that. We're all worried, but now is not the time to panic."

Robin and Sam exchange glances, ignoring Casey's words.

Casey turned toward Scott. "Maybe he's just waiting for us to come home."

Sam nodded to her younger sister and faced the kid from the tent. "I'm sorry, but we have to go now. Our grandfather is in a hospital, but we don't know which one, and we have to find him." Sam spoke with a conviction that puzzled Jacob. Why was she jumping to that conclusion when it was based on an eight-year-old's speculation?

The boy took it in stride. "In Connecticut? Maybe I can help. We have a contact with most emergency rooms in the towns we visit. I designed a spreadsheet so I can pull it up all at once."

"We?" Sam asked.

"I travel with the carnival during the summers." Ducking his head, he added, "I remember you from last year, but in another town."

After a moment, Sam closed her mouth. "Fine. Let's go."

He beheld her determined pink face, and for a moment looked like it was difficult to breathe. *The right girl will do that to you, kid,* thought Jacob.

"We...we should tell the others where we're going," said the kid.

"You're right." Sam turned toward the group, saying, "Hey, me and—" She turned back to him, blushing. "I don't know your name."

"Christopher." He grinned. "And you're Sam."

"Samantha." She corrected him with a shy smile. "Hi, Christopher." Sam turned back to her family. "Me and Christopher are going to check the Connecticut hospitals for Grandpa."

"No!" chorused Jacob, Casey, and Scott.

Samantha and Christopher were taken aback by the force of their collective response.

"We need to stay together," said Scott. "Now is not the time to go wandering off."

"You don't even know him," said Jacob with previously untapped parental caution.

Robin interrupted Casey's response. "It's okay." Squirming out of her big sister's arms, Robin ran over to Christopher. Tugging on his hand, she brought his face within reach and patted him on the cheek. "He's going to love Sam."

"Robin!" Sam snatched Robin's hand away. "I'm *so sorry!*"

"*I* don't mind." Christopher laughed, for once not ducking his head. "Stranger things have happened, right?" He stepped toward the others. "We weren't leaving the fair. I have a spreadsheet with the hospital numbers. We can divide them up between us and call."

"That's a great idea, Christopher, but I have a better one," said Casey. "There are no worries any more, right, Uncle Scott? I'll just call Hanson, and he can—"

"Hanson?" shouted Jacob. "You'll just call *Hanson*?"

Scott looked at the O Casey's astonished mouth formed, and the identical Os being sported by Robin, Sam—correction, Sam*antha*—and some boy. "Now *this* I'm gonna enjoy."

"What is wrong with you?" Casey stared at Jacob as he seized her by the shoulders.

"Who's your grandfather?"

"William Hatch. Do you know him?"

Jacob released her to slap his forehead and pace. "Do I know him? Jeez! I don't believe it. After all this time…. So *you're* his secret project. I completely forgot they were trying to get to Greenwich—"

"*Jacob!*" Casey grabbed his arm and spun him around to face her. "What are you talking about? Do you know our grandfather?"

"Know him? He's my boss! Honey, we have to talk. But, first, Robin's right. He's been taken to Greenwich Hospital, and we have to get there right away."

"I got this." Scott shifted into FBI mode. "Meet me by the parking lot exit. I have a siren that'll cut through traffic." Hand to his ear, they could hear him issuing orders as he ran off.

Samantha spun toward Christopher, indecision all over her face.

"Go on, Samantha. I'll find you again."

Samantha grabbed his hands and babbled. "I know you don't understand, but I've been hiding for so long, I feel like you'll never be able to find me. I don't have an address or even a real name."

"Samantha, I've got the Internet on my side. You're the granddaughter of someone named William Hatch who lives in Connecticut. How hard can it be?" He cupped Samantha's face. "*Don't worry*. I'll find you," he repeated before brushing her lips with his.

Jacob stared at them in disbelief. *I'm no Don Juan, but I'm pretty sure you don't kiss a girl in front of her family.*

"Woo*hoo*, Samantha!" Robin's teasing broke the spell as they jumped apart.

"We gotta go!" Jacob scooped up Robin and took off with Casey running beside him. The only thing that mattered now was William.

***

"Go on." Christopher spun Samantha toward her retreating family and gave her a gentle push. She broke into a sprint, waving to him before she disappeared behind a booth.

Well, that was different. He planted his interlaced fingers on top of his head. *What am I getting into?*

Chris staggered as his friend, Gnat, materialized out of nowhere and pounded on his back.

"Dude, are you crossing the fence here or what?" Gnat shifted his lanky frame from one leg to the other.

He thinks he saw me kiss a guy. Irritated, Chris shrugged Gnat's hand off his shoulder. "What's the matter, Nathaniel? You worried about being seen with a 'fruit loop'?"

"Nah, it's all good. Cradle to grave, and all that. But, seriously, dude, what about the squeeze you've been moping over all year?"

Chris shoved his hands into his pockets and jerked his head in the direction of Samantha's departure, a half grin on his face.

"No way. Really?" Gnat whistled softly. "Dude, why didn't you tell me you were batting for the other side?"

He turned toward Gnat, a retort on the tip of his tongue, and paused. A quick search of his friend's pale-blue eyes revealed only mild indignation.

"I woulda stopped trying to fix you up all the time if I had known."

Grabbing Gnat around the neck, he grated his knuckles on the redhead's spiky hair in an affectionate, time-honored noogie. Gnat might have a few shortcomings, but he was a loyal friend.

"Hey, dude, watch the hair!" Gnat squawked.

"Number one, stop calling me *dude*." Chris let him go.

"Number two, I'm not batting for the other side. And number three, stop fixing me up. The only one I'm interested in is the little morsel that just left."

He grabbed a fistful of Gnat's shirt and pulled. "C'mon. I have to Google someone named William Hatch." Draping an arm over his friend's shoulder, he intoned, "By the way, 'Sam' is short for Samantha."

"No way," Gnat hollered as he smacked Chris's chest. "And she let you kiss her? That's one *helluva* birthday present."

"You have no idea." He made an exuberant leap up to tap a sign as they trotted toward their trailer.

Over by the Karaoke Tent, he spotted Miss Ana standing in the entrance beaming at them. He altered their course, waving as he approached, wondering if she had seen him kissing Samantha. "Hey, Miss Ana. How's the stage working?"

"Perfect, Christopher. Is perfect. Is working very right," she said with delight. "Is such a wonderful idea Nathaniel had, to use part of Kissing Booth for Karaoke Stage. And so nice of you boys to build for me."

Gnat's freckled face tinged. "You're welcome, Miss Ana. I just figured you could get more income if you upgraded a little bit." He leaned over and kissed her weathered cheek. "Besides, who watches out for us all summer long?"

"I do, *dude*." She winked at him as Chris chuckled. "Where you two off to?"

"We have to go Google someone for his birthday." Gnat drummed him on the back again.

"Oh, yes, my dear. Today be the anniversary of your birth." She clapped her hands together. "You wear you good luck charm I make you?"

"I got it right here." Christopher pulled a chain out of his shirt. It held an intricately designed wooden rune Miss Ana had carved from a piece of the old Kissing Booth floor.

"Excellent, my dear, excellent. Nathaniel, you must be next. When is you birthday?"

"I'm a December baby. December 1st at your service, ma'am," he said, clicking his heels and bowing at the waist.

"Hmmm…December. Hard, but not impossible," she murmured to herself.

The boys exchanged puzzled glances over her head.

"Not to worry," she said, patting Gnat on the arm. "Now, if you not busy after you google, you come for birthday cake, hmmm?"

Chris replied for the both of them. "Miss Ana, nothing could keep us away." He bent down and kissed her cheek as Gnat did the same on her other cheek.

Straightening, Chris gave a theatrical sweep of his arm and proclaimed, "Let the googling begin."

The two boys trotted off.

"Wow, dude. Not only do you find the squeeze you've been moping over since *last summer*," Gnat counted on his fingers, "but the guy turns out to be a girl. *And* she gives you a birthday kiss. *And* you get one of Miss Ana's famous cakes." Gnat grinned at Chris. "Did I leave anything out? Oh, yeah, *and* you've been accepted into college, *and* you have me for a best friend. Is this your best birthday ever or what?"

"*Dude*, you have no idea." Christopher jumped up to smack another posted sign and raced off to the computer.

***

A smile stretched across her face as Ana watched her two newest projects disappear into the crowd. She patted the floor of the former Kissing Booth. "No, *dude*, you have no idea."

Chapter 38
Back to the Hospital

Jacob halted the car at the hospital emergency entrance. Glimpsing the shell-shocked faces of the three sisters, he shook his head. *William Hatch is their grandfather.* As far as he could tell, his efforts to keep his two worlds from colliding had caused more harm than good. William's breakdown most likely came from searching for the very girls Jacob had hidden.

Casey covered his hand with hers. "This is not your fault," she reminded him before she jumped out of the car. "These wheels were in motion long before we ever met."

He responded with a curt nod. She slammed the car door and rushed inside.

He ignored the clamor broadcasting from the rear seat about being left behind. Instead, he pointed the car toward the parking lot. "Casey will find out what we need to know faster if she doesn't have us with her," he barked at her siblings.

He pulled into a parking space and jumped out. As soon as they were out of the car, Sam grabbed Robin's hand. With his hand held high, Jacob punched the remote car-lock button, and led the charge to the imposing white building that now housed William.

Casey met them at the door. "He's been taken to the Cardiac Wing." Her calm exterior masked any inner fears. "But they wouldn't tell me anything except which floor."

He ushered them onto the elevator, clasping Casey's hand in his. She smiled up at him. If she could be calm, so could he. When the doors opened, the two made a beeline for the nurse's station, the younger girls trailing close behind them.

"Excuse me," Jacob and Casey chorused.

An overworked nurse raised her head and sighed. "May I help you?" she asked, returning her attention to her paperwork.

Jacob swallowed his irritation. "We're looking for William Hatch."

"One moment, please." She remained intent on her work.

Casey tapped on the counter. "*Excuse me!*"

The nurse glanced up, lips pursed.

Without warning, the alarms went off in one of the rooms down the hall. Before their very eyes, the low energy, put-upon drone buried in paperwork transformed into an energized, efficient professional intent on saving her charge. Scooping up papers and issuing orders, she disappeared in seconds. A variety of formidable machines followed her into the room where she had disappeared.

"What if it's Grandpa?" Sam tried to follow, but Jacob seized her arm.

"No, Sam. Wait here. We'll only get in the way." He held her as she struggled. When she sagged against him, he wrapped his arms around her in a hug. "We'll wait together." He led the anxious group to the waiting area. Casey followed, her arm draped around Robin.

Thirty minutes later, machines and people trickled out of the room. What a relief to see the satisfied expressions on the staff, even though they still hadn't found out William's location.

Jacob released his accumulating tension with a noisy exhale and checked on the others. Seated by his side, Casey slumped into her chair, legs extended along the floor. Sam and Robin sat behind them, back to back. Jacob felt Samantha sit bolt upright, her body rigid against his shoulder. His questioning eyes collided with her panicky ones.

Where was Robin?

He swiveled his head toward Casey as she shot to her feet. By the time he jumped to his, Sam and Casey had already fanned out, military fashion.

"Hold it!" commanded Casey. "We are no longer on alert. Robin probably went looking for Grandpa. She's around here somewhere, and she's safe. We simply have to locate her. I'll check the restrooms. Sam, you take the north side. And you...." She faltered as she addressed Jacob.

He gave her a wry grin. This was the group he wanted to protect? They sure didn't seem like they needed protecting. "Yes, sir?"

Casey returned his smile. "And you check the west wing. We'll meet back here in five minutes."

***

All of the rushing around and noise made Robin more and more nervous. She wanted to see Grandpa. Something was wrong with him. If she could just hug him, he'd be all better.

Robin looked over at the others. Why weren't they doing anything or asking somebody something? She sighed with impatience. Waiting was stupid. Stealing a glimpse of Sam slumped beside her, Robin decided her sister wouldn't notice if she left for a minute. She slid quietly off her chair and stole across the waiting area to the closest hall. She shrugged at the sight of the very big hallway stretching out in front of her with all those rooms. Like Casey always said, "It's a tough job, but someone's got to do it." Happy to be doing something at last, she started toward the first door.

She reached the end of the corridor, peeking into each room as she went, but none of them yielded Grandpa. She crossed the hallway to try the rooms on the other side. As she approached the next door, excitement bubbled up inside her. Grandpa's room! And he would be better as soon as he saw her. She stepped into the room, quiet as a mouse.

Is that old guy my *Grandpa?* She stared in stunned silence. It *was* Grandpa. His eyes were closed, and his face looked so pinched and sad.

What happened to him? What is all that stuff sticking out of him? Frightened, she needed to find her sister. *Casey will know what to do.*

"I knew you would come." Grandpa's soft comment forestalled her flight. Robin crept toward his bed.

"Don't be frightened, my little love," he said, eyes still closed.

"Grandpa?" she whispered.

He opened his eyes.

"Oh, Grandpa!" she cried, closing the distance between them. She stopped short, focused on the hand he reached toward her.

"It's okay, my darling girl." He wiggled the tube taped to it. "It doesn't hurt, and it makes me better."

Robin reached out a fingertip to test his words herself. One delicate touch satisfied her. She spun around and dragged a chair over to the bed.

"Move over, Grandpa," she ordered as she scrambled up onto the chair. "You need hugs."

She maneuvered onto the bed and snuggled under the offered arm. They sighed in unison and then gazed happily at each other.

"Did you hear me come in, Grandpa? I tried to be quiet."

"No, I didn't hear you, sweet thing. You're not the only one who *feels* things."

She raised her head in surprise. "Really?" She frowned. "I told them you were sick, and no one would listen to me." Distress flooded her at the recollection.

"Everything's okay now." Grandpa hugged the bad feeling right out of her. "Seeing you has made me much better. I've been so worried about you. This is the first peace I've had in a long time."

***

William didn't know how his youngest grandchild had gotten there, and, for the moment, he didn't care. They were together, and if Robin was here, the rest had to be close by. He gazed at one of his precious three. His wait was over at last. Now, they could be a real family. After all these years, the sounds of children would fill his empty home.

He smiled at the top of her head, his throat tight. "What have you done to your hair?"

"Do you like it?" Robin patted her short black locks. "It was blonde before." She raised herself onto her elbow so she could see him. "Why do grownups say I'm s'poze to have more fun when I'm a blonde?"

"Did you?" William chuckled.

"Well...." Her brow furrowed as she thought it over. "Camping was fun, but then Casey got sick, and *that* wasn't fun." She smiled brightly. "Staying at Mr. Kent's was fun, but today wasn't fun." She buried her head and snuggled close to his side again. "Nope, not fun at all."

William took it all in, trying to sort out the meaning of her words. *So Casey was sick? 'Mr. Kent?' She couldn't possibly mean Jacob.*

"Do you know what Mr. Kent's first name is?"

"I dunno," she shrugged. She paused. "Wait! Maybe it's Clark. Clark Kent. Yeah, that sounds right."

William gave up after her reference to Superman's secret

identity. He'd have to wait until he talked to someone older. As intuitive as she was, she was still only eight years old. "Where are the others?"

She gestured toward the door. "They're coming. When they get here, can we go to your house, Grandpa? We've been trying to get to you *forever*!"

"Well, little love…." He hesitated. "I'm not sure when I'm going to get out of here."

"Then I'll stay here and take care of you."

"Oh, no, you don't." He ruffled her hair. "A hospital is no place for healthy people."

"That's what Mrs. Fuller said," she exclaimed.

Mrs. Fuller? Margaret Fuller? How could she possibly know Margaret?

"Grandpa," she said, her face anxious. "Don't you love me anymore?"

"Where did *that* come from?" he asked, baffled.

"They...somebody said you didn't want me anymore." Her lower lip trembled. "That you didn't need a bunch of kids running around."

"Well, whoever 'they' are, they're wrong," he said firmly. It pierced his soul to see her relief. She had experienced too much loss for one so young. In an effort to lighten her up, he teased, "I think I have just enough room in my heart to love *one* more person. Plus, *you* are rather small. I think you will fit in nicely in my home. You don't take up much room, do you?"

"Oh, no, Grandpa, I don't." She nestled against him again.

He wearily closed his eyes again. "I just wish everyone else would go away and leave us alone."

***

From the doorway, Samantha's heart dropped. Grandpa wanted just Robin? *I knew it. I just knew it!*

First Daddy and Mama died. Now Grandpa didn't want her. It wasn't fair.

She backed out of the room undetected, the lump in her throat and the sting in her eyes directing her escape.

Well, I don't need him either!

***

Casey paused in the doorway of the earlier cause of alarm. An exiting technician informed her the patient inside was not William Hatch. Relieved, she continued on her quest, making a quick sweep of the restrooms. Her search did not produce Robin, so she set out once again for the nurse's station. By the time Jacob joined her, she had obtained Grandpa's room number. Grabbing Jacob by the hand, she led him down the hallway where Samantha had disappeared earlier.

They entered Grandpa's room to find Robin snuggled up in the crook of his arm. Expecting both girls to be there, Casey shot a bewildered glance at Jacob, who shook his head and shrugged. Casey forced herself to relax. In all likelihood, the nursing station would redirect Sam back here.

Casey tiptoed over to the bed with Jacob on her heels. Grandpa was asleep. He looked so pale and weak, a lump formed in her throat. When she looked at Robin, she received a bright, sunny smile. *Well, she doesn't seem too upset. Can she tell if he's okay?* She heard Jacob take a shaky breath.

"This is like déjà-vu," he muttered. "He was all wired up like this the last time, too."

"The last time?"

"That night I found you on the side of the road, I was trying to get to William because he had been rushed to the hospital."

Appalled, Casey whispered, "This is the *second* time this happened?"

Jacob briefly described the previous incident. "I wonder where Hanson is." He pulled out his cell phone intent on tracking down William's right hand man.

"*Mr. Kent!*" whispered Robin. "You can't use cells phones here. This is a *hospital.*"

"You're right, Robin." He snapped the phone shut. "I'll be right back."

As he strode out of the room, Casey moved closer to her sister and put her hand on the little cheek. "You knew at the fair, didn't you?" She spoke softly so as not to disturb Grandpa. "You weren't guessing about Grandpa. You knew."

Robin's eyes filled as she nodded.

"Tidbit, I am so sorry I didn't listen to you at the fair. I didn't understand."

"I was scared." Robin heaved a tremulous sigh. "Nobody would listen."

"I know, sweetie." Casey wanted to hug her, but was afraid of being disruptive. "I was too excited. But I think I understand now. How is Grandpa?"

Robin slipped her hand into Casey's. "He's better because he hugged me."

Casey retrieved a glimmer of the original relief created by Uncle Scott's news. Was it this morning they had stopped being fugitives? It seemed like a lifetime ago.

She heard Grandpa shift and caught his loving gaze. Were those tears? It was hard to tell with her own vision so blurred. "Oh, Grandpa!" Ignoring the jumble of wires, she reached over to hug the two of them.

"There, there now, pet." He murmured into her hair as she tried to control her tears. "This won't do. This won't do at all."

"You are supposed to be cheering up the patient." She

looked over her shoulder to find the reproving voice belonged to Dr. Don. "Well, you seem to have made quite the recovery. How about letting me in there so I can see my new patient?"

Wiping away her tears, Casey straightened, revealing Robin tucked in next to Grandpa.

Dr. Don grinned at the little girl. "How's my patient?" He angled his stethoscope toward her chest.

"*I'm* not sick," she exclaimed. "*He* is!" She turned to her grandfather, her brow creased. "Grandpa, are you sure he's a good doctor?" she whispered.

"He says he is," he whispered back.

"We'll wait outside." Casey squeezed the hand of the doctor who had been so helpful during her own hospital stay. She extracted Robin from Grandpa and the tubes.

"We'll be *right* outside, Grandpa." Robin gave Dr. Don a warning glare.

"Wait, Casey," called Grandpa. "Where's Samantha?"

"She's around here someplace. I'll go get her."

"Are you sure? I need to see her for myself. Please bring her to me right away." He extended his hand toward her in his plea.

"Right away, Grandpa," she said past the lump in her throat.

Where is *Samantha? She should be here by now.* Spotting Jacob at the end of the hall, Casey aimed for him, Robin in tow.

He glanced up at their approach.

"Did you find Samantha?" they asked each other in unison.

Casey sighed. Would this never end? Robin reached out, and Jacob slipped his free hand in hers.

"No one at the nursing station has seen her, and I can't get ahold of Hanson or Maggie," Jacob murmured.

He bent down to Robin's level. "Robin, Sam went to find you. Did you see her?"

"Un-uh, but something's wrong with her."

Now what? "Do you know what it is?"

She hung her head. "I promised not to tell."

Casey looked around the room, trying to decide what to do. With no real enemy anymore, she was at a loss as to how to approach this situation.

Jacob's phone rang. He glanced at the screen. "It's Maggie." He flipped it open.

Casey watched relief flood Jacob's face, and an answering comfort filled her.

And something else. She placed her hand over her heart in surprise. She could love him now. She had been fighting it all these years because.... At this moment, she couldn't remember why.

He hung up and hugged her. "Maggie and Hanson are with Sam. Something upset her, and she tried to leave the hospital. Maggie saw her go down the stairwell and followed. Hanson followed Maggie, and now they're all in the cafeteria."

"There's a light at the end of this tunnel," said Casey as she let Jacob steer them toward the elevator. "All we have left to do is figure out Sam."

"Hah," snorted Jacob. "That's not going to be easy."

***

Chapter 39
Together Again

As they stepped out of the elevator into the cafeteria, Jacob once again experienced déjà-vu. About two months ago, he had stood here watching Maggie with two skinny girls disguised as blond boys, lost and alone. Tonight, dressed in clean clothes and well-fed, a brunette Sam looked worse off than she did that first night. *What the hell is going on?*

"*Miss Casey!*" Hanson stood near the elevator. He held out his arms, and Casey rushed into his embrace. Bowing his head over hers, Hanson encircled her in a fierce hug as they rocked back and forth.

Wow, that's something you don't see every day. Robin pressed against Jacob, and he reached down to stroke her hair.

Hanson looked up, his face a wreath of smiles. He released Casey to scoop up the smallest of the sisters.

"Oh, Miss Robin!" He wrapped around her, happier than Jacob had ever seen him, while Casey lent a supporting hand to help him hold Robin up.

Robin's little arms encircled his neck in a stranglehold. She kissed him soundly on the cheek and tucked her face into his shoulder. "*My* Hanson."

Hanson's eyes brimmed with joyful tears.

Jacob's eyes widened with disbelief. *Is this the same Hanson I know?* He pointed toward Samantha. "What's going on over there?"

Hanson shook his head with a sniff. "I'm sure I don't know, sir. She won't talk to me or Marg—er, Ms. Fuller. She keeps saying she has something to take care of."

"Well, she better talk to me." Casey patted Hanson's back and marched toward the table where Samantha and Margaret sat.

***

Casey felt Jacob's gaze on her, but ignored it. *First things first.*

"What's going on?" she demanded, her hands on her hips as she loomed over her sister.

"Well, I've been thinking, and...." Samantha swung her gaze toward the huddle by the elevator and started over. "Are you going to marry Mr. Kent?"

Margaret lowered her head and froze in the presence of such a private conversation.

Where did that *come from?* Casey crossed her arms. "What?" she floundered. "Well, I...I...." *Wow, it's warm in here.* She swung her gaze back and forth between Samantha and Margaret, clutching her arms, too flustered to notice Jacob crossing the room. So when he slid his arms around her waist, she jumped out of her skin.

"Whoa!" she squawked then stood stock-still, arms half-raised. How odd to see Jacob's hands clasped around her middle. He had never been affectionate in front of her family before. With her heart thudding loud enough for them to hear, she tried to collect her thoughts.

Okay...Okay...wait." It was difficult to draw a breath with Jacob trying to cuddle her. His touch occupied all of her attention.

"I...I...." Swallowing, she tried to focus. "What I mean is...I...." She gave up. "What did you ask me?"

"Never mind." Samantha shifted her sullen gaze in another direction.

"Yes, she is," Jacob answered for Casey.

"Yes, I am *what*?" Casey was still trying to calm her thumping heart. She really wanted to turn around in the circle of his arms and kiss him. Trying to act nonchalant with the rest of the world looking on was proving to be extremely difficult. She gasped as he bent down and kissed the nape of her neck.

"Yes, she's going to marry me." She could hear the smile in his voice. "She doesn't know it yet, but she loves me."

***

Jacob was way out there on a limb. He had just laid his cards on the table in front of everybody. Now, it occurred to him discussing this with her in private first might have been a better idea, but it was too late to take it back. With Casey's back still to him, Jacob couldn't see her reaction to his words.

"What?" squeaked Casey.

Not exactly the response he was hoping for.

She grasped two of Jacob's fingers. *Uh-oh.* Sam had shown him this maneuver. He knew what came next, and there was nothing he could do about it.

"Oh, no, mister. You got it totally wrong." Casey wrenched his fingers, forcing him to release his loving grip on her waist.

"*Oww!*" he cried, for both his fingers and his dignity.

With a neat little twist, she was out of his arms, still gripping his fingers in her painful vise. He contorted his torso in a vain attempt to relieve the agonizing pressure from her dainty little hand. She released him, and he stepped away, shaking his arm.

Definitely not the reaction he had been hoping for.

"You got it totally wrong," she repeated.

Entranced by the warmth radiating from her beautiful brown eyes, Jacob stopped shaking his hand. An emotional tidal wave enveloped him.

She sauntered toward him, holding him with her gaze. "I *do* know I love you." She placed her hands on his cheeks, drawing his head to hers, offering.

He accepted. *This* was the reaction he had been hoping for.

His lips brushed hers gently as he watched her. Eyes half-closed, she slid her hands around his neck. For a moment, they regarded each other. Unable to help himself, with a groan, he crushed her to him, pouring all of his hopes and dreams into one kiss. He could hold her like this forever….

"Ahem."

He thought he heard —

"*Ahem!*"

He definitely heard—

"Get a room," said Hanson.

Remembering where they were, Jacob broke from Casey, embarrassed at having become so lost in the moment in front of others.

Hanson grinned at them from the doorway as Robin hopped up and down in front of him. Maggie's hands were clasped under her chin as she beamed at them.

"I knew it!" Samantha hissed.

Oh, no. She's pissed. Jacob glanced back at Casey. Her slack jaw conveyed she had no more of a clue how to deal with this than he did.

"Samantha—" she began, but Jacob's cell phone interrupted her.

He dug it out. "It's Dr. Don." He read the urgent summons. His quiet "*Oh, no*" made everyone turn toward him.

He shoved the phone into his pocket and grabbed Samantha by the arm. "C'mon! We got to go, and we got to go, *now*!" Whatever problem Samantha had with the idea of Casey marrying him would have to wait. William was in trouble.

Responding to the urgency, Samantha jumped to her feet. Jacob and the sisters ran to the elevator. As Hanson held the door open, Jacob noticed his executive assistant standing by the table. It was the first indecisive move he had ever seen from Ms. Fuller.

"Let's go, Maggie!" he snapped. "Like it or not, you're part of this family, too."

She hurried over to them. "Oh, but I like it, Mr. Kent." She sounded somewhat breathless as they all scrambled for a place in the waiting elevator. As the doors closed, Jacob's cell phone vibrated again.

"Yes, Don, we're in the elevator. Tell him I have all of the girls with me." He hung up and turned to the enigma.

"Samantha, I don't know what's going on...." Jacob began sternly, but tempered his tone. "And I'm sure it's important, but right now you're going to have to think about someone else's needs. Your grandfather needs you."

"He doesn't need me." Samantha glared at the floor.

Jacob grabbed her by the shoulders and gently turned him toward her. "Sam, he *needs* you. He's worked himself up into a state, and the doctor is very worried."

"What's his problem anyway?" Samantha refused to meet his eye. The doors of the elevator opened.

"You're his problem." They started off the elevator. "He hasn't seen you yet and doesn't believe you're really safe. We were supposed to bring you right back with us."

He collided with Samantha, who had stopped short at his words. "Me?"

"What is it with you?" asked Casey in exasperation as she pushed Samantha the rest of the way off the elevator.

"*Where is Hanson?*" William's weak bellow came from his room. "I want my Samantha!"

"Grandpa," breathed Samantha. Without a backward glance, she dashed down the corridor.

"No, I will not calm down," William continued to rasp. "Something is wrong. I can feel it! What's that? No, don't sedate me! I want my family!"

"Grandpa!" shouted Samantha as she burst into his room. "It's okay. I'm right here."

Ignoring the constraints of the hospital bed and its writhing tubes, she flung herself upon him, sobbing like her heart would break. Don and the nurse who had been trying to restrain him barely got out of the way.

"What's this? My beautiful girl?" William hugged her as tightly as he could. "Oh, my dear, where have you been? I thought they were keeping something from me. Shush now. We're together, and no one is going to separate us again."

"Oh, Grandpa, you want me, too?"

"Does he want you, too?" squawked Hanson from behind the doctor. "*Of course* he wants you, too. That is all he has been working on for the past three months. The way he has been driving himself…. No wonder he ended up here."

"That's crazy. The Herd was William's big project?" Jacob stood in the doorway, feeling displaced.

"Okay, everyone," interrupted Don in his firmest Dr. Don persona. "All's well that ends well. You can sort this out later. Right now, my patient needs some rest. We still have more tests we need to run to see what's going on."

He began to pry Samantha off of his patient. "C'mon, young lady, you can talk to him in a little while."

"Wait. *Wait!*" cried William, clutching at Samantha's arms.

"It's okay, Grandpa," Samantha sniffed. "We're not going far. Just call if you need us."

"That's right, Grandpa," confirmed Robin, sniffling by the door. "We'll be right out there."

"My beautiful girls." William wiped a tear from Samantha's face.

Hanson came over, and William released her.

"They're home, Reginald." William settled back in his bed, smiling at the man who had stayed by his side all these years.

"Yes, old friend." Hanson wrapped a loving arm around Samantha's shoulders. "They're finally home."

***

A wave of relief washed through Don as he witnessed the immediate transformation in his patient. Happiness always factored into a speedy recovery. Don watched with Mr. Hatch as the sisters claimed Samantha in a tight hug by the door. It was the first time he had seen them together. Their dark hair was a little startling, but there was an obvious family resemblance.

Hanson and Jacob guided them out. Don waited until they stepped beyond Mr. Hatch's view before he pulled the curtain around his bed.

"Now we can start a new chapter, together." Mr. Hatch rubbed his hands together, the dancing tubes reflecting his joy.

"This sounds like a helluva story, sir." Don was gratified to see a hint of Mr. Hatch's perpetual twinkle returning. He'd always liked the old guy.

"You have no idea, young man."

Don pulled a chair next to the bed. "And it looks like Jacob and The Nameless Wonder are going to write their own chapter."

"The nameless what?"

Don grinned at Mr. Hatch's confusion. "Apparently, I have a couple of missing chapters to share with you." He leaned toward his patient. "Like the chapter where Jacob has been hiding your granddaughters at his place for the last couple of weeks."

"They've been here? At *his* place? All this time?" The elderly man's jaw sagged.

"I don't know about 'all this time,' but I'm pretty sure they've been there for a couple of weeks."

A hearty chuckle replaced Mr. Hatch's incredulous expression. "Bless my soul. What else? I can tell from your face there's more."

Don beamed. "Jacob and your granddaughter have fallen for each other." This was the happy ending he wanted for his friend.

"No, no, no." Mr. Hatch frowned. "It's much too soon. They've only known each other for a couple of weeks."

"Yeah, well, about that…."

***

Chapter 40
That Was You?

William's dream had finally become reality. His two younger grandchildren sprawled on the floor working on a puzzle. Margaret held the door open for Hanson who carried a laden snack tray. Through the open door, he could see Jacob stealing a kiss from Casey in the hallway. Everyone was home, and, for the first time, they were a family. A real family.

He raised his head to the cherished portrait of a dimpled young woman with raven hair and ebony eyes so much like Samantha's. He winked at her, saying, "We did pretty well, didn't we, Livy?"

Hanson laid the tray on the table by William and looked over his shoulder at the portrait.

"You certainly did, sir. She would be very proud of your family."

"*Our* family, old friend."

"Who are you talking about, Grandpa?" Robin came over to inspect the tray of food.

"My wife, your Grandma Livy. That's her in the painting."

"That's your wife?" asked Jacob as he entered the room. "I didn't know you were married."

"Well, of course I was married! Where do you think grandchildren come from?" William fidgeted with the arm of his chair. Confession time had arrived. "Not many people knew because we married in secret. My family didn't approve of their blue-blooded son and a Gypsy girl." William frowned. "As a matter of fact, I didn't even know I had a son for many years because of their interference."

"I know." Casey came up behind Jacob. "Daddy told me all about it when I was younger."

"He did?" Funny how the topic had never come up at the fair rendezvous.

"Yes, well, I was pressuring him to tell me why you and GrandAna didn't get along."

"GrandAna?" asked Jacob.

"You know the lady who runs The Kissing Booth?" said Casey. "She's my great-grandmother. She'll be here later."

Jacob turned to William. "That Gypsy lady is your mother-in-law? And all this time, I thought you didn't have any relatives."

William cleared his throat. "About that, Jacob—"

"Please, William. You don't have to explain. I understand. It was too risky for you to tell me about your family."

"I told you he would understand." Hanson's smug tone grated. "He has been quite concerned about how you would take the news, Mr. Kent."

"Hanson!" admonished William.

"I am simply saying—" retorted Hanson.

"Don't you two start." Robin wagged her finger at the two scowling men. "Or Ms. Fuller will be in charge of your time-out while we have dinner."

His irritation melted away as Hanson walked over and kissed her cheek. "Yes, Miss Robin."

Might as well get it all out in the open now. William beckoned Jacob over.

"It's okay, William. I understand," said Jacob as he approached.

"No, Jacob, this is important. I've never said you were like a son to me because, for a very short time, I had a son, and no one can replace him. But I've also never told you what you are. You have been family to me and Hanson while my blood family was in hiding. You are the grandson I never had. I couldn't be prouder of you."

"I feel the same way." Jacob leaned over and enveloped him in a gentle hug.

Expecting a handshake, William hesitated then returned the embrace. Relief filled him. He should've known the boy would take it all in stride.

Hanson heaved an unsteady breath. "I wish you would warn me when you are going to do something like that."

Jacob straightened up and put a hand on Hanson's shoulder. "I had been without a family for a long time before I met you two. I will always be grateful you came into my life." Jacob reached over and wrapped his arms around the older man's stiffened shoulders.

"Yes…well…thank you…Jacob." Hanson awkwardly patted his back.

"Relax, Mama Bear," laughed William.

"I am *not* the mama bear." A sniff accompanied Hanson's mutter.

Margaret discreetly slipped a tissue to him.

Jacob turned to Margaret, gave her a kiss on the cheek, and hugged her. "I owe you so much, Maggie."

"Oh, dear," sniffed the unflappable Margaret Fuller. She accepted the tissue Hanson slipped to her.

"Hey, what's wrong with everyone?" Robin scooted over and squeezed next to William on his chair.

Poor little thing. Adults in tears made her nervous. "These are happy tears, my dear," he said.

"Well, you better dry off before the others get here. They'll think something's wrong." She gave Margaret a hug and bounced over to her eldest sister. "Casey, who else is coming to Grandpa's welcome-home party?"

"Dr. Don and his wife—"

"Are here!" Don poked his head into the room. "Rita is anxious to meet everybody." He propelled his blushing wife into the room. "You, of course, know our esteemed host, Mr. Hatch."

"Oh, I'm so glad you are feeling better, Mr. Hatch." Rita warmly embraced her boss.

"Call me William. No formalities here. And that's what having children around does for you. Let me introduce you to my family." He paused for a moment, savoring the novelty of happiness. "My family. It feels so good to be able to say that aloud. These lovely ladies are Robin, Casey, and...." He scanned the room. "Where's Samantha?"

"Oh, I'll get her," said Robin. "She's on the phone with that Christopher guy again, telling him what to do."

***

Casey smoothed the front of her blouse again. Something felt a little off, but she couldn't quite figure out what. With the attention focused on Don and Rita, Casey tried to feel like a normal person at a regular party. She reminded herself to relax. After all, there was no reason to keep her guard up anymore.

Jacob's warm hand nestled in the small of her back. He whispered, "No worries, Casey. Rita's going to love you."

Casey smiled uncertainly at Jacob. It must be a case of nerves. She wasn't used to so much attention being focused on her and the girls. For the hundredth time, she reminded herself to relax. Nevertheless, the feeling persisted.

Sam and Robin pranced into the room. As Samantha was being introduced, Rita raised her palms. "I'm sorry, but I don't see how any of you could have been mistaken for boys."

For some reason, Casey's guard shot up.

"Oh, they can be very clever when they want to be," Grandpa chuckled.

"And last but certainly not least, The Nameless Wonder herself," Don announced as he steered Rita toward Casey.

"Knock it off, Dr. Don," said Rita.

Casey froze, putting voice to face. "It was you!"

"Excuse me? What do you mean?" Rita put her hand to her throat.

"In the hospital. It was you. I heard *your* voice in the stairwell."

"Oh, no, my dear," corrected Grandpa. "Rita wouldn't have been at the hospital. Don's the doctor."

"Umm, actually, yes I was." Rita rolled the hem of her sweater. "I just really wanted to meet you, Casey. Jacob has been mooning over you for so long I wanted to see you for myself. So I stopped by on my way to work."

"That's great!" cried Jacob. "If Rita was the one you heard in the stairwell, then there isn't another player in this game."

"What do you mean?" asked Rita.

"I thought you had been sent by the people stalking us," explained Casey. "I heard you say, 'Knock it off, Dr. Don,' so I thought he was the one who had betrayed me. I pulled another disappearing act and hid out at Jacob's."

"Oh, no!" Rita covered her cheeks with her hands. "I'm so sorry."

Casey grabbed Rita's hands and held them in her own. "Please don't, Rita. Everything is fine now. That's all history. Let's pretend this is our first encounter instead of the second."

"You mean the third encounter." Grandpa had a mischievous grin on his face.

"Third?" Rita's brow furrowed.

"Put a blonde wig on Casey, and *voila*. My first trip in the mom-mobile." Grandpa clapped his hands, delighted by their expressions.

"That was you?" An astonished Jacob turned to Casey.

"The day I lost my job?"

"That was you?" laughed Casey, "At the limo place? Were you the driver who stuck up for Grandpa?" Warmth filled her at his dazed nod.

"Then it was you who smacked my boss," Rita hooted.

"That was the best part of the research." Casey giggled at the memory.

Jacob ran his fingers through his hair. "I thought you looked familiar that first day at the fair, but I couldn't place you."

"Misdirection," Casey reminded him as she hugged his waist.

"Look who's here," interrupted Hanson as he ushered in Mrs. Tucker, Isadora, and Gregory.

As Jacob strode forward to welcome them, Robin barreled past him and flung herself in their general direction. They collected her in a group hug, making her squeal.

"Where's Samantha?" asked Gregory.

"Her cell phone rang while we were in the foyer," said Mrs. Tucker. "I think it's that boy, Christopher, the one she met at the fair."

"Well, she can talk to him later." Casey headed for the door to retrieve her.

"Oh, I'll get her." Mrs. Tucker put a detaining hand on Casey's arm.

Casey acquiesced with a quick hug, and rejoined the others.

***

Wondering who else was expected, Samantha peered through the frosted glass of the front door before she opened it. A pleasant looking, middle-aged man stood there with his hat in his hand. Although his demeanor was relaxed, his eyes were sharp, and, right now, they were zeroed in on her.

Uh-oh.

"Hi," he said, his nonchalance transparent. "You must be Mr. Hatch's granddaughter. Samantha, right? Is Mr. Hatch in?"

Their presence had not yet been revealed to the public. Suspicious, Samantha slipped into her blasé teenager persona. "I wish." She snorted. "My mom's the day maid here. I was on my way out, but I can announce you if you want." She gave him a cheeky grin. Calling over her shoulder, she hollered at the top of her lungs, "Someone's here! Heads up, everybody!" She casually strolled past him as if leaving the house anyway. About to break into a run, she heard Mrs. Tucker in the foyer.

"You!"

Alarmed, Sam looked back to see Mrs. Tucker and the stranger staring at each other. "What are you doing here?" the two chorused at each other.

"*I* was invited." Mrs. Tucker gave the man a frosty glare. "Were you?"

"No, not exactly. I'm here to see Mr. Hatch on business."

Hanson quietly appeared and stepped between Mrs. Tucker and the stranger. "May I help you, sir?"

"Yes. I'm Derrick Rivers, and I want to see Mr. Hatch about a business matter. I understand he's home from the hospital." Although the man offered the identification he had dug out of his pocket to Hanson, he watched Mrs. Tucker.

Hmmmm. Samantha's interest was piqued.

"Mr. Rivers, is it?" Hanson reached over to receive the card. "Yes. My name is Hanson. We spoke on the phone."

"Oh, good, Hanson. We have a few matters we need to discuss." Mr. Rivers glanced at him, but returned his gaze to Mrs. Tucker.

"I'm afraid this will have to wait, Mr. Rivers. Mr. Hatch is unavailable at the moment."

Mr. Rivers tore his eyes away from the housekeeper. "Oh, no you don't, buddy. No one has returned my calls, and I want to know what's going on. I think that young lady," Mr. Rivers nodded toward Samantha at the bottom of the stairs, "might know the people your boss hired me to locate."

Samantha straightened in surprise.

"Mr. Hatch *hired* you?" Mrs. Tucker echoed Sam's thoughts. "So that's why you were watching the house?"

"I'm not at liberty to discuss the case. I'm sorry."

Interesting. That's another piece of the puzzle.

"I thought you were following *me* that day." Mrs. Tucker blushed.

"Well, I was." Mr. Rivers ran his finger around his collar. "But only because it was part of my job."

"Your job?"

"Uh, yes. I was searching for someone else, and I thought you could help me."

"Oh," said Mrs. Tucker in a small voice.

Hmmm, very *interesting*. Even Hanson had paused to watch the uncomfortable couple. *I wonder what Robin will think.*

"Not that I wouldn't want to follow you," Mr. Rivers amended.

"Really, Mr. Rivers!"

"I mean, if you were single. I'd want to follow you if you were single. Not that I would follow you if you were single. That would be creepy. I only meant that—"

These two obviously need some help. "She's a widow." Samantha called from the bottom of the stairs.

"Samantha!" admonished Mrs. Tucker.

Hanson quirked a conspiratorial brow in Sam's direction.

She and Hanson were usually on the same page. She smirked back.

A red-faced Mr. Rivers turned toward her. "Look, I didn't say I wanted to do anything with her."

"*Oh!* Well, that's just fine by me!" Mrs. Tucker spun on her heel and headed back into the house. "Now I'm glad I sicced the police on you!"

"That was you?" Mr. Rivers looked awed.

"Nice going, Sherlock," commented Samantha.

Ignoring her, Mr. Rivers started after Mrs. Tucker. "Hey, wait a minute!" he called after her stiff-backed exit.

"Just a moment, sir," said Hanson.

Dr. Don appeared in the doorway, putting up a protective wall between Mr. Rivers and the departing Mrs. Tucker. "Well, hello. Mr. Rivers, isn't it? I seem to remember you from the hospital."

Mr. Rivers knows Dr. Don, too? Sam grinned. *This guy sure gets around.*

"Uh, yes. Dr. MacNamara. Nice to see you again."

Ignoring the pleasantries, Don loomed over him. "What are you doing here?"

"I'm here to see Mr. Hatch on business." Mr. Rivers sounded aggravated. He turned toward Hanson, who now had Robin peering out from behind him.

Mr. Rivers regarded Robin's beaming face until Dr. Don gently pushed her behind him, his large frame filling most of the doorway.

Mrs. Tucker reappeared behind Dr. Don. Samantha's ears perked up again.

"Mr. Hatch would like to see you, Mr. Rivers." Mrs. Tucker delivered her curt message with an elevated chin and marched back inside.

"I got to hear this." Samantha sprinted up the stairs to join the others. *Oh, yeah. This is going to be really interesting.*

"Day maid's daughter?" Mr. Rivers said under his breath as Samantha caught up to him.

"It's good work if you can get it." She giggled as she raced inside ahead of him.

***

Alerted by Samantha, William watched Hanson and Don escort the private eye he had hired. The man entered the richly decorated room, taking in its details with an arched brow. William felt like he was holding court *and* getting judged. That was all right. It was time to own up to his contribution to the fiasco. "Mr. Rivers, how nice of you to join us."

"Hello, Mr. Hatch. I see you have company. I hate to interrupt, but if we could talk privately for just a few minutes to finish up some loose ends, you could return to your guests right away."

"We're not guests," piped up Robin, who had returned to the puzzle on the floor. "We're family." She studied the pieces as she spoke.

Rivers examined her before scanning the room. His gaze rested on Mrs. Tucker for a moment. She harrumphed and turned her back on him. His lips thinned as he scratched his chin.

"I assure you all is well, Mr. Rivers," said William, worried the man would misconstrue what had actually transpired.

"With all due respect, Mr. Hatch, I need a bit more information before I'll be satisfied."

"*You* hired him, William?" Jacob scowled in Derrick's general direction. "He scared the hel…." He glanced at the preoccupied little girl. "Uh, he scared the heck out of me at the hospital. I thought he was one of the stalkers."

"So did I," added the good doctor.

"No wonder I couldn't get any information out of you," snorted Rivers.

"Oh, no, Jacob. He's one of the good guys." A wave of guilt engulfed William. "I needed to find my granddaughters."

"Jacob Kent, eh? That would make you Mr. Hatch's biz-wiz kid." He waved at William. "No disrespect, sir, but you have to admit the story you fed me sounded pretty fishy."

"What story?" asked Robin.

A thread of panic tightened William's chest. What if Rivers said something inappropriate in front of her?

But Rivers furrowed his brow at the smallest member of the group. "Well, Mr. Hatch hired me to find three granddaughters under pretty unusual circumstances."

He seemed to be selecting his words with care, but William's hands clenched.

"You didn't actually find anyone, did you?" Samantha snickered from her chair.

"No, I didn't. But if this case is to be closed, I need to make sure these granddaughters want to be found. So, I'd like to hear the story from them."

"What's the problem?" Robin focused on the adults' conversation.

Rivers regarded her innocent face. "I, um, need to make sure the grandpa is one of the good guys. If everything is good, the granddaughters could start by introducing themselves."

"Sure! I'm Robin. That's Samantha, and that's Casey. We're all good guys."

William began to relax a little. No doubt Rivers would see the family resemblance between the girls. He glanced at Casey, who was shifting her weight from foot to foot, the picture of discomfort.

"And that's our grandpa," Robin waved toward him. "And that's our Hanson, and they're both good guys."

She continued to point. "And those are our new best friends. That's Miss Isadora—she makes the best food in the world—and that's Mrs. Tucker. Oh, you know her…and that's Mr. Gregory."

"We've met," said Gregory shortly.

"Ah, yes, when my salesman routine failed to get me into Kent's condo."

"They're Mr. Kent's family, but we're sharing them," Robin explained. "Hah! A corner." She snatched up a piece of the puzzle.

"Uh-huh." Rivers paused to survey the three girls. "And, uh, who is Cassie Thatcher?"

William and Hanson exchange confused glances, but Don and Jacob grinned at each other.

"That would be me." Casey hesitated then stepped forward. She laughed, shook his hand, and resumed more boldly. "I'm still not used to sharing the truth about myself yet. My real name is Casey Hatch, but Cassie Thatcher was the name I used in the hospital."

"Your Witness Protection ID?"

"No. The one I took after the accident." Her eye contact with Rivers never wavered, but the color drained from her face at the reference to the tragic loss of their parents.

His own chest tight, William followed Rivers's glance at Samantha. She sat rigidly, her face devoid of expression. He looked at Robin's head, still bent over the puzzle. Had she heard?

After clearing his throat, Rivers had the good manners to change the subject. "Perhaps this should be saved for another day." He addressed William. "But before I go, for my own satisfaction, do you mind if I ask a few more questions?"

Exchanged looks and shrugging shoulders lent unspoken permission, so William braced himself.

Rivers turned to Samantha. "Who is going to take care of you from now on?"

His choice of question surprised her. "Why, Grandpa, of course."

He studied her face and nodded.

"And this is where you want to be?" he asked Casey.

"Oh, yes. We've worked hard to maintain our family for as long as I can remember. Now we can finally live together like a normal family."

"I don't know about the *normal* part," muttered Derrick as he flicked a crystal vase, producing a melodic *ting*. He hastily put his hands behind his back and stepped over to Robin. He squatted next to her, spied a straight-edged piece, and handed it over. "And you, missy. Where would you go if you were in trouble?"

"Straight to my sisters. They always know what to do."

"What if your sisters were, umm, out of town? Where would you go then?"

"To Grandpa and Hanson." She leaned toward him and lowered her voice. "They have lots of money, so they can fix things fast."

Laughter erupted around the room. William's anxiety diminished a bit.

"What? Aren't I supposed to be telling the truth?"

"Yes, Tidbit. You're doing fine." Samantha gave her a thumbs-up.

"Good. Usually, we have to lie about who we are all the time."

"But we don't have to anymore, Robin," said Casey.

"You mean, we have to tell the truth now?"

"That's right, Tidbit. From now on, we always tell the

truth. No more *Who Am I?* games."

"Wow. *All* the time?" Robin pressed as if she was trying to decide something.

"Oh! No, no, no. Not *all* the time." Samantha ran over to squat in front of Robin.

"Well, when?"

"What's with you?" Jacob asked Samantha.

"We'll explain later, okay? Please?"

He looked at Casey, who appeared uncertain.

Rivers raised his palms in a calming gesture. "Okay, it seems like you still have a few kinks to work out, but I get the gist of it. These young ladies are healthy and happy enough. I guess I can wait to hear the rest. Thank you for your time, everyone." Rivers shook Hatch's hand. "Congratulations on reuniting with your family, sir."

William finally allowed himself to relax.

"Wait!" cried Robin. "You can't go yet. You have to tell us the fish story Grandpa told you."

"I think that'll have to wait until another day, little lady."

"Mrs. Tucker!" wheedled Robin.

Mrs. Tucker nodded at Rivers and took Robin's hand. "I'll tell you the story in the kitchen if you'll help me get some more food."

"Sure!"

Robin skipped alongside Mrs. Tucker as they headed for the door. Skidding to a stop, Robin turned to Rivers. "You promise not to leave while we're gone? You have to make up with Mrs. Tucker first."

Samantha grinned at Robin's words. "Are you sure?"

"Oh, yes. I'm sure."

Samantha's grin widened.

Rivers looked at the blushing Mrs. Tucker. "I promise."

"Cool," Sam murmured under her breath as Robin took

Mrs. Tucker's hand and exited the room.

What was that all about? William indicated a chair. "Very well, Mr. Rivers. Have a seat. Let's sort out the rest of this story."

"Grandpa," interrupted Sam, plopping on the floor at his feet. "Did you really hire a *second* private eye after the first one scared us into hiding?"

"I know, I know. I should have waited until our next fair rendezvous like Hanson warned me. I was too impatient for us to be together. But I didn't hire Mr. Rivers here until after Casey missed our phone call. We knew something had happened at that point, and we were—"

"Freaked out. I get it, Grandpa."

"Quite freaked out," injected Hanson.

"Right you are, Hanson. We were quite freaked out."

"But we contacted you. *Twice*," said Samantha. "I snuck into your house and left you two different *Save the Children* ads."

"I don't believe it!" Jacob raked his fingers through his hair, his face pale. "*I* took them. I'm so sorry! I gave all the junk mail to Connor. I was trying to get your grandpa to take it easy by rerouting his mail to his office."

Hanson cleared his throat.

"Don't say it, Hanson," ordered William. The poor boy was feeling guilty enough.

"Don't say what, William?" Jacob didn't look so good.

"Let's put everything on the table, shall we, sir?" Hanson ignored William's glare. "Jacob, the day he had his *episode*, we found one of their messages balled up on the floor. We realized we had traveled to the wrong fair and missed the rendezvous—"

"Oh, William, that triggered it?" Jacob covered his temples with his hands. "Jeez! I almost single-handedly killed you with my good intentions. I hid your grandkids. I took their messages. I—"

William waved his hands. He had to put a stop to this immediately. "Nonsense, m'boy. You had no way of knowing. As much as I hate to admit it, Hanson was right. I should've told you the situation once Maletti was killed, but I was too used to keeping the secret."

Hanson cleared his throat again. "All the cards, sir."

"There's more?" Samantha's cry interrupted William's fresh wave of nerves. He didn't have much of a choice. Hanson would tell them if he didn't.

"Yes, well…. I was also concerned about how you'd respond to my having a secret family." There. He had said it.

"Please, guys, I get it," scoffed Jacob, his face drawn. "They're your real family. They always have to come first. It's cool. I was only borrowing you for a while."

"Oh, no, you don't, Jacob. You're a part of my family, and nothing is going to change that." He stared intently at his young protégé until he nodded. The boy still looked distressed, but time would heal that.

Satisfied, he turned to Samantha, still seated at his feet. "Darling girl, is that why you thought I didn't want you? Because I didn't respond to your note?" He lovingly stroked her bizarre hair.

Samantha lowered her head a little. He waited patiently.

"I heard you yelling at Hanson."

He had to lean closer to hear her soft words.

"You said you didn't want anyone living with you in your house."

He chuckled. "I wasn't talking about my precious girls. I was talking about him." He jerked his head toward Jacob. "That hovering boy would not leave me in peace, and—"

"Mr. Kent is not a boy," corrected Samantha and Hanson

at the same time. Sam giggled as they shared a grin.

"I apologize." William bowed his head in deference to them. "Sometimes, at my age, the other generations seem very young. *Jacob* would not leave me in peace, and I couldn't figure out how to get him to leave. I had to hide what I was doing so he wouldn't know I was looking for you three."

"Grandpa, you should have trusted him after all these years," Casey reproached.

"Oh, no, Miss Casey. It wasn't about trust," intervened Hanson.

"Hanson's quite right. I was worried about how Jacob would take the news."

"Does his secret family hurt your feelings?" Samantha asked Jacob.

"Nah, I'm made of stronger stuff than that." He smiled. "I knew your Grandpa and Hanson were hiding something, but I thought it was bad news about his medical tests. That's why I was trying so hard to keep his workload down." He chuckled as he raised his palms like two sides of a scale. "Bad news from the doctor or a secret family. Which one do you think I'd rather hear?"

"Mother hen," muttered William. He patted Sam's hair, and smiled at his adorable Casey.

***

Casey's heart swelled with love and happiness. Across the room, Jacob reflected her emotions like a mirror.

"To think we met at the fairs all those times because you were driving Grandpa to meet me." She laughed. "I kept wondering if it was cosmic or if it was because of that birthday kiss before Uncle Scott tackled you."

"Hey, I remember that," said Samantha. "That was him?"

"That was Jacob?" asked William.

"C'mon. The Kissing Booth thing's a story. A myth," snorted Jacob.

"Do not dismiss because you not understand, young man," advised a musical voice from the doorway. "You hip.… Is good today, yes?" In the doorway stood a petite, elderly woman dressed in colorful skirts. With one hand, she leaned on a decorative cane. The other was on the arm of her escort.

"GrandAna!" cried Samantha as she ran across the room.

"Your hip?" Casey grinned at Jacob as she went to her great-grandmother.

"She hit me with a bucket at the last fair," said Jacob. "I didn't know she was related to you."

"GrandAna, it's so strange to see you someplace besides a fair," said Casey as she hugged the dear woman.

Samantha had stopped short in the middle of the room and was staring at GrandAna's companion.

"Hi, Samantha." Christopher smiled broadly. "I told you I'd find you again."

"What are you doing here?" Samantha sounded somewhat breathless.

"I drove Miss Ana to see her great-grandchildren. I didn't know you were one of them."

Samantha broke into an awkward grin. "Well, since you are here, come meet my grandpa." She took his hand.

Casey swallowed past a lump in her throat. It looked like Samantha was going to get to act like a teenager after all.

"GrandAna!" Robin dashed into the room with Mrs. Tucker trailing behind her.

Amid the commotion, Jacob quietly slipped his arms around her waist and pulled her close. She leaned her back against him, a happy calm saturating her very being.

What an incredible difference there is between feeling fairly safe, and feeling absolutely safe.

Today, with everyone she loved nearby, everything seemed possible. After all those years of living like nomads, pushing Jacob away, but thinking about him constantly, she was ready. It had been over a week since he had announced his intention to marry her. She was ready to give him her answer.

"Yes," she whispered to him, her heart overflowing with love.

Jacob understood her. He always did. Reaching into his pocket, he pulled out the ring box for the last time and slipped it into her hand. He re-laced his fingers around her waist. She rested against the security of his chest, the box making her palm tingle. As soon as Uncle Scott and Aunt Patti arrived, she would share what he already knew. She was going to marry Jacob Allan Kent and spend the rest of her life being happy with him.

Fact or fantasy, The Kissing Booth prediction of a Christmas wedding sounded perfect.

Chapter 41
Epilogue

"What the…?" Stunned, Casey grabbed Jacob's arm, shook it as hard as she could, and pointed at The Kissing Booth.

Jacob turned in time to see Derrick Rivers place both hands on either side of Helene Tucker's sturdy waist and lift her up onto the platform. Her astonishment escaped with a *whoosh*. A raucous cheer accompanied the private investigator as he clambered onto the platform next to the rigid housekeeper. The girls manning The Kissing Booth giggled as their line of customers scattered to make way for the middle-aged couple.

Ignoring the enthusiastic and noisy support from the crowd, Derrick kissed her. As he lifted his head, she stared at him in breathless bewilderment. He smiled down at her.

Uh-oh! Casey could see it coming.

"Mr. Rivers!" the woman spat out, her cheeks flaming.

He kissed her again, longer, more lingering. He drew away and gazed at her upturned face and her closed eyes. As the hooting of the crowd rose in volume, her eyes flew open.

"Mr. Rivers! Contain yourself!" She tried to pull away from him, wildly seeking an escape. "What do you think you are doing?"

Casey and the crowd held their breath.

"I...I just wanted to say Happy Birthday, Helene." He gestured toward the sign.

"How did you know it was my birthday?"

"I know a lot of things about you." His face turned red, but his gaze didn't waver.

"Oh, Derrick," Helene fluttered as she tilted her head and leaned forward.

He responded by sweeping her into his arms. "Gotcha!" He planted another kiss on her.

Casey joined the crowd chanting "Birthday Kisses! Married by Christmas!" She snaked an arm around Jacob and Grandpa, feeling happy and secure as she watched Uncle Scott lift his son, Simon, onto his shoulders for a better view. On the other side of Jacob, Christopher was taking advantage of the confusion to sneak a kiss from Samantha.

Robin jumped up and down in front of Hanson. "Old people are so cute!" she cried.

"Old people?" he spluttered. "They are neither old nor cute. I'll show you cute old people." Despite the crowd, the ever-proper Hanson reached past Casey to grab the impossibly prim Margaret Fuller by the hand, and started tugging her toward The Kissing Booth.

Casey clapped her hands over her mouth, hoping the dear man would not get shot down.

"Mr. Hanson!" Margaret hissed at him as he dragged her past Casey.

Oh, no. Casey's stomach dropped.

Hanson ignored her and kept on course.

"Mr. Hanson!" Margaret said louder. She grabbed the hand pulling her and tried to resist without creating a scene.

Squaring his shoulders, Hanson kept going.

"*Reginald!*" she shouted, digging in her heels and bringing them both to a grinding stop just shy of The Kissing Booth.

Fearing the worst, Casey clutched her hands as he turn toward a pink-faced Margaret.

"I...I just wanted to say I would like to do this myself."

Oh, yes! Another happy ending. Casey poked Grandpa and Jacob to make sure they weren't missing history in the making.

"Hanson?" Jacob's mouth hung open. "And Maggie?"

"It's about time," Grandpa exclaimed as his friend offered her his arm.

Margaret slipped her own through his, and they primly ascended the stairs together, surrounded by the cheering spectators. Once they were on the stage, Margaret Fuller got up on her toes and kissed him. They smiled at each other.

"Wahoo!" Hanson grabbed her by the waist, and twirled her around amidst the applauding booth attendants and the good-natured shouting of the crowd.

Attracted by the uproar, fair attendees came running from all directions to join the fun, chanting, "Birthday Kisses, Married by Christmas! Birthday Kisses, Married by Christmas!"

"GrandAna and Robin strike again," Casey sang out. No doubt today's events had been orchestrated by her clever great-grandmother, but Robin didn't look surprised. Not at all.

"Hey! Is today Ms. Fuller's birthday?" called Uncle Scott over the happy noise. "Nah, Maggie's birthday isn't until next month," yelled Jacob.

"I wonder if something happens if it's not their birthday." He was personally acquainted with the legend of The Kissing Booth.

"Doesn't matter!" shouted William over the din. "Today's Hanson's birthday!"

"Robin. Hey, Robin!" Casey flagged her attention. "Did you know?"

Robin paused her jumping. "Sure I did," she hollered. "Looks like it's going to be a busy Christmas!"

***

"Good night, my dear Livy," murmured William Randall Hatch III as he gazed at Olivia's face from across his bedroom.

This was his favorite picture of her, depicting her laughing, rosy mouth and her sparkling, dark-brown eyes. He had captured her standing in front of The Kissing Booth at some carnival, memorializing the day they had been wed in secret.

Tonight, the weak light on her portrait made her vibrant eyes appear to be gazing back at him as if sharing a special moment. They had indeed been destined, regardless of the social barriers of the times, meeting secretly for years. Every summer, her family had swept into town for a couple of weeks, bringing fun and excitement to the otherwise mundane existence of local farming communities...and bringing her, his secret love.

William smiled softly to himself as he adjusted his position to one more comfortable. *No one knew about us, my dearest love....* William drifted off to the novelty of another peaceful night's sleep...*at least not for the first few years. Now, everyone knows.*

The End?

THE LEGEND

If it be the anniversary of your birth when you first kiss, that blessed moment over the ancient rune becomes your union of destiny.

Long ago, before time had forgotten, an ordinary tree was forever changed when a magical rune was carved into its trunk. To keep its power out of the hands of those who would abuse it, the tree was taken down and cut into boards. Although the boards were used to construct a Gypsy's mystical Kissing Booth, many said the destruction of the tree was the undoing of its magical power. Or was it?

What do you believe? Read the tales in the *Love of Fairs* series, and decide for yourself.

Deborah Ann Davis
www.DeborahAnnDavis.com

RANDOM FACTOIDS

Alice fell down a rabbit hole in the book, *Alice's Adventures in Wonderland* (commonly shortened to *Alice in Wonderland*) is an 1865 novel written by English author Charles Lutwidge Dodgson under the pseudonym Lewis Carroll.

Blond- (adj.) various shades of yellow hair

Blonde- (noun) a person with various shades of yellow hair

Casey, the Utterly Impossible Talking Horse by Anita MacRae (1960) unfortunately is no longer in print. When the talking horse needed a name, he chose Kitty Cat. The children protested, so they reached a compromise: K.C., later changed to Casey.

Clark Kent is Superman's secret identity, characters created by Jerry Siegel and drawn by Joe Shuster. He first appeared in print in the late 1930s.

Lyme disease is a deer tick-borne ailment, caused by the bacterium *Borellia burgdorferi*. The symptoms include joint pain, fatigue and flu-like symptoms. Left untreated it can cause anything from irreversible heart failure, debilitating brain fog, to sudden arthritis, and even death. It is especially prevalent in Connecticut.

The Perseids are an annual meteor shower visible from the northern hemisphere around the second week of August. On a moonless night, it is not unusual to witness fifty or more shooting stars, depending on your location.

Yale University is located in New Haven, Connecticut.

WHAT WAS IT LIKE BACK THEN?

1938- USA President was Franklin D. Roosevelt.

Nylon was patented, it's first use in toothbrush bristles; Teflon, Ballpoint Pens, Photocopier, Freeze-dried Coffee were invented; the first use of Seeing-Eye Dogs; Families gathered around a radio at night since TV had not been invented. *The War of the Worlds* by H. G. Wells radio broadcast panicked many people on October 30; Howard Hughes set a new Round the World record: 3 days, 19 hours; Action Comics issued the first Superman comic; Gas was $0.10/gallon; Phones were Candlestick style with a separate earpiece and mouthpiece using landlines only.

www.thepeoplehistory.com/1938.html

1998- USA President was Bill Clinton; he gets caught cheating on his wife.

The first Harry Potter book is published; the Euro is adopted; the court case against Big Tobacco is won, the biggest legal battle in history; the UK reports; 150 countries signed Kyoto Protocol at a Global Warming Conference in Kyoto, Japan. Sadly, the USA did not sign; The UK reports a link between the MMR Vaccine and Autism Spectrum disorders; Google begins; Viagra is approved for use; Gas was $1.15/gallon; Phones are mostly landlines, but many adults had remote phones, cell phones, caller ID and answering machines; Public payphones abound.

www.thepeoplehistory.com/1997.html

1999- USA President was Bill Clinton.

European Union bans USA beef because of the unhealthy hormones put in it; MySpace and Napster begin; Gas was $1.22/gallon; Cell phones are prolific; Businesses and government are scared their computers will malfunction when the calendar changes from 1999 to 2000.

www.thepeoplehistory.com/1999.html

2002- USA President was George W. Bush.

The Senate votes to build a Nuclear Waste facility at Yucca Mountain, NV, ignoring the fact that it's on a fault zone; Kmart files for bankruptcy; Kelly Clarkson wins first American Idol; Gas was $1.61/gallon; Blackberries, Treo Palms and Motorola abound. Public payphones are scarce.

www.thepeoplehistory.com/2002.html

1938 Minimum wage was $0.25/hour
1998-2002 Minimum wage was $5.15/hour

www.dol.gov/featured/minimum-wage/chart1

PLAYLIST FOR FAIRLY SAFE

One Way or Another   by Blondie

That's Not My Name   by The Ting Tings

Dude (Looks Like A Lady) by Aerosmith

Ray's Rockhouse   by The Manhattan Transfer

Wipeout   by The Surfaris

FAIRLY SHORT LIST OF FAIRS

The Big Eastern States Exposition, West Springfield, MA
(The Big E)

The Connecticut Renaissance Fair, Norwich, CT

The Skowhegan County Fair, Skowhegan, ME

The Barnstable County Fair, Barnstable, MA

The Stowe Foliage Arts Festival, Stowe, VT

The Four Town Fair, Somers, CT

The Renaissance Faire, Guilford, CT

The *Love of Fairs* Series

Different Time Periods…
Different Characters…
Same Legend…

I hope you enjoyed reading **Fairly Safe**, the second tale in the **Love of Fairs series,** as much as I enjoyed writing it. Here is an excerpt from **Fairly Obvious**, the third tale in the **Love of Fairs series.** Sign up for notification when it's published at www.DeborahAnnDavis.com.

Fairly Obvious

"Pardon me, ma'am. Have you seen these kids?" The officer held up a family photograph in front of the elderly carnival Gypsy. A *Happy Sweet Sixteen* banner crowned a ring of happy faces. The glow of a candle-lit cake radiated from below.

The old Gypsy woman grasped his wrist and angled the photo to a more comfortable position. The picture was of a petite lady with classic Roman features wrapped in the arms of a tall Black man. They both gazed proudly at a cluster of three girls and a boy. The photographer had caught the eldest girl preparing to blow out the candles, one hand holding back a generous mound of dark curls. A boy resembling the man loomed over her. Two grade school girls flanked her.

"They do a bad thing?" the Gypsy asked.

"No, ma'am." The young cop gently tried to tug himself free from her hand, but she tightened her grip while she examined the faces frozen in time. "The kids are runaways. We're just trying to locate them."

"They *all* runaway? They parents do a bad thing?" She squinted at the picture.

"What? No, not at all. They died in an accident earlier this year."

She frowned. "Ahh, they run away from family who take them in. Why? They do a bad thing?"

"No! No one did a bad thing, and they don't have any family. They ran away from foster care."

"Foster care." Straightening, she rolled the unfamiliar phrase around. "Explain, please."

"Yes, ma'am." He tried to extricate his wrist again, but gave up. "Foster parents are paid by the state to take care of kids whose own home is unsuitable, until a permanent situation can be found."

"Is a lot of people for one foster house."

"You're right. They had to split them up."

"They all missing?"

"Yes. We believe the oldest rounded them up and they took off together."

"So, they together now." She smirked. "You think they run away to join carnival, eh?"

His older partner spoke for the first time. "We are just checking out all possibilities, ma'am." He reached over and plucked the photo out of the younger cop's hand.

She released his wrist. "Ay, no. I no see these people."

"If you do see them, please contact us immediately."

"And then?"

"And then they will be returned to the system."

The older cop snorted behind him. "Yeah, if they don't end up in Juvie for running away."

The elderly Gypsy wrapped her shawl around her shoulders and nodded. "Is not good they run away. Children need good home. If I see them, I take care of it."

The two men glanced at each other while she beamed at them, her hand extended.

"Good day, ma'am." They shook her hand, and headed for the next carnie.

A few minutes later, the older cop returned. "Excuse me, ma'am. Did you find that picture we showed you? I seem to have misplaced it."

She shook her head and flashed him a mischievous grin.

"Thanks again." He patted his pockets, shook his head and trotted off.

She pulled a white square from her shawl. "I not find it. I take it," she chuckled. The police always underestimated the elderly. She headed for the wagon. The faces in the picture were the same as the ones in her dream. She didn't have much time to prepare.

DEBORAH ANN DAVIS began writing when a particularly nasty bout of Lyme disease put her on the sidelines. Until then, she was a proud Science Geek who tried to convey the coolness of the universe to others (AKA, a Science Teacher). Trying to speed up her recovery led her to Fitness for her body health, and Writing for her happy health. She currently is a happy and healthy Educational Speaker and a Certified Personal Trainer.

Even though they had followed separate paths, Deborah reunited with, and married her childhood sweetheart, twelve years after their first kiss. She and her husband coached their daughter's AAU Basketball Team, which swept States two years in a row. (Yay!) Then, for several years their daughter and their money went to college.

Deborah currently resides on a lovely lake in Connecticut with her Beloved, where she is completing a workbook for teenage girls, her **Girl's Guide to Good Guys**. She enjoys writing novels for her **Love of Fairs** series, dabbling with living a sustainable life, dancing, playing outside, and laughing really hard every day. She promotes increasing the amount of movement throughout your day via Wiggle Writer posts on Merry Meddling, her blog at www. DeborahAnnDavis.com. With an insightful and quirky approach to life, she shares life lessons with wit and compassion.

Follow her on Facebook, Goodreads, LinkedIn, Pinterest, and Twitter @DeborahAnnDavis and @WiggleWriter.

You can sign up for her quarterly newsletter, Merry Meddling, at www.DeborahAnnDavis.com.